THE TIGER AND THE DOVE
BOOK THREE

CONSOLAMENTUM

BY
REBECCA HAZELL

IM • PRESS

ACKNOWLEDGEMENTS

I would like to thank every historian, alive or deceased, who traced the culture and history of the Mongols, Iran, and the Frankish Crusades and Crusader States. As well, thanks to the historians of Antioch, Byzantium, Venice, medieval France, and the Inquisition and Cathari. I would like to thank Professors Trudy Sable, Ruth Whitehead, and Peter Conradi for their encouragement and advice; my many manuscript readers; my husband Mark, who tirelessly read and re-read my seemingly endless revisions; my sister, Candace Ammerman, who drafted the maps for all three books in this trilogy; and my daughter, Elisabeth, who finalized the maps, laid out the interior of two of the books, and helped me design two of the covers. A better family no writer could have.

DEDICATION

This trilogy is dedicated to Sakyong Mipham Rinpoche.

This novel is dedicated to my beloved family, past, present and future.

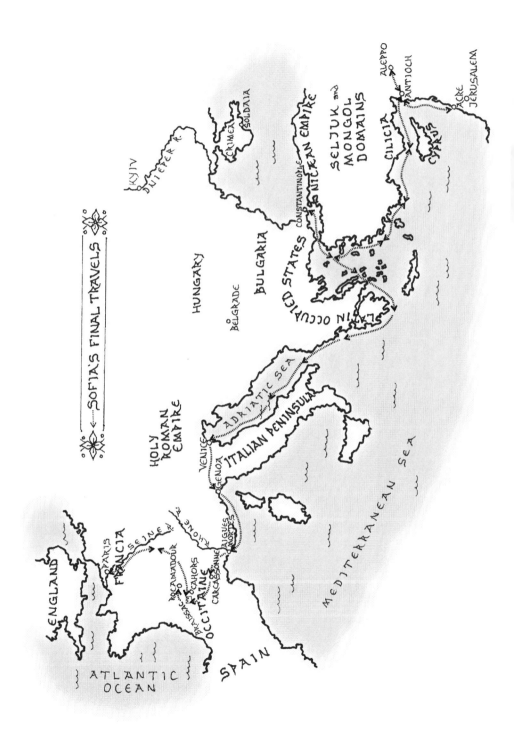

I count him braver who overcomes his desires
than him who conquers his enemies;
for the hardest victory is over self.
–Aristotle

Many troubles have sprung from a foolish tongue.
–Medieval French proverb

"Kill them all. God will know his own."
*–Papal prelate Arnold Amaury's reply when asked
how to tell Catholics from heretics in Bezier*

SUMMER TO WINTER
ANNO DOMINI 1249

A sea of lies indeed—of lies and deceit. I was soon awash in them, beginning with my lies to myself. When Caterina's physician first told me he thought I was carrying a child, I was not convinced. I had always believed I was barren. But when on his next visit he listed the signs, I was forced to admit he was right. I was stunned at first and then gladder than ever that I had not told the exact truth to my Uncle Vasily, or Basil as he now styled himself, and his wife Lady Caterina.

Once I had accustomed myself to this strange turn of events, I was surprised at how elated I felt: I was carrying my beloved's son! But again came the deceit: I felt I had done nothing wrong in lying with Sir Joscelin. According to what I had gleaned from the Frankish court ladies on Cyprus, even private betrothals were as sacred and binding as a marriage. Having exchanged vows privately with him the day we lay together, I simply wished away the fact that he was still married in the eyes of the Church. I told myself that it did not count anyway since his marriage had never been consummated and would soon be annulled.

Still, while I felt I had not strayed too far in saying I was already wed, the untruth hung between my new family and me.

At first I was too sick each morning and too sleepy during the day to care much about anything anyway, but when after a few weeks I was feeling better, I realized that things were somehow not right. Certainly Caterina was kind to me and most attentive to my health, and Uncle Basil, as I was learning to call him, was concerned and affectionate on the rare times he was home. I wrote a long letter to my beloved telling him, among other things, that he was to be a father soon. Basil promised to send it to Cyprus with a reliable captain.

And once I felt better, I was so enjoying getting to know my niece and nephews that I did not notice that Basil and Caterina seemed in no hurry to take me around Constantinople or even to make my presence known to anyone else. I saw not a soul beyond the physician and my servants, and my world was as bounded by the four walls of the courtyard as it had been in Selim's andarun or the Nizari and Hospitaller castles. I could only hope that once I felt better, everything would change and I would be free to explore Constantinople and, after my visit, to return home to await the return of my beloved Sir Joscelin.

Then my cook disappeared. Leo had been preparing special delicacies and sending them to me, but as I was feeling better, I thought nothing of it when Caterina's maidservant stopped bringing them.

However, when I asked burly Bardas how his brother was doing, he looked at me a little strangely. "He is doing well now. He is employed at an inn in the city."

"He left my service? Why? And why do you say 'now'?" I asked.

"She," he tilted his head toward an imaginary Lady Caterina, "turned him out, said the household didn't need two cooks, that he would have no trouble finding work elsewhere. Lucky he had saved a little working for you, because it wasn't easy at all. This is a city of ghosts, and he was finally forced to find work under Franks at a pittance. I wondered if you knew, Lady, but you were so unwell that I could not bother you. But we both are furious. She is not our mistress; you are! And so I told her when she tried to dismiss me at the same time. But Leo left anyway. He was too insulted to stay. He said he's a better cook than hers is and if she can't tell the difference between an artist and a peasant, he won't waste his breath arguing."

I was annoyed, of course, but I supposed Caterina's logic made sense. After all, when would she have tasted Leo's superior fare, and why keep two cooks? With me so ill, she might have decided to act on my behalf and then forgotten to tell me. It was clear that she was not well, too, so

I must forgive her on those grounds alone. So as her guest and feeling beholden to my hosts, I said nothing to her. I did send Leo a couple of old silver coins of original Byzantine mint, Latin coins being terribly debased, and a message that I hoped he would return to me when I sailed back home. And then I tried not to resent Caterina's interference.

Until the day she slapped my servant Banjuu, whose loud cries drew me out of my room to the head of the stairs from the courtyard. She ran up to me, weeping, threw her arms about my waist, and sobbed her story into my skirts. Slapping my child I could not tolerate!

But when I rushed down to confront Caterina, who was sitting on a bench embroidering something, she smoothed her crimson silk gown and looked up at me with shockingly cold eyes. "She refused to obey me when I ordered her to do a small task for me."

"Well, first of all, she is my servant, not yours, and next, she is but a child from a faraway land and is still learning how to serve!"

Caterina's eyes narrowed and she leapt from her seat, her work spilling to the paving stones unheeded. "What monstrous ingratitude! We take you in, nurture you, protect you from your wrongdoings, and this is what I get?" She stormed inside.

Wrongdoings? I could understand her feeling a little piqued about Banjuu, but rage and accusation were not called for. I followed her inside where she was busily straightening her barrel-shaped chairs, which were already in strict order.

"Caterina," I said as contritely as I could, "I never meant to offend you. But you confuse me utterly. What wrongdoings have I committed that you protect me from?"

"That child you carry is a bastard! And worse, its father is a known seducer and liar! We have been at a loss over what to do ever since we found out, for surely you believed this Sir Joscelin's falsehoods or you'd never have lain with him—I can only hope so, at least. But you endangered my entire family's reputation with your heedless conduct. While you were so ill, your uncle Basil took steps to protect you, even established himself as your guardian. But we still have no idea how to untangle you from the web this man wove around you."

By the time she had finished speaking, she had calmed down considerably, but her words were hammer blows on my heart. I sat down on one of her chairs to gather my thoughts. When I finally spoke, I could not hide the quaver in my voice. "Where did you hear such things?"

"Basil has many connections in Antioch and beyond. It took only a month to discover the truth from his agent in Cyprus. He had to quell the terrible slanders he heard about you. His man says you are the butt of jests in every tavern, but my husband would not believe his dear niece was anyone's concubine—and that is the kindest word he heard used about you! But the more Basil heard, the more alarmed he became.

"He first thought to take you to our country estate as soon as you were fit to travel. But I urged him to wait, to put out more enquiries into your holdings and so forth, and to set about protecting you in case your seducer might have seized anything through some trick."

"Good God, these slanders, I assure you, are utterly unjust. Both of us behaved with the greatest restraint for over a year, always considering ourselves betrothed to each other. But then he was forced to marry that terrible girl, which was a disaster for us all, even for her. Their marriage was never consummated, and Sir Joscelin only awaits news of its annulment, and with the blessings of King Louis himself! He has behaved with complete virtue toward me, and we are truly betrothed, which is as good and binding as marriage. Indeed, we are married in the eyes of God if not the Church.

"And if he lied to me, why give me not one but two rings, one of the utmost value to him? I am certain the evil rumors you heard about him merely stem from the death of his first wife, for which he utterly blames himself. He has been paying for that tragic death ever since. He even went to the Holy Land hoping to die in battle, a death I am so glad our Merciful Lord refused him!"

Caterina looked at me as if I had grown another head. "You are sadly mistaken, Sofia. It was bad enough at first when I learned of your previous marriage. No one who has been widowed should remarry—and you already told us you were widowed—but I thought this last marriage had already taken place and that there was no more to be said about it!"

I paled, afraid of what would come next. Why had I ever tried to cover my tracks by mentioning I was a widow? I had not even told the exact truth about the so-called marriage, just that I'd been married to a merchant who had died on our journey west. They'd have been far more horrified had they known I had wed not one but two Muslims, Selim and then his son Kerim after Selim was murdered. Ironically, both marriages had been temporary and not true unions, at least from my point of view. They simply took advantage of a custom among the Shi'a, first as a way for me to belong to Selim's family and then to escape Alamut with Kerim. Neither had been consummated, though a little guilt flitted through my heart. Had Kerim not been murdered, too, I might have relented one day and lain with him. I had been celibate for so long and was so ruined already that the sin of it would not have stopped me.

Caterina was continuing relentlessly, "But worse, in the eyes of God you committed fornication and this Sir Joscelin committed adultery, no matter what lies he told you about betrothal. And only confession and penance will wipe out that stain on your soul! I will send you my confessor. That at least I can do for you.

"But your uncle and I agree that it would be best for you and your precious servants to remove to our country villa. There you can bear your bastard and give it away in secret. After that, out of respect for my husband—do not think I feel the same for you, but you are family—I will bring you back into society and even find you a real husband if you wish. Not that I would force anyone upon you, of course." She smiled in what I supposed was meant to be a friendly way.

I was reeling by the time she had finished, and so upset that I had overlooked a vital fact she had let drop. Trying to keep the rage out of my voice I merely replied, "If my presence is a hindrance to your welfare, I will go at once. I am wealthy enough to find my own way, and my business interests are flourishing. And I can find my own confessor."

She smiled again, this time with no pretense of friendliness. "You are under your uncle's guardianship now, Sofia. You will have to go through him for monies or permission to go anywhere. And neither of us wants you to leave. You are, as I have already said, family." She did not wait to hear my response, as her little daughter Cecelia ran into the room at that moment, pursued by her nursemaid and crying that her brother Paolo had hit her. Without a word, Caterina turned and swept outside, every step radiating moral triumph.

I stayed, though, my mind a blank, my heart beating out of my chest, and every fiber of my body screaming protest. After many deep breaths to calm myself, I faced the reality of my new life. I had walked into yet another trap, this time of my own making. I disbelieved anything Caterina said about Sir Joscelin. I knew his heart. But I had put myself at the mercy of people I thought I could trust before I even knew them.

Now I saw how I had misinterpreted my welcome. Caterina's solicitude for my welfare had hidden a mercenary mind. Worse, either my uncle was under her influence or was just as mercenary. And I had been trying for a good ten years to reach these very people! It made me sick that all those years as a slave among the Mongols and then as a virtual prisoner in haram and in Alamut, my one goal had been to find my uncle, the last of my family and my last link with my beloved Kyiv, and to make a happy home with him.

Rage and disappointment gave way to dark fears. Did they hope I would die in childbirth? Or, having removed me to the country, would they keep me prisoner while using my wealth to profit themselves? There was only one way to learn my uncle's intentions: to confront him and read his signals, a skill I had learned as a translator among the Mongols and had happily abandoned after finally reaching what I thought was safety. That was another mistake I would never make again!

I didn't need to find an occasion to speak with him. That evening after a silent supper—neither Caterina nor I would look at each other—Uncle Basil said, "Sofia, it is time for you and me to talk alone." A significant look passed between him and his wife.

"Indeed yes!" I glared at Caterina, but she was carefully avoiding my gaze.

He led me to his office, crowded with a lectern and stool, a barrel-backed chair across from it, cupboards, and shelves stacked with documents.

"Please sit here, my dear," he began, waving me to the chair and placing a cushion at my back, all most courteously. Instead of seating himself, he stood before me, a troubled expression on his face. "I understand you and Caterina had a misunderstanding today."

"Oh, I think my understanding was quite clarified!"

He held out his hands in a mollifying gesture. "My lady wife can have quite a spicy temper sometimes, and I fear you tasted it today. She is ashamed now and only wishes for your forgiveness."

"Why does she not come to me herself?"

"Alas, her other besetting sin is pride. She wants me to prepare the way for her."

"Well, I am happy to accept her regrets once she offers them, but that does not touch on the matters we quarreled over, and those will not go away!" This time, it was I who held up my hands to show I would stand for no interruption—a trick I had learned from more than one man.

"First of all, and I may have been wrong to do so, I lay with my beloved on the clear understanding that our betrothal, of much longer standing than his unconsummated marriage, was as good as a real marriage. I know he believed it so, for he called on God Himself as his witness.

"Sir Joscelin may have committed many sins in Occitaine, but he confessed all those twice over long ago, both to his priest and to me, and he has done penance to atone for them! He has led a chaste life for many years, and he went to the Holy Land to die for God in reparation for his sins. He never meant to hurt me. And when he returns, God willing, we will be Church married straightaway. It is most likely that he is no longer even married, since before he left on campaign he and his so-called wife sought an annulment with the full consent of King Louis! So let me be clear: in my eyes we are already wed, and if that offends Caterina, there is nothing for it.

"Furthermore, I intend to write my will now, and I will leave all my wealth to him and our child; the only other provisions will be for my servants and my orphans. I want to make that clear because Caterina let slip that you think you have taken on a guardianship over both me and my possessions that I neither asked for nor want! I am of age, and I have been handling my own affairs for years.

"Uncle, I am beyond angry. If there is anything I signed when ill, which I do not remember doing, I will seek court redress for it. I do not know the laws here in Constantinople, but I have powerful friends in Antioch who will support me in my suit. Think well before you answer, for I am a woman of the world and a good businesswoman, too!"

A storm of successive emotions had swept across Basil's face: dismay, outrage, and even, briefly, shame. "It seems not so to me, Sofia, for you were taken in by a sly fox. This whoreson's by-blows are scattered across the Holy Land. Ours is too small a world for gossip not to spread. Whatever lies he told you, I ferreted out the truth soon enough. I am only protecting your interests and those of your unborn child, for I feared some such folly on your part. You may go to court if you wish, but my authority comes straight from the king himself. Until you are safely wed to a proper husband, I am your guardian whether you will it or no!"

"King Louis would never do that!"

"I speak of my king, King Baldwin of Constantinople. Here is his document—" He started sorting through a sheaf of official-looking papers as if to show me, but I stayed to hear no more. Fleeing to my room, I found Alexander loitering about laughing with the girls, tossing his dark hair back and looking less like a boy and more like a youth. My heart almost stopped with love for my three dearest orphans, all so happy together: him; Banjuu, so dark-skinned and lovely; and fair Marguerite, whose hair was still as pale as wheat. Who knew what fate awaited us all? Straightaway I ordered Banjuu and Marguerite to start packing.

"And Alexander, go tell Bardas that we leave for Antioch straightaway, and then return here to help us."

Alexander, looking worried for a change, hurried off.

"What has happened, Lady?" Banjuu answered.

"I will tell you later. Do you still have the little chest I entrusted to you, the one with the gold coins?"

"Yes, I kept it safe and secret for you."

"Good, we'll need it! I think my uncle has robbed me. At the very least, he may control a good deal of my wealth, and we must escape here and return to Antioch before he does more damage." At that, tears of rage and disappointment insisted on flowing, though I wiped my eyes and set to with a will. I was weary of tears.

It was not until we had finished packing everything that I stopped to think how I would escape. "Girls, we may have to climb down over the balcony from the outside window. Go to Bardas and tell him that he and Alexander must await us outside. And why hasn't Alexander returned, anyway?"

We found out when she tried to open the door: it was locked from the outside. And when I looked out the window, a guard stood below. Tears gave way to simple rage. I had had enough of being kept in thrall like some slave!

When the door was unlocked the next morning, I faced my jailer—Lady Caterina, of course—followed by servants bearing food for the three of us. I so wanted not to give into rage, but I could not restrain myself. "This is an abomination! Do you hope to rid yourself of me in secret if I do not die in childbirth?"

She had the grace to look shocked. "No such thing. Your uncle and I simply want to protect you from making some terrible mistake. You should never have conceived, if I may use the word, of writing your will in such a wayward and childish manner. Basil fears for your sanity now!"

Looking around at the room, she added, "Ah, I believe you have already packed, perhaps to flee? It is a good thing, anyway. Today we remove you to our country estate, just beyond the outer walls of the city. There you can rest and bear your bastard in secret. Perhaps you can even send it to one of your orphanages." She smiled slightly. "I understand that two of your lover's bastards live in one of them. Oh, you didn't know? A boy and a girl. But don't worry. Basil will ensure that all your homes are well endowed. He lauds your charity and prays it will be counted in your favor on Judgment Day. In that way at least, you are unlike your father."

And she left.

I sank onto the bed again, feeling as stabbed in the heart as if she had struck me with a knife: Caterina must mean Rotrou and Agnes. Why had Joscelin not told me the truth? But wait—perhaps she and Uncle Basil were mistaken, perhaps misled by false rumor. It was too soon to lose heart. And what could she possibly mean about my father? Well, there was no point in wondering about that now. Until I could find a way to escape, I saw no way forward but to seem to yield to their plans. I still had money and friends in Antioch. I would find a way to flee there and ask Lady Helene for refuge and advice. Matthew of Edessa would surely help me, too.

Later that day I was taken, closely guarded, out of the house and across the city. Uncle Basil led the way astride a horse, while my girls and I were confined to a gauzily curtained, gaily painted mule-drawn wagon. His guards rode beside it, so there was no hope of simply hopping off and escaping. Of Bardas and Alexander there was no sign. What would they do now? Did they know what had happened to me? Caterina had doubtless turned them out without a word.

We were headed toward the lowering sun, and when I turned my head against the glare, I could just make out the cathedral of Saint Sofia in the far distance on my left, glowing like a pink jewel. We turned right onto a broad, dirty street, and my uncle dropped back to tell me its name, although I scarcely welcomed anything that traitor could tell me.

"This ancient thoroughfare was once called the Mese, built by Emperor Constantine himself. It was the life's blood of the city." I pretended to ignore him and he rode forward again, but what he had said caught my imagination. Along this street emperors and generals had ridden in splendor past cheering crowds. Now it was almost empty, pot-holed, and garbage-strewn. Where was this Heaven-brought-down-onto-earth that Papa had told me about when I was small? The avenue was lined with burnt buildings and broken-down arcades, their columns tumbled and battered. This sad wreck of a city looked more like an outer Hell.

I was caught up in such dark thoughts when out of the corner of my eye I thought I glimpsed Bardas and Alexander. My spirit rose a little. I scarcely dared count on them to rescue me, but there was nothing to be lost by boldness. "Marguerite," I whispered, "Look to your right. Do you see? Is that not Bardas and Alexander?"

"Yes, Lady! I think so," she whispered. "What shall I do?"

"Part the curtain and ask the guard where they take us, then look straight at my men and nod, and see what they do. Then we'll know."

She did as she was bid, trembling the entire time. The guard curtly told her to get behind the curtain again. She sat back in the litter, again enfolded in our gauzy prison.

"I did it, Mistress," she whispered, still atremble. "They signaled, but then they turned away. I think because we are in this big place." She was referring to an enormous public area of some sort, oval in shape, in the middle of which stood a tall pillar looking rather lost on its huge, many-stepped base. From what I could see, this area was being used as a market or public meeting place. At least there were more people here, some hurrying along looking down as if lost in thought, while others were gathered in clusters, talking about who knew what. Stalls had been set up haphazardly and were displaying wares, while a small but busy open air market hosted several merchants selling pack animals: a camel or two, some donkeys, mules, horses, and even a few sheep and goats and pigs. Other stalls held fruits and vegetables, and a few displayed items like fabrics, pottery, and jewelry. The cries of venders calling out to passersby seemed lost in that huge space—nothing like the crowded markets of Antioch.

One area even had a kind of stage set up for various forms of entertainment: the usual jongleurs, musicians, tumblers, and a chained bear with bald patches on its dusty coat. At a nearby booth, painted whores danced or sang obscenities and displayed their private parts to any man who would look their way. I was reminded of the Mongol camps and the painted whore I had seen there. Some things were the same everywhere, it would seem.

I saw no more of Bardas and Alexander and prayed that they had not lost us in the crowd. It seemed as though there was little they could do, but I still felt faint hope.

After passing through several great empty rectangles littered with a few scattered remains of statues or the burned-out ruins of houses, we turned aside and passed through a set of gates guarding the city's somewhat tumbledown inner walls, and over a weedy wasteland to reach a second set of walls and gates. Both sets of walls rose up, majestic yet somehow forlorn, and clearly in need of repair. The gates looked poorly maintained, too. Given the few guards patrolling them, I wondered if these Franks could actually withstand a serious attack.

By sunset we had reached our destination, a country estate indeed, but quite close to the outer city walls, with farmland and vineyards surrounding it. The grain was turning gold and would soon be ready for harvest. We passed peasants wending their way back to their villages. For a moment I envied them, for they had true homes, however humble.

By the time we arrived, it was dark and I saw little beyond the usual courtyard arrangement of buildings. I was handed over to servants and my uncle was turning to depart with scarcely a word, but I panicked at the thought of being left so alone. On impulse I caught at the sleeve of his robe.

"Uncle, you do me great wrong. Do not simply leave me here without more farewell than this. You can at least have the courtesy to take supper with me."

"Of course, niece. I know how angry you are with me; I merely thought to spare you my presence until you calmed down and showed some sense. Truly, I am only trying to keep you from harm."

So we supped together, though without much cheer. At one point, though, I remembered to ask what Caterina had meant about me being different from my father.

Uncle Basil sighed. "Caterina belongs to an old Venetian family with strong ties to the Church. She was brought up strictly and, I might add, in ignorance of the corrupt politics of certain elements in the Church hierarchy; she has never wavered in her convictions. She finds it too easy to stand in judgment on others, even on your father."

"But why? Did she ever even meet him?"

"Only once, on his last voyage here. He let slip in her presence that after years of grief, he had finally found comfort in the arms of a new woman. While he would never remarry, she was willing to live with him as his concubine. I imagine you knew her."

"No, I never had any idea!" Several memories suddenly fit into place, beginning with my servant women gossiping about some "wicked harlot." I remembered the exact words: "She lives happily outside the sacred bonds of marriage, parading her finery and strutting about his palace like it's hers. Bent for hell, she is." It had never occurred to me that this harlot might be my Papa's woman.

And the love letter I had thought was meant for me, as though any of my father's half-literate knights could have written that: he must have written it for her! I blushed for shame over my arrogance, but even worse was the feeling of betrayal. My beloved Papa who had always seemed so brave, so pious, had led a second life away from my eyes, full of event and secret. What else had he kept from me?

"Did he say she had red hair and green eyes?" I asked. I might be mistaken....

My uncle looked surprised. "Yes, how did you know? You might have seen her and not known who she was."

"No, I never knew her. Papa never let his city life mingle with his country life, I think. It explains why his city palace always seemed filled with whispers and hidden eyes."

We fell silent for a while.

"I imagine she died when Kyiv fell," he finally said. "Perhaps she gave him comfort in his last days. I never held it against him; a man has his needs."

"I envy her," was all I could say now that my life both past and present was as reduced to rubble as my beloved Kyiv.

He said nothing to that. "It is too late to leave tonight. I will stay until tomorrow morning, but you need not rise early—I know you need your rest."

Once I was abed, deep melancholy threatened to settle on me. I had thought I had finally found my life's path, but it had turned not only into an unwelcome byway but also into one that seemed full of threat.

No, I could not afford such silliness anymore! Bardas and Alexander were free, so I still had a little hope. I would not give up, and I would find a way to flee to safety, if only for the sake of my unborn son.

The next morning soon after dawn, the noise of Uncle Basil's departure woke me. It was a truer abandonment than when Selim had left me in Alamut to face the Grand Master, but I knew the futility of pursuing and pleading this time. I arose and looked out the window to take in my new prison, an aging villa in what I later learned was the Roman style, still found across the Mediterranean. My room was on the second floor facing the city walls, and I could make them out in the distance, their towers gleaming pink and gold where they caught the rising sun, while the walls themselves were draped in the last blue shadows of night. Banjuu and Marguerite stirred and sat up from their pallets.

"Good morning, Mistress. What is your pleasure today?" asked Marguerite, as if we were still at home and nothing was amiss.

"My greatest pleasure would be to escape right now back to Antioch," I exclaimed, "but how to do it? I must think on a way to free us all and to reclaim my wealth. I still cannot believe that my own family has robbed me."

"I knew they were bad people," Banjuu burst out, "that Lady Caterina especially. She called me a little black monster and she slapped me when I wouldn't obey her, but I would never serve her, not ever!"

"Well, Marguerite can serve us all by going downstairs and seeing about breakfast, perhaps do a little looking around at the same time. I heard my uncle leave, so he is out of the way at least. We must hope that Bardas and Alexander followed us and can find a way to free us. Perhaps they will be able to lie in wait somewhere nearby. It seems rather empty around here except for the peasants, though I do see another villa in the distance. And if I can take walks, perhaps they can overpower the guards."

This idea cheered us all, but though Marguerite was well treated when she timidly went downstairs—indeed, during my stay so were we were all—our several jailers were courteous but tight-lipped. That morning we were allowed to roam about freely inside the villa courtyard, but none of us were able to discover anything useful beyond the fact that some of the servants spoke Frankish. We each hit a wall of silence whenever we asked questions that might be useful. And while the villa's grounds were extensive and I could see tiny villages and farms in the distance, it straightaway became clear that strict bounds had been set on my movements: I was not allowed farther than the courtyard.

I spent that first day unhappily exploring what I thought of as my prison, though it was as well appointed as the house in Constantinople. I must have looked out every window of the house, but I saw no sign of my men or of any way to escape. After that I gave up, unpacked my belongings, found my sewing box, and sat in the large courtyard with my girls, each with our own project. Since I was labeled a sinner now, I would embroider a new altar cloth to give the confessor that Caterina had insisted she would send me.

My outer quiet meant nothing, however. My mind was racing with absurd plans for escape, while underneath them lay a dull cloud of worry: had Sir Joscelin lied to me? I could not even bear to think about what I had learned about my father. Finally my hands fell idle. So many arguments fruitlessly chased each other inside my head, not just whether my beloved might have lied, but if so, how he could have presumed to judge my past?

But was that not an argument for his having some good explanation for these rumors Caterina had brought to me?

At one point I realized that since arriving, I had taken no notice of my surroundings beyond what they could do for me. I looked around. We were being kept in quite a golden cage. The courtyard, easily as large as Selim's andarun garden in Iran had been, was designed for ease and delight, with a fountain in its midst, trees for shade, and lovely flower and herb beds laid out in graceful fashion. Farther away were the usual outbuildings for horses, storage, kitchen, and so forth, but they were cleverly screened by the plantings. Birds were singing out joy, the sky was purest blue, the air was moist, and the light itself laid a golden hand on everything it touched. But none of this had power to gladden my heart. Nothing would, except the return of my beloved along with the end of all deceit, that and finding safe haven for us and our son.

A series of warm, golden days passed, so alike that I might be drifting down a river of endless time. Each day I would wander from room to room, gazing out of one window after another, especially if it faced the city, and each day my hopes of escape dwindled further. Were Bardas and Alexander out there somewhere? Perhaps they had given up and abandoned me to my fate.

The priest came and went: a Dominican, a gray-faced stick of a man with a mouth as puckered as a dried fig, which made him seem even more disapproving. It grew even more puckered as he questioned me about exactly what Joscelin and I had done together. It was so mortifying, as if he was looking in on our most sacred acts of love and pouring shame on them all. He had a long list of questions that he looked at from time to time, and each thing we had done together that was wrong in the Church's eyes—which was everything—was counted against me. I could not help feeling deeply ashamed and aggrieved over my faults, but I also felt violated and angry about losing the purity of my memories. The whole thing, man and confession and contrition, made me long for my old Orthodox priest—he whom I had once so resisted!

At the end of my unwilling confession, this priest shook his head at my sinful and degraded behavior and absolved me, but his full penance I never performed because it seemed even more degraded than my sins: bread and water for a year, plus I should scourge myself every day. At least he taught me a prayer of contrition to be counted many times on paternoster beads while kneeling before an alarming crucifix that he gave me. It was an especially gory Christ in agony. He did approve of the altar cloth, which I quickly finished and sent on to him—I regarded it in the light of a substitute for the scourging, since having anything to do with the man seemed like a scourge to me.

And I did the prayer of contrition for several sessions every day—but while on my knees, I also prayed for deliverance, most of all for my unborn child! I even tried to pray for forgiveness for my uncle and his wife, but that came harder. As to the bread and water, I saw no point in abjuring every meal and so contented myself with making that my breakfast custom. Who knows if I did wrong, but I was content with my compromises, as I felt that my love and loyalty for Sir Joscelin must count against my sins with him.

My jailers, whose names I never even learned, apparently decided that I had resigned myself to my lot. One day they let me outside the compound, accompanied by a guard, where I was relatively free to wander about the grounds with the girls. I didn't like the way the man kept eyeing me, but it was such a treat to be outside. The grounds were clearly laid out for delight: soft grasses surrounding paths that led to vistas, including of the city walls; old crumbling statues tucked among trees and shrubs of great beauty; air sweet with flowers and birdsong. I wondered what Greek nobleman had once owned this property and where he was now—which made me think of Uncle Basil again. I might be a pauper now. And despite my bluster, even were I to escape I had no idea how to get back to Antioch, much less regain control of my wealth. After that, the scenery meant nothing to me and I turned back.

In the middle of that night I woke to a click: the bedroom door, always locked from the outside, was slowly opening. Starting up and seizing a candlestick, I edged out of bed and stood before my two sleeping girls. I prayed that the intruder—would there be more than one?—was not there to murder us. Hopefully it would be that sly guard, and I would be able to protect us all. Surprise would be my first weapon.

The door swung fully open, the light of a candle lit up a face, and there indeed stood the guard—behind Bardas! My man put his finger to his lips and motioned to me to waken the girls. I lowered the candlestick and silently set it down, thankful I hadn't hit my own servant. I gently shook the girls, shushing each when she startled awake. They rose sleepily, but when Banjuu saw Bardas, she ran and embraced his waist, whispering, "I knew you would come." I could gladly have done the same. He gently set her aside, helped us to pack hastily, and led us down the stairs. There was no sound anywhere. The house itself seemed dead asleep.

The guard left us outside the villa gates, nodding at the faint jingle from a purse Bardas handed him. I could just make out Alexander and Leo past the hill on the road, holding the reins of four muffled horses.

Once mounted, with the girls seated before the men, we galloped off into the night guided only by thickly clustered stars. I turned to Bardas. "Please accept my deepest gratitude. But how did you manage to find us … bribe the guard … get us out so quietly?"

The brothers both laughed, but it was Leo who spoke. "Everyone in the villa is sound asleep and will waken with a head they'll regret. I'd have done worse, but I knew you would not approve, Lady. All it took was a cask of my very special spiced wine. I've made deliveries here at the villa a couple of times to lull everyone into trusting me—they thought I was working for your uncle. The man we bribed gave it to his fellow servants at supper. And serve the whole lot of them right tomorrow when they waken late with sore heads and thick tongues!"

Bardas added, "I have more good news for you, Lady. When Alexander came to me that evening, he knew only that you wanted to return to Antioch; but servants do gossip, and we heard all about your quarrel with your aunt and uncle. It was clear from what they said that you were in the hands of those who wished you no good, and we knew it for certain when Lady Caterina turned Alexander and me out into the street later that night. Well, they should have delayed doing that until after you left, told us some lie or other. Thank God they didn't, or we'd never have found you! We waited nearby until the next day, and out you came the next morning, guarded on all sides.

"We followed you, and when Marguerite looked out of that wagon straight at us and nodded, we knew for sure you were in it, too. We fell back and kept our distance, especially after leaving the city. As soon as we saw where they took you, we went back to your uncle's house and watched it. Sure enough, that afternoon the both of them left, and we simply went back in through the servants' quarters. They were all out in the stables drinking that bitch's best wine together and complaining about their poor wages and poor treatment—they dip into a cask, top it up with water, and move onto a new one all the time. She doesn't know the difference.

"We drank with them awhile like old friends. But after taking our leave, we headed straight to your uncle's office with none of them the wiser. We are sure we found the very paper he told you about. What a jest! We know no Latin, but while there were many papers that looked like merchant's business, only one looked official enough. And as far as I could tell, it was unsigned! King Baldwin is with King Louis right now, begging for gold or selling holy relics, so he cannot approve any such thing for some time. We left it just as it was so as not to alarm anyone, but we've kept a watch on the house most of the time ever since.

"Last night was our first chance to get back in. Your uncle and aunt were out, we got her servants nicely drugged with Leo's special wine, and your uncle was so sure of himself that the paper still lay in the same place. We took it and all the other papers on his desk, which I hope will cause him plenty of trouble! And now that you are free, my Lady, you only need tell us where you want to go!"

"I want to go back to Antioch. I want no more of this terrible place! And please accept my gratitude to you all from the bottom of my heart. If I have indeed lost nothing to my uncle, I'll soon be able to reward you handsomely!"

"Many thanks, Lady, but money could never buy our loyalty to you. It is the way you treat us.

"And … I found something else." Bardas pulled something from inside his robe and reached over to hand me not only the document but three letters from Sir Joscelin. "I know his seal. It was on his other letters when I brought them to you in Antioch. And I kept those other papers I took, too. They await you back in the city."

"Thank you again," was the most I could muster.

I spent the rest of the mercifully short ride avoiding thinking about the letters and the perfidy of my uncle. Instead, I tried to make a plan. It would be easy to find me in that ghost of a city once he learned about my escape, so I had little time to take ship. At least I still had my little casket of coins to pay for the passage back to Antioch, but where would I go? To Helene? In my disgraced state, would she befriend me or judge me? I knew nothing of Frankish attitudes about bastards, and even if she were to help me, what would my son's fate be? Well, I would just have to wait and see.

Dawn was almost upon us by the time we sighted the city gates. Realizing that we must not enter together or we would too easy to trace, I said, "Bardas, Leo, where did you get these horses?"

"They come from the inn where I cook," answered Leo. "The innkeeper keeps a stable where you can hire them. Yesterday I got the stableman and his son drunk on my special wine, and once they fell asleep I took these four. I only need to bring them back this morning before they waken. They may notice signs of travel on the horses, but they'll be too ashamed to say a word!"

"Well, you had best stop with that wine! You might make trouble for yourself one day!" Leo just smiled. "But do you think we could stay at this inn—or at least meet you there later? I think we should separate before we enter the city. We cannot all be seen together." This time they all nodded.

We soon sorted ourselves out. Marguerite and I would arrive first, riding side by side, with Bardas on foot as my guard. I was well dressed, our entry would excite no comment, and we would arrive long before the others did. Alexander and Banjuu would enter on foot a little way behind Leo, who would ride in leading the extra horse. It would almost be like the time I had entered Derbent disguised as a boy!

Separating was easy enough, as peasants and farmers were already lined up before the gates with cartloads of produce or skinned lambs. Marguerite, Bardas, and I passed through without difficulty, though I felt a moment of panic when it came our turn to pay the entry tax. By drawing my veil close over my face, a common enough custom in the city, I kept my hair and eyes well hidden while Bardas paid the sleepy guard. The tender light of dawn made even the damaged city glow as my man led the way toward Leo's inn. We stopped well down the street from it and waited while I tried to master my slow panic. Finally everyone else arrived.

After suggesting I go to another hostel nearby that served only Greeks and other so-called foreigners, Leo led the horses into the stables, promising to disappear from the inn quietly. Suspicion was bound to fall on him, anyway, so he had decided to leave straightaway.

My servants and I made our way to the other inn on foot, Bardas ordered good rooms, and I was able to get upstairs without being seen. Once I was safely hidden, my man went off to find out about departing ships. It could have been a dull day of waiting, but there was too much tension and even a little excitement among us to feel anything else. Indeed, we spent the rest of the morning listening to Alexander recount his adventures.

And adventures there were! "I was almost kidnapped," he proudly declared. Banjuu and Marguerite exclaimed in alarm. "Lady, do you remember that strange looking man we saw the day we arrived, the old one with long limbs and a baby face?"

We all three nodded.

"He is what they call a eunuch—do you know what that means?" And he made a snipping gesture in front of his privates.

"Yes, I know what they are." The girls clearly didn't, and I saw no reason to tell them. I doubted they knew much if anything about how men's and women's bodies differed.

"Well, I learned a lot about them through him. For centuries they used to be common here. Rich families would have one of their boys snipped, sometimes even have all of their privates shaved off completely, so they could get the best work in the palace or the government. Every emperor surrounded himself with them. The idea was that since they could never beget children, none of them could betray him and take the throne for their families. Stupid idea if you ask me! What's to keep a powerful eunuch from sticking a brother on the throne or at least getting his relatives into positions where they control everything?"

"I imagine that might happen," I said, amused, "but what makes you say so?"

"John of Epirus—that's his name—said it. He's one of the few eunuchs who remain in the capital. He works in some ministry or other, since the Franks know only how to loot—or at least that's what he says. He seems rather bitter. He said they banished or killed most of the other eunuchs."

"Well, what about this kidnapping?" Banjuu finally burst out, her eyes round with curiosity and alarm. "Did he try to seize you and make you into this eunuch kind of person?"

"Do you mean he wanted to make you into a girl?" Marguerite chimed in, looking horrified.

Alexander laughed. "As a matter of fact, that's what I do think! And more, too!"

It took much tracing back and filling in, much like repairing one of my damaged mosaic floors in Antioch, before his story came clear. Bardas and Alexander had roamed the streets for the first few days, trying not to be seen loitering near the villa and sleeping in a cheap inn near a wharf. In keeping an eye on my family's comings and goings, they ended up seeing a great deal of Constantinople. Little did they know that someone else was keeping an eye on their comings and goings.

This John of Epirus approached Bardas one day.

According to Alexander, the man said, "What a pretty boy you have there! I could lead him to great riches if you agree to put him under my tutelage. Please accept my invitation to dine with us any time you would like to know more." And having told Bardas how to reach his home, he bowed and departed with his men.

With little to do but wait for the right moment to free me, Bardas and Alexander decided they might as well get a good meal from the eunuch. John's house lay near the southern city walls, close to the grounds of a palace called Bukoleon, in one of the parts of town that had survived better than others. "Indeed," Alexander continued, "this palace is where the king sometimes lives on the rare occasions he is in Constantinople. Much of his government is located around there, too, and many of his ministers and officials live nearby.

"John treated us to a real feast! And he told us that there were many ways for a handsome boy like me to prosper, with such curling dark hair and fine eyes." Alexander hooted with laughter. "He said that under his guidance I could become wealthy in Nicaea or Epirus or even Trebizond. We politely refused and thanked him for his hospitality, and we parted on friendly terms."

"And where did the kidnapping come in?" I laughed. "It seems a mild enough adventure, and you were with Bardas the entire time."

"Oh, I knew what he really wanted," Alexander airily replied. "I once went home with a man who offered me money to use my body. I think that's all this John of Epirus wanted, too! But I never liked what that first man did to me, so I never did it again! I'm more of a man of the world than you think I am, Lady."

"I suppose you are, and I am saddened for it."

Alexander just laughed.

Horrified and concerned though I was about all this, I admit that one part of me only wished to send everyone away and read Sir Joscelin's letters.

Bardas returned late in the morning, having scoured the city. There were no ships leaving the next day, as it was Sunday. But that was not such a long wait, and in fact I was glad: I could visit the Cathedral of Hagia Sofia for Mass! It was located far from the church where my uncle went, and I wanted at least to see this wondrous palace for God before I left.

The rest of the day passed like an eternity. Leo appeared with his huge bundle of kitchen gear, settling into a corner of my room and falling deeply asleep against the wall despite Alexander teasing the girls and being silly. Bardas planted himself outside the room like an immovable statue, having armed himself with one of Leo's kitchen knives. That made me smile. He would hardly use it!

I did look through the documents Bardas had stolen from my uncle. Basil's certificate of guardianship was indeed unsigned, and I could only thank God that this King Baldwin's signature was necessary. Likely Basil had paid dearly for it, another way for the king to get his hands on more funds for his ravaged realm. I felt a dark delight imagining my uncle losing his money, which gave me a rather wicked idea.

I gave the task of destroying it to Alexander and the girls. They gaily fed every last scrap of that hateful document to the candles, a small and happily distant reminder of another fire I had once fed in order to escape.

Then I turned to my uncle's other documents. They certainly gave me an understanding of his business dealings, as well as showing me a way to get back at him. I was too angry to see how my outlook was hardening.

Finally, after an early supper brought up to my room, I sent Bardas, Leo, and Alexander to theirs.

And my girls having fallen asleep, I could turn to Sir Joscelin's letters. I opened them with trembling fingers. The seals had been broken on every one, which made my blood reach fever point. The first was dated April 30, 1249:

> *Beloved Sofia,*
>
> *We sail soon and I have little time to write, as Lord Gilles and I are overwhelmed with last details, there being some 1,800 ships to deal with, for the armies and for provisions and siege engines and so forth. Something always seems to happen to delay us or to complicate matters—for instance, the ships the Genoese and Pisans supplied for us are the wrong kind, and we will be forced to wade ashore once we arrive in Damietta. I pray this reaches you in time for you to reply and that you have found happiness in the bosom of your uncle's family.*
>
> *As soon as I return from this campaign, I will seek you out, we will take our vows in public before the church doors, and I will bring you home to Languedoc. I pray your parting from your second family will not bring you too great a grief when that time arrives, for it will by my happiest day. My annulment petition has been presented before the Pope himself and should be granted before this war is over.*
>
> *I pray and hope that there will be little fighting and that you and I will be united for eternity within the year.*
>
> *With a pledge of my eternal love,*
>
> *Your Joscelin*

Here was the fair and courteous knight I remembered. It was hard to reconcile this image with the one Caterina had painted of a lascivious scoundrel. Yet she had set doubt in my heart where it gnawed at my faith in him.

I turned to the second letter, dated June 15.

Beloved Sofia,

Greetings from Egypt. I have so much to say and so little time to say it. Our fleet was scattered in a great storm, so less than half of our ships arrived before the walls of Damietta. Even so, the Saracen army awaiting us melted away as our knights poured out and waded ashore. My king leapt from the ship and his men had to hold him back from attacking the enemy single-handedly, he was so eager.

We took the city with shocking ease. Its gates were wide open, which bodes well for a quick and easy campaign. Spies tell us that the sultan of Egypt is dying, which explains why his troops retreated so hastily. With no one to lead them, they are lost. We will be in Mansourah soon and then march on Cairo, where King Louis can name his terms and secure Jerusalem in perpetuity. Then I can return to your side. Meanwhile, we await the rest of the ships, which are expected any time now.

I often see you in my dreams at night. Once I saw an angel hovering over your shoulder, and it gave me comfort. Strangely, though, it was female, although I supposed when I awoke that it made sense, for would not a motherly angel bring you much comfort? I, alas, am without further comfort, for I got no word from you before I left. I pray that all is well with you and that it is only the vagaries of ships and weather that keep your letters from me.

With all my love,

Joscelin

My heart burned with frustration for a moment, but then a little common sense forced its way into it. Perhaps Basil had sent my letter and Joscelin had simply not received it. And at least my uncle hadn't destroyed my beloved's letters to me.

But mostly I felt relief and regret. The relief was that if there must be a "holy war", and I really had no idea why there should—it seemed to be a peculiarity of Western Christendom—it would be short, and not only for my sake but for all those involved, from the nobility to ordinary soldiers. And remembering the villages I had seen ruined in Iran, I prayed for all the humble people whose lives are always shattered by war.

My regret was for the time that had been lost. Now he would be too far away for my letters to find him. I sighed and turned to the third letter, dated August 2, only five weeks earlier.

Beloved Sofia,

The march on Mansourah is delayed, as the other troops have not arrived. Meanwhile, we have learned that Queen Marguerite is with child, though she insisted on coming with us. Someday I hope to have you with me wherever I go, too, with our own children by our sides.

While we wait, we suffer. The heat is enough to broil our brains. We all itch to be on with it but must simply bide our time and scratch fleas with our swords, so to speak. But my king takes careful steps and will not move until we are ready.

The only good thing about the delay is that he has completely taken me back into his favor. He has granted me my family lands and received my homage. Now I am Lord Joscelin, Baron of Braissac, a modest barony but large enough for us.

Surely it will be but a month or so more and I will be with you.

How I yearn for a letter from you. For all I know, you have received none of mine.

Your faithful Joscelin

I blew out my candles and went to sleep, eager for the next day. Surely if letters could come from Damietta, they could go the other way as well! And on the morrow, having called for a goose feather, ink and paper, I sharpened the quill and wrote:

August 24, 1249

Dearest Lord Joscelin, for such I may call you now,

First, joyous felicitations on your new title and on regaining your king's trust. How good it must feel to have your lands secured to you.

It seems that things have not gone according to plan for either of us. I only received your letters late last night, all three at once, and I am torn between gratitude that you are alive and well, and outrage at my uncle and his wife—I will not dignify her with the name of aunt—for withholding the letters you sent me, among other things! There is so much to say and all of it hard to put in any kind of order.

First, and most important, if you never received the letter I sent you before, you will not know that I am carrying your child, a son, God willing. I am both delighted and fearful, for the future is so unclear.

Next, I am no longer staying with my uncle, for he and his wife not only kept your letters from me, they kept me in seclusion while my uncle set out to discover who you are. They claim that you are a scoundrel and seducer who tricked me into thinking our betrothal counts as marriage so that you could get your hands on my wealth. They said I had committed a grave sin in lying with you. Worse, they imprisoned me in their villa outside Constantinople. I only escaped last night with the help of my faithful servants, who also rescued your letters from my uncle, or I'd never have heard from you!

Now I will seek refuge with Lady Helene in Antioch. I only pray she is not as judgmental as my own family. My uncle also sought to seize my wealth for himself by making himself my guardian, but now I am free from the both of them and all their plots.

But worst of all, his wife claims that Rotrou and Agnes are your bastards and that you left a trail of misbegotten children across the Christian states of Outremer. I could not answer them, and yet I cling to my faith in you. I pray this reaches you before you go to battle and that you never come to harm. And I pray that there is a guardian angel watching over you, too.

Your loving Sofia

I know just what it said, for I made a copy of that letter, thinking not only that I might have to wait until I reached Antioch to find a ship to send it, but that I might try sending it twice, something I never had never tried before. Instead, I kept it all these years and now I can finally part with it. Writing it eased my heart considerably.

Early the next morning, beckoned by the sound of church bells, I gathered my children and Bardas together and announced that he, Marguerite, and I would all attend Mass that morning, but that Banjuu and Alexander must stay behind with the door locked. I told them that as she was Muslim she need not go, and that Alexander must keep her safe. I did want her to feel safe, but I had an unspoken aim: her dark skin was unusual enough in Constantinople that it might give us all away.

Bardas found a litter for Marguerite and me, and we hastened to the great Cathedral of Sofia for Mass, my bodyguard on one side and my cook on the other. She seemed most uneasy and at one point said, "My Lady, do you not fear discovery? What if your aunt and uncle attend Mass here?"

"They always go to a little chapel near their home, but I would be very surprised to find them at any church today. They most likely have received word of my escape and will be caught up in what to do next."

And so it was: they were not there, which was a good thing since so few people were. The cathedral was in dismal disrepair. Someone kept it clean, at least, but the ikonostasis was gone, some of the walls were wantonly damaged as high as a tall man's arms could reach from horseback, and the altar looked makeshift and barren. Yet the cathedral was still amazing, with the largest dome I have ever seen—indeed, it is the largest in the world—floating like a cloud above the windows on which it rests. The windows allowed honeyed light to pour in and light up the upper walls, all of which are decorated with magnificent glittering gold and colored glass mosaics. Farther down, more mosaics were set aglow by enormous hanging lamps—at least where they were lit. Lofty stone or marble pillars, some banded with iron, divided the space, and a great gallery ran in a half circle along the walls opposite the altar.

There was too much to take in, though I bowed and crossed myself whenever anyone else did, tried to follow the priest's barely audible sermon, recited the Creed, received Communion, and kissed the book of Scriptures as the other worshippers did, and offered silent prayers for Sir Joscelin, my dependents and myself. I had meant to stay afterwards and pray further, for by the end I was deeply moved by this sad, beautiful place, so full of sacredness despite everything that had been done to it. But Marguerite was near tears and began tugging at my skirts to leave as soon as the Mass was over. Well, she was so young and vulnerable. So we left.

We were outside the cathedral staring at the tallest column and statue I had ever seen—it was almost as high as the cathedral roof—when I caught sight of that same eunuch who had hosted Bardas and Alexander. I suddenly had an idea. Turning to Bardas I said, "I wish to meet this John of Epirus. Come, present me to him." And I boldly stepped toward the man, who was stopping to share some witticism with his companions. My bodyguard looked most unhappy, but he did as I commanded.

"I understand that you took a friendly interest in my boy," I said in as neutral a voice as I could muster.

He looked a little abashed, but he kept his poise. "Yes, a handsome and most promising youth. I only wished to do him a good turn, but perhaps he and Bardas here misunderstood. I hope you do not think I intended anything else. I often act as an agent for well-placed government officials in Nicaea and Epirus, as well as Trebizond, so I am always looking about me to see where I can make a profit for all concerned.

"Perhaps I can even do you a good turn," he added in a pacifying voice. "I know the city well, and I have many Frankish friends in the ministry where I work."

"I thought as much. And I understand. Quite well." I smiled coolly.

"Well, you know," he smiled back slyly, "it is always better to make friends than enemies."

I laughed. "All right, John of Epirus. Tell me where I can write you and I might contact you. I could use someone to act on my behalf in this city, so perhaps we can do business. Is there anyone here who can vouch for you?"

"Indeed there is." He gave me the names of a pair of men I had heard my uncle mention in passing as trusted business partners. "Both have used my many services in the past. If you ask them about me, you will hear only the highest praises of my work. I am utterly trustworthy."

For once I looked at all the body signals I had learned as a translator and saw nothing to make me disbelieve him. We parted in cautiously friendly fashion. Indeed, that very afternoon I sent Bardas to the homes of the two men John had mentioned to ask among their servants, who are always the most reliable sources of information. He returned, his head a bit the worse for the wine he'd shared with them at my expense, but with the good news that the eunuch was actually well respected for his business acumen, even though they mocked his unmanned condition.

Bardas also learned John's story: a younger son in a noble family, he'd been made into a eunuch as a boy and sent from Epirus to Constantinople to take service in the court, unaware that within a year the Franks would storm the city. It had been hoped he would rise in the bureaucracy and find ways to benefit his family, but those plans were cut off as surely as was his future as an ordinary man, and he was lucky to survive the killings and starvation that followed the Frankish conquest. A wealthy Venetian merchant took pity on the starving, homeless boy, and took him in first as a servant and later, when John proved himself so useful, as a trusted assistant in his business. When the merchant decided to leave Constantinople for Epirus, he arranged for John to stay on as his agent as well as to take on a minor role in what passed for government under King Baldwin II.

So, reassured by these findings, I began to shape my plan.

The next morning we all left on a merchant ship, in a convoy heading to Antioch. I looked back with such mixed feelings: though too much had gone wrong there, anyone could still see Constantinople's greatness. Indeed, I doubt any other city on earth comes close to what she must have been in her glory. I had seen so little of her, but perhaps I could return some day with Lord Joscelin. I rolled the word "lord" in my mouth like sweet wine. A lordly husband, a home, a safe haven at last!

It took a few weeks to reach Antioch, as we had to seek refuge in a small island port when a sudden and frighteningly violent storm struck. This time I wanted to survive. We stayed in an inn and, by what seemed a happy chance, met a stout Pisan merchant who was on his way to Damietta with several of his ships carrying supplies for King Louis' troops. I could not have asked for better and gave him a second letter for Sir Joscelin along with my first. He assured me that he and his men were all expert sailors who would have no trouble making their way there swiftly and safely, that he himself would put the letter into my husband's hands.

Alas that he began to be overly friendly; I felt his eyes roaming over my figure every time he thought I wasn't looking, so I was glad to set sail again. I seemed to be increasing daily and could only be grateful for the loose Oriental-style gowns favored in Antioch. I could already feel my son stirring inside me.

It was early October when we arrived in Antioch, and I was never so happy to be back in a city. We spent the first night in a noisy inn, but the next morning Bardas went off with a message for Lady Helene while I waited, torn between impatience and fear. Would she think I had lied when I'd assured her that Sir Joscelin and I had been celibate with each other? Would she let me explain? And what would I do if she abandoned our friendship? I was close to showing now, and not even loose garments could hide my condition for much longer.

Bardas returned mid-morning with Lady Helene by his side and two of my first orphans, Irene and her brother Fotis, following behind. Both seemed half a head taller than when I had last seen them. They were as happy to see me as I was to see them. Helene and I having embraced with many tears, she promptly said, "You must not think of staying anywhere but with me."

I stopped her, though, and whispered, "You must wait until you have heard my story first. You might change your mind."

She shook her head and laughed. "Tell me, then." So we walked slowly up to her house, and I explained a little about my uncle and his wife. Irene shyly took my hand, and my friend merely smiled indulgently. Fotis sidled up close to my other side, and she said nothing. She had always been kind to her servants, and both brother and sister were clearly petted.

After hearing of my uncle's and Caterina's misdeeds, Lady Helene looked satisfyingly shocked. She put her arm through mine and said, "You were right to come back here. What terrible people! And I can think of no reason why you should not stay with me."

"Well, there is more," I said. "I would rather share the rest when we are alone with each other."

She looked at me with a question in her eyes but merely nodded. "We are almost home. I can wait."

At last, having sent my servants off with hers, she led me up to her little solar and waved me to a window seat large enough to share. "Now, tell me all." And so I did, praying that she would understand and at least forgive my sin.

"Worst is the fact that I cannot answer their attacks on Sir Joscelin.

And I know so little about how the Franks and the Church of Rome view betrothals and remarriage that I feel helpless. Please believe me, Helene, had I known I was sinning so deeply, I'd have fought temptation and won." This was not exactly true, but I so wanted her to take my part—after all, I was not some harlot. She need not know that I could not regret my interlude with my knight or its result. "But by now the annulment has surely been granted. And once this war is over, God willing, Lord Joscelin will return to me and make it all right again."

Helene looked somber. "Yes, God willing." And we crossed ourselves. "I know so little about church law," she added, "but this priest of Caterina's has absolved you and set your penalties for what you have done.

"Truth be told, I never had to think about those things. I was given in marriage at thirteen to Lord Gilles—he was twenty-eight. I grew up here in Antioch and knew nothing about marriage but that I must obey my husband without question. His offer for my hand was a boon from God according to my family, what with his connections to King Louis, and I always counted myself among the fortunate few, for he never beat me. We grew to love each other. I think he is a rarity in another way, too, for most men tend to meddle on the side with women of low degree, and he never does."

She fell silent for few moments. "Indeed, I wonder if that is not the truth behind these tales about Sir Joscelin. If so, it can hardly matter." Her explanation did not help me feel better, especially after what I had endured as a slave.

"But what worries me," she added, "is that you are held in high repute in Antioch, and that will change if word spreads that you are carrying a child out of wedlock. It seems to me that you had best remove to one of your orphanages as soon as possible. I have a good physician who can keep his lips sealed, and I will send him to you. And when the time comes, if Sir Joscelin has not yet arrived back here, annulment in hand, and the marriage taken place straightaway, I'll send you my midwife and find you a good wet nurse if you wish. A few coins in their palms and they will remain silent, too. And you are doing penance. That is the important thing."

Seeing the distress on my face, she added, "No need to despair, Sofia. How rare is a love like yours, both in spirit and in body. It is what the Church preaches—and," she laughed, "we are told that procreation is the only reason to lie with one's spouse, so in one sense you are fulfilling Mother Church's commands, just in the wrong order."

I smiled, too, though I felt less than reassured. But Helene turned to other matters. She had received news from Lord Gilles, who said that the remaining ships still had not arrived. She thought it strange that warships could disappear like that, considering how many letters sailed back and forth courtesy of the Genoese and Pisan fleets that brought supplies to Damietta.

At one point she stopped. "Oh, you could write Sir Joscelin now! Here are quills, ink, knife, and paper. I will leave you to it; I hear little Gilles crying," and up she jumped and left me alone. From below came a baby's lusty yells.

I suddenly began to tremble. Would I soon be presenting my beloved with a lusty son? God willing?

So I moved in with Helene, and another letter sped on its way the next day. I too sped straightaway, to see Matthew of Edessa. He jumped up in surprise when I entered his cluttered office, but he sent a servant for refreshments and closed the door on his clerks. We spent the entire morning together going over my dealings, all of which had done very well.

"God lays a protective hand over everything you touch, for rarely have I seen such profits made time and again. I have begun sending my own wares on the same ships I use for your goods, as they never seem to run afoul of bad weather or pirates."

"Well, let us pray that my good fortune continues, for I have need of much money and of trusty agents."

"Oh, do you plan to open another orphanage?"

"No, I plan to buy good land in the Languedoc if there is any to be found. I know nothing of its customs, but I intend to establish myself there shortly."

He frowned and shook his head slightly but said, "I will see what I can find out for you."

"One more thing," and I handed him a list of certain goods scheduled to arrive in Constantinople; it came from my uncle's stolen papers. "There is a shipment I am interested in that is expected to arrive in Constantinople in the next few weeks. I particularly want to buy the fabrics and dyes, and the herbs and spices. If you have an agent there, one who could be trusted to keep close counsel, I need someone to bid on them for me. Of course if the bidding goes too high, I would want him to bow out, but I would like to try."

"I am sure these goods are of highest quality—I know who these carriers are, and they handle only the best. I will send a message by my own couriers and arrange it all." Smiling, he stood and bowed. "As always, Lady Sofia, I am happy to help you, and I am glad you are here again. What news of your uncle?"

"Oh, he was gone most of the time I was there. I decided it made more sense to live here after all. If you have ever been to Constantinople and seen its ruination, you will understand."

He nodded. "Indeed I do," and we parted with him none the wiser about my uncle or raising questions about my wanting those goods, which I never intended to purchase.

Nor did he know anything about a certain letter I wrote to John of Epirus. I sent Bardas down to the port with it, where he found a willing shipmaster about to sail for Constantinople. And now the dice were cast. Or perhaps, better said, the lure was about to be cast!

My next visits were to my three homes for orphans, to visit Efrem and Mary and Jonah and the other caretakers and warn them that I might be followed and not to give away my whereabouts. Foremost, of course, I wanted to see that all was well with my young wards. Coming back to the first home, the one the Hospitallers still so graciously allowed me to use, brought back such memories, not only of my first children, most of them now in service with others, but of my beloved Sir Joscelin. How could a man of such generous heart be lying to me? When I met with the caretakers, they asked about him and spoke of our upcoming nuptials as if there was no war or other possible hindrance.

Mary was now happily nursing her first son. "One of many, I hope, Lady Sofia. And I hope I do no wrong in wishing the greatest happiness to you and your fine lord when he returns and for many sons of your own."

She mistook my deep flush for modesty.

I did spend a little time talking with Agnes and Rotrou, all the while trying to discover any resemblance to Sir Joscelin, but other than their both having his eye color, I saw little. Neither knew anything about their fathers, as they had different mothers and came from different villages.

At one point Agnes said in a curious tone of voice, "Do you think the fair knight who found us might be our father? That would be pleasant." And I had to drop my questioning for fear of revealing how I felt about that.

The last home I visited was the villa near Daphne. It was so peaceful up there, with lush woods, sweet streams flowing down to the Orontes, sweeping views of Antioch and its valley, and glimpses of the far-off sea. There were fewer children there, too, most of them older and almost ready to find work in the trade they had learned. The buildings with their repaired walls, some of which still bore traces of elegant mosaic murals, were graceful and placed in such harmony, and the air was sweet and soft—not like Antioch, which stank horribly on hot summer days from the river and the garbage.

Helene was right. I must bear and raise my child in secret, and clearly this was the ideal place. I felt no desire to stay in Antioch, not with those two children nearby and with the ghost of my happiness with Sir Joscelin there to haunt me. In Daphne I could be safe, and after the birth I could keep my baby with me while leading the outer life of a virtuous widow.

Why, my son could pass as one of my orphans! A sudden chill passed through me. I crossed myself and whispered a prayer for my beloved.

I returned to Helene's house with several plans in mind. After the evening meal, I excused myself and wrote to Anna and Maryam. Given all we three had been through, I felt I could trust them with my secret, and I also wanted to ask Maryam about any contacts she might have in the Jewish community. I had decided to expand my trade connections into the interior of Syria, and Matthew of Edessa had too few of them. He thought me strange for wanting to deal with "pagans", as he called them, but I only saw another business opportunity. No matter what happened to me, I wanted to make certain that my child would be wealthy enough to enjoy a good life.

Helene understood, at least, and threw herself into helping me make plans. A few days later, having showered her with gifts of gratitude, I left for Daphne and settled in, taking the time to make it as homelike as I could. The children were no trouble, and I even began teaching letters to a few of the likelier ones.

Cool weather arrived, and so did a missive from Lord Gilles, which Helene brought up to share with me. He mentioned Lord Joscelin in it, and it was clear that my beloved had received nothing from me. Most of the letter was an account of what the army was doing. It seemed that the missing ships, which had been arriving piecemeal, were now all accounted for, so the army was preparing to move south along some river toward a city called Cairo by way of this Mansourah that Joscelin had mentioned. The men, soldier and knight alike, were eager to get on with the invasion, but the king was nothing if not cautious—not counting the time when he leapt from his ship so eagerly!

I also heard back from John of Epirus in Constantinople, whose letter was also full of eagerness: to serve. He accepted the terms I had suggested and would gladly do as I had asked. Now I must await the results.

They came in November, and I was filled with unholy glee. Looking back I blush, but I was still so angry. My uncle had gone to the warehouses that held the goods I had asked Matthew of Edessa to bid on, expecting to have the shipment all to himself. Instead, he became mired in a bidding war, not only with Matthew's agent but with my own, someone John of Epirus had hired. Both agents withdrew when the price grew so high that little profit was to be made, and Uncle Basil was left to pay a staggering sum for the goods and none the wiser that he had been tricked. Straightaway I sent monies to John through the Knights Templar banking system, which has branches in every major Frankish-held city.

Indeed, I was so pleased that I wrote John asking him to seek out other similar occasions when goods arrived that my uncle might try to buy. But he must wait a few months, as it would not do to play the same trick too soon. And this letter he did receive and act upon as well.

ANNO DOMINI 1249-1250

It was mid-December and snowing lightly when my baby was born. I had made my will and commended myself to God. In truth, I was terrified of giving birth. But Helene's midwife was there, and a likely wet nurse who supposedly resembled me in looks and temperament, for that is the Frankish way. Helene was by my side, along with Banjuu and Marguerite and Irene. But seeing how upset and useless the girls were, asking questions about whether I might die, I sent them away when my labor began to really pain me.

And it did hurt! Now I understood why Helene had howled and wept so much when little Gilles was born. At one point I lost all sense of waking or sleeping and thought I saw the ghosts of my Mama and my cousin Irene looking on and it was not clear whether they wanted me to join them by dying in childbirth as they had or to live on! Well, I had never so wanted to live. The birthing seemed to go on for days—in fact, it only took two, the second of which was the fiery pain of hell—but in the end I was delivered, not of a son but of a lustily screaming daughter.

What I had not expected was that despite the fact that she was not a son, I fell entirely in love with her. Nor had I expected to feel such a fierce and protective love. Indeed, as I lay there holding her in my arms for the first time, I was almost overcome with terror for this tiny being who was already nuzzling blindly to find my breast. I wanted nothing more than to ensure her happiness, even if it meant sacrificing my own life. I remembered Sir Joscelin saying he had seen a female angel hovering over me, but he had been only partly right: she was not a woman but a girl. Now it was up to me to see that she was not only safe but that she kept her angelic innocence in this dark world. I named my little darling Anna.

To Helene's horror, on impulse I decided to nurse my daughter myself, recalling how to start the flow from witnessing my fellow slave Tsetsegmaa nursing little Kuchan in the Mongol camps. And a few days later, I sent word to Anna's namesake and to Maryam, for who else was there to rejoice with me? And I chose Saint Anne, mother of the Holy Virgin, as her patron. She seemed ideal.

The Christmas Holy Days passed quietly. Soon it would be 1250! I was not able to attend church for over a month, as Helene had warned me that women were banned from entering church for that long after giving birth. My new religion seemed to offer surprises on all sides, many of them meaningless to me, but I bore with the custom. Besides, Mass offered little comfort for my situation, though I of course had Anna baptized. Helene and the three girls took her, which was hard, for I'd have liked to be there.

However, it meant that no one would question her origins, as Helene let the priest think that Anna was just another orphan I had collected for my children's home. But when they returned and my darling daughter nuzzled at my breast for her milk, I almost wept with the joy of feeding her. She was already beginning to put her tiny hand up to touch me, right over my heart.

It was not long before my first Anna wrote back and asked me to visit her when I felt recovered enough. I did so in early March, accompanied by my servants and a few guards hired in Antioch. My tiny Anna and I went by covered litter so as not to be recognized in the city, although in hindsight I think I was being too careful.

The journey took all day, and it was exhausting. I began to realize that I had made a mistake bringing such a young baby so far in one day: little Anna cried half the time and nearly drove me so mad that I almost wished I had a wet nurse after all! At least I no longer feared to be outside. Indeed, if I had to choose, I now felt safer where I could see all around me and knew what the dangers were.

Finally she fell deeply asleep just as we arrived at Adar al-Mas'udi's castle, where my former servant now lived in splendor with her husband's family. What a change for a Hungarian peasant! It gave me faith in my own future. All the women turned out to greet me. I was put straight to bed, my infant by my side, my girls nearby, and Alexander and Bardas somewhere with the male servants.

The next morning Adar al-Mas'udi came to the women's quarters and welcomed me. He stayed until the afternoon. I watched him and his Anna closely and was glad to see that he seemed as happy as she was, for their union flew in the face of all custom. Their son was crawling and trying to stand, and it was clear they both adored him. And his older half-brother did not seem too jealous, even held him up by his hands and led him around in little awkward, stumbling steps.

"Your Anna looks as beautiful as her mother," Adar smiled. We laughed softly, recalling the time when he had so gently but relentlessly taken my first Anna from me. How glad I was for her now.

After a happy two weeks with my friends, they sent us off with so many gifts that they had to send a mule and extra servants with me to bring them all back. Soon after I returned to Daphne, Helene came to see me. She had received another letter from Lord Gilles. The news seemed hopeful, dated February 5. As best as I can recall, it read something like this:

> "The sultan of this godforsaken place has died, his subjects have lost all heart, and their soldiery is faint with fear! It will not be long before I greet you and our firstborn son, dear wife. We are now deep into Egypt, and we have made camp on the north bank of a river called Nile. Across the river is the city of Mansourah, though for now Egyptian forces block us.
>
> "It is turning dangerous, though. Several soldiers, not paying attending to their duty, have been killed at night, throats slit. Even a few knights never wake to see the day. We arose once to find several with heads severed from their bodies."

Though this detail made me shiver, I also had to smile at the grim irony: those locals, so faint with fear, seemed to be waging quite a successful secret war on the camp.

"But I was guarding King Louis' pavilion when a local Bedouin was brought before him. From what the translator said, it sounded as if for much gold the man will show them an unguarded ford where the army can cross in secret. I asked the translator later why this man would betray his own people, and he told me that the fellow is a heretic who believes that some man named Ali is God—Ali instead of Allah, ha ha—and that he hates the sultan. Anyway, later that day a battle plan was devised. In a few days a vanguard will cross the ford. Once they take the enemy camp by surprise, our main army will follow, and then on to easy victory in Mansourah!"

There was more, but it was not meant for my eyes. Glad though I was to learn that the war might soon be over, I felt such sadness at not being able to hear from Sir Joscelin. If he had sent any letters, they would go to Constantinople and be seized by my uncle. I wished he would send something by Sir Gilles, who seemed to have no problems with his letters! Then I wondered if any of mine had even reached him. He might be despairing of me by now.

And when would I find out the truth about his "bastards"? When would the annulment free us to marry? When would our daughter, already so laughing and curious, be freed from the taint of bastardy? There was no way of finding out unless Sir Joscelin learned where to write me. But I could hardly contact my uncle and ask him to redirect any letters. My heart insensibly hardened even further.

As well, the reference to the Bedouin who worshipped Ali made me realize that Shi'a and perhaps even Nizari were everywhere in the Outremer, as Helene called it. It gave me shivers to think about them. Here they were called Hashishim, or Assassins, for their political murders reached at one time into every corner of this world and even threatened kings.

When I asked Helene about their presence in the Holy Land, she confirmed it and added some strange tales about them, too. She claimed that only someone who was drugged with hashish and seduced by lies could be possessed by such fervor. Men were supposedly willing to throw themselves off cliffs if their Grand Master ordered it! The truth was both more complex and sadder. And I could see little difference between a Muslim holy war and a Christian one: both driven by fear, hatred, and misunderstanding, and both justified by faith. But that was simply a thought that

I soon dismissed. I was far more interested in getting revenge on Basil, which I suppose made me as guilty of wrongdoing as anyone.

In mid-March a messenger arrived from Constantinople with the news that John of Epirus' man had tricked my uncle into another bad bargain; I rejoiced.

It was the last time I was to rejoice for years.

❦

Lady Helene came to visit me in mid-March; we were preparing to celebrate the New Year on Lady Day and Easter directly after it. Her face was streaked with tears. "A ship arrived from Egypt," she cried as soon as we were alone. "Dear God, King Louis' army is somehow destroyed and he is taken prisoner."

"What? How can that be?"

"No one knows. All I know is that he and a few of his closest knights will be ransomed, but most of the troops were slaughtered or sold into slavery—and their wives, too. Dear God, I'd have gone with Lord Gilles had I not been pregnant! Where is my husband now, and where is your betrothed?" She subsided into sobs that racked her body.

I turned to stone.

Then the tears began. Arms around each other, we wept.

The Holy Days passed like a dark dream.

Over the next few months, news trickled in as more ships arrived in Acre, some carrying soldiers who had escaped Damietta with nothing but their lives and, on occasion, their families. Queen Marguerite had left for Acre after personally overseeing the exchange of ransom for prisoners, and King Louis had followed on another ship, penniless and wearing clothing borrowed from the new sultan. Of his brave knights taken prisoner, some were now free but others must wait until monies arrived from their homes to redeem them. Would Joscelin be among those already freed? Or might he be languishing in a Saracen prison? I could not let myself think of him dead. Perhaps I should write to Acre, or even go there.

I settled for writing. Anna was too young to leave behind. I never found out what happened to my letter, though, for there was no answer. I tried not to despair, for things were surely in a tangle there and I had not known how best to direct the missive. And storms on the Mediterranean might have taken its ship—and many unfortunates—to the bottom of the sea, as it was such a stormy year. There was no way to find out.

Despair lay over all of the Christian princedoms, for we were all touched by the loss in one way or another. Beyond worrying about Lord Joscelin's fate, I could only imagine the pain of the lowly soldiers, the squires, and the women and children who were not on the queen's ships. They were likely either slain or sold into slavery. My heart twisted remembering the orphan boys I had allowed Sir Joscelin to take on as servants. They had probably been on this campaign, too, and were all dead, my efforts to give them a good life gone for naught.

Word reached us that King Louis had reached Acre a broken man. Some of his faithful retainers were staying with him along with those mercenaries who had survived, but most of his knights who could were returning home to fields and family. Had I not been afraid to go that far with my little Anna, who was just learning to sit up by herself, I'd have leapt aboard the next ship, somehow gained entry to the king's presence, and begged—nay, demanded—to learn my beloved's fate!

As time crawled past spring and into summer, Helene felt less and less hope that her husband was still alive, but I refused to give in to my own fears for Lord Joscelin. I sometimes visited her and her circle of friends in Antioch, but I felt uneasy away from Anna. I became a recluse except for business every few weeks with Matthew of Edessa, or seeing to my orphanages, or finding places for my older orphans as servants or skilled workers. I would never let any of them serve a knight again!

I think it was late July when King Louis sent Helene a message from Acre that Lord Gilles had been killed in battle. She came to me and wept in my arms. At one point, she lifted her blotched wet face and whispered, "I did keep myself together long enough to ask about Sir Joscelin, but the messenger shrugged and shook his head. I could get nothing from him."

She left, but a week later, unable to be alone with her grief, she shut up her house in Antioch and appeared at my villa in Daphne clad and veiled in the white of mourning, holding little Gilles in her arms and looking like a ghost. A few of her servants had accompanied her and were looking around curiously. All she said was, "May I stay with you so that we can comfort each other?"

Embracing her, I said, "You are welcome to live with me as long as you wish. But other than Irene and Fotis you'll need no servants here, as I have trained my orphans to serve me. They can serve you, too."

She took my meaning and sent her people straight back to Antioch.

For the next year, she cut herself off from all her other women friends, as none of them had lost her husband. They regarded her grief as excessive, but then they felt little love for their spouses. During that time we clung to each other, not a day going by without our tears. I did what I could for her, but she was prostrate with grief, and sometimes seemed half-mad. She grew thin and listless, and her interest in her little son Gilles veered from none at all to clinging to him in a way that made him push away and cry.

But after doing what I could for her and knowing no other remedy for my own sorrow, I turned to what I had always done when hope was lost: I threw myself into activity. There was my charming Anna to dandle, there were Helene and Gilles to look after, and there were the orphanages and my business to keep me busy.

I did all these things with a leaden heart, all but dandling Anna. She became my sole joy in life, and I spent far more time with her than most mothers do—and likely petted her far too much—but she so loved to smile and wave her tiny arms and legs, to open and close her little flowers of fingers and to grasp just one of mine, and to make all the usual infant noises from cooing to screaming. I found them all novel and charming. Banjuu and Marguerite and Irene loved and petted her, too, so she grew fat and cheerful if rather demanding of her way, from food to anything shiny she could put in her mouth.

And my fledgling empire did expand. Maryam wrote back with letters of introduction to merchants in her community, and I soon found a reliable agent who helped me extend my trading ventures as far away as al-Mawsil. This was not easily accomplished, given the unstable nature of the relations between Muslim atabegs and sultans and caliphs and the like; I had never really learned to distinguish between all these titles, though they were important to those in the throes of their rivalries and battles, small and large. And al-Mawsil itself was slipping ever further under the Mongol yoke, though trade was still possible.

As the summer slowly passed, Helene began to show some signs of life again, though she sometimes forgot her son unless he came to her. Luckily, with the other young ones about to play with him, especially Fotis, who was the most forbearing, little Gilles was growing into a sturdy, boisterous child. Fotis once told me that he had never realized that a wealthy child could lose its parents as easily as a poor child could—it was why he felt like an older brother to Gilles.

Indeed, it seemed that Gilles and Anna both had a happy effect on the other children, who seemed to delight in caring for them when the three girls would let them.

I brought no new orphans to the villa in Daphne, and over the following years as the children grew up and I found places for them, I made it my first proper home since I had lost mine in Kyiv. Little by little, I found a chair here or a table there. One by one, I embroidered curtains and tablecloths and bedspreads and cushions. It began to feel like it truly was home, full of life, and a haven for my best memories. I might sew a new cloth or cushion and embroider it in a style I had learned from one of my lost friends, honoring her and feeling her presence. I sometimes imagined them with me, sitting side by side on their special cushions: Q'ing-ling, a Chinese noblewoman who had been my second mother, Perijam, a playful little Persian wife and the closest to a sister I had ever had, and even the slave women whose lives I had shared in the Mongol camps.

In mid-October came a small break in the clouds of sorrow that over-hung Helene and me. It began when an unwelcome visitor arrived and asked for me by my full Rus' name. When a servant brought me the message I almost turned my uncle away. I had no use for him anymore; he was no longer family to me! But curiosity outweighed disgust, and I admitted him as far as the courtyard.

"Basil," I said, as neutrally as I could while waving toward a bench under a pomegranate tree. Anna was in my arms, though she wanted only to wiggle and reach away from me now that she could crawl. "How did you find me?"

"Matthew of Edessa told me where you were." I saw my error. I had not thought of warning him.

"And what brings you here?" Helene looked out one of the doors to the courtyard and gave me a questioning look, but I waved her back. I was not afraid of him anymore.

He looked much older than when I had last seen him, with flabby pouches under his eyes like empty coin bags and the flesh on his face sagging and creased, his complexion as gray as the new streaks in his hair. He walked heavily to the bench and almost fell onto it.

"Grief, niece, grief twice over, for first I lost you, the last of my old family, and now I have lost my wife and to all purposes my children. Caterina died of a fever almost three months ago, and I have sent our children to Venice to be with her family. I cannot raise them alone.

"Is this your child? She is beautiful; she has your green eyes, and such red-gold curls!"

"Yes, she is: my bastard, the one you wanted to disappear." But, never able simply to say something harsh without regret, I added, "On the other hand, I understand, Uncle Basil, how hard it is to lose someone you love."

He frowned and sat looking down at the ground for several heartbeats. "Well, I suppose I deserve that. And as you may have guessed, love was less the bond between Caterina and me than money, though I do miss her and the children."

After another long pause, he looking up at me and added, "But as for you, is there any hope that we might reconcile? I truly seek to make amends. I feel so ... empty of purpose now that there is no one left in my life. I only wanted my family to be well off and safe, but God has stripped me of that lie. The wheel of fortune has turned downward for me. My business dealings have been a disaster all year: overpaying for goods, ships lost, bad debts falling on my head all at the same time.

"Your servant—it was Bardas who stole papers from me, yes?" I nodded. "That is what my servants thought. He did me a bad turn. He took a sheaf of my business papers along with the document that gave me guardianship over you, though I doubt he knew what they were and just wanted to cause harm. And a few letters from your Sir Joscelin that I had kept from you—only for your protection, I swear it on the Holy Cross!" This he likely added because I must have looked as angry as I felt.

He sighed when I did not answer. "I imagine he simply threw my papers away."

I shrugged. If my uncle's losses extended beyond my acts of revenge, well and good. He deserved to suffer! I felt no regret for what I had done, nor would he ever find out my role in his undoing.

"But that is all in the past. Today I humbly ask your forgiveness, for I know I treated you ill."

I was not impressed. My trust in him had been too violated. But while he was speaking, he was removing several folded pieces of paper from his wallet and holding them out to me. "Perhaps these will soften your heart toward me."

I took them: three letters from Sir Joscelin, each with the seal broken. "Did you read them?" I asked, my face flushing.

"I did, and I have finally had to admit that he truly loves you." He coughed: a hoarse, rasping sound. "Perhaps you could spare me something to drink and have a servant see to my horse." I could not even speak, merely nodded to my girls, who had crept out behind me. They returned shortly bearing trays of fruit, wine, water, and two cups. I handed Anna to Marguerite and sent them away with orders for a stable boy to tend to the animal.

Accepting his cup, Uncle Basil said, "I will just sit here with my own thoughts while you read your letters, Sofia."

I moved over to another bench and sorted them out. The first two covered the same time span that Sir Gille's had and carried the same general descriptions of the conditions in camp. But I also gleaned a little about the politics surrounding King Louis' strategic missteps. In one Sir Joscelin wrote,

> *"The king's younger brother, Robert of Artois, is as always a swaggering bully who glorifies battle and heeds no one with real experience. It is thanks to Robert's advice that our army has not captured Alexandria first to make sure no one could attack at our rear. We move inland toward Cairo instead…"*

I knew the aftermath of that decision all too well! Rumor and report had supplied the details of the disaster: the secret river ford Sir Gilles had mentioned crossed, the successful attack on the Egyptian camp and Count Robert's insistence on pursuing fleeing soldiers into Mansourah, there to be cut down along with almost half of the king's army. The failure of the entire war could be laid at that man's door, though he would never know.

It was the latest letter that gripped me, though, mind and heart. It was dated August 30, 1250, only two months earlier.

Beloved,

I pray that nothing amiss has befallen you, as I have received no word from you at all. I almost despair, but I feel I would know if you were taken from me completely.

I am with my king in Acre, I will come to you in Constantinople as soon as he gives me leave, and I will bring you back here with me before we return to Braissac. He is so ill and low in spirits that I almost feel like a traitor for wanting to go, but there is little I can do for him. He blames himself entirely for the failure of his holy mission, and indeed it was a bitter loss. Thousands of men died, and I pray that they all now rest in Heaven.

But having survived, I seek a heaven on this earth where I spend the rest of my life in your sweet embrace, the hope of which kept me alive during the darkest of times. I will not go into those times now, trusting that soon enough we will be reunited. Then there will be time to tell you all.

So look for me in Constantinople no later than October. I hope to have heard by then about the annulment, a matter that is never far from my mind. As soon as I arrived in Acre, I sent letters to Rome to find out the course of my petition.

With deepest love,

Joscelin

Hope and fear chased each other through my entire body. He would not have found me in Constantinople. Would he have thought to look for me here in Antioch? Why, he could be looking for me right now!

"Uncle, when did you receive this last letter?"

"Shortly after Caterina died. I was bereft at first, and having to send my children away took what little energy I had, but when I came to my senses and read it—well, losing her and seeing how you and your Sir Joscelin might so easily lose each other … It was what decided me to seek you out. I would see you married to this man and your daughter protected by the Church and the law. I am no monster, after all!"

I sighed and felt such a burden of anger roll off my chest. "Well, then, I forgive you. But on one condition: you must never lie to me again. Bardas did find the document granting you guardianship over me, and it was unsigned! You never had any power over me but that of force and deception, so you can see why I mistrust you."

My uncle's struggle was visible and took some time. I sat and waited, and finally he straightened up and said, "You are right. I must make a clean start in life. First of all, though I know it won't be good news for you, your Sir Joscelin never came to me, so I have no idea where he is. But you can count on me to direct him to you if he finds me. I swear it before Almighty God Himself.

"For now, though, there is more I would ask of you. You once offered to be my business partner. If you are still willing to undertake it, I would be happy to work with you as equals. Matthew of Edessa says you have the golden touch for business, which is something I seem to have lost. Perhaps I can find it again."

I was loath to make such an arrangement, but then it occurred to me that my uncle had a dangerous hold over my future. If he returned to Constantinople with enmity between us, he might want revenge. Sir Joscelin might be anywhere, even in Constantinople waiting for Basil to return from Antioch. How easy it would be for my uncle to mislead him and keep us apart forever.

So I answered, "I must consider your offer from all sides, Basil, and I would speak with Matthew first and see what he advises. Give me the name of the inn where you are staying, and I will give you an answer in a day or two. Too much is happening at once, and I must sort it all out."

"Fair enough, Sofia."

We parted on friendlier terms than I could have imagined an hour earlier, though it was based more on his power to do me further harm than on any true warmth toward him. Indeed, though hope had blossomed at the news that Sir Joscelin was alive, I also felt a rush of fear: who knew when we would be reunited? A small shiver ran down my back, although the afternoon was mild.

ANNO DOMINI 1251-1252

The next day when I asked Matthew of Edessa for advice about setting up a partnership with Basil, I had to tell enough about my flight from Constantinople to explain my doubts about him. Having assured me that though Basil was a tough businessman, he was an honest one, Matthew put me at ease by explaining that he would write up a contract for a limited partnership to cover any and all rights and obligations that might arise between us.

"Your uncle is usually so clever with his monies, but this last year did not go well for him. And I now realize you were bidding against him on that one lot of goods, though my agent realized when to stop—I think Basil let pride get the better of him that time! But from now on, you two must work together, yes?"

In the past I'd have blushed and regretted my vengeful actions, but I only needed to think of how close I had been to losing my darling Anna and the moment passed. "Of course. It's in everyone's best interests."

So Basil and I became partners. To my surprise, over the next year I found him to be both capable and straightforward, and many decisions I had burdened Matthew with I could now entrust to him. He never learned about my trickery, and I wrote to John of Epirus to tell him to stop. Instead, John became my eyes and ears just in case my uncle tried to betray me in some new way. At the same time, though this may sound paradoxical, he proved his worth as an agent for both Basil and me. Thanks to John our trade connections extended ever further, across the Black Sea to the remnants of the Eastern Roman Empire: the Crimean cities and Trebizond, and Epirus on the Greek peninsula.

And thanks to Basil's family connections, we also penetrated further into the secretive world of Venetian banking and trade. Although Basil often went to Venice, with Anna still so small I could not join him, but I promised myself that someday I would visit the famous—to me, still, infamous—republic that calls herself La Serenissima.

However, and this must have been shortly after Basil had taken much of our business in hand, he learned that I was trading with Jews. He was most displeased and tried various means to discourage me. Finally, I put my foot down and simply kept that aspect of my business to myself. I often corresponded with Maryam, and soon after Easter in the spring of 1252, feeling that Anna was now old enough to be alone for a few weeks, I traveled with Bardas to Aleppo, as I had learned to call it, to see her and to meet my business partners. It was a tiring journey—although this time I was not imprisoned in an enclosed howdah—and the caravan I traveled with was heavily guarded, so there was no trouble from bandits. It was also the first time in months that I had been so far from home.

Once we reached Aleppo, Bardas hired two Muslim guards who knew their way around it and were not afraid of entering its various quarters: here each race—or rather religion—was given its own area where it could follow its own ways. Antioch was a little like that, too, although the areas allotted for Jews and Muslims there were a mere handful of mean-looking streets.

Early the next day, which dawned warm and clear, they led us to the Jewish quarter. Thick walls and a heavy, door-like gate protected it, and a man with a Jewish-style imamah and long robes stood guard, a sword by his side. He had a small black box bound upon his forehead just like the one I had seen on the rabbi in Antioch. After hearing my reasons for wanting to enter, he opened the gate and allowed me through, and I glimpsed another box attached to his upper left arm with thongs that wound down his arm and over his hand. Curious, I thought, before turning my attention to my surroundings.

We were in a largish square with a well in its center where two veiled women were drawing water. What I took to be a temple occupied one side.

It was taller than the other buildings and decorated with arched windows, a colonnade, and lovely turquoise tiles. Other than that, it almost could have passed for a church or mosque. Much as in Iran, a few dark-clad men were gathered before it speaking in low tones, although here the men were Jews. A boy of perhaps eight, wearing a little black skullcap, a shawl, and a short garment bound by a blue and white striped sash, ambled over to the gate when the guard called to him. In exchange for a coin, he guided us through narrow, twisting lanes to Maryam's house, which was guarded by a plain wall that I first mistook for one side of her house, as it was a full story high. There he left us.

My two guards looked around, crossed their arms, and stood on either side of its heavy wooden door as if expecting trouble, though it was hard to imagine what trouble could befall us other than not being able to find our way out again. A slender little half cylinder of silver—as if it had been split longwise—was nailed to the right side of the doorframe. After Bardas had rapped sharply on the door a few times, it opened, and there stood an older, grayer, much happier looking Maryam, though her tears welled up when she saw me. She embraced me warmly even while looking around at the street most anxiously. I turned around to look, too, but saw no one beyond a boy leading a goat by a string.

"Come inside quickly. You never know who might be watching us." Her voice sounded wispier than ever. "Good that you brought guards. You both keep watch out there," she said to them, "and I'll have a halal meal brought to you later." One of them nodded thanks.

"Bardas comes in with me," I said. "He guards my person and is dear to me."

She nodded and waved him inside, where we found ourselves in a little courtyard.

"We have woman things to talk about, but you are welcome to shade yourself on that bench there, and my servant will bring you some sherbet." Bardas nodded, sat, and crossed his arms, looking about with something between interest and wariness.

After leading me inside her little house, shutting the door, and embracing me, she whispered, "Good that you brought stout guards, Sofia. Those Nizari are everywhere—all over Syria—they go in all sorts of guises, and who knows what they might be up to. I have learned that the Grand Master was not pleased that you left Alamut with a traitor to his cause, and his Syrian followers know who I am and about my connection to you. I had to use the services of one of their lot to get a letter to my son. He replied once, but when I sent another letter, nothing ever came back." She sighed dolefully. "Anyway, you should be very, very careful."

She turned toward a thin, youngish woman in black who had just entered the main room and who seemed as still and composed as earth itself. "Sofia, this is my friend and sister, Rakhel." We smiled and greeted one another, but when Maryam gave Rakhel a meaningful look, the woman straightaway said she would see to the refreshments their servant was preparing. She left by another door. I noticed another silver half cylinder nailed on that door's frame as well and decided it must have some religious meaning.

"Come, sit here." Maryam led me to a bench built out from the whitewashed wall and covered with a striped wool blanket. I looked around the room. Its furnishings were few and simple: a chest on which sat a seven-branched candelabrum, a brazier, striped carpets on a hard earthen floor that shone from years of sweeping, another bench built out from the opposite wall—all in all a pleasant place. After the maidservant, with Rakhel hovering over her, had offered us sweet wine and dried fruits, we three settled down together. An awkward silence fell. It had been such a long time since Maryam and I had seen each other, and I did not want to say anything about my life before a stranger.

But it was Rakhel who smoothed the way into easy speech by asking me about my journey and urging more refreshments on me. She soon excused herself and left us alone. Straightaway Maryam began to ask me all about my little Anna, what she looked like, whether she was a good quiet child and healthy.

Having exhausted those questions, she came to the one she really wanted to ask: how I could have fallen into sin with a married man. So, haltingly, I tried to explain. She surprised me at the end of my story by saying, "God has his own ways of loving and testing, and of forgiving us, Sofia. Do not lose heart." And she was done. I had expected a lecture, truth be told, and was glad to escape it.

We of course also spoke about our mutual friend Anna and the fact that she had become Muslim, a fact that shocked Maryam almost as much as discovering that Maryam was Jewish had once shocked Anna. "I still cannot believe that one so in thrall to her Christian beliefs could betray them like that. But I would never tell her so. I still hear from her from time to time, which is a comfort. And I have entirely forgiven her for the misery she once caused me. Even though I cannot understand, I do rejoice in her happiness, you know. Love makes for strange bedfellows."

"Yes," I agreed. "I, who once despised Catholics, am now reborn into that faith, and it was out of love." We sat in silence for a few heartbeats, each contemplating the mysterious twists of love and of faith. "But tell me about your life here, Maryam. You seem much happier."

"Indeed, how happy I am in my own home! As you can see, though she is much younger than I am, Rakhel is a good and kind woman. Almost like a sister but without the jealousies of sisters—I remember mine, all older than I was, all dead now. And I am surrounded by a loving community and able to practice my faith freely, such a gift."

But then the talk turned to her painful past, to her lost son, to the fearful misery of not knowing what had happened to him. There were tears, and I held her hand and tried to offer comfort. Truth be told, dear though she was to me, I found her ramblings trying in the extreme, for she repeated the same things endlessly. Perhaps it was age, for she must have been over sixty by then, almost twice the age most of us could realistically expect to live. I never showed my restless feelings to her, of course, but I realized I had lost the patience I'd learned as a slave and which had been sorely tested when I was confined in Selim's andarun and at the Hospitaller castle. My daughter was the only person I really felt patient with anymore.

However, amongst her lamentations, Maryam also gave me an alarming picture of the larger world, a world I had ceased to feel connected with since Anna's birth. It seemed that the Mongols had laid a heavy hand on the nearby Muslim states, none of which would stand together to fight them due to the usual family and dynastic and even religious rivalries. It reminded me of the fate of Rus'.

"It is strange, too," she said, "when they have the example of the atabeg of Al-Mawsil before them. As you know, he wisely submitted to them a few years ago when he saw their long arm of conquest stretching toward it, so the city has enjoyed a good deal of freedom and peace—if you don't count the soldiers he has to send them from time to time. But there is no telling how long you'll be able to keep your trade connections with that city alive, Sofia. War is coming this way and will sweep over us all, I fear."

Prophetically, she added, "I know that one day this city will fall to them, too, and I only pray that I will already be dead when that happens. We Jews are always the first to be slaughtered, no matter who takes a city, and it never matters how much we have given to it—or to the sultanates or caliphates or Christian principalities or any of them!" What could I say? It was all too true, and I could justify none of it.

Late that day we parted with embraces and blessings and I went back to my inn, ill at ease at the thought of Nizari spies possibly following me. But nothing happened, and I decided that Maryam had allowed her imagination to carry her away.

The next morning I returned to the Jewish quarter to meet my three business partners for the first time, all with fine long beards and the small boxes bound to head and arm. They led my guards and me to a warehouse where they showed me some wonderful goods: a kind of cotton cloth called muslin, named for al-Mawsil where it was produced; some blown glassware made by local Jews, very fine; and wonderful metalwork pieces, some from al-Mawsil and some from there in Aleppo. These last items were enchanting, from candlesticks to platters to basins, made of bronze. They were inlaid, often heavily, with silver decorations that were not only the usual floral designs but also of people and animals, most unusual, considering how Islam is so firmly set against portraying people. I could commission anything I wanted and have it all decorated to order. And some fine spices had just arrived from India. I ordered many items and bought others and was ready to leave when on impulse I turned and asked about the little boxes they wore.

One spoke for all. "They are called tefillim. Each of them contains a parchment with lines from the Torah written on it both for blessings and to remind us of how we were delivered from Egypt by Yahweh, whom you call God but whose true name cannot be spoken for it is, like Him, beyond human speech." They all looked at me challengingly, but I merely thanked him, nodded respectfully, and took my leave.

As I made my way back to my inn, it struck me for the first time that we all assumed that God was 'He'. I supposed it was a matter of language, for surely if God was beyond human words, God was also beyond male or female. Or was that heresy? I didn't know, nor did I feel strongly about my question, so I thought no more about it.

I returned home in another large, well-guarded caravan, carrying goods that would enrich me further, and meeting with no mishaps whatever. No Nizari followed me, no Mongols swept down upon me—although I knew they were not that far away. Now that Maryam had alerted me, I still felt vulnerable, though. The many shifting alliances and betrayals among the princes and governors of the region would mean nothing but trouble for us ordinary people: they invited lawlessness and banditry and, for me, disruption of trade routes. I prayed to be spared all three this time! And I also prayed that these Muslim princes would set aside their quarrels. Their politics would lead to their downfall if they did not put them aside and fight side by side against the Mongols when the time came. I imagined finding the right sultan or prince and explaining what had happened to Rus', but then I realized that I did not want to think about any of it. I only wanted to arrive safely home again and hold my little Anna close to my heart.

Still, it was a rare respite for me, that trip. I rarely left Daphne except to go to Antioch or, once, to Constantinople on business. My only other long journey took place long before that, in 1251, to search for Sir Joscelin.

For he never arrived, not in Constantinople or in Antioch; nor did I receive any word.

I had waited for him all through the rest of 1250 and for half of the next year. After a month I even overcame my suspicions about Basil and asked him outright if he had ever received further letters from my beloved. My question seemed to outrage him at first, but after that, whenever he and I met he made a point of assuring me that Sir Joscelin had neither written nor come to him.

When more time passed with no word, I asked Matthew of Edessa to alert his agents for news of any ships arriving from Acre—or that were late or known to be wrecked. And when that failed to tell me anything, I sent Bardas to Constantinople to talk with anyone on the docks who might have seen Lord Joscelin there. I even queried John of Epirus, who sent assurances that my uncle had had nothing to do with my beloved's disappearance and that aside from traveling on business or visiting me every few months, Basil led a quiet life in Constantinople. John even set his own men to searching the docks and inns in the city for word of Lord Joscelin, but they too found nothing.

Again I sent Bardas out, this time to Acre; but from what he could discover, my knight had taken ship and it had arrived at Tyre, its first port of call, but then had vanished without a trace. This much he had learned from the ship's agents, who feared that a storm or pirates had sent it to the bottom of the sea. Still, ships were known to turn up long after all hope had been lost for them. So he had traveled to all the other coastal cities, only to meet with more disappointment. But my heart cried out that my beloved must still be alive. I refused to give up hope.

How I wanted to be searching for him myself! But Anna was still so small, and I had learned my lesson after trying to take her only as far as Adar's castle. I could not see how to bring her with me without endangering her. So it was not until September of 1251, having deemed Anna old enough to be without me for a month—she was now almost two—that I sailed to Acre with my faithful Bardas. Though sailing could be dangerous that late in the year, I simply could wait no longer, for who knew how long King Louis and his people would remain in the Holy Land? Happily, the journey was uneventful. I was comfortably hosted in one of my own ships in a large, well-armed convoy, and we always stayed close to the shore and put into harbor every night. And we had to face only one minor storm.

Once we had arrived in Acre and settled at an inn, I discovered to my frustration that the king was not even in the city but in Caesarea to the south, where he was overseeing a project to strengthen its fortifications. I did locate the castle where he always stayed when in Acre, and that evening I sent Bardas to the nearest tavern to gather what gossip he could. He came back with an odd assortment of newsy morsels.

"Lady, from what I can make out, the king's court is now very small; most of his family returned to Francia. A few of his mercenary knights who survived battle and captivity still remain with him, and because he is well respected, others from around here still serve him. For one thing, he always pays them on time! I heard his name on the lips of several men, always in praise of his generosity and dignity.

"But what I think will interest you most is that his Queen is still here in Acre. I believe she looked on you kindly once, yes?"

"Yes indeed! Thank you, Bardas. Now I just need to gain entry to her court. I'm sure she would help me."

With my heart more at ease again—this journey might not be useless after all—I slept well that night and dreamed of ships streaming into safe harbor. For the next day or two, I wandered about the city with Bardas, observing the repair work being done on its fortifications, looking into the busy markets to find proper gifts for the queen, and listening to what people around me were saying. It was a strange city, full of people from all lands, not to mention several military orders. It seemed that the Templars dominated it and that the Hospitallers were not well liked—indeed, the few times I tried to ask after Lord Joscelin, I was rebuffed if I made any reference to them.

I began to place all my hopes on the royal family. Once I had seen how to go about it and paved my way with carefully placed bribes and a courteous letter sent up to the queen, I was soon invited into her presence.

I entered the little solar where she and a few other ladies were at their embroidery while one played the lute and sang a doleful song. To one side of the queen, a maidservant played with a boy just a little younger than my Anna.

The queen looked up and exclaimed, "Ah, Lady Sofia! How glad I am to see you. It brings back memories of Cyprus and happier days. Come sit by me and tell me the news. So Lord Joscelin did return to us and has brought you with him. Truly I thought he might stay on in Constantinople instead."

It was all I could do to remain composed. Having bowed and offered gifts and seated myself on a stool an attendant set out for me at the queen's feet, I said, "Good queen, it is for news of him that I come to you. Indeed, Sir Joscelin was to find and bring me here many months ago, but he has vanished. I put out queries from one end of the Holy Land to the other, and I can discover no trace of him. Now I come to beg for your help. Perhaps you or King Louis will know something that could direct my search."

She frowned in surprise, gazed on me with pity. "Good lady, this is terrible news indeed. Your knight stood by my king and husband in the darkest hours, defending him even as they were surrounded by infidels on all sides while King Louis lay too ill to move." She paused and added mournfully, "But in this past year I have witnessed too much death and loss to hold out much hope to you. Lord Joscelin left here over a year ago, but ours is a cruel and godless world, and so much could have gone awry. Still, if you would care to stay here tonight in our humble borrowed lodgings, I will see what I can discover for you."

I declined her hospitality with grateful words and said I would return on the morrow. In truth, I could find a dozen inns in the city that offered better lodging than their castle. But I spent the afternoon there, listening to her story of that disastrous time.

"Yes," she answered in response to one of my questions, "while I lay abed in labor, I did indeed keep an elderly knight by my side to behead me if the Turks should take the city. My ladies in waiting and my sister Beatrice were also by my side, she with her own tiny son in her arms—she too gave birth in Damietta—and while I endured the punishment of Eve, she wept and prayed aloud that she and her baby would not meet such a cruel end."

Perhaps by way of explanation for her sister's lack of bravery, the queen added, "She lost the son she left behind in Cyprus, you know, so her new son must be doubly precious to her. But we all escaped harm, thanks to our Merciful Lord. And soon I hope to return to Paris and my other children, although Jean Tristan will always be special for me as the son I almost lost, born in tears and travail. His name means sorrow, for that truly was a time of sorrow and nightmare, both sleeping and waking." She smiled sadly at the boy, who caught his mother's glance and straightaway reached his arms out to her. I smiled, too, sharing the queen's sense of how easily our children might be lost to us, and wishing I could tell her about my child.

I returned the next day to learn what Queen Marguerite might have discovered.

"I wish I had good news for you, Lady Sofia. Last night I asked my guardian knights about Lord Joscelin, but they only knew what we all know: that he left here by ship. He had just received monies from home—he now has a title and holdings—did you know?" I nodded. "I myself recall that Lord Joscelin took his leave with many expressions of loyalty and gratitude and a promise to return, although my good husband bade him go home after finding you. But as to what ship it was or where it might have stopped between here and Constantinople, no one knows."

It took all my strength not to weep, and she reached over and took my hand. "You would have made him a much better wife than Lady Ysabel, now Sister Mary since she took the veil."

"Does that mean their marriage was annulled?"

"Yes indeed. Did you not know?"

I shook my head. Here at least was one piece of good news. A dark thought intruded: if my beloved were indeed lost, it would not only break my heart, but my little Anna's life might be haunted by her bastardy. If only she at least could be spared some of the pain I had undergone. And now, who knew what the future would hold?

I decided to await King Louis' return, as he was expected shortly. And there was the compensation of being welcomed each afternoon as almost a friend by the queen, a respite after spending so many desperate months seeking some trace of my Joscelin. By means of lavish gifts, I also helped ease her poverty a little, for the king was spending what monies they had on strengthening fortifications in the Latin-held port cities. But I also missed Anna terribly. I was just about to give up and sail home when Queen Marguerite announced that King Louis had returned and that she had arranged an audience for me in two days.

The time crawled until at last the day arrived. I was led to a small room, empty of furnishings but for a little altar with a crucifix on the wall above it and a simple chair. A changed man rose from his knees before the altar. King Louis had been scourging himself, and there were streaks of blood on his coarse white monkish garment. Ashen-faced, stoop-shouldered, and with worry lines etched into his forehead and around his mouth, he seemed a ghost of himself as he walked over to his chair. When the formalities of greetings were over, he looked at me sadly and asked, "How do you fare, Lady Sofia?"

"Not as well as I could wish, Sire."

He nodded and sighed. "It seems that woe lies everywhere. I am sorry you cannot find your fair knight. Only God knows what fate has in store for each of us...."

Silence stretched out, for I did not feel I had the right to speak first and the king seemed lost in thought. Suddenly he said, "Do you remember the Mongol envoys who came to court on Cyprus? You were still in the city when I sent my trusted advisor André de Longjumeau to Karakorum to convert the Great Khan Kuyuk to Christianity and save Mongol souls. He spoke kindly of you to me."

I nodded, masking my mixed feelings. "That was good of him."

"Yes. So I know you will be glad to hear that just before I left Caesarea, he returned safely from his mission. Alas, the Great Khan Kuyuk was dead by the time he reached Karakorum, and his widow was regent. She sent me an insulting message saying that I must submit to her completely and in person. I am deeply disappointed that his mission was a failure. Things are in a sorry state now, and I pray for guidance from Almighty God and our Holy Savior, since Mongol forces press from every side.

"In a way I wish I could visit that faraway land, so full of wonders. André told me about all the fantastic places he had been, the horrifying sights, too—bones lining roads, and more. But losing an entire people to the true faith is the greatest of sorrows...." He seemed to drift into a world of his own.

I waited in silence. I had nothing to say about this mission to Karakorum. It had always seemed a mad dream to me. It was interesting, though, to hear that Kuyuk had died so soon after becoming Great Khan. From murder or too much drink? I didn't care, though I wondered who would replace him. The king's voice jolted me back from my musings.

"But my thoughts wander. So my dear knight and friend, Lord Joscelin, disappeared on his way to find you. It was yet another burden of sadness upon an already heavy heart when I learned of this. Is there anything I can do for you? My circumstances are somewhat reduced, but I would find a way to help if possible, for you both have suffered needlessly over this issue of marriage."

"I can think of nothing you could do, Sire. I have already sought for him everywhere I could think of—well, you might know the route of the ship he took, whether he might have debarked and continued his journey by land."

"I thought he planned to go by sea straight from here to Constantinople. I do know that his ship would have been Pisan or Genoese, as we have little to do with Venice if we can help it. But you know, Lady Sofia, that there are no safe journeys, ever, in this world of woe. So much could have befallen him; he could easily have departed this life, you know."

"I cannot accept that, my lord. Were he dead, I know I would feel it in my heart, in my very bones. I will keep searching until all hope is lost."

The king sighed again. "I honor your loyalty to him. I have learned something about humility in the trials my Savior set before me this last year, and I can only tell you this: if you find him, he already knows he has my permission, nay, blessings, for you two to marry. It was a sore test for him to be married to Lady Ysabel, and I regret that I did not allow the power of your love for each other to guide my judgment that one time. The needs of Francia were not so great that much of value would have been lost.

"Of course my intention was to honor my loyal subject and friend, but, just as I did so much harm on my failed campaign, so I also did harm to one I care for very much. Therefore, I promise you this: if Lord Joscelin still lives when I am ready, I will not call on him to follow me on my next campaign. Instead, I will see to it that you and he are settled happily in Braissac."

"Your next campaign, Sire?"

"Yes. For now, I can only make amends in the ways I know: by strengthening the walls of Acre and some other Christian cities, but I have also vowed to lead another holy war to free Jerusalem from the Saracens one day, and I will repeat none of the mistakes I made this time.

"Indeed, as I think on it, perhaps I should try once more to reach the Great Khan—word has reached us that a new one has been chosen, I believe he is called Mongke—and see if he might be more reasonable about converting to Christianity. Perhaps we even can ally with each other; several Mongol missions have sought one with us."

It was all I could do not to stare at the king in horror. After all the thousands of lives lost, the monies wasted, the land itself trampled and harmed, he wanted to go on a "holy war" again? And he still wanted to convert, perhaps ally himself with the Mongols? Well, after all, this was the man who had refused an honorable treaty the old dying sultan had offered right after the fall of Damietta, a treaty that would have handed the Christians Jerusalem in exchange for returning it. The result would have been no further losses on either side. Had Louis accepted the offer, two peoples would have benefited instead of being thrown into the winds of death like mere chaff! But the king's ideas of chivalry had blinded him.

I think I understand now, though I still believe it was folly: Louis had come to the Holy Land to fight what he thought of as an honorable war, not for easy victory and peace with Saracen enemies. Well, war he had certainly gotten. As soon as I could, I left as gracefully as possible, thinking never to see him again. In that I was wrong, though many years would pass first.

The only thing I had gleaned of interest was that Mongke Khan was the new Great Khan, a distinct improvement over the drunken Kuyuk. At least he could read.

So I returned to Daphne, to my children, and especially to Anna, who seemed to have forgotten me at first. She was more interested in tottering away from restraining arms and laughing, a game she played happily with anyone. When she finally reached out her arms to me that night as she lay abed with me, I could have wept for joy.

Other things had shifted while I was away, too. When I first arrived home, to my surprise Basil was there in the courtyard with little Gilles, carrying him on his back and bouncing him while the boy screamed with delight. And Helene was looking on with a pleasure in her eyes that I had never thought to see again. She had become so thin that I worried about her, but that day she seemed fair and fragile. When they saw me staring, they both blushed and Basil set Gilles down and gave him a clap on the back, ordering him off to play with the boys, while she rushed forward to embrace me and make much of my return. She asked so many questions that I had no time to think about what I'd just seen.

But there was more. After I had been home for a few days, Alexander, who had grown into a lively, handsome youth with a head of dark curls, came to me holding hands with Banjuu. "Lady, with your permission, we would like to marry," he announced, shyness and joy mingled on both of their faces. I was caught by surprise. I knew that Banjuu had become a woman recently. She must be thirteen or fourteen by now and Alexander might be as old as sixteen, so both were old enough to wed, but how long had they been in love? I'd seen them together so often that I took their play for granted, especially since Marguerite had usually been with them, too.

But then, I realized, I had scarcely attended to anyone else's doings for a year and more. All my heart and mind had been directed to finding Sir Joscelin and to securing Anna's future as best I could. Of course I granted their request, as it made them happy and hardly made any difference to our daily lives.

I wondered if Marguerite would be sad to lose her close friendship with Banjuu when, after the quiet wedding a few weeks later, I gave the couple a room of their own. But she shook her head. "It was I who made them ask your permission to marry. They've been coupling ever since that day you took us to Mass in Constantinople, but when her moon cycles began, I grew afraid he might get her with child and she would suffer as you have. I didn't want that."

So much going on that I had never seen, and some of it not what I'd have wanted—but then, who was I to judge?

As for Marguerite, a new bond grew up between us, for I was touched that she would care so much for the welfare of both her mistress and her friends. Indeed, she threw herself entirely into caring for Anna and me and seemed content with her life.

Contentment was something that too often eluded me. Now that I was back in Daphne with my search for Sir Joscelin a failure, I felt trapped. In the past, whenever I'd been a slave to circumstance—not to mention a slave in fact—I had found something to do. Now I was a slave to my love for Anna. Beyond playing with her or riding in the forest or visiting Antioch on business, and the one necessary trip to Aleppo in 1252, there was little to do besides sew clothes for everyone or embroider more cushions and altar cloths.

So after the journey to Aleppo, I turned to the journal Lord Joscelin had given me. I hadn't written anything in it. Alas, I had far fewer happy memories to put in it than my beloved had predicted, and I scarcely knew where to start. Other than having nothing else to do, I had no real reason to bother writing at all. So I set it aside after one attempt.

After Acre it took months before I could face each day without a shroud of gloom trying to wind itself around me so tightly that I could scarcely move. And there was nothing, nothing at all that I could do. Sir Joscelin was either alive or he was not. I believed he was, felt in my heart that we would find each other someday, and I desperately clung to that hope. After my visit to Maryam, I knew I must relearn patience, an art I seemed to have lost. But night or day, I ceased to dream.

I had never completed all the penances Caterina's priest had given me, so I decided to start there; to my surprise they helped ease my heart a little. Once in a while, I also tried that little practice of peace that Dorje had taught me. Truth be told, I had mostly forgotten how to do it and felt a little foolish trying. My restlessness often got the better of me, and I would find I had gotten up to do some small task before I even realized what I was about. So I practiced it seldom, thinking each time that I would try again later when I was less distracted.

In essence I led two lives: an outer one where I carried on as if all was normal, where I could laugh and talk and behave like anyone else; and an inner one, where an invisible wire of sorrow was wound tightly around my heart, always cutting into it a little. Alexander and Banjuu were so happy to be together without having to steal away anymore, Marguerite was so happy tending to Anna, and Helene was so happy with Basil: in all this I could take only mild pleasure.

ANNO DOMINI 1252-1253

Basil's visits became not only regular but also too often to be just about business matters, especially when those were literally sailing along so well. It was clear to me that he and Helene were in love, but I had to wait, feigning ignorance, until the autumn of 1252, when they finally announced over supper that they had become betrothed.

"Let me be the first to wish you both happy, and for years to come," I smiled.

"Oh, we thought you would object!" exclaimed Helene.

"And why would that be?"

They both hesitated. "I suppose for many reasons," Basil began. "First, your mistrust of me."

"And your sorrow over losing Lord Joscelin and mine over losing Lord Gilles," Helene added. "I feared you might disapprove of me for remarrying, or even begrudge my happiness—well, more the former than the latter. In some circles," and here she glanced over at Basil, blushing, "people firmly believe that the widowed should never remarry. What if you felt that way?"

"I cannot pretend not to envy you, but I could never begrudge either of you finding love together, whatever Church and custom dictate. I hope you find the kind that Lord Joscelin and I shared. Nor have I given up all hope of finding him, just most of it. Besides," I added, hoping to lighten the mood, "now you can keep an eye on my uncle for me!"

We all laughed, Basil perhaps a little less heartily than Helene and I did.

So preparations began for another wedding, to be held in Constantinople, where Helene and her household would settle into an entirely new life. It was better thus, for both Daphne and Antioch would always hold sorrowful memories for her, but how I would miss her! With no new orphans coming to my villa and my having found places for the remainder who wanted to leave—all in towns where I was not known, for I wanted no tongues wagging about Anna—it made for a very quiet life.

Basil and Helene married on a warm blue day in late April of 1253—it was hard to find a month and a day in it that the Church had not forbidden, and there had been banns to make public and a betrothal ceremony to hold before the cathedral doors in Antioch, all this only after they had gotten priestly sanction for remarrying. Helene, young Gilles, Anna, our closest servants, and I arrived in Constantinople a week early and stayed in a house that Basil had found for us. This was where the children would stay during the ceremony and the festivities, which they were too young to attend.

Anna was three now, and I'd have loved to take her to the wedding, but it was perilous enough for my reputation just bringing her to Constantinople. At least she had proven herself to be a fearless little sailor, sometimes getting into mischief with the ropes or leaning out over the water in a way that made my heart stop. I decided to take her on all my journeys from then on, which would broaden both our lives. With Marguerite, Banjuu, and Alexander watching over her, I felt she would always be in good hands.

Marguerite began looking fearful the moment we landed, while Bardas cast his eyes about in a fierce manner that bespoke his resolve to defend me from all attacks, quite ridiculous now that Basil and I were on friendly terms again. Only Banjuu and Alexander seemed at ease. But in fact we all enjoyed ourselves that week more than I could have hoped, for though I sometimes felt a keen contrast between my friend's happiness and my single and thus sinful state, there was too much to do for me to nurse dark feelings. When not helping Helene and her servants unpack various chests of clothing and plate and the like at Basil's villa, I was sometimes able to explore the neighborhood at my leisure. It at least was an area that was not damaged at all, and it held many gracious homes, often set around a central public square with a fountain.

There was little else to do, as I had already helped sew and heavily embroider Helene's wedding gown, leaving only the last stitch to be put in on the day of the wedding. She had a chosen a pale, silver-threaded blue samite to salve her guilty feelings about remarriage: a virgin could wear blue, but as she was no longer one but had remained a chaste and faithful widow, the fabric, white and silvery blue mixed together, was a gesture of respect for Lord Gilles, gone for well over two years now.

The morning of the wedding, I assembled a bouquet of flowers and herbs for her to carry—they represented various virtues—and helped her dress while she eagerly told me the meaning of each detail of her attire, all based on Frankish custom. Basil, in token of his love for her, was giving her a traditional Frankish wedding.

As befitted a second marriage ceremony, a modest party of some thirty people—mostly Basil's business partners with their wives and grown offspring—arrived at the door to escort us to the local church. It had been a long time since I had seen such gay fluttering ribbons and bright costumes, heard such singing and cheering while musicians led the way with flutes and trumpets and tambours. I noticed the youths and maidens in the procession eyeing each other with interest, and a few meaningful glances passing between some of them. They must all know each other.

Basil and the priest were waiting at the church door. My uncle was attired in rich red brocade embroidered in gold, a blue ribbon tied around his sleeve in token of his fidelity to Helene. To my surprise the priest performed most of the ceremony before the church doors; it dwelt mainly on ensuring that no one objected to the marriage. Basil and Helene also exchanged vows and rings before entering the church for a solemn wedding Mass.

Both ceremonies included customs I had not seen before, as when the couple knelt before the altar and were draped in a white veil, and that the candles were red instead of white. But I had lost interest in the endless chanting and singing by then, was wondering how my golden little Anna was getting along by herself. She had wept and held out her arms to me so piteously as we were leaving. Besides, while I rejoiced for Helene, I could not help contrasting her happy state with mine, unwed and with only dim hope for future happiness, at least of the marital kind.

Afterwards, we all followed the newly wed couple back to Basil's villa for the wedding feast. More guests had gathered there to greet them, spilling out from the main hall into the courtyard and even standing on the yard stairs that led to the second floor.

The celebration feast was beyond bounteous. There were at least six courses, including a sanglier, stuffed and roasted. With so little forest remaining outside the city, doubtless Basil had paid quite a round sum for someone to hunt down a boar! There were also the usual stewed and roasted meats and various birds, including a peacock with its feathers re-attached to look alive, plus cheeses, nuts, fruits, breads, pastries, a spicy mulled wine that brought back less than pleasant memories—though this time there was no opium in it—and sallats made of various herbs and root vegetables seasoned with vinegar and olive oil.

I remember it all too well, since according to Frankish custom we were obliged to eat until everything was gone, the reasoning being that nothing would keep. I tried to eat slowly, all the while secretly wishing we could give some of this abundance to the needy men lurking outside the villa walls, drawn in hopes of largesse—wealthy grooms might be generous on their wedding day—but as far as I know, they were only given the usual bread rolls after the feast was over. Despite my temperance, I soon felt like a stuffed roast beast myself.

A Frankish nobleman was seated by me, richly dressed in Oriental style even to a sort of imamah, which was adorned with a ruby clip and did not hide his long, festively crimped hair. He seemed determined to serve me more food and drink than I could possibly want, meanwhile eating three dishes for my every one.

His face was somehow familiar. Sir Reynaud was his name, and he reminded me that we had first met in Antioch at the home of Lord Gilles and Lady Helene. I remembered then. It would have been at the gay festivities they had often held before King Louis' war called Lord Gilles and my beloved away. Helene had seated him next to me on purpose, I was certain: a strongly built, blue-eyed giant of a man with light brown hair, a combed and trimmed reddish beard, and courtly manners. He made light conversation and even drew laughter from me with some comical stories.

"You had no eyes for any of us men," he said at the end of that endless meal, filling our goblets with the last of the wine. "We had all fallen hopelessly in love with you at first sight, but…." He sighed.

"How disappointed we all were to learn that you were already betrothed to Sir Joscelin."

Hearing his name, I sat up straighter and asked, "Oh, do you know him?"

A closed look passed over Sir Reynaud's features, but he only said, "Yes, slightly, and I knew his younger brother Robert, too."

"Will you tell me what you remember about them both? I long to know everything about them, you see."

"Perhaps another time, for the dancing is about to begin. Would you honor me by joining me in a round?" I accepted and soon found my head awhirl in the steps and my body awhirl in his arms. After several such dances, I finally had to seat myself again or fall over from dizziness and sore feet. Sir Reynaud sat beside me and made me laugh by fanning me with a bunch of fern fronds that he had found among the table decorations; his absurdity was charming. Nor did I mind my feet. Dancing had been a rare treat. Helene caught my eye and smiled, no doubt pleased that my partner had proven his worth.

However, at one point a minstrel strolled by and composed a song on the spot that made me blush and recoil a little: something about hot maidens and the hotter men who pursue them. But Sir Reynaud saw my pained look and waved the man away with a scowl.

He turned to me and smiled. "But now I must leave you, lovely lady, as there is important business to attend to. The happy bride and groom have drunk their wedding cup and are retiring as swiftly as they can! How eager he must be, or else protective. I must try to get the bride's garter from her. It guarantees my future bride's fidelity." He looked straight into my eyes before leaping up to pursue Basil and Helene, as did several other eager men. I shrugged inwardly. If he meant me, he was mistaken.

I now witnessed the strangest custom of all: poor Helene was nearly mauled in the rush to strip her of the ribbon I myself had tied around her knee. Had I known how brutally she'd be handled, I might have refused to help her, especially when Sir Reynaud emerged the victor. Luckily, he did not—or could not—seek me out, as he was carried along like a leaf in a river by the other guests' sudden rush up the stairs, where many flooded into the bridal chamber, a man in the lead carrying a goblet filled with some kind of potion and the rest of them laughing, calling out coarse jests, and throwing seeds at Basil and Helene. Standing near the bottom of the stairs and a little fearful that I might be pushed backwards by the unruly, bawdy crowd above me, I pulled at the sleeve of the lady in front of me and asked her what was happening.

"You don't know? The men will force the Bride's Broth down their throats, to make sure they enjoy fruitful issue, tonight especially but also throughout their marriage. The seeds are for the same." I must have looked puzzled. "You know: children! Not to worry, Lady ... Sofia, yes? It's not anything too nasty, just mint and parsley in mulled wine. Perhaps you'll be tasting it yourself soon." She laughed and rejoined the rowdiness, and did not see how my face fell. I did manage to avoid Sir Reynaud when everyone returned downstairs, though I saw him searching the feasting hall for someone, perhaps me, as he went down the stairs.

It must have been midnight by the time the guests began leaving. So, having spent too much time trying to avoid Sir Reynaud, which was not very pleasant, I mingled with a large family and darted out into the court-yard. Happily, Bardas was patiently waiting at one side of the yard with a litter and our guards to escort me back to my house. I heard some rustling and soft laughter in a dark corner of the yard but did not stop to look. In the litter I took off my little silk slippers, shredded by dancing, and rubbed my raw, aching feet. They would have blisters by morning. Why must I always pay so for my small pleasures? At least it had been far easier es-caping Sir Reynaud than eluding Qabul all those years ago when he had pursued me so relentlessly.

Or so I thought until the next day! Anna had wakened me twice at to-tally unreasonable hours; she had arisen noisily at dawn and run off to play, only to come racing back into the room a little later to clamber back into bed with me. Marguerite was right behind her, ready to shoo her back out, but though I groaned, I returned my darling's embrace. She lay there contentedly just long enough for me to doze off, a headache behind my eyes, when she began shaking me and crying, "Mama, come play with me!" until I gave up and obeyed.

Thus when a visitor came to the house, I had dressed and breakfasted and was sitting with Anna and little Gilles. He was defending her favorite doll, one I had sewn for her so long ago that it was now faded and torn. While he flailed about with his stick sword, she shrieked and made my head spin with pain, so I did not hear the knock on the door or even footsteps in the hall outside the room until the door opened.

I looked up in surprise. Sir Reynaud, clad today in Latin garb and a modest cap made of felt, had brushed past Bardas and was now crouching down and looking into my daughter's eyes, saying, "And who is this delightful young creature?"

Bardas appeared behind him, looking red-faced and fingering a coin in surprise.

"No matter, Bardas. I know Sir Reynaud."

The knight looked up at my servant and asked with firm courtesy if he would see to his attendants. He then returned his gaze to Anna. She stood and reached up and tugged at Sir Reynaud's beard. "Who are you? Not my father."

Laughing, he encircled her with an arm and said, "No, child, I am not. Another of your orphans, I see, Lady Sofia. What a charming child."

Anna struggled free, muttering something about her ghost father that I didn't catch.

I blushed and let the falsehood stand as we rose and smiled at each other. "You are the first man I have met since Lord Joscelin who seems to like children."

"Oh, well, were we not all once children? We would be disliking ourselves not to like them—in their place, of course," as Marguerite and Banjuu came forward at my sign to take Anna from him and lead Gilles away, her clutching her doll and him his makeshift sword.

But Anna, so abruptly removed from the center of attention, wailed, "Mama!" and held her arms out to me.

I wished I could sink below the carpet, I was so put out of countenance, but Sir Reynaud simply said, "I heard that you treated all your orphans as your children. Now I have proof that it is so."

Gallantly spoken, and I let this falsehood stand as well, of course, but I could not help wondering if this strange man was a heaven-sent innocent or if he knew my secret. He was, after all, Helene's friend and perhaps Basil's, too. While I knew that Helene would guard my secret, and Basil had much to lose and nothing to gain by sharing it, it took an effort to shake off my mistrust of my own kin. No, surely Caterina had covered Anna's birth in enough shame to keep his tongue from wagging.

"I know it is forward of me," Sir Reynaud continued, "but I wish to ask you to stay for a few more days while I show you what remains of this wreck of a city. It is a fascinating wreck, at least, and my responsibilities have given me a long view of my beloved home. And I can tell you more if you would care to accompany me around Constantinople today or tomorrow, as my king sends me on an errand in a few days."

"Oh, you serve King Louis?"

"No, King Baldwin. I am, I suppose, both guard and emissary for his treasures, those that remain. He tries to keep the city alive by selling the few treasures he can still find here, and I am entrusted with the task of accompanying them to their destinations. Indeed, that is the mission that will take me away this time. Who knows when our paths will cross again; hence my hastiness in approaching you."

"I must decline with thanks, Sir Reynaud. Last night was delightful, but I am still feeling the effects of too much food and drink. And I plan to leave shortly, so my time remaining will be devoted to my uncle and his bride. I doubt...." He looked at me with such disappointment that I almost relented.

"Besides, I think we should become better acquainted before I accept such an offer. I will be back in Constantinople on other occasions, and instead of your proposal, may I make a different one? I will ask Basil and Helene to invite you to sup with us before I leave, which would be better for now, anyway."

He looked a little disappointed, even annoyed, but he quickly masked his emotions and smiled, revealing surprisingly even white teeth. A nasty memory of another man's white teeth thrust itself into my mind, but I shook it off. "Agreed, then," he replied. "I will show you around the city another time and also provide dinner at an inn well-known for its excellent cooking."

I smiled an agreement, and he bowed and took his leave while I found myself, to my surprise, looking forward to a pleasant evening with a gallant gentleman. I would simply be careful not to send him any false signals!

That afternoon, having brought Gilles and Anna to Basil's villa to play—strange to think that this was now Gilles' and Helene's new home and that I had once thought it would be mine—I completed some business with Basil and then spent the rest of my time with Helene, who was already settling into her new life.

I was helping her unpack her remaining chests from Antioch and wondering how to ask her about Sir Reynaud when she suddenly said, "These men from Rus' are a lusty lot," and blushed redder than a beet. "I imagine I'll be presenting Basil with another son soon. Which reminds me: I've persuaded Basil to summon his other children from Venice. It will seem strange to have a stepson only a few years younger than I am, but I think Gilles will be glad to have brothers and a sister. He grew lonely in Daphne, I think, with no brothers or boys his age to play with him."

I had nothing to say to either comment. But I fumed a little inwardly, thinking of all the time and love we all had lavished on Gilles when his mother was too distraught and lonely to think of him. Clearly she had not even been aware of our efforts. And I prayed that Basil's children would not mistreat the little boy, who might well be regarded as a rival.

"By the by, I hope you didn't think ill of my sending Sir Reynaud to you this morning. He came here thinking you would be staying with us, and I sent him to the other house. Oh dear: Anna! I didn't think—was I wrong?"

"Not to worry. He mistook her for one of my adopted orphans. He was a little hasty in his plans to get to know me better, though. He wanted to take me around the city, which surely would be improper of us, yes?" Helene nodded. "But I told him I would ask you and Basil to invite him to supper before I go, and he swallowed his disappointment. Would you be willing to invite him? I know it imposes on you, but I felt a little sorry for him."

"Of course. I will ask Basil, but I am sure he'd be delighted. They haven't known each other long, but Sir Reynaud has the king's ear, you see, and that makes him a valuable asset to my husband's business ventures—and to yours."

"That is perfect, my friend. And then I must return to Daphne and my quiet life."

"Why? Do stay at least another week. I will be so bereft without you. Please?"

These thoughts were parents to the deed, and within the hour Basil had sent off an invitation to Sir Reynaud to dine in two days, while I had given in and sent Bardas to arrange for a different sailing date.

The dinner went splendidly. Sir Reynaud was a great storyteller and had us all laughing almost to tears; and when Basil learned of his guest's idea of taking me around the city, he straightaway decided that we should all go the very next day. "After all, my sweet," he said to his bride, "Constantinople is your new home and you have yet to see it!"

So, early the next morning, having arranged for Anna to stay with Gilles and his nurse, I was waiting with the newly wed couple and our respective servants when Sir Reynaud arrived with a huge retinue of his own plus fine horses for us all. Our host seemed to be in a pensive mood, though he put on a cheerful face for us.

There was much to see, though Basil and Helene were so wrapped in each other, they scarcely paid attention. I was left to ride with Sir Reynaud most of the time, and he made an entertaining companion. We first rode east to the harbor to look out of the same gates where I had first arrived some four years earlier.

"This water passage is called the Golden Horn," Sir Reynaud told me. Across it was another settlement with a damaged tower standing near the water. He said no more, simply turned and led us around the curve of the walls. We headed more or less south, the thick walls looming protectively over us. Sir Reynaud said little while we rode, which suited me at first, for I was awestruck. I finally exclaimed, "How on earth did the Franks capture the city? It seems impregnable to me!"

"I am glad you asked. First they captured that tower you saw across the Golden Horn. It held a mighty winch to wind and unwind a massive chain that could stretch under the water to the city to keep enemy ships from entering. The Franks captured the tower and broke the chain, and then with the Venetians they breached the walls by land and sea, struck down the emperor, swarmed in, and began looting and killing."

A strained look crossed his face. "You cannot imagine the wealth that was carried off: precious metals and gems, works of art, sacred relics. My father was among the looters, and he made himself wealthy indeed, even took a Greek noblewoman to wife—my mother—she agreed to wed him rather than starve on the streets—and he allowed her family to stay in their home, which he and his knights had taken for their own. So you see, I am half Greek myself, though few hold it against me—or perhaps my strong arm convinces them. Doubtless my Greek blood is why I love this city so much and wish to share its glories with someone. You must forgive me if I speak about it with passion."

"Not at all. It does you honor."

As we headed away from the city walls and toward a high hill, we passed abandoned homes, empty public squares, parklands gone wild with benches half-hidden in weeds, smashed statues, wild dogs and cats, and refuse. Behind us, Helene exclaimed in alarm several times, as did my girls and Irene. I heard Basil murmur something soothing to Helene before riding up ahead of us and looking left and right as if to scout out further dangers. He then dropped back to her side, looking rather self-important as we passed him.

Sir Reynaud spoke for all to hear. "These abandoned city blocks were the Genoese and Amalfian quarter, but the Franks and Venetians drove everyone out with little but the clothing on their backs. The Pisan quarter was seized by Venice, and that is where you live, Basil."

He turned around in his saddle and smiled.

I looked back, too. Basil seemed unsure whether to be amused or irritated. "Well, best to make use of what we find before us. All that happened long before I came here."

Braving a pot-holed thoroughfare up the hill, we reached what our guide called an acropolis, crowned with half-ruined buildings and surrounded by a crumbling wall. It was the same one we had seen from our ship on first arriving in Constantinople, and it commanded an astounding view of the entire city, the surrounding sea, and the far shore across a wide stretch of water that Sir Reynaud called the Bosporus.

We all stopped to admire a great streaked marble column. "This may be the oldest Roman relic in the city," he said. "It once supported a statue commemorating some long-forgotten war. Nowadays it is called the Column of the Goths. And over there is something else I thought would interest you, Lady Sofia." He pointed to one building that was in better shape than the others. A few boys were practicing some kind of carpentry outside its doors, overseen by serious-faced, white-and-black-clad monks. Basil and Helene glanced over but turned back to the view. "That is the orphanage of Saint Paul, which is now run by Dominican monks. Since you are a patroness of orphanages in Antioch, I thought you might like to see it."

"Thank you," I said quietly. "It is good to know that the Franks have done some good here."

He smiled politely. "Yes, some. The only two hospitals that remain open are now run by Templars and Dominicans—not like what they once were."

"Oh?"

"Once there were many across the city, each with its own public baths, and hospices for the old and dying, and dispensaries; all were supported by public coffers. The entire empire offered the best medical treatment in the world. Now they are like any Frankish hospital, dirty and foul, with barbaric notions of treating patients. And most of the medical books were lost to fire and pillage."

I looked a question.

"One of my uncles is a surgeon, and nowadays he also provides physics for the ill since so few men of medicine remain. He still works in the Sampson Hospital, which I will show you, and he remembers what it was like. He does the best he can."

Leaving the acropolis behind, we continued on through empty squares where specialty markets had once flourished: farm products or silks or armor, or glassware that had mostly been produced in the Jewish quarter. "The Jews are all gone now, of course, slaughtered or fled elsewhere. And good riddance, eh, Basil?" Sir Reynaud turned around and shared a smile with my uncle, but I froze a little inside.

"Our next goal is Hagia Sofia," he told us all.

We passed another lovely church, which Sir Reynaud called Hagia Eirene. "If time allowed, I would show it to you. Another time, perhaps," and he smiled at me. "I will say that to me it symbolizes how little some people value art—its beautiful mosaics are lost forever. Iconoclastic prelates and even emperors destroyed many other wondrous works, too. It was nothing but a waste. Luckily there is still much of beauty here that has survived the ravages of time and man ... and occupiers."

Basil frowned, Helene looked mystified, and I alone spoke, though I had no idea what iconoclastic meant. "You feel such losses strongly."

He laughed without real humor. "I do. It must be because I am to deliver yet another treasure taken from what little is left. But power, greed, and faith were and are always a deadly mix, and the winner always claims that God is on his side!"

He might have said more, but Basil spoke sharply, as if he thought Sir Reynaud blamed him. "Well, you cannot blame the Franks alone for all these losses! Tell her about the palace intrigues and murders, the riots that burned down parts of the city, the dark secrets behind your splendor! It was not as perfect here as you might have thought, Sofia, given how we Rus' once felt about what the Franks did here."

It sounded to me as if Basil now identified as little with being Rus' as with being Orthodox, but then he had long ago converted to the Catholic faith for business reasons. We Rus' had always regarded Constantinople as almost our mother city. Her missionaries were venerated as saviors who gave us true religion along with written language, and her sack had always been spoken of as one of the blackest deeds of mankind.

"You are right, of course," Sir Reynaud answered mildly. "Do not think I blame the Franks alone. They only damaged the visible, but especially in recent times rot was undermining the empire already, particularly here in the capital. Too many power-mad claimants to the throne, too much territory lost both to enemies and to so-called friends, too much corruption all around."

Basil still looked ill pleased and Helene perplexed, but Sir Reynaud seemed too wrapped up in his story to notice.

"When I was little, my mother often took me around the city and told me what it was like before the Latins captured it. She loved Constantinople, and in its times of power and glory it would have been amazing. The emperors and empresses supported schools, libraries, monasteries, arts and architecture, stadiums and hippodromes and more. I still see what remains of its greatness and beauty because of my mother. And much still does remain.

"Indeed, Basil," and here he turned in his saddle to face my uncle, "you can take pride that the Varangian guard, mostly drawn from Rus', died to a man, axes in hand, guarding the last emperor. There will never be another force like them."

Basil now looked pleased, so Helene smiled happily.

We stopped briefly at the Sampson Hospital, which lies next to Hagia Sofia, to meet our guide's uncle the surgeon, a wrinkled, stooped, white-haired man whom Sir Reynaud brought out of some bad-smelling room. Groans of such pain echoed from its walls that I almost turned and left. He led us to a quieter area, but after exchanging pleasantries, he excused himself. "You may look about if you wish, but I must return to my duties: a limb that has begun to rot awaits me. With so few of us left ..." He sighed. "Well, I do what I can."

He bowed and left. Most of our party took no interest in the hospital and went back outside to wait, but Sir Reynaud, Marguerite, Bardas, and I did look into a few of the wards, mostly empty, dirty, and strewn with debris. There is little to say about it: I left feeling grim and sorry for all the ill and dying men who lay in rows on filthy beds or even on the floor. Most of the people attending them were monks, but here and there we saw a nun tending to some miserable person who could have been a woman. Illness and death are great levelers of us all. Marguerite seemed deeply affected and kept brushing away tears.

Sir Reynaud shook his head as we left. "What you saw in this once-great hospital is but a shadow of the past. There were clean rooms, baths, dispensaries, and the best of care for all who came here, even the poorest— and it cost them nothing. Medical men gave half their working time to these public hospitals and practiced privately the other half. It was taken as a given that their Christian duty was to look after those less well off. All that is gone; now it is every man for himself and God against all." He smiled sweetly.

We entered a small building near the Hagia Sofia cathedral. Inside, our guide's servants lit torches and held them aloft to reveal marble steps leading underground. Marguerite appeared by my side and gripped my hand, and her tremor of fear almost made me stop. But Basil exclaimed, "I have heard of this but never come to see it. Go forward, ladies. You will witness a wonder."

What awaited us at the bottom of the many steps was a cool world of magic, a vast room with hundreds of fine columns holding up its vaulted ceiling. It took a moment to realize that this underground vault was a cistern, where water lay like a still, secret sea. It seemed strange to think of the city sitting above us as if unaware. I walked along the edge, strain-ing to see beyond the light from the torches. Some columns matched, but others were one of a kind—one was covered in a pattern of peacock feathers, and I thought I glimpsed a woman's head at the base of one of the columns, with hair like snakes.

Sir Reynaud broke our awed silence. "This cistern is several hundred years old, and water still runs into it from a great viaduct that begins in the faraway hills. I would love to take you to it someday. It was for royal use, I believe. The city has always had many cisterns, and until recently no siege could break its people's will. Constantinople was once the home of a million people from all over the known world, and they needed water!"

Helene exclaimed, "I cannot imagine that many people!"

"I think there are scarcely 35,000 of us living here these days. In 1204, when far more people lived here, over 50,000 people died at the hands of bloodthirsty soldiers. Thousands more fled." Helene shuddered. Sir Reynaud went on. "I sometimes think about all those people who once lived and thrived above us, loving, hating, celebrating, mourning, fighting or making peace, and all of them now dead, as we will be someday."

I shivered, too. Nor could I imagine a million people in one city, either, much less the numbers who would have lived in Constantinople alone over the centuries. 35,000 seemed like so many, but Antioch might well boast that many people; I thought I recalled hearing that it too had once boasted a population of over a million. And to think that the Mongols had killed many millions of people in Cathay, and millions more elsewhere! But Sir Reynaud was right: all of us would pass from this earth in our turn, having lived a life better or worse.

He cut my musings short with a light jest about being glad to be still among the living before leading us up into the blinding sunshine and onto a great open area laid out before Hagia Sofia. I had passed through it before without really noticing it—just one more public meeting space outlined by a columned arcade—or what was left of it, with so much tipped over, smashed, and shattered.

"This was once the heart of Saint Constantine's new city, called the Augustaion after his sainted mother Augusta Helena. A pillar here once bore her statue aloft."

We passed by a damaged structure that must once have been lovely, with columns, arches, and domes. Sir Reynaud waved toward it. "The Milion, it is called. The True Cross was said to reside in its cupola, but as you can see, it was terribly damaged by the Franks. And the main thoroughfare, the Mese, begins here. You have all used it, I am sure." I certainly remembered it: the Mese was the route we took when Basil and Caterina kidnapped me! "It runs to what was once the main entrance through the city walls. There is a wonderful ruined porphyry column in Constantine's forum along it that I would …" he caught a glare from Basil and raised his eyebrows, "love to show you some other time." However, he could not resist adding, "It is topped by a cross these days, and its base is filled with holy relics like Noah's axe and Mary Magdalene's jar of ointment."

Helene crossed herself piously but also whispered to Basil loud enough for us all to hear, "We've seen so much already!"

Sir Reynaud did not respond to her, though. He was wrapped in his passion for ancient ruins. "I am certain that the massive column and statue in the agora over there has caught everyone's notice before this." We all turned toward a tall column of bricks that had once been completely covered by some kind of brass plates, though many had been pried off on its lower half. Marble steps led up to it on four sides. We all stared in awe. This was the column and statue I had noticed before, almost as tall as Hagia Sofia is high.

"Do you know who it is, Basil?" asked Helene.

"Of course; that is Saint Constantine."

"Well, many men think so," said Sir Reynaud, "but in fact, that is Emperor Justinian in triumph on horseback. Even from down here you can see that the statue must be at least the height of three men. See, he holds the globe and cross of the universal emperor with his left hand. It is said that it holds the city's genius—its guardian spirit, Lady Sofia—and that as long as he holds that globe, Constantinople will never fall into foreign hands." He laughed to himself.

Basil snorted. "Are the Latins and Venetians not foreign?"

Sir Reynaud smiled pleasantly. "Well, at least they are Christians." But standing nearest to him, I heard him mutter, "More or less."

My guide gestured toward another ruined palace standing to one side of the forum. "Over there is what remains of the Magnaura Palace, where the Roman Senate once—" Helene let out a loud sigh that not even Sir Reynaud could ignore. "I see I weary you with detail. Let us go inside the cathedral, then. It is not to be missed. But first we can cleanse hands and heart at this fountain, built for just that purpose." He swung off his horse and did so himself, obliging us to do the same. The fountain was elaborate and beautiful, but the water was rank.

We entered Hagia Sofia and crossed ourselves. It was almost empty but for a few monks and priests and even fewer worshippers. Leaving our servants behind, we climbed some stairs hidden from the common view, up and up to a semicircular gallery that overlooked the massive floor. From there the people looked like small dolls. "Here is where the empress and her court ladies listened to the Mass conducted far below." The queen's throne still stood in place, though it was much defaced: jewels pried out of it and gold stripped from it.

"And look over here." We followed Sir Reynaud to another spot where a simple tomb sat on the marble floor. "Here lies the author of Constantinople's misery, the blind Doge of Venice whose idea it was to storm the city: Enrico Dandolo." And he spat on it.

Turning to see our shock, he added, "Please do not take me too seriously. It is a little secret I share with you: Greeks do this, and remember I am half Greek."

He smiled sweetly, as if spite in such a holy place held no threat to anyone, and led us through a series of halls that had once been the sole preserve of the emperors and empresses of Byzantium. Mosaic decorations were everywhere, covering upper walls and outlining delicately painted ceilings. High up, where the looters had not been able to reach, gold and ruby and emerald and lapis tiles still glimmered. We passed glowing murals, mostly portraits of Christ or Mother Mary, sometimes flanked by the emperors and empresses who had commissioned them. Some walls looked as if the murals had been bodily removed, for there were great damaged empty spots. But on the remaining ones, the tiles were so perfectly placed and so delicately colored that everything came alive, from the lift of an eyebrow to the flush of a cheek. The rooms might be empty and neglected, pillaged of the wealth that must have adorned them, but I was struck dumb by the beauty that remained: marble doorways, pieced marble floors, columns topped with intricately carved capitals.

Sir Reynaud came up beside me. "You will find some of the missing mosaics in Venice if you ever happen to visit there." I thought I caught a note of bitterness, but when I looked up at him, his smile told me nothing.

By then even I was feeling weary, and he finally seemed to sense that we had all had enough. "Time for a meal," he declared, "at the finest inn the city has to offer. It is quite close by." And he led us, to my surprise, straight to the same hostel where Leo had once worked!

As we trooped inside, where the innkeeper awaited us with barely concealed impatience, Sir Reynaud said, "Of course the food is not as good as it was when they had a Greek cook a few years back, but his kitchen boy was alert enough to note what he did. He got himself advanced to cook when the Greek left, so we have a hint of what it was like."

I hid a smile. My Leo had struck a blow at the Frankish world in his own way: on its tongues!

The dinner was good indeed, and I recognized one of Leo's favorite receipts, somewhat modified and not as tasty as when he made it. After an hour or so of food, drink and rest, Basil and Helene regained their good humor. But rather than bid us good-bye, Sir Reynaud declared that there was still more to see: the Great Palace. Helene and Basil agreed that this would be interesting, so we set out to see as much more as Sir Reynaud could cram into one afternoon. We returned to the Augustaion to enter the Great Palace, which was surrounded by thick walls and massive doors topped with a small chapel and some statuary. Its uniformed guards recognized Sir Reynaud and waved him through, though we had to leave our horses at the entrance. It reminded me of the main entrance into Kyiv, and I stifled my own sigh. The Golden Gates and their chapel were all gone now, I imagined.

"This is the Chalke Gate." I could see that Sir Reynaud wished to say more, but Basil and Helene were not paying attention, so he simply waved us through and into the palace yards. The Great Palace turned out to be a complex of buildings, some in ruins and others turned to new purposes. So many buildings, some of them huge! Papa's palace in Kyiv would have been lost there. But what desolation lay before us.

Sir Reynaud spoke. "All this was ravaged in 1204, and much of it has fallen into complete ruin, though King Baldwin sometimes stays in the Bukoleon palace—that one over there, built right into the sea wall. But we cannot go inside it today, as he is in residence right now." No one seemed disappointed. "Do not be surprised when you find that most of the buildings are now open to the sky. In order to raise money, he recently stripped the lead roofs from the disused buildings and sold it. Over there are the barracks, which he does use, and you can still see traces of the imperial gardens."

In awed silence, we began to wander about. I was in a daze. Alexander and Banjuu disappeared together, looking, I suspected, for a secret corner to be alone with each other, but Marguerite and Bardas followed me like shadows. Here and there I recognized the remains of a church; and inside what must have been an enormous library, I came upon the moldy and torn remains of several scrolls and books that had escaped burning only to be destroyed by weather. Everywhere walls were defaced, with holes in the mosaics where tiles had been pried out, perhaps. Innumerable statues lay in heaps, some smashed into shards, and others with limbless or headless torsos, like dismembered corpses on a battlefield. Marguerite gave a sob of horror, and I felt like joining her.

Sir Reynaud appeared at my side. "Some of those statues stood for a thousand years before the Franks smashed them, and many of them were sculpted by the greatest artists of antiquity." He pointed around us. "Many sacred ceremonies took place in these great courtyards, and some of these buildings were only used for a single annual holy rite. Also many festivals and games were held here, each with their special arena. It once must have been a place of such elegance and beauty."

Helene and Basil and their servants rejoined us, and together we wandered through ruined meeting halls, throne rooms, banquet halls, tiny chapels, and bathhouses. In an abandoned orchard, new fruits were forming while old ones rotted into the ground. Birds had left droppings on fabulous marble mosaic floors. Some buildings were left open to the sky by design and others were clearly the victims of King Baldwin's desperate search for monies, but everything was falling apart. Sir Reynaud named a few palaces here and there: the Pearl Palace, an old heap called the Daphne, and the Hall of Nineteen Couches are a few names I recall. Corridors, courtyards, and walkways overgrown with weeds or half-buried under rotting leaves led us on. One marble-walled throne room in particular took my breath away, at least what was left of it.

"You who hail from Rus' will be interested in this room," Sir Reynaud told us. "Many years ago, your prince sent envoys to the emperor to decide whether to accept Orthodox Christianity. That emperor had a throne built with pulleys that raised it up as though ascending toward Heaven, just to impress visitors. Brass lions at its base spat out water with a great roar, and sheep spouted perfumed water. And a silver bejeweled tree with singing metal birds stood somewhere in the room. I understand that your envoys saw the throne carried up into the air with the emperor sitting there like a golden angel and decided that it and the other wonders they saw must be reflections of the true faith."

"What happened to it all? Did the Franks take everything?" I asked.

"No, the metals were all melted down long ago to finance some war or other. It was just a whim on the part of one emperor, after all. Another was more passionate about food. The dining table in one feasting hall, I am told, was of solid gold, and gigantic fruit bowls, too heavy to lift, were carried from guest to guest by gold-encased ropes and pulleys hanging from the ceiling."

"Surely you jest with us. How could these things be?"

"Oh no, I promise you, I speak only the truth."

Basil nodded solemnly. "What a sight it must have been."

We all followed Sir Reynaud to the last sight of the day. Helene and Basil fell behind; clearly they felt they had seen enough. But this was worth seeing! We passed through a once-fine hall that led to a spiral staircase. At its top landing were worn, heavy doors that had been stripped of their decorations—much of them ivory, given the bits that still clung to the damaged surface—and came outside onto a covered porch, once fine and now ruined, above a race course shaped somewhat like a long, narrow oval and surrounded on three sides by tiered marble benches and broken columns that must once have formed an arcade. The fourth side might once have led to stables or the like, but its buildings were so ruined that it was hard to tell until Sir Reynaud explained it all.

"We are standing in the imperial box, or what is left of it, where the Emperor presided over events. Below you is the Hippodrome, used for state ritual occasions, as well as for chariot races and public meetings. It could seat 40,000 men. No women were allowed, of course, but the empress could watch from within the Great Palace."

Helene's only comment was, "I doubt much of what they did there would interest a woman, much less an empress. I've heard about gladiators and such, and throwing Christians to lions—terrible!"

"Well, that was in Rome and even longer ago. Saint Constantine changed much of that, certainly throwing Christians to lions," Sir Reynaud smiled. "He was the first Christian emperor of the Roman Empire, after all. But try to imagine the sights this course has seen: holy processions, races, war games, cheering crowds, and even riots."

We all laughed mildly, but though I was familiar with knightly jousts and melees, or the war play of Papa's warriors, or even Mongol battues, all this racing and fighting for sport would always seem most strange to me.

But in that I may be alone; many women also delight in violent sport.

I could hear our young servants murmuring together, and then Alexander and Fotis were racing each other, leaping down the steep stairs. Banjuu called to him to take care. Her voice and his laughter echoed emptily as if into a huge, empty well.

"And what are those pillars down there along that central divider?" I asked.

"Two are ancient obelisks brought from Egypt. The brick one was entirely covered with bronze plates before the Franks pulled off the ones they could reach, which is why it looks so strange now. And the bronze snake column over there was brought here long ago from the Temple of Apollo in Delphi—a famous city in Greece. The serpents' heads supported a great golden salver once used in pagan rituals. The Franks stole it." The pillar, shorter than the obelisks, was shaped like three intertwined serpents unwinding as they reached the top, where each head lunged out, hissing forever, in a different direction.

"There used to be more statuary and monuments all along the spina— your divider—including bronze statues of famous race horses. Four of the most ancient were carted away by the Venetians to adorn their city. Much else was carried to Venice, too, the wealth and artistry of a thousand years and more. But better than letting the Franks destroy them, I suppose."

We all stood in silence, each lost in our own thoughts, until Sir Reynaud spoke abruptly. "I must escort you all home now and, as it turns out, leave tomorrow on my mission for my king. I had thought to have another day to show everyone more if you wished, but King Baldwin's plans and therefore mine have changed."

Helene and Basil looked distinctly uninterested, though they murmured something polite, but I felt a little disappointed. "I would indeed have wished it."

"As would I, and someday I hope to continue showing you all the wonders of this city. But for now, I must deliver another splinter of the True Cross, encased in an ivory reliquary of great antiquity, to another monastery, this one in a German county. I suspect that if all the splinters King Baldwin has sold were put together, along with the chunk the Pope possesses, there would be enough to make two or three crosses." He tried to sound as if his statement was a jest, but the sneer in his voice was unmistakable.

"You believe he is selling false relics?" Basil asked in surprise.

"Who knows? He must make difficult choices if he and his kingdom are to survive. But the reliquary is a rare work of great beauty. It belonged to my uncle, the man you met today, who was persuaded to donate it." Was there an edge to Sir Reynaud's voice? His face revealed nothing.

The silence of a wearying day fell between us as we rode back to Basil's home. Finally Sir Reynaud said, "I hope to see you again, Lady Sofia. You were most attentive to my little stories, and I value your interest."

"I am grateful for everything you did for us today. You brought Constantinople back to life in my imagination. I begin to understand what it must have been like here before so much was destroyed, and it grieves me to think of all that was lost. My father once said it was like heaven brought down to earth."

"That was exactly the intent of what Western Christendom calls Byzantium: to make Heaven manifest on Earth. It once extended to the borders of Persia in the east, and in the south, in Africa, from Egypt to Carthage. Even after the Western Roman Empire fell into pieces, it still thrived, grew ever more glorious while wars raged between barbarians and Rome, Pope and Emperor. There was no quarrel between sacred and worldly here. I wish I could show you everything that remains this city alone, so many shadows of a great dream that stretched all around the Mediterranean and beyond."

"What you say is like poetry, but you sound rather bitter. Is the dream entirely dead? After all, there are Greek states in Nicaea and Trebizond and Epirus."

"Bitter? Please forgive me. No, some dreams never die. And I have no doubt that one day one of those little claimants to Byzantine glory will succeed in breaking the Latin hold, here and elsewhere, too." He smiled and turned to light topics, to jest, and to frothy flattery.

Sir Reynaud left us at the entrance to Basil's villa. He would not come inside when Basil invited him—not that Basil showed much real eagerness. "I must finish preparing for tomorrow's journey. I hope we meet again soon." And he bowed and left.

I returned to my lodging soon thereafter, too, feeling a mixture of emotions, none of them as happy as I had expected. It had been such an interesting day, but I felt saddened as well. Of course seeing and learning about such ruination was disheartening, but there was more. I felt discomfited by Sir Reynaud's bitter edge and diminished by some of the stories, especially the one about the throne that rose in the air. It felt as though our Rus' ambassadors had been tricked and my people been fooled into converting to Orthodoxy.

But then I wondered if the Roman Emperors, as they had still called themselves then, had simply wished to display their superiority, not to trick anyone exactly. After all if they could command that such wonders be built, perhaps that was an act of their faith. Well, there was no one to ask now; it would remain a mystery. And Sir Reynaud was, all in all, a mystery, too.

I also felt a little guilty that I had not thought about Sir Joscelin except in passing, I had been so entranced by such amazing yet painful sights, each a little prick by itself, but all together like being stung by a swarm of bees, that I had been blinded to everything else. Possibly I had missed a special opportunity, since Sir Reynaud had said he knew my beloved and his brother. On the other hand, it would not have been a good time in such a crowd. But the fact remained: I had not even thought to ask him about them, and now we were both departing.

.

ANNO DOMINI 1253-1254

The morning before I left Constantinople, I received a most unexpected visitor, one who made me glad I had lingered on for that extra week. It began with yet another knock on the door, but this time I heard it. I was overseeing the packing, so I thought it was Helene, whom I was expecting to come help me. Instead Bardas led in a sturdy-looking monk who introduced himself as Friar William of Rubruk.

"I hope I don't disturb you. I am soon to leave for Mongol lands on a mission for His Majesty King Louis. I was given your name some time ago by my friend, whom I hope you remember: a fellow monk, André de Longjumeau. He said that if I ever went to Karakorum, I should first contact you and a knight you may know, Sir Baudouin of Hainaut. One of Friar André's last requests was that I should to give you his greetings and tell you that you were right about Mongols. His visit to Karakorum was a blow to his heart, one from which he did not recover. He died recently."

A glance at Banjuu and Marguerite sent them scurrying off to find refreshments. "That was very kind of him. I am sorry to hear of his death," I said as I led my guest to the chair of honor and pulled a stool forward for myself. "He meant so well and had such large dreams. I will light a candle for his soul when next I go to church.

"And I know of Sir Baudouin, I think. Is he the envoy King Baldwin sent to Karakorum to arrange an alliance? I heard my uncle speak of him.

He returned recently, did he not?"

"Yes, I hope to speak with him before I leave, since Friar André was so disheartened. I wish to learn as much from as many people as I can."

A short silence fell, during which the monk began looking around the room. So I examined him. He seemed to be in his mid-thirties, with a ruddy face that bespoke health, and a muscular build that his cassock of unbleached wool could not conceal. A white rope was bound about his waist, and the ring of hair on his tonsured head was a light brown. When he caught my glance, he smiled warmly. Somehow I felt at ease with him, as though I was sitting on the earth. In some way his presence reminded me of Dorje, though he seemed to feel no desire to chatter and ask questions. Words did not even seem necessary. I had not felt that with André de Longjumeau, whose head had seemed to float in clouds of blind faith.

Alexander soon appeared with a tray on which sat carafes of wine and water, cups, and some fruit. Once served and with my people dismissed to other tasks, Friar William finally spoke. "If you do not object, I will speak straightly with you." I nodded my permission, wondering what he could me. "Friar André felt that you knew more than you were willing to reveal when you spoke with him. As he put it, if the danger has passed for you, you might be able to tell me of your experience."

I drew back. "What experience could I possibly have that would interest you?"

"Among the Mongols, of course. Friar André told me about your encounter with the Mongol envoys. He was a good reader of people when his faith didn't carry him to extremes, and he said that not only was he certain that you knew more Mongol speech than you said you did, but that you knew more about Mongols in general. Given what the envoys had said about you, he did not blame you for keeping close counsel. But now, in honor of his memory, I ask you to relent and tell me anything that would help me on my mission, for he feels his was an utter failure. He believed it might have caused more harm than good."

"Oh?"

"Yes, Kuyuk Khan's widow was regent at the time. André told me that her arrogance and rudeness were even greater than what he reported to King Louis when he returned. She took as a given that the king's gifts—you know he sent a scarlet tent embroidered with saints to be used as a chapel, and of course missionaries?" I shook my head. "Well, she saw them as gifts of submission! She demanded that the king go to Karakorum to submit in person or face the most terrible consequences.

"Of course such a journey would be impossible, but as it happens, King Louis need not fear any so-called consequences! By the time Friar André left, a new Great Khan had already been elected. Word has crossed the endless miles of a continent: the new Khakan, one Mongke, despised Kuyuk and his family, and most of them are now dead, including that woman. She especially died horribly."

This news of retribution was shocking, for I remembered Mongke as possessing more dignity and calm than most of his fellow khans. But he was also a tough warrior. Well, who knew what the politics among the Golden Kin were like these days? I must at least help this kind monk. So I took a deep breath and said, "Yes, I also heard about Mongke Khan's accession through one of my business agents. And yes, I do know more than I admitted to Friar André—it was for my own safety. But I will speak now. All I ask is that you never reveal that you ever even heard of me. Nothing I tell you came from my lips. Is that a promise you can keep?"

"Indeed, I can. I am a man of discretion, for my king would have no other kind of advisor around him." Again I masked my feelings. It was good to know that Friar André had held no hard feelings toward me, but I still thought him a little too full of religious certainty to make a reliable advisor to King Louis or anyone else.

So I explained what I knew, and in greater detail than I had meant to reveal, for the monk had such a sympathetic way of listening that I ended up in tears a few times. But he was most interested in Mongol customs and took note of all the bans I could recall, as well as forms of greeting and respect and so forth.

I also told him what I remembered of Mongke Khan and Mongol family politics. And I tried to explain that their tolerant policy toward all religions was just that: a policy, which gave them more control over their subject nations.

At the end I added, "Please to not try to convert anyone or argue with the other holy men there, for no one truly wins."

Friar William smiled. "On that point I must keep my own counsel."

"Well, I have given you everything I can to help make your journey fruitful, and now it is up to you. I admit to feeling some relief in telling you all this after feeling so helpless on Cyprus."

After few more pleasantries, he took his leave. At my request he blessed me, afterwards adding, "May Almighty God look after you."

He departed. I never met him again, but a few years later I did learn that he had returned safely and even written a history of his journey. How I would love to read it and compare his recollections with mine.

But now I was homeward bound and leaving with no regrets.

However, to my surprise, life seemed surprisingly dull back in Daphne. No more weddings to look forward to—although considering the pangs they caused me, that was not much hardship—but also no guided visits in the company of a mostly pleasant companion, and still no way of finding Lord Joscelin. How I regretted not asking about him when I had the chance!

Not only that, but in several ways, I felt rather useless. Of course there was Anna, who was not only growing but also changing almost every day and providing me with endless delights. And as always, I had something in hand to sew or embroider, or I could read in my breviary. At least I could pray for those I loved and for forgiveness for my sins. I went to Mass every Sunday and celebrated all the Feast Days and so forth.

But with the last orphan grown up and gone from Daphne—only a few had stayed on as servants and guards—and trustworthy subordinates looking after the other two homes, even to finding new children on the streets, I had little to do with them anymore. I scarcely knew the orphan children in Antioch, as most of the ones I had first taken in were gone. And Basil had become such a good business partner, especially in dealing with the Venetians and the Greek states, that I was left with little to do with business, either.

I kept in touch with John of Epirus, of course, who reported dutifully on what he saw and heard—like Mongke becoming Great Khan. He had nothing of import to say about Basil, who seemed totally happy: a new wife, his children returned to him, and business flourishing. After a few weeks of brooding, watching Banjuu and Alexander openly in love, and enjoying Anna's endless discoveries—including many new words and so many questions that went with them—I realized I must do something more with my life or I would go mad.

So I began writing again. It started when I came upon my Papa's wooden book, stored in a little-used chest. It was my last memento of him. I sat down and began to read. Much of it brought me to tears, but I also realized how much I had changed since then. My childish hopes and terrors and despairs seemed like someone else's.

That was when I decided what to do: I would rewrite it and add my other memories, of Alamut and Castle Sa'amar, of my beloved Joscelin and so forth. Perhaps I could make some sense of all those lost dreams and hopes, perhaps find solace in the good memories. Since I had long given up using the language of Rus', I would write in Latin, the universal speech of the world I now lived in.

So I began with the day I set my fate in motion, as I had called it so many years ago. I undertook to turn this second attempt into more of a story, so there would be a flow from one episode in my life to another. From then on, I spent hours each day writing, without realizing the passage of time and only a cramped hand reminding me to stop.

Right away I felt benefit from my new task: going over what I had written in my first journal also inspired me to try that practice of peace again, in honor of Dorje if nothing else, and I began to use it in the mornings when I arose. It seemed to give me strength.

We passed the Christmas Holy Days quietly. I took my wards to all the ceremonies, even Banjuu. She and the others liked attending religious festivities because they were full of color and splendor, and even humor, what with all the unruly traditions of overturning tradition. I doubted any of my orphans were especially religious, though of course they always attended Mass with me. But they were not alone in that, for most people I knew came to worship more out of fear or for a desire for entertainment or the good opinion of others than they did from deep devotion.

Nor did the particular religion matter: even at the Hospitaller castle, Muslims had come for miles around to witness every holy occasion. They found these events most entertaining and interesting.

A pair of women came begging at my gates one chill day late in January. Their hair was shorn, and their simple habits and veils were of the coarsest, most colorless cloth. They told me they were nuns, and they sought permission to build a hut on my land by a stream they had found. Of course I gave it to them and even sent Bardas back with them, bearing many provisions. Such small events seemed momentous in my quiet life, and in this case I was right, though years were to pass first.

But things suddenly changed and became very interesting indeed! In February just before Lent, Sir Reynaud suddenly reappeared in my life. And once more I was playing with Anna. He seemed to take no notice of my blushes as I sent her away with my girls, simply greeted me courteously and asked after my wellbeing. After I had in turn asked after his latest mission and he had offered very little about it, he said, looking about the courtyard, "I heard you lived almost like a nun here. But no convent ever held such a pretty space as this. Look at the embroidery on these cushions and the way you have laid out your flowerbeds. Enchanting!"

"You have an eye for beauty," I responded, remembering my long lost friend Q'ing-ling with a tiny twist of my heart. She had once said the same to me.

"Yes, that is what drew me to you," he laughed.

He had seen Basil and Helene before he left, which was how he knew where to find me, and he brought their greetings along with a packet of business documents from my uncle and letters from them both. He encouraged me not to wait to open them, so I broke the seals on Helene's and read. She wanted me to come to her for a long visit after her husband's plans for me were concluded. So I read his letter next, as I knew of no plans.

To my great surprise, his was another invitation: to accompany him to Venice right after the New Year that spring. "It seems that our Venetian trading partners, some of whom are my cousins-in-law, want to meet my mysterious partner. I know you prefer to stay hidden in the background, but if you come with me, you can slip under their guard, charm them with your beauty and wit, and we'll be the richer for it, as I have a daring plan," was how he phrased it. It only took me a moment's hesitation to decide that I would go. Daphne had grown too dull.

Thanking Sir Reynaud for his patience, I asked him to dine with me. As luck would have it, Leo prepared the same dish Sir Reynaud had ordered for us in Constantinople. My guest commented on the fact, adding that it tasted even better this time and attributing it to the pleasant company of his hostess.

I laughed. "Indeed, that is not why. My cook was the author of that receipt, and of course he prepares it better!"

"He hides his talents here, just as you hide your beauty."

Seeing me blush, he passed on to other subjects. "Basil's children, as you know, are home and settled back into their old life, and I am happy to report that the older boys torture Gilles only a little—no more than brothers ordinarily do. Cecilia and Paolo, being younger and knowing how it feels, are a little kinder. They defend him from their brothers when it suits them, but then Paolo goes off and Gilles is left to Cecelia's mercies. She dresses him up like a doll, which makes him miserable. He'd rather be tortured by the boys, whom he follows around like a faithful hound when they let him. They even made up a game: they are the knights and he is their page, but he is glad to run silly errands for them, bring them fruit from the kitchen and so forth." Sir Reynaud spoke in such a mock-sad way that I had to laugh.

"Oh, and King Louis has finally returned to Francia. After his mother died, there was no one he trusted to be his regent. Just as well. His kingdom needs him, and he used up all his wealth on fortifications here in Outremer, as they say in Francia." I suppressed a sigh: an entire world of memory, of lost hopes, rose in my breast.

After the meal we went riding in the forest, with Sir Reynaud's attendants and Bardas trailing behind. It was a soft day for that time of year. We passed my pair of nuns busily working on their hut, which was built out from a rocky outcrop. "Nuns?" he asked. I nodded. From a fissure in the rock poured one of the mountain's many streams, reminding me of a happy afternoon alone with my beloved Joscelin, a sweet dream from long ago, and far removed from these nuns' sacred world. But that did remind me to ask Sir Reynaud about how he knew him and his brother Robert.

As before, a veiled look flitted across his face, which I took for a moment of jealousy. "We both fought at the battle at La Forbie, where Robert died. But I first came to know them both in Ascalon after the disaster of Lord Thibaut's campaign, which I had nothing to do with, thank God!

"I was there seeking the same thing they were: monies, in my case for King Baldwin. Why I had to go there is a long and tangled story, but suffice it to say it included a holy relic. We met quite by chance before the door of the Templars' offices and fell into conversation together. After our business was done, we went to an inn to drink together. I fear Robert was not very good at drinking, but he was more of a girl than a man, anyway."

"What do you mean by that?"

"Oh, I thought you knew already. He'd have been fine in a monastery, could have been some bishop's Ganymede and been happy. Not much real fight in him at all. But of course, his brother made up for that! I enjoy a good brawl myself, and we ended up drunk and with fists flying when someone insulted Robert." Sir Reynaud laughed. "We got the worse of it, too, I fear, nor was our friendship to have much future, for Robert left a week or so later with some Knights Hospitaller and I returned to Constantinople.

"And that is as much as I can tell you."

Clearly there was more, but what he had said fit well with what I already knew, so I didn't pursue the subject. It sounded as if Robert had not made a good impression on Sir Reynaud. And I did not understand what he meant about Ganymede—all I recalled was that he was cupbearer to Zeus.

My friend, for more than that I would not allow, visited me several times over the next fortnight. It seemed that his king was on the move again and for the present was in Antioch visiting holy places before celebrating Easter. According to Sir Reynaud, King Baldwin rarely lived in Constantinople, and these days he spent most of his time on pilgrimage or as a guest in foreign courts—or as a beggar in them, I gathered from my friend's veiled words. The king was forever in need of money, had once even pawned his own son to Venetian bankers in order to survive, although a fellow king had taken pity on them both and redeemed the boy. I looked over at Anna, playing as she often did with invisible friends, and wondered how anyone could part with their child—the boy's life must be so sad.

But Sir Reynaud spoke in such a lightly jesting way when telling me about his adventures in the king's retinue that I had to laugh. For instance, they had spent two years in the capital of the Franks, Paris, whence had come a goldsmith I had saved from the Mongol sword all those years ago. Batu Khan had sent the man back to Mongolia as a gift for Mongke Khan.

"Paris was a muddy mess," Sir Reynaud told me. "And it is also rather barbaric. I once saw a pig escape from the market right into the city's great cathedral, Notre Dame. It was so clever at doubling back and worming out of its pursuers' grips that it took a pair of monks, three priests, and four merchants to chase it out. The owner of the pig fell flat on his face and spewed out a stream of the filthiest oaths I ever heard! I think the holy men were more shocked by that than by the pig." We both laughed.

Although Sir Reynaud did not say so, I gathered from his words that daily markets are held not only in the square in front of the cathedral but even inside the church entrance. Certainly he went on to describe all the things that can be bought, from foodstuffs to books to amulets and holy relics—and, I supposed, livestock.

"And King Louis was building a truly wondrous church to hold various holy relics, especially the Crown of Thorns. I wish I could see it now; it must be lovely, and now the crown rests there. Years ago King Baldwin pawned it to the Venetians, and it ended up in King Louis' hands, brought to Paris by one of his advisors, a rather opinionated monk named André de Longjumeau."

"Oh, I knew him: he was the same man the king sent to convert the Great Khan of the Mongols to Christianity."

Sir Reynaud barely nodded, for he was thinking of his own story. "The church is called Saint Chapelle, and it was already sublime—surely it is even more so now that it is completed. However, that crown does not convince me, even if it turns out to be the one that was venerated for centuries: it is made from woven rushes, with thorns arrayed within the circlet, the ones that have not been given away to various kings and prelates. The reliquary that holds it is worth much more than it is! I can think of more arguments against its being the true crown, since my king is known for—but I see I disturb you with my saucy talk."

"Yes, I am disturbed, and almost as much by your lack of respect toward your king as by the thought that the crown might be a false relic."

Sir Reynaud seemed taken aback. "Pardon me, Lady Sofia. I have let an ill habit guide my words. I of course worship the true Crown of Thorns devotedly, which this may be, and I deeply respect my king."

He smoothly drew my attention to some cluster of early flowers and began praising the beauty of the day, but I could not believe his protestations. And he raised doubts in my mind that would not be easily laid to rest, both about him and about false relics.

On another visit he told me about going with his king to Hungary and Germany, where Baldwin had raised an army to take back the lands that once formed his empire, as Sir Reynaud ironically called it. "It marched all the way to Constantinople before melting away without doing much but eating the countryside bare."

Such stories, while told laughingly, began to make me wonder if Sir Reynaud was carrying some secret burden of outrage, or if he was just a man of the world in a way I was not familiar with. Because he was always charming and attentive to me, I could not help but like him. Still, his attentions were sometimes subtly familiar. He never said anything of a personal nature to offend or to draw back from, but I would suddenly feel ill at ease without knowing why.

However, I could only feel grateful for Sir Reynaud's help in arranging my journey back to Constantinople after Lady Day. He had done everything for me; indeed, he had found me passage on the same ship he was sailing in, which was part of King Baldwin's convoy. I even saw the king for the first time on the morning my servants and I embarked. The king was black-bearded, dark and grim of face, and saturnine in demeanor as he strode aboard his own ship, looking neither right nor left.

My hesitations about traveling in Sir Reynaud's company never came to pass. He was good at keeping Anna from falling overboard and distracting her into more moderate play, and at times he seemed to enjoy her company more than mine. With fair winds behind us, it only took ten days to reach Constantinople, and within days we were aboard a ship to Venice with Basil.

I say we because to my uncle's dismay, I insisted on taking not only Anna but also my favorites among my household: my first three orphans, of course, and a charming, eager youth named Thomas whose golden thatch of hair no brushing could tame. We had taken to calling him Golden Thomas. These young people were my family now, and nothing Basil or Helene could say would persuade me to leave them or Anna behind with her. Alas that this meant the journey was less than pleasant. In his irritation Basil spoke as little to me as possible, reminding me a little of Oleg both in his brevity and his ability to hold a grudge overlong.

I spent some of my time studying the Veneziano I had learned while traveling with Batu Khan's translators. I had written many Veneziano words and phrases in the final pages of the journal Papa had given me, as a way to pass the time, and then had forgotten it. Happily, I had remembered at the last minute, dug out my book, and brought it with me.

But more came back to me than speech: memories, too. Where was my teacher Maria now? Had she and her Kipchak Kchiia fallen in love, perhaps married? I hoped so, given how few were the pleasures of a slave. It made me glad that I had decided to write down everything I could remember.

Too often, though, I had to make sure Anna was safe. She seemed to be happiest when she was close to falling overboard or climbing up the forbidden rope ladders that led up to the sails. Mercifully the sea was no problem at that time of year, and in fact sailing among those lovely Aegean islands again brought back memories of another journey, a hopeful one, when I had not known I was carrying a child or that my beloved Joscelin would vanish from my life.

We arrived in early May. The sun was well past her zenith when our ships glided past a barrier of long, sandy, islands that reminded me of protective walls. Each boasted at least one settlement and a chapel. As if in happy greeting, church bells began ringing over the water. We were now in a wide lagoon, with more settled islands dotting the water and many boats of various sizes heading to destinations near and far. And as if it had stolen color from the sky, the water was a sparkling mosaic of little blue and turquoise ripples. In the distance a mountain range gleamed like a hazy pearl.

We docked at a wharf that led straight onto a long open market place full of people and lined with stalls. "The Piazzetta of San Marco," Basil told me in a rare fit of talkativeness. On either side of its entrance, two tall pillars stood guard, on one of which stood a winged lion with one paw on a book. "That is the symbol of the patron saint of Venice," he said when he saw me staring, "the Lion of Saint Mark. Someday someone will put something on that other pillar, too. Probably something sacred and stolen." He laughed to himself. "Venetians like nothing better than adding to their collection of stolen relics—they take pride in their exploits, the more daring the better."

Between the pillars were colorful striped stalls where I heard rattling sounds mixed with shouts of glee or horror. I realized why when we passed by them: they held gaming tables, and men were crowded about losing or winning at dice and other games of chance, or encouraging their friends to try their luck.

A well-guarded castle with a crenellated roof marched along the right side of the piazzetta, flanked by a columned and arched arcade; other buildings linked together by similar arcades lined the opposite side. Beyond us the piazzetta led to a much larger square, which was bordered on one side by a large, fanciful church. From where I stood, the castle hid most of it. I was not expecting such a handsome city, and I raged a little in my heart at how it outshone Constantinople. Even the pavement was beautiful, set in a herringbone pattern with bands of stone near its edges to make a decorative ribbon-like outline, though that was mostly covered by merchant's stalls crowded around the margins. Every imaginable kind of goods stood on sale: foodstuffs, salt, spices, armor, swords, heavy silks, damasks, brocades, filmy tissues, inlaid caskets, perfumes, cosmetics and more, all set out in dazzling array. Behind the stalls, jewelers and goldsmiths beckoned from the doorways of their workshops and called to me when they saw me staring.

I had thought Antioch wealthy, but this market alone carried items of such richness that I was reminded of Batu Khan's city of Sarai. However, here all was more orderly and more elegant, and the goods of even greater variety. We were clearly in Western Christendom, though plenty of Veneziano men wore imamahs—I later heard them called turbans—and Oriental style clothing. And there were as many races of men as in Antioch, too: black, yellow, and even a few who might have just dismounted from a steppe pony.

We also passed an area where slaves stood naked and shivering—many boys and pretty young women who might well have been from Rus'. My heart twisted for a moment, but I quickly turned away.

Having pushed our way through the crowd without losing anything to pickpockets, we reached the end of the piazzetta and turned into that vast square I had glimpsed, which Basil called the Piazza of Saint Mark. The surrounding buildings dwarfed us, including the church: a fanciful structure indeed, with pointed domes, arches, pillars, balconies, mosaic decorations and more. Work was going on both inside and out: columns and slabs of marble being carried inside and someone up on a scaffold laying tiles into a gilt mosaic.

A tall bell tower stood nearby, surrounded by what seemed to be barracks and watched over by soldiers all wearing the same red and yellow colors and insignias. Even more stalls crowded around the margins of this piazza, and merchants and servants and men—and women—apparently from all around the world were everywhere, talking at ease, bargaining with sharp voices, walking purposefully. This huge long space dwarfed them all.

Basil found a litter for Anna and me, but everyone else walked. Leaving the noisy square behind, we followed a maze of little streets, sometimes passing over canals via pontoons or wooden bridges. I could not help gaping at the fine churches and handsome buildings. Their walls of red brick, white stone, or colorful stucco, adorned with arched windows, iron balconies, and colonnades lined with pillars, looked somewhat like those in Constantinople. Flags of many colors bravely flew from some of the balconies, often bearing that image of the bookish winged lion, a motif that was also often carved in relief over the doors of several of the churches. Where there were gaps between the grand buildings, I glimpsed orchards and vegetable gardens behind or beside them, and sometimes Persian-style gardens contained by fences.

I saw perhaps two horses. Almost everyone walked or rode in litters like mine, or else rode in long, narrow, flat-bottomed boats guided by a pilot. He always stood, pushing the boat along with a long pole, perhaps so he could both steer and see what was coming around the next bend. The finer buildings had landings with private docks, often with those narrow boats tied up to them. Indeed, I soon realized that this was a city of islands and boats, most of which lay so close to each other that surely they had been enlarged to leave only water lanes for passageways. Only a few bridges linked a few of the larger islands. These waterways are how Venice differs from her mother city, for clearly Constantinople was her model.

The waters of course stank with refuse, drowned rats and the like. But the fine ladies and a few well-dressed men passing by combated the stench by holding fragrant flowers to their noses, a custom Helene and I soon adopted.

I was soon lost in a labyrinth of alleys, squares, canals, and people building or bargaining or transporting something or someone by water. Even the women I saw were adornments: so elegant, so finely attired in rich silks velvets, heavy damasks, and filmy tissues that my womanly vanity was aroused. If only I could look like that, too! It had been so long since I had cared for such things or had needed to.

Venice was a floating dream. So much, so much beauty all around me that I fell into a trance: ornately trimmed buildings reflecting in rippling water; a song floating from a church, sung in many interweaving voices and new to my ears; the scent of incense; little shrines at corners of lanes devoted to the Virgin or to a saint, each with an unlit lamp before it; gold and pink air; and soft sunlight. The dream faded when we passed a large modern church with workmen and artists hard at work inside and out and I realized what I was seeing. This had to be a new home for treasure Venice had seized from Constantinople! Sir Reynaud has told me that it would take decades to find the right places to put it all. As soon as he knew where I was going, he had straightaway begun describing Venice to me. All its naval power, its wealth, its great churches, centered on this city, and the rest of the Republic consisted only of the lagoon islands, certain forested coasts along the Adriatic Sea, and several wealthy island ports across the Mediterranean.

And how had a mere city grown so rich, so powerful? There could only be one answer: with untold spoils seized from her mother. Uncountable amounts of gold and silver must still fill Venetian coffers. Sir Reynaud had even told me that the huge church I had seen on one side of the Piazza, dedicated to Saint Mark, was being expanded and decorated further with marble tiles and porphyry pillars ripped straight from Constantinople's heart, and I soon would see them for myself! My heart quickened with righteous anger.

He had also mentioned that a "treasury" had been established right inside the church to protect some of the most sacred valuables "removed" from the churches of Constantinople. He had added with a rueful jest that the holy men accompanying the Franks, and especially the Venetians, had been very careful to take the most sacred relics, thereby at least preserving much that ordinary soldiers would have destroyed.

We came to a large river that seemed to curve around inside the city, and which was bordered by many fine buildings. "The Grand Canal," my uncle announced, so perhaps it too was man-made. We all embarked in several of those long, colorful, narrow boats—gondolas, he called them—and glided dreamlike past mansions and palaces, churches and squares and docks until we reached our destination: a cross between a palace and an inn. "Here is our fondaco, where Greek merchants stay. Visiting merchants stay with their own people at the city's expense, but since there are no Rus', I come here."

"What a fine colonnaded arcade—" I began, but he cut me off.

"It is called a portico," he said impatiently, turning to his heavily laden servants to tell them where things should go. It seemed that a side door under the portico led to storerooms. While he was thus occupied, my young people and I wandered through a graceful gated opening into a large courtyard that reminded me a little of the inns of Iran and Syria, although instead of stalls or pens for animals, it boasted a lovely garden. Basil soon joined me, looking a little happier.

"Whenever I stay here, I am impressed. Excellent storerooms—Venice thinks of everything. Come, the innkeeper awaits; he will show us up to our rooms." A modestly dressed man standing behind my uncle bowed and waved his hand toward a staircase that led to rooms overlooking the courtyard.

Upstairs our host showed Basil and his servants to his room, and me and my people to mine. I had stayed in many places in my life, but rarely had I met with such a fine guest room as this. The girls, especially Anna, were almost overcome by the enormous canopied bed. She found a stool that also served as a bed-ladder and was on the bed in an instant, leaping off, and running back to her stool to try again. Marguerite and Banjuu straightaway sought out our linens and quilts and, shooing Anna off, set to spreading them on it. "You must act more like a lady," Marguerite cautioned her. Alexander and Thomas were meanwhile exploring a painted cupboard and a carved chest where we could store our things. Bardas and Leo merely stood just inside the door with their arms crossed, looking fierce.

Basil looked in, crossed the room, and opened a door on the opposite wall that let in a cool spring breeze. When he stepped outside, I followed him. He was leaning on the railing, looking out at the city, which was now glowing in the setting sun.

"Oh, how delightful! Another portico—"

"No, a loggia."

I ignored him. Leaning over the low wall, which was flanked by elegant pillars and graced by arches, I again entered a dream. Below us flowed the canal, on it an endless parade of boats and people. As the sun set behind us, the sky softened to amethyst and deepened into sapphire. Golden stars came out in a sky as clean and rich as new velvet. Lamps blazed into light all over the city, along the alleys, canals, and squares, large and small. Below us a monk was lighting a lamp before a little shrine set into the wall across the way, so now I understood. It was as if the city was proclaiming that if the sky was God's heavenly firmament, then she was its mirror, reflecting its glory in hundreds of wayside shrines.

We dined that night in a large refectory, surrounded by other merchants, all of them Greek but us. When I thought on it, I was a little surprised that Basil's relatives by marriage were not hosting us, but I did not ask. Today was the most my uncle had said to me in one day since we had left Constantinople. Even then he had mostly just corrected me when I called something the wrong name. But perhaps he could not ask his relatives to host my large retinue—or perhaps it was because of Anna and the questions that might be asked about her. That would explain his grudge against me.

After supper we bade each other good night and went to our rooms, where Anna slept between Marguerite and me, while Banjuu and Alexander lay on a pallet at the foot of my bed and Bardas, Thomas, and Leo lay as guards just outside both my doors. I doubted they would ever trust my uncle. But I slept well, still feeling the rocking ship in my bones.

The next morning Basil and I took a boat to an ornately decorated palace—he gruffly told me I must call it a Ca'—to meet his Venetian trading partners. As soon as we entered the large room that served as office and meeting room, I realized why he had brought me along, even grudgingly tolerated my willfulness in bringing my own people. Several of the men turned and gaped. No one had guessed that I would be a woman: this was his jest at their expense. And I was from Rus' as well! I saw the look of sly triumph on Basil's face as he said in Latin, "Please welcome my business partner and niece, Sofia Olga Volodymyrovna."

I nodded graciously before looking around. I could almost hear their thoughts: how could barbarians like us be so canny in our dealings, have amassed such wealth? What contempt they must have shown him; what a sacrifice Caterina had made in marrying him just to extend their trading empire into Rus'—and then it had completely vanished! And now his partners were being forced to swallow their pride and welcome me. Perhaps that was why we were staying in a fondaco, not here: Basil was not considered worthy of such personal hospitality.

After recovering from his surprise, his brother-in-law, one Patrizzio Girardino Falieri, who I later learned was related to a line of Doges of Venice no less, stepped forward. He seemed to be in his late thirties, was tall and thin with a nose that reminded me of Caterina's. Like her, he seemed to enjoy rich fabrics, for his surcoat was of deep brown brocade heavily embroidered with gold, his hose and fitted shoes were black silk, his long silken tunic was black with roundels of gold, and he wore a black Oriental-style turban. On his chest a heavy gold crucifix flashed from an equally heavy chain. Nor was he alone. All around the room, my eyes met the glitter of precious stones, the dull richness of silks, damasks, samite, and more Oriental-looking attire. And I realized that my few items of jewelry and my simple garments, which I had sewn myself, must make me look outlandish to them. I suspected Basil knew that, too, from the gloating look he cast at me when Patrizzio Falieri bowed graciously and greeted me in Latin.

"Because you and your uncle do not understand our Venetian speech, we will try to use whatever language you understand, Lady Sofia—Greek? Latin? The Frankish tongue?"

I nodded yes to all three, clearly impressing him. "And a few words of Veneziano." This information seemed to take him aback. I looked around the room and saw that I had just changed the playing board.

He nodded. "Forgive us if we sometimes use words strange to you. Let us know and we will try to explain."

With all formality, he gave me the names of the other men; clearly, these were the foremost merchant nobles in the city. How ironic that they should look down on Basil, who was, after all, once a prince himself, and who was certainly as wealthy and as well dressed as they were. Like them and unlike the Franks, we Rus' had never thought of trade as a barrier to nobility, so why would they be so haughty? With presentations over, the patrician, who insisted that as family I must call him Girardino, led me to a chair near one end of a large table while the men all found seats around it—the barrel-like chairs reminded me of Caterina's, too—and we set ourselves to business: how much each of us, Basil and me in particular, could invest in our mutual venture.

When my uncle told them our figures, there was a hushed silence, as if we had reached the holiest moment of the Mass. But these men worshipped Mammon. I almost laughed, for while I was always happy to make more money, it was not for its own sake but for Anna and my orphans. However, when Basil offered to put our monies into Venice's shipbuilding industry rather than into goods, there was general surprise at his boldness, though it made perfect sense to me.

I was able to follow most of the discussion, which was mostly held in a mix of Latin and Greek, though sometimes someone slipped into whatever speech fit the needs of the moment, usually the Venetian dialect. What they could not know was that my practice on the galley had prepared me better than I had let on. I understood clearly whenever they tried to think up some subtle way of tricking us. Deciding that they must think me more like an extra limb or tail for Basil, on the rare occasions that I spoke I weighed each word carefully to show that I knew what I was talking about. I was able to surprise them, not only since they clearly had expected me to remain silent but also because I was catching them at their games. And from the nods and raised eyebrows I noted, it seemed that I was gaining their grudging respect. After a long discussion about various approaches that might allow this type of partnership, it was decided that the next day we two should pay a visit to a place called the Arsenale to see the shipyards.

By this time it was midday, and we all repaired to a dining hall of great magnificence. There a hearty repast awaited us, hosted by Girardino's wife, another woman with a powerful nose and fine eyes whose name was Beatrice. What riches she displayed in her attire: a bejeweled crucifix hanging on a gold chain around her neck; more jewels at her ears; a deep red brocade gown with full sleeves trailing almost to the ground; a golden, pearl-embroidered, close-fitting cap that revealed her artfully twisted, abundant dark hair; and a sheer golden veil. She seemed entirely friendly, and we spent some time recalling Antioch together, a city she had once visited on pilgrimage years earlier. Happily, she knew enough Latin and Greek for us to understand each other. Once when I tried slipping a Veneziano phrase into the conversation, she almost applauded me. "How delightful that you can already speak a little of my language. We must become friends, for you are so unlike other women. They only know about children and housekeeping!"

"It would be my great pleasure," I smiled.

In truth, though, her cook was not as accomplished as Leo was. He was never happier than when preparing something new, and he had already found his way to the fondaco kitchen to learn from the cook there. I decided that Basil and I must host our partners at a dinner to repay their generosity in letting us enter into partnership with them. It would be my sly jest when they discovered we could even command better feasts than they could! And I would invite Beatrice, too, even if it did mean outshining her a little in one way.

The next morning I arose to soft sun shining in through the pillared loggia. Today I was to see ships being built! I wished I could take Anna to see; she would doubtless be climbing up the nearest ladder, she was such a little sailor. But I would have to leave all my people behind, Basil had told me, as it was very difficult to gain entry into the Arsenale. Only he and I would be allowed in, and under escort. It made sense, of course. A city built on trade must have a merchant fleet and navy, beyond which Venice also supplies ships to other nations, so shipbuilding would be something of a state secret.

Indeed, the price of her ships lay behind the invasion and sack of Constantinople. The Frankish armies' inability to pay for all the galleys they had ordered put them at the Venetians' mercy, and they had led the Franks, step by step, to abandon their original purpose. What a strange and horrifying way for these warriors to pay off their debt, or so it seemed to me. But Venetians are nothing if not sharp when it comes to their own profit, and how they go about it matters not at all to them.

After breakfast we embarked on the Grand Canal and, by way of a series of smaller canals, arrived right before the heavily guarded entrance of the Arsenale, where Girardino and another of Basil's partners were waiting. This man's name, I recalled after a few moments, was Maffeo Polo. I had first seen him at Basil's wedding but had not met him then. During the conversation at dinner the day before, Maffeo had mentioned two brothers, Marco and Niccolo, and he had even spoken to me once. He was about my age or a little older, with a trimmed beard and dark brown curling hair that was cropped rather short. I read intelligence in his eyes, which seemed fixed on me when I glanced his way.

Before us reared a high-walled city within a city, if size and noise meant anything. Such pounding and clashing and clanging bursting from inside it! We were granted entry through a thick, iron-bound gate, and there I beheld the largest and busiest shipyard in the world: smithies, carpentry workshops, rope factories, storerooms, barracks, and more, spread out in all directions and divided by a few canals and what amounted to an artificial lake that led into the lagoon, clearly where the ships were launched.

"Please come this way," said Girardino. He led us to a half-finished galley. It seemed almost like a huge skeletal beast with a skin of wood being hammered onto its great curved ribs. "Here you see what is special about our building methods. We create a frame first and then complete the galley around it, which saves time and makes for a stronger, more uniform ship. This one will be a merchant ship, though it will have many of the same elements as one of our fighting ships. And in the same way, no war vessel would be complete without storage for trade goods or anything captured at sea from our enemies."

I held my tongue.

Somehow as we walked from sight to sight, I found myself beside Maffeo Polo, while Basil and Girardino moved ahead, already deep into a discussion about various aspects of shipbuilding. I heard something about forests and distances, and Maffeo began to speak to me. I was just as glad, for I would rather look about than engage in talk about the costs of shipping lumber.

"How do you like La Serenissima?" he asked politely.

"It is a beautiful city. I hope to see more of it, for there is nothing I like better than seeing new places and meeting new people." He smiled in such a gratified way that I feared he had mistaken my intent, which was certainly not to behave lightly with him!

But the moment passed. We spoke of his various trade connections in Constantinople and found that we knew many of the same people. He recalled seeing me at Basil's wedding, too, but I was so engaged with Sir Reynaud, whom he also knew, that there had been no opportunity to meet me.

"I am often there," he told me, "though my brothers and I were born on the Dalmatian coast. We have another home and offices in Constantinople. I also have trade connections in the Crimea, and I plan to go there this fall to trade with merchants from Sarai. The Mongols do not know what to do with all their wealth, and I hope to help them part with some of it," he laughed. I smiled politely.

"But my greatest dream, one which I doubt I will ever see realized, would be to travel into Asia along the Silk Route. I would like to see Sarai for myself, and who knows what may lie beyond it? I would love to find out. And how I would love to see Cathay, that fabled land of riches on every tree."

I turned aside the subject by randomly asking something about the shipyard. He most obligingly explained that and whatever else I asked about, so I learned that the Arsenale was not just for shipbuilding but for crafting and storing weaponry of all sorts, and that the skilled craftsmen and carpenters live as well as work there and are fed and clothed and entirely cared for by the Republic.

At one point, though, I stopped in my tracks. Ahead of us several workers were loading four metal statues of horses onto four large boats in that little lake, balancing each carefully before wrapping it and securing it with heavy ropes. I remembered Sir Reynaud's telling me about just such horses. "What are those men doing over there?"

Maffeo looked where I was pointing. "Oh yes, those are four ancient bronze horses that Venice took from the Hippodrome in Constantinople. We stored them here for years, until the present Doge remembered them. They are to be set high up over the entrance to the Basilica where a suitable base is being built for each of them. I expect it will be quite an occasion, an excuse for the entire populace to turn out and celebrate La Serenissima's greatness.

"And speaking of such things, there will be a great festival the Sunday after the Feast of the Ascension. You and your uncle must witness it. I will arrange it all, if you and he will accept my humble invitation."

I kept my own counsel, for after all, Maffeo had had nothing to do with the events of 1204, had not even been born yet. But how strange it seemed to me that men could speak so lightly of the ill deeds of their forefathers, especially this man who knew what Constantinople was like nowadays. I thanked him politely, but he read my mind.

"I see by your face that you wonder at the boldness of us Venetians—like pirates or bandits, you think. No need to blush; you would not be the first person to arrive in Venice from our mother city and feel the same. And in part you would be right, for is it not true that taking from our enemies is the way of the world?

"However, I would wager that you also do not know the full story behind what happened all those years ago before Constantinople fell to the Franks. Has anyone told you of the massacres, the persecutions Venetians endured repeatedly for almost fifty years before the Franks turned from their purpose and captured and destroyed much of the city? For it was they who did the greatest damage. Venetians have too much respect for beauty to smash statues, and for holy places to deface and burn down churches—even heretical ones, which of course was the excuse given for that madness."

I shook my head, but not for the reason he thought. I was remembering something Lady Q'ing-ling, long dead, had once said—and Qabul, too—about the strong crushing the weak as if it was their right.

"No, I thought not. There is always more than one side to any story. Arrests, seizures, blindings, massacres not only of men but also of women and children, sometimes engineered by the emperor himself. Still, we Venetians had not realized what true barbarians could do to a city or perhaps our Doge would have pulled back from his revenge. He had grown to hate Constantinople when he acted as emissary there more than once, trying to free members of our merchant community and get its goods released. It is a maze of a tale, too long to tell here and on such a lovely day. But I sometimes wonder if his blindness kept him from seeing how terrible the destruction really was, or perhaps he could not control it once the looting started."

He paused. "I see we have fallen behind our companions and that the guards eye us with suspicion. Perhaps we should join them."

I walked on feeling a little sick at heart.

Maffeo Polo applied himself to entertaining me from then on, banishing all thoughts of war and revenge from my mind with his light way of speaking and his quick wit. He and Girardino even guided us back to the fondaco at the end of our tour, pointing out certain churches or the Ca' of such and such a patrician as we glided along.

For several days I had time to explore the city with Anna and the servants, visiting modest chapels to pray or wandering along the booths lining the Piazzetta. I even bought a few lengths of brocade and velvet, thinking I might stitch them into garments one day. And for Anna I bought a pair of earrings and a matching necklace, both of a green stone new to me called peridot. The color was softer than emerald and just right for her coloring, plus the set was modest enough for a girl on the threshold of womanhood. She was enchanted.

Once we also went out with Beatrice, who insisted on taking us to buy yet more beautiful goods. I felt almost overwhelmed by her zeal, but Beatrice justified the amazing expense of my purchases by insisting that I would not be taken seriously if I did not dress for my role. And she arrived the next day with her favorite seamstress, who within a week had made both Anna and me much more suitable garments for attending public events.

Like the marriage with the sea. Basil had accepted the Polo brothers' invitation to the festivities on the Sunday after Ascension Day, so, dressed in our new finery, we witnessed a grand ceremony indeed. It had something to do with celebrating some long-past victory over pirates, and something about a Pope and an emperor. After Mass the Doge led pretty much everyone in the city in solemn procession over to the docks of the Piazzetta. There he took ship on a gaily-decorated barge. As guests of the Polo brothers, we boarded an elegant barge, too, and were part of the Doge's water parade, happily avoiding the general chaos behind us. It seemed as if every boat in the entire city was behind or around us. According to Maffeo, who kindly explained everything before Basil or I could even ask, "We sail to the Lido, the long island that guards the entrance to the lagoon. When we reach the lagoon entrance, the Bishop will bless the waters out of gratitude and to seek peace. And then the Doge will cast a ring into the sea. This ceremony has been held every year since the Year of Our Lord 1000 or thereabouts."

The port soon filled with boats. Horns blew, people called out greetings to each other, and a few fights broke out over whose boat was there first, but when the great moment arrived, a reverent silence fell. The Bishop blessed the sea and then blessed a golden ring, which he handed to the Doge. Crying his loudest, "We wed thee, O Sea, in token of genuine and lasting power," the Doge threw it into the Adriatic.

A great cheer arose, and after everyone got themselves turned around, we sailed back for a rowdy general celebration: noise, crowds, flags, and music as both Piazzas filled with noblemen and their families, all the members of the merchant and craftsmen's guilds and their families—not

to mention pickpockets and peddlers and peasants come in from the countryside. The city leaders, not content with the Doge's achievement, stood on
a great platform before the Church and made one overlong speech after another, often drowned out by laughter and rude witticisms. Vendors offered
sweets, and pigeons circled overhead. Anna, who had been beside herself with
joy on the boat, made herself sick on something sticky Alexander had bought
her and had to be taken home—so like her namesake in her love of sweets.

Maffeo Polo hosted Basil and me for a great feast afterwards. His digni-
fied elder brother Marco was there, dressed in black with gold embroidery, as
was his younger brother Niccolo, handsome in brown velvet. And I met their
wives. Marco Polo's wife was a drab, quiet woman named Lady Agnesina,
settling into middle age, clad in pearl-embroidered black, and already using a
cane to walk. And then there was Niccolo Polo's young wife, Juliana, dressed
in deep blue brocade, with a little jewel-studded cap and a gossamer veil covering her elaborately bound brown hair. Her garments could not hide her
pregnancy.

The three brothers were so alike in looks that only Marco's graying hair and
Niccolo's lighter hair set them apart from Maffeo. The two younger brothers
were eager to talk with Basil about their forthcoming trip to the Crimea, as
he had been there more than once. Juliana, who was clearly not happy about
the voyage, sat in sullen silence during this conversation, though she seemed
pleasant the rest of the time. I could not blame her, but then men did what
they did without regard to such details as wives and children. These harsh
thoughts on her behalf, sprung seemingly from nowhere, surprised me, but I
felt no shame for them.

The talk then turned to the Mongols, to Asia, and to Cathay. It seemed
that Niccolo Polo shared his brother's fascination with the Orient, and he
grew ever more animated while recounting tales of fabulous kingdoms, amazing beasts, strange races of men and the like as if they were all true.

Alas, Basil had drunk far too much wine all day, and he lost control of his
tongue. Perhaps the heat was partly to blame, but I think pride was also at
fault. He knew, because I had told him much when I had first stayed with
him and Caterina, that the young man was getting carried off by dreams.
Finally he burst out, "What nonsense you talk, Niccolo. You need real advice
if you wish to travel so far! My niece has been in Sarai, and in Iran, too! You
should consult her if you truly want to make such a journey. You'll get lost in
some desert if you base your travels on these absurd tales! Go ahead, ask her

yourself."

How I blushed. Every eye at the table was on me. "Perhaps some other time," was the most I could utter. I sent such a glare of outrage to my uncle that he straightaway closed his mouth and said not another word the entire time we were there. I was the one who had to offer thanks to Maffeo Polo for his hospitality.

As I had feared would happen, Maffeo visited me the next morning. After exchanging courtesies he embarked on a less than subtle quest to find out just what I knew. I'd not have minded that, but his inquiries bordered on territory I considered forbidden: how I knew, why I had been to those places, and so on. I finally said that it was enough to know that war had forced me to take the most roundabout route to my uncle imaginable, and that it had not been pleasant. This seemed to satisfy him, especially when I added that if the time ever came when his journey became a reality, I would share everything I thought might be of use to ease his passage.

"And when do you think to make such a journey?" I added.

"Oh, no time soon. For now it will be enough to go to Soldaia. My brothers and I plan to live in Constantinople for a few years before we can even think of being gone so long. The special privileges we receive under the Latin king make it worth the sacrifice of leaving Venice for an extended stay. Frankly, given his desperate poverty, I think King Baldwin is foolish to give so much away; but if we Polo brothers don't seize such opportunities, others will, and they will gain the advantage over us."

That month in Venice was full of event. We dined with our partners and hosted them in turn and impressed them, I think. We saw much of the Polo brothers, and Maffeo was always attentive and courtly but very correct, which was the only kind of attention I wanted. Basil took me on endless trips to various merchants to buy local goods, ranging from rope to salt to iron nails, which might all be worth bringing back but truly held little interest for me.

He also bought furs and slaves from what he dismissively called the Slavic countries—the slave countries. Had he looked closer, he'd have seen that some of his slaves, mere boys and girls, were Rus', or perhaps he knew and didn't care. Nor would he let me buy them from him. He claimed to be acting on a partner's behalf back in Constantinople and that the boys were destined for Egypt where they would be made into stout palace guards. The girls would fetch high prices in Muslim-held areas if he couldn't sell them in the Christian cities. He thought it would be a very good life for them all, better than shivering naked in a slave market.

I gave up arguing, though I knew that the so-called palace guards were none other than the Mamluks who had defeated King Louis' armies. They might well be used against us someday. And the girls were probably destined for brothels.

I had brought goods of my own to sell in Venice—the muslins, Aleppo glassware, and inlaid trays and candlesticks and so forth—and for those he did help me find the right buyers. In turn I bought delicate blown glass articles and colorful beads made on an island called Murano. Though the blown glass pieces needed the most expert and gentle wrapping to survive being shipped, they would fetch a fantastically high price in Constantinople or Antioch. All in all, despite the slaves, Basil and I worked fairly well together, but we ended up needing another ship for the return journey just to hold all the merchandise he bought!

Happily, Juliana and Beatrice both befriended me and, when Juliana asked about Anna, they accepted my story of her adoption without even a raised eyebrow. They were already friends with each other, and they were most helpful when I tired of Basil's quests for more trading pacts to seal, more goods to buy. Whenever I could get away, I would make some excuse and hire a gondola to take me to Girardino's Ca', where Beatrice was usually able to free herself from her duties. Then we would visit Juliana, often rousing her from slumber in her tree-shaded flower garden, and then simply wander about looking at this and that with Anna and my servants. Except Leo. He preferred to stay behind, cooking. He was growing quite stout, proof of how much he liked his own receipts!

We talked freely about children, for Juliana was eager to learn what to expect, this being her firstborn child. "We have already chosen a name for him," she once said with supreme confidence, "Marco, after his uncle. Marco the Elder and Marco the Younger. Does it not sound gracious?" She was such an innocent, and she was so in love with her handsome young husband. "Alas, the price for our good life is that we must be separated for a year or more at a time. I only hope my little Marco will be born before Niccolo leaves."

This conversation happened while we three were in Beatrice's home. I was being fitted for more new garments. My two friends had decided that my old clothing looked both too rustic and too truly Oriental and that they must dress me properly. So womanly vanity was given full reign, and several seamstresses were employed to stitch the garments my friends had so eagerly designed for me, using the fabrics I had recently bought.

Even more than the pleasure of new clothing, I found a brief release from the loneliness I had felt since Helene had left Daphne. It felt good to have woman friends. I must return often to see them, for they could hardly be blamed for what had happened to Constantinople. What point was there in holding endless grudges against the wrong people?

We also went to the Basilica of Saint Mark together for Mass every Sunday. The first time I had entered it, I was so overwhelmed by the splendor of the church that I could scarcely pay attention to the holy service. Gold mosaics covered almost every wall and ceiling, surrounding or enhancing sublime mosaic sacred portraits and scenes. I wondered if any of them were the ones stolen from Hagia Sophia. The richest altar screen I had ever seen, made of gold and adorned with gems, stood like an ikonostasis, though this was a Catholic church. Porphyry pillars— pillaged from Constantinople, of course— reached to the fabulous ceilings, pillaged marble tiled the floors, and on and on. Some of the things of beauty, like the screen, were even gotten honestly.

There was that same unfamiliar, almost Oriental singing, too: the choir seemed to weave tones together like fine silk, so lovely.

And the cathedral does indeed have a treasury, most appropriate for Venice, which contains not only worldly wealth but also many relics of saints. And of course there is the actual tomb of Saint Mark, his body reputedly having been stolen from Muslim-held Alexandria, supposedly hidden in a barrel of salted pork to keep it safe, as no Muslim would touch pork.

I think the best thing my new friends did for me, once they recovered from their surprise at my wanting to learn, was to teach me more Veneziano speech. How I loved learning new languages, and the ladies were gratifyingly impressed with how quickly I mastered it.

One day we were idling in the Piazzetta looking into goldsmiths' workshops when I noticed some poorly dressed men and women, a few carrying baskets of bread or other foodstuffs, passing in and out of a heavy door in one section of the Doge's castle. It was the homeliest part of the castle, with barred windows on two floors, but it was always heavily guarded. Thinking it might be another storehouse for treasures, I had never before questioned its use. But my curiosity was awakened by those baskets. I turned to my friends and asked what was going on in the Doge's storehouse. They both laughed.

Beatrice said, "In a way, it is a storehouse. That is his prison. On the ground floor is where petty wrongdoers are kept, and this is a day when their families can bring in food and such for them. None of them stays locked up for long, for what greater punishment can there be than to be separated from family and to lose time earning a living?

"But on the floor above, the Doge keeps political enemies and captives awaiting their ransom monies. That must be a right hard thing; many die of broken hearts, I hear, before they can be redeemed. These days there are few men in it, for we are in a lull between wars."

Curiosity satisfied, I thought no more of it. Another day we passed a hospital run by Benedictine monks, a sad-looking building that looked as if it might seal the fate of anyone ill enough to enter it. At that moment my distaste for Venice arose again. What if those long ago conquerors had brought back surgeons and physicians instead of loot, had thought about healing instead of killing and robbing? It was not until years later that I learned that such men had indeed been brought back to Venice to serve new masters and to teach others. And I was twice lucky that this was so.

The greatest surprise came a few days before we were to depart. Basil knocked on the door to my room early one morning, and my heart sank. I did not want to go with him to yet another island to see yet another blacksmith's wonderful ironwork! Instead, he dismissed my servants and daughter, saying we would join them at breakfast shortly.

"Niece, I must speak with you about an important matter that cannot wait, as we leave so soon! I only wish he had come forward before now."

"What is it, Basil?" I still refused to call him uncle, though I did wave him to the one chair in the room.

Basil shifted in the hard chair as if uneasy with what he was about to say. "Last night after you went to bed, I received a visitor. Can you guess who it was?"

"No, nor do I care for guessing games this early in the morning."

"Come now, who have you been spending most evenings with, who is it who makes you laugh and puts the bloom back into your cheeks?"

"Anna? Juliana? Beatrice?"

Now it was Basil's turn to look annoyed. "Well, none of them are about to propose marriage to you, are they?"

I felt my cheeks go hot, but tried to stay calm. "I know of no suitors, no special attentions being paid me. Nor have I encouraged any! You know where my heart lies. So who is it?"

"Maffeo Polo, of course, and a better match for you I cannot imagine. I know Sir Reynaud also courts you, but he's half Greek and as slippery as any of them—and a match with Maffeo offers many advantages."

"I was not aware that Sir Reynaud was any more a suitor than Maffeo Polo," I said coldly.

"Well," flared Basil, "that is exactly why men call you the ice queen! There is more than one way to let a man know you are interested, and while I value your circumspection, particularly with a bastard child in the background, you cannot deny your interest in those two!"

"Yes, I enjoy their company, but no, I never thought of them as anything more than pleasant companions, and in Sir Reynaud's case, as a friend!"

"Don't be a fool! Men and women can never be friends! And you are even more of a fool to think that your Lord Joscelin will ever return to you. He is dead, and the sooner you admit it, the sooner you can return to a normal life instead of shutting yourself up in that villa like a nun!"

I cried, "I am joining my family now, my true family beyond blood ties. You can stay here and spin stories to yourself about me all you like, but with such ideas you will never truly know who I am. And Lord Joscelin lives; I know it in my bones!"

I stalked out, fuming. Ice queen? Who had called me that, and why? If I did not reveal myself frankly, was it any wonder? I had never misled either man into thinking I was open to a marriage proposal, either. As for Maffeo Polo, I supposed I must seem like a perfect wife for a merchant, with such a trading empire to my name. And I knew he liked me. It was not such a surprise when I thought on it, but nonetheless unthinkable. Even beyond my loyalty to and love for Sir Joscelin, still intact, I had no intention of moving to Constantinople. I must give him a gentle refusal.

This I did on my own, for Basil and I were not on speaking terms for the rest of the day. We dined with the Polo family that night, and after the meal when everyone else was seeking the fresh air of the loggia, I asked my suitor to stay behind for a few moments to talk privately. He nodded and slowed his pace so that we would be the last to leave the room.

In a low voice I said, "I do not know whether I violate custom by speaking to you directly, but I fear my uncle has been less than honest with you when he encouraged your proposal of marriage to me. I am already betrothed to another, someone he … dislikes … without having ever met him. I do want you to know that I feel a high regard for you."

Maffeo Polo responded most graciously. "I confess disappointment, but I had wondered why such a lovely widow would remain unmarried as long as I've heard you have been unless she was most loyal to Church strictures. With wealth such as yours, even an unlovely widow would tempt any man. I am glad to learn you will be safely wed soon, for in a man's world you are at risk in so many ways.

"And if something ever goes wrong—or if you change your mind—come to me, I beg of you. Beyond friendly regard, you won my heart in a very short time."

I had to turn away to hide the tears that sprang to my eyes. What a good man!

"Thank you. I will always be grateful for your kindness. I imagine we will see each other from time to time in Constantinople, and I look forward to that with pleasure."

Our conversation over, we went out to the loggia in the most natural way and passed the rest of the mild evening in talk and laughter with friends.

And if Basil was disappointed, he had the good grace or good sense or perhaps outrage not to say anything to me, about marriage or much else.

It was late June, on a perfect day of sun and fresh breezes, when we finally bade farewell to our partners and my new friends. They all came out to the dock where our increased flotilla lay waiting to carry our huge stores of merchandise. I had embraced Beatrice and Juliana and bidden goodbye to their husbands, Maffeo had gallantly kissed my hand, and I had lifted Anna into my arms and was almost aboard my ship—happily, Basil and I would sail separately on the journey home—when I thought I heard a man call my name. I turned and looked around, but my friends were already leaving and no face was turned toward me. I thought I heard it again, and I looked around the Piazzetta but no one there was paying us any heed. Did I glimpse a white face and perhaps a hand waving from the upper story of the prison? It vanished before I could tell whether I had imagined it. Anna, however, was waving back.

"What did you see, Anna?"

"My friends and the ghost of my father." I turned white and scanned the windows of the prison again, but saw nothing. It must be some whim of Anna's, for she often spoke of her father's ghost, to which she spoke from time to time. I had never had the heart to tell her anything of substance about my beloved.

We were well under sail before it occurred to me to wonder whether the Doge might be holding any foreigners for ransom.

⁂

Though I could have pinched myself for not thinking of it sooner, I knew it would not be hard to find out if I was right. As soon as we arrived in Constantinople, I sent to Beatrice and asked her to get her husband to find out who was being held prisoner by the Doge's. If by some miracle Lord Joscelin were there, I would simply return, pay his ransom, and be reunited with him. My heart lifted at the thought, and not only for the sake of reuniting with my beloved. Once married, we never need reveal Anna's bastardy to her, for it would be wiped out before she was even old enough to ask for the truth.

Of course life is never so easy. It took months to hear back. Meanwhile, instead of lingering on and stretching relations with Basil to the breaking point, I left for home, to put away my lovely garments, useless in Daphne, and to return to my simple but practical attire. Though daily life passed in apparent calm, I felt as if suspended in amber while I waited. My heart retreated further into my breast, and soon I could scarcely feel it.

To my surprise Sir Reynaud returned in late July, this time for the wedding festivities of Prince Bohemund of Antioch. King Baldwin was attending them, so my friend had much to do in Antioch itself and could only stay for an afternoon. This time his manners were so pleasing, his humor so contagious, that I was sorry to say goodbye to him. He had come to invite me to join him for part of the celebration, which was month-long, and I was tempted to go, for the bride's father was the same King Hetoum whose sister, Queen Stephanie, had befriended me on Cyprus. I was mildly curious to see the king who had not only submitted early on to the Mongols but also gone all the way to Karakorum to prove his loyalty. I hoped he would never regret his actions by being drawn into some war one day. But I decided that satisfying curiosity was not a good enough reason to mingle with nobles and their ladies, though many were familiar to me. I could never shake my fear that they might ask questions.

Finally, in late November, I received a reply from Venice. Lord Joscelin was not among the prisoners in the Doge's palace, but a fishing boat had strayed into Venetian waters shortly before our departure. One of the men aboard had clearly been a spy, but rather than execute him, his thrifty captors had demanded ransom from him not only for himself but also for the entire crew. Indeed, by the time the news reached me, he had returned to his home city of Genoa.

This was frustrating because he had news of another kind: according to the man's jailers, whom Girardino himself had questioned on my behalf, he had claimed he was no spy. He insisted that the crew of the fishing boat had rescued him after he had escaped an attack by pirates, having dived from his own ship and swum for his life when it caught fire and sank. But according to him, others less fortunate had been aboard and had either been killed or enslaved. Some Frankish knights had been among the captives, one of them his special friend: a baron called Joscelin!

My heart leapt at this news until good sense prevailed.

Though I was certain that this must be my Joscelin and I prayed that he had survived, even if he had there was simply no way to reach him—though I gave free rein to dreams of seeking out pirate lairs, of rescue or ransom. I could certainly afford that. However, there were too many kinds of pirates in the Mediterranean, and I had no idea whether these were Adriatic or Arab or who knew what other kind? I could not count on anything.

Suddenly I saw how I was riding up and down some wheel of hope and fear, all to no purpose. And just as suddenly, it was as though veils of cobwebs and dust that had been drifting down on my inmost being all along hardened and encased me in a little tomb of memory and lost hope.

Especially when I read the sad news that Juliana Polo had died of childbed fever shortly after giving birth to a son. The child had been named Marco Polo the Younger as planned. In his name Juliana had been right, but none of us who has given birth ever takes it for granted that we will survive. Poor soul, she had never imagined dying. I wept and prayed for her and her orphaned infant. As Niccolo had already left for Constantinople, Marco the Elder and

Lady Agnesina would raise the child.

Little Marco was doubly orphaned: Beatrice had added that Niccolo was so heartbroken that he did not even want to see his newborn son. How sad. I also prayed that his grief would pass and that one day they would be happily reunited, perhaps even travel together to those faraway lands with my once-suitor Maffeo.

ANNO DOMINI 1254-1255

I saw Sir Reynaud again when my entire household spent Christmas with Basil and Helene. He was waiting at the dock when my ship arrived, with a musician playing a lute and singing a Christmas song with a sad refrain: Oh Come, Oh Come Emmanuel. He graciously escorted me to Basil's home but declined my uncle's polite invitation to join us.

"No, it was enough that you agreed to my meeting your niece at the dock. I would not intrude on your happy reunion with her. I have been invited to sup elsewhere tonight, but I wanted to welcome her today, at least. And you have kindly invited me to your final Christmas feast." He turned to me. "I look forward to seeing you then." He saluted us and was gone.

I thought I heard Helene murmur to Basil, "Look out for that one," but there was so much noise of joyous welcome from the children that I could have been mistaken, and its meaning was unclear, anyway.

I had not seen Basil's children since before Anna was born, and how they had grown! Little Cecilia was no longer little, nor did she remember me, but she was much taken with Anna; and the compliment was returned. Basil's boys seemed to have grown as tall and thin as bean stalks. They all bowed in their most formal and courtly fashion before bounding back to some game of their own making. Gilles ran off in the train of the older boys after giving me a little embrace and Anna a pat on the head that she did not want.

And Helene was pregnant with a second child—the first had been a daughter named Heloise, born last January—and looking as content as could be. Her pregnancy was the excuse Sir Reynaud had used for meeting me, for she was loath to leave the house until she knew the baby would not miscarry, and Basil was likely happy not to have to greet me by himself.

Gilles soon returned while we adults were sitting in the main hall at our ease. He seized Anna by the hand and insisted she play some war game. But Cecilia was already making much of Anna and had begun her own game. A quarrel ensued. We had to send them off with our respective maidservants, but Anna looked well pleased. And in the days to come, the three of them would often go off to play some game wherein the two older children vied for the right to direct the next move.

How quickly and pleasantly the days passed, with a mixture of solemn holy occasions, the usual rowdy festivities, and merriment at home.

Sir Reynaud came to Basil's Christmas feast along with our closest business partners and their families. After the meal, while Helene and Basil were attending to other guests, he appeared by my side and gave me a little gift: a ring that he called a poesy, for a line of verse was inscribed inside it. It said, "On her lips blossom roses."

"Thank you, Sir Reynaud, but I cannot accept such a token, for it implies a love that you must know...."

I could say no more, seeing how his face fell. "I found it among my family's belongings," he replied after an awkward moment of silence. "It is worth nothing sitting in a casket where one of my younger brothers might find and sell it for some silly thing they want. It would be better worn on your little finger. It is only a token of my happy memories of sharing my city with you."

So I took pity on him and accepted it and wore it when I saw him next. After that I put it away.

But I should not have done it. Sir Reynaud's intentions became clearer and clearer, no matter what I said or did to discourage him. He often came to visit, claiming too much of my time while maintaining that he was there to see the entire family. I did enjoy outings with him and Basil and Helene to see more of the city: the viaduct of Valens, which brings water into that great cistern all the way from some faraway land called Thrace; the Blachernae palace, the second, much damaged palace that the king and his court used when in the city for very long; the various forums through which the wide street Mese ran—the very ones I had passed through on my way to imprisonment in Basil's villa; and the Golden Gate, which served as the city's main entrance. Once only emperors and favored generals could enter by it, and it was certainly imposing with its three arches, its pillars, its carvings, and above all its size. Now everyone used it, from peasant to pauper to prince.

But Sir Reynaud never breached the walls surrounding my heart. When I left for home, I had given him not one chance to speak to me in private.

The only one who could truly breach those walls was Anna, who was growing into a cheerful if strong-willed little beauty. As an example of her power over me, the summer after I returned from Venice, I had begun teaching her letters. At our first lesson, though, she insisted that her friends must join her. I had never paid her spirit friends much mind; they kept her busy and happy and that was enough. But this time she tried to point them out to me, worried that I had nearly stepped on one of them.

"This is Blade," she said. "He has a long beard. And this is Sheep. She wears a scarf on her head. And she has a bird bill for a mouth." I felt all the blood run from my head and had to hold onto the handles of my bench to keep from falling. "And my ghost father is here, too."

I politely greeted the air where she had pointed, unable even to ask about her ghost father. "How long have you known Sheep and Blade?"

"Oh, they came to stay with me when Gilles moved away. They fight a lot over me, like Gilles and Cecelia did."

"Sheep and Blade are no strangers to me, though I never thought to meet them here. They were once my friends when I was your age, but I can no longer see them, I am sad to say."

"Where were they, then?"

"In Rus', where I was born."

"Since they were your friends first, does that mean you are my real mother?"

"Of course. What did you think?"

"Marguerite always says I am an orphan like her." Anna's eyes welled with tears. "I want to be an orphan like her!"

I took her in my arms. "Anna, we are all orphans, me too. We can be orphans together." We both spilled a few tears before I tried once more to turn back to her lessons. But her stubborn streak flamed up.

"No," she cried, "I want to know more about Sheep and Blade and Rus' and—and when you were little like me!"

So in order to get her to attend to lessons, I had to make a promise: at the end of each month, if she behaved well at lessons, I would tell her a folktale from Rus' or a story about my own childhood, along with stories about her—our—lost family. I made only one rule. I would tell her only about what had happened when I was her age. And each year on her birthday, I would begin telling her stories of myself at her new age.

And I told her about the memoir I was writing, lying a little and saying it was for her. After all, I thought, by the time she reached twelve, either she would be old enough to understand my travails or she would have lost interest. For now she was thrilled. I promised to show her what I had written so far, knowing she could not read it, and with that she settled down to learn in a serious way. The ghost father I never did mention. Anna was eager for her first lesson and I did not want to think of Sir Joscelin as a ghost, nor did I want to tell her about him yet. And another occasion never arose, mostly because of my lack of resolve.

Instead, we formed a further bond over her joy in learning and mine in teaching. Over the next few months, I came to realize how much I had to offer her. If I had never turned into Sofia the Wise, I was certainly Sofia the Learned and Sofia Full of Memories.

This new task of teaching led to another interest: collecting learned books and scrolls. I soon amassed a large collection by finding orphans in my other homes who could become scribes, a truly fruitful calling for them and for me, and one that ended up profiting the orphanages. Not only did I use their services to copy and thus preserve old, tattered finds, but when men—and not a few women—learned that they could find reliable scribes at the orphanages, they began coming to commission letters, for few could read and even fewer could write.

That idea led to another: those children who showed a talent for calligraphy I sent to a monastery in Antioch to learn illuminated lettering and illustration. Rotrou was among them, and he was also among those who took the tonsure and stayed on, to the loss of my orphanages and the gain of the Church. I didn't really mind, though. I still felt uneasy about the possibility that he was Lord Joscelin's son.

There was also much demand for copies of the Scriptures and breviaries and so forth by monasteries and well-educated laymen alike. My scribes were soon known for their skills in both Latin and Greek, though the latter language was still much suppressed along with Greeks themselves. With so much income, the orphanages began to thrive even more, though beyond using the copyists' services for my own collection, I had even less to do with them than before. My only contribution was to buy yet another house where even more children could find refuge. It was old, but I hired workers who improved it enough that it could be used right away, and I made plans for it to be rebuilt over time.

I was always happy to lose myself in new manuscripts. I discovered the ancient Greek philosophers: Socrates, Plato, and Aristotle, in the original Greek. Aristotle I admired the most as being so earthy. But my favorite discovery was modern.

Adar al-Mas'udi had at my request been sending me manuscripts that I might find useful to copy and sell. Usually he sent me medical texts, but with one package he added some poems written by a Muslim mystic named Jalal al-Din Rumi. From what I could gather, he lives in Konya, a city somewhere in Rum that has been subject to the Mongols for some time. But his fame has spread even to Antioch, and it is no wonder! Such sublime language. Here is my favorite poem, though my pitiful translation cannot do it justice:

> *Dearest friend,*
> *Never abandon hope*
> *When the Beloved*
> *Bids you leave.*

> *If you are forsaken,*
> *If you feel hopeless,*
> *Another tomorrow will dawn*
> *And you are bid come again.*

> *If the door shuts*
> *In your face,*

Wait on with patience
Stay on longer.

Seeing how you wait,
Your Beloved will
Call to you gracefully,
Raise you like a hero.

Even if all paths
Lead to naught,
You'll be shown the secret ways
No one understands.

My Beloved
Gives without thought
Solomon's entire kingdom
To a tiny ant!

My heart has sought
Throughout this world again and again,
But never has it found
Nor will it ever find
Such another Beloved.

Ah, I should stay silent.
I know that this eternal love
Will come someday
To you and you and you.

I know nothing of Rumi's Beloved, though surely it is God. But I also thought of my Joscelin when I first read it, and it gave me a glimmer of hope and a feeling of renewed patience. It is strange to think that this master poet still lives under the Mongol yoke. How it gives me hope, to think on how even in the midst of war, plague, hatreds and cruelties, such a voice can ring out, quenching all the fires of evil in an ocean of love.

ANNO DOMINI 1255-1256

Marguerite became a woman that summer. She came to me one day, weeping with fear, and I showed her what to do. "So this is the curse of Eve," she said wanly. "Lady, I see nothing good coming of it for me. With your blessing I wish to enter a convent and devote my life to God."

I had known she was more religious than Banjuu, who had little knowledge of Islam other than what I remembered from living among Selim's women and had passed on to her. But this came as a surprise.

"How Anna and I will miss you!"

"Then you consent?"

"Of course. You have served me long and faithfully, and I know how timid you are in the world. From all I hear, the life of a religious is difficult, but it might suit you well. Do you have anywhere in mind?"

She mentioned the tiny convent in the forest above Daphne where the two nuns lived. We only saw them when they came to the villa to beg for more food. "But I will wait until Anna is older. She is like my little sister, and I know it would grieve her if I left now. I will need to prepare her."

So it was agreed that when Anna turned seven, Marguerite would enter the religious life. I went with her to the hut to speak with the nuns. They lived there as penitents under what they called the Order of Poor Ladies, and they said they would be happy to welcome Marguerite in the name of their founder, a sainted woman named Clare, who had recently died. This Clare had in her turn been sheltered by and then inspired to follow the example of a Saint Francis of Assisi, who had formed an ascetic order that is now known as the Friars Minor or the Franciscans.

Theirs sounded like a harsh life to me, and I also suspected it could be dangerous. I didn't know why I hadn't thought of it sooner, but I decided to support them more regularly and to have my own guards keep a protective watch over them, for holiness is not always respected.

The autumn of 1255 and the Holy Days of Christmas passed in peace. It was a snowy winter, so I rarely went beyond the bounds of the villa, leaving it to Leo to go into Daphne on market days to bring back what we needed. Antioch seemed like another world, and I gave it little thought. I knew I could trust Matthew of Edessa and my uncle to do what was best for my little empire. I signed documents from Aleppo, wrote to my friends, sewed, taught Anna, and took walks or rode into the forest on milder days. 1256 arrived. Things could have gone on in the same way for endless days, my activities laid out neatly, my world self-contained, my future reduced to simplicity, even sameness, had it not been for what happened late that spring.

The warmth and a series of cloudless days had drawn me outdoors, and I had arranged an outing for my entire family, servants and all—even Leo was going. Only one man was to stay behind to guard the villa. We had all gathered in the courtyard, my mules were already harnessed to my two carts, which were filling up with people; an outdoor feast was being loaded into one cart, and Anna was already inside the other beside Marguerite. I had just mounted my mare when she whinnied and abruptly shied sideways, nearly throwing me. At the same time, the mules began to bray and shift in their cart shafts. All birdsong stopped.

Then a rumble as if invisible rocks were tumbling down, and the ground began shaking as if a monster under the earth had wakened and, enraged, was trying to claw its way out of the earth. One of the oldest sections of wall surrounding our compound cracked and crumbled, and again came a convulsion of crashing rock. I turned toward the noise, still trying to control my horse.

One side of the house was simply falling apart from the shaking, the roof sliding and sinking inward, clay tiles shattering, the walls crumbling. Crushed furniture inside lay exposed like torn organs in a wounded animal, while in the courtyard mosaic paving stones ground together and lifted, tilting the pomegranate tree sideways and tipping a pot of flowers that burst, scattering color across the stonework. Dust billowed up like a dry fog.

We were screaming—all of us, even the men—while I tried to keep my mare from bolting. And then silence and stillness but for Anna and the girls weeping. The mules stood trembling in their traces, my mare froze in place, trembling; I dismounted, trembling. Much of the villa was, for all purposes, a ruin. All I could think, over and over, was 'Thank God no one was hurt.'

Anna was somehow in my arms, hers wrapped around my neck, her head buried in my bosom. She had stopped weeping, but her body still shook like an echo of the quake. We began to wander about as if in a daze, none of us daring to approach the remaining walls of the main building, the plaster having crumbled away to reveal rocks and bricks that had shifted and were ready to fall. The stables were leaning like bent old men. Leo's kitchen, which was separate, was intact so far as we could tell, and he and Alexander and a few other young men approached it timidly, pushing at bricks or stones here and there to test them. I was too dazed to realize what they were about until they began dragging out pots and pans, food stores, wood, and so forth.

Leo approached me. "Lady, we can build makeshift shelters for tonight, and I have found enough supplies to last us for several days, plus the barnyard animals are fine. But I think someone should go into Daphne to see what the damage is like there, and perhaps go to Antioch, too. It has suffered terribly from earthquakes in the past."

Bardas added, "And the other orphanages…."

"My God, you are right. Bardas, you take the mules and hasten down with a few of the other men to see about them. Take care—the roads might be unsafe. Alexander, you go into the village to see how it does."

We sat in the carts and waited. Another, smaller quake shook us again, sending more bricks and stones tumbling. The stable groaned and fell apart, but Leo's kitchen held. It was the newest building; the others were much older, some perhaps as much as three or four hundred years, though I really had no idea. I had never thought to ask when I bought it.

Alexander was back from the village within the hour. "The newer buildings survived well enough, but the chapel was a little damaged," he told us.

"And no one was killed, though everyone is afraid to go back inside their homes in case there are more earthquakes. Mostly people are afraid they won't have enough food and water. But I don't understand that. No crops or animals were harmed, and the weather is so mild that we can all live outside for a few days and start rebuilding. I stopped at the villas nearest us and it's the same story there. But we seem to be the only ones who lost any structures."

All in all, it could have been much worse. Everything would take awhile to rebuild, but with the number of strong and willing arms, we might even begin the next day. That was until Bardas returned in the middle of the afternoon, looking severe.

"This is not one of the great earthquakes that killed hundreds of thousands of people, but several buildings did fall in Antioch, and there are riots in the marketplaces. Many people are panicked over food and water, but others are no better than bandits. They are looting warehouses and even homes, and blood has been spilled. I went to the orphanages, and I am sorry to tell you this, Lady, but the last house you bought is rubble. Some children there were killed—you knew none of them, so names will mean nothing to you. But Jonah and Efrem and Mary are unhurt, as are—"

I leapt up. "I must go to them now! We must bring the survivors up here, we—"

He held his hands up. "No! Lady, if you truly wish it, the other men and I will bring them up; but I cannot let you go down there. It is too dangerous. We had to defend our mules just to get back here. A beautiful woman would be a target for rape and worse. I saw such things in the city already, and more will likely follow in the next few days. You must stay here." He looked around. "If I take Alexander and three others, your women can help Leo and the rest of the men set up shelters here. There will be much to do."

Leo, having come up to listen, nodded his head and firmly agreed.

I had to bow to their superior understanding and let them take charge. A few men were soon on their way in the two carts, heavily armed, to rescue the children in the destroyed orphanage. The rest, under Leo's direction, began building simple huts for us all, using the very wood, bricks, thatch and stones that had just fallen. It was a small blessing that the carpentry tools were stored in a wooden shack; nothing had been damaged when it fell.

Anna suddenly struggled loose from my arms. "Where are Sheep and Blade? They might be hurt!"

"Anna, sweet, spirit friends never get hurt."

"Then where are they?"

So, still dazed with shock, I looked around the villa with her until she cried that she had found them. It was strange to see her embrace nothing that I could see. Had it not been for their names, I might have wondered if they were even real.

Marguerite had disappeared by the time we returned. According to Banjuu, she had gone to see about the convent in the woods.

"She goes there to bring the nuns extra food and to seek their guidance every chance she gets, so it's no surprise, Lady. Here, let me take Anna for a little while so you can think on what else needs doing. The huts that the men are building are good enough for now, but you must decide what to do in the long run."

I thanked her and went to look at the shelters, to get as close as I could to the ruined main building, and finally to ponder the future. I wandered around in the courtyard, avoiding the worst part of the house. One wing was still standing, and I could see in the windows that the beds were undamaged, their bedding dusty and littered with rubble but useable. If there were no more earthquakes and the building still stood, we might be able to get inside and bring things out.

But as far as I could see, overall there was little worth saving. Across the courtyard was the ruination that had been my rooms. My pretty wall hangings and curtains were ripped and soiled; my tables and chair and bed, where Anna had always slept beside me, were smashed. Books lay spilled across the floor, some torn and others dirty. I turned away, set a few flowerpots upright again, and tried pushing the pomegranate tree back into place, but it was too heavy. One of my servants came running up. "No, Lady! Leo says please do not touch it. What if it crashed down on you? All would be lost! You must not stay near the building, either. It is still dangerous."

So I was reduced to standing aside, for no matter what I put my hand to, someone held me back for fear I might be harmed. It brought back memories of slavery when I had not been allowed to put my hand to anything useful. Now I must endure the almost equal burden of being mistress to others while feeling equally useless!

Bardas and Alexander and the others arrived near sunset. Both carts were full of children, some of whom were badly wounded and sobbing with fear and pain. It broke my heart, especially since I knew not a single face. I didn't even know the woman who oversaw them and who was also injured. Her husband had been killed, but she was concerned only for her little wards. A kind of self-hatred welled up: why had I bought that house, why had I not paid more attention, how could I have gotten so wrapped up in my own little life that I knew not a single child there, or even their guardians?

And worst was the voice of an implacable judge lurking in the back of my thoughts that condemned me for thinking I could ever help anyone.

But this was no time for excess, for there was much work ahead of us. The sun was already setting and creating fantastic shadows among the ruins.

A few brave fellows went into the undamaged part of the house and brought out everything they could: beds, blankets, unbroken platters and jugs, wooden chairs and tables, anything that looked useful. The others threw up more makeshift shelters for the injured children—thatched roofs with no sides so that if they shook down again no one would be hurt. I could at least help clean the children's wounds, with water that at my insistence had been boiled in Leo's makeshift outdoor kitchen. I had read something about boiling water in one of the medical texts that Adar had sent me, written by the famous physician Ibn Sina.

Marguerite reappeared with the two nuns, who seemed to know as much about nursing hurt children as I did, and who straightaway began helping with them. When I saw Anna gaping at a little girl her age whose arm had been torn apart and who died screaming, I told Marguerite to take her away and shield her from the worst sights. I could scarcely see through my tears, but I myself carried the little body away and put it in a cart. Tomorrow we would take it and any others—we all prayed there would be no more—to the village chapel for burial.

Most of us spent that night under thatch tents, with the stars shining serenely over us. My servants insisted I take one of the beds, so I cradled Anna all night, only leaving her side to insist that someone else rest a little while I took a turn tending to the children. Some slept, but there were nightmares. Most of the injured children were in too much pain to do more than slip into sleep and then jerk awake, terrified and wailing. It was like some small corner of hell.

In the morning we took two corpses to the village; the second one was the woman caretaker, who had given her last ounce of strength to comfort others and who simply slumped over and died. The priest took the bodies and put them with one other that had been brought to him. I suppose he and his servants buried them, but I was already on my way back to the villa. The day passed in a blur, but we were fairly well off, as was Daphne itself. It was, after all, a community of the wealthy, so buildings were stronger, supplies were more abundant, and injuries were few.

Several days passed. Bardas still would not let me go down to the city, though I wanted to see if Matthew of Edessa was safe. I had ships that could bring grain and other staples to the city, and I could afford to pay for them myself. It felt right to do this, and certainly it was the Christian thing to do.

Marguerite, with my permission, had left with the nuns to see to out-lying areas of Daphne in case someone was in distress and had no one to help them. Indeed, it was over a week before I saw her again, which surprised me a little. By then most of the healthy children were getting over their first terrors and would actually play in the ruins if not watched, while the injured ones were recovering fairly well. No more would die, hopefully, though a few would be crippled or maimed for life. We had enough food to last a few weeks and we were already rebuilding a little, but my heart was not in it.

Marguerite appeared at the gates one afternoon, borne on a stretcher by the nuns. Anna ran straight to her. "No, little girl, do not come near!" the one called Sister Clemence shouted. Anna did not listen but put her arms around her beloved maid—or rather her gown, which was befouled with what looked like thin mud. The nun shoved her away with some force, and Anna began to wail.

I rushed up. "What is the shouting about?" Then I saw Marguerite. "What is the matter? Marguerite, you look terrible. You have soiled your gown! Are you ill?" It was a stupid question, for of course she was. She smelled terrible.

"She is ill unto death, and we count it a miracle that we got her here."

We hastily made up a pallet for her away from the others, while the other nun, Sister Adela, told me everything. "There was nothing to do in

Daphne, so we went down into Antioch."

"But the riots!"

"Prince Bohemund's knights quelled the riots the day after they started. We went to work in a hospital. Disease had broken out, and there was much to do cleaning people who vomited or soiled themselves without let, and who must be given water or broth to drink until they either recovered or died. Marguerite worked with us like a saint, but she started vomiting this morning, and then … well, you can see for yourself. She will most likely die, so she begged us to bring her back here to be with her own people. She is a true daughter of Christ. You should call the priest to offer her the viaticum. She will go straight to heaven; of that there is no doubt."

Bardas hastened off to Daphne while I ordered Leo to bring Sister Adela hot broth, salty as she ordered. "If we keep her sipping it, a little at a time, we may be able to save her. I will see to that and keep her clean. At the hospital in Antioch, a Greek physician who studied with Muslim hakims told me that this is the best thing to do. And you must go back to your children."

A hakim! Three thoughts occurred, each chasing the other: I could ask Adar to come help us; what if he and his family—Anna!—had been injured or killed?; how was I to reach them? I felt sick with dread, for there was no way to find out how they were until things had settled down. Meanwhile there was so much to do.

I turned to find that my little Anna had crept back and was staring down at Marguerite. She was trying to wipe something off her hands and when she could not, she started to lick them. "Nasty," she cried, and tried to wipe her tongue with her arm. She spat, ran to the water bucket, and took a great mouthful of water from the dipper. I turned back to the other tasks at hand while too many thoughts, all of them painful, ran rampant in my head.

The priest arrived; the viaticum was given, though Marguerite, in such pain from cramps of some sort, seemed only barely aware of what was happening. He had stood and would have left, but she seemed to revive a little and called to him, "Please, I want to take the veil before I die!"

He nodded and knelt next to her, crossing himself. "Repeat after me," he began, and I turned away. I was too overcome even to weep, though I knew this was what Marguerite had always wanted, that this was a good way for her to end her life. And there was much else to do, so I joined the other nun, Sister Clemence, who could not be older than sixteen or seventeen. Together we fed and settled the other children. Stillness descended on me as the day dimmed, perhaps because the sister seemed to radiate a quiet confidence.

Night fell, and after putting Anna to bed I returned to Marguerite's side. Sister Adela was still there feeding the girl hot broth that Leo had made especially for her from a freshly killed chicken. The nun looked up at me. "I thought she would be gone by now. Certainly she has been at peace ever since taking her vows. And she is dead to this world even if she recovers. She is Sister Constance now, and if she lives we will take her back to the forest with us." I nodded and knelt to stroke Marguerite's— Sister Constance's—forehead. Her eyes were sunken, with dark circles under them, and when I took her little hand, her skin looked as wrinkled as if she had turned old in one day. Banjuu crept up.

"She is like my sister. Please let me help."

Sister Adela nodded and showed her how to drip broth slowly into her friend's mouth. "If she soils herself again, call me. Do not touch her! And Lady Sofia, let this be a time for the two of us to pray for her."

And so we did until a half moon rose, casting a gentle light over that scene of woe. I finally went to bed on my pallet in my crude shelter, my arms wrapped around Anna. We had all done what we could, and my servant's fate was no longer in any worldly hands. A kind of fatalistic peace arose like a lake of calm, and I slept until the rising sun woke me.

To everyone's joy and surprise, Sister Constance was much better, and even better the day after that. Within the week she was able to walk about a little; and once things had settled down somewhat, the other nuns departed for Antioch with promises to return for her later.

This was because things grew more tense for some time after she recovered. Three days after Sister Constance arrived, Anna fell ill with the same dread disease: first vomiting, then soiling herself, and then the cramps, the wrinkled skin, the sunken eyes. I was mad with fear for her, again was not allowed to do anything but to sit by her, feed her, hold her small hand when no one was looking, and pray to God to take me instead of her.

At one point Sister Clemence reproached me, "You cannot cling to worldly objects of love, you know. Children die, and to love them so much is to ask for pain heaped upon pain."

I snapped back, "Get out of my sight!" and the girl retreated, looking both self-righteous and hurt.

Later, regretting my temper, I pondered what she had said and rejected it. The possibility of loss would never stop me from loving Anna or anyone else. Such an attitude seemed cowardly. Were any of us so important that we should put up walls around our hearts so we needn't feel the pains of life? Though my nursemaid Baba Liubyna had lost her entire family to plague, she had not only told me the truth about love and loss—that the pain of loss is part of love—she had shown it to me in the way she loved me, raised me almost as her own, and bidden me farewell forever. As for the possibility of losing Anna, it had been one of the first things I realized when she was born: one of us must die first. And even if they outlive you, few daughters remain at home. They marry and leave you. I cared nothing if I were to die on the spot if only Anna would recover.

I don't know why I bothered trying to tell Sister Clemence any of this—perhaps to temper my harshness—but I did. She looked surprised.

"Perhaps if you can broaden your love to include us all in the way you love your daughter, you would see God's love pouring out into this world as I do."

Not wishing to quarrel further, I simply said, "Undoubtedly," and went back to tending Anna. Our interchange had only made me feel as if nettles had brushed across my heart. What was wrong with wanting Anna to recover? Had I become so narrow in my outlook that I needed chiding by this girl scarcely older than one of my orphans, or did she think that only nuns and monks felt universal love? What about everything I had done for my forsaken children? Did that not mean anything? And why should I care for her opinion when I was weary and frantic with worry for Anna and all the other children!

I got no further chance to think about such things, because three more children got sick that day. The able bodied took care of them, and Bardas and Leo and the nuns directed it all, for I would not leave Anna's side. The irony was not lost on me: my servants thought I was their lodestone, but everyone was perfectly capable of deciding and doing what must be done. They didn't need me except as a way to give meaning to their tasks. Sister Adela and I patiently dribbled broth into my little girl's mouth for hours each day, while I watched her clean and wash her, always with boiled water—a task she reserved for herself—always wishing I had such a steady hand and serene mind.

And after three of the longest days of my life, Anna began to recover.

In gratitude I vowed to endow the little chapel in the village in perpetuity as soon as I could get to Antioch and make the arrangements with Matthew of Edessa. In the meantime I sent one of my servants to the village chapel to pay for candles and ask for the priest's prayers. The rest would have to wait until Anna was fully well again.

Indeed, she recovered with surprising swiftness, and in a week or two she was running about as before. But when she was first able to sit up and take real soup, she said something that almost stopped my heart. "Mama, my ghost father came to me again while I was so sick, but he said you still couldn't see him."

I stroked her hair. "No, I cannot. What does he look like?"

"Like a ghost, silly Mama! And he said to tell you something. I thought it was a secret when he told me before, but he said no, I should tell you."

"And what is that?"

"He says he loves us and he is coming for us both, but that we must wait. Do not lose heart. He said that before, too! But this time I asked him if you and I were going to die and he would come for us from Heaven, and he said no, not at all. Because he is not really dead. And then he went away."

I began to tremble; my mind began to race. I had never given Anna reason to think Joscelin was alive, and she knew that orphans are those who have lost their parents, so it would be reasonable for her to think he was dead. Clinging to hope, I had avoided thinking about her visions of her "ghost father."

Did what she had said ring true, or did it simply confirm my own hopes? But what if she somehow saw past the veil of this fleshly life? Perhaps her youth and innocence made it possible to bridge minds, to hear him when I, so full of hope and fear, could not. If so, that would be a miracle and a blessing. I crossed myself and whispered a little prayer for his safety. And I offered another prayer of thanks for Anna—for her recovery, her ability to pierce my heart, and for her filling my empty life with love.

"So Mama, does that mean that I'm not an orphan anymore?" She looked rather wistful.

"You are until your father finds us. Then you will have the kind of family that all orphans dream of, full of love and joy. When that happens, you'll be glad not to be an orphan anymore."

She nodded gravely. "But Marguerite tells me that she has a new name—Sister Constance. She says she'll soon be leaving me, so I will be an orphan in that way forever. I love her very, very much."

"Yes." In truth, I hadn't given much thought to Sister Constance, partly because of worry about Anna and partly because I could not admit how I felt toward her. In my heart I was angry that she had brought plague back to the villa and been the cause of other children's deaths and endangered us all, especially my little Anna. I knew I was being unfair.

Once Anna had been able to get up and needed me less, Sister Constance had come to me with hands held in supplication. "Please, Lady Sofia, forgive me. I would rather have died than bring plague here. I will always blame myself for what happened, and all my prayers from now on will be dedicated to your welfare. I went to Antioch because I remembered all those sick and dying people at that hospital in Constantinople. I only wanted to help."

I'd had no choice but to forgive her, no matter how I felt. Taking her hands, I had said, "I understand, and I laud your for your charity, too. As for bringing plague here, it was only natural that if you thought you were dying, you would want to return to the place where you were loved. You will always have a special place in my heart." After that, I went out of my way to be kind to her, as I knew she still quietly blamed herself.

Of the remaining sick children, one died. That child, a boy who had been badly injured and had been clutching to life, was sent to the priest to be buried. It grieved me more than I could say that I never even learned his name, or those of the other victims. And while I blamed myself to my core for buying an old building, at least I could make sure it never happened again. I would hire only the best stonemasons and build a new home and a new orphanage that could survive earthquakes! And looking at my damaged villa, I could see that having my orphans perform work that required such skill had been a huge error on my part, for the oldest parts of the house that I'd thought they had repaired were exactly what had fallen. It was truly a miracle that none of us had been hurt.

On the other hand, plague and earthquake were always cited as a sign of God's displeasure with a sinful mankind.

Well, I had learned a painful lesson. I could protect no one fully, not even my darling Anna. Some survived and some were lost, beyond any thought or design on anyone's part. So, had what happened been a miracle, or a punishment, or was it simply the way of this world?

Another week passed before I finally got to Antioch. We needed to go down to buy food, as with so many mouths to feed and most of the chickens slaughtered for broth, we only had milk, butter, a few early vegetables, and a little flour left. But also I wanted to see Matthew of Edessa, if he had even survived, to discover what state my finances were in, and to learn what damage had been done to the city. And perhaps I could still help in some way.

As we followed the road down the mountain, I saw some damage in several older neighborhoods, but looking down from the last turn in the road I realized that most of the city had survived intact. Not only that, the prince's soldiers had already cleared the rubble away and there was much rebuilding going on.

I have not mentioned Prince Bohemund very often, as he was never part of my life. He was a youth of fifteen when he took full possession of his two principalities, and he was therefore required to travel between Antioch and Tripoli. He was now only eighteen, so I was impressed by how well he had taken his responsibilities in hand. Since his marriage, much beautifying of Antioch had occurred, possibly under his wife's influence. And I had heard that he was also repairing forts and roads throughout his holdings.

After sending Leo off to bargain for food—there was plenty in all the markets, though from the grumbling we overheard in passing, merchants were overcharging for everything—I found Matthew alive and well in his office by the Orontes quay. It had been slightly damaged: mostly documents fallen from shelves, and there were ink stains on the floor here and there. A few little round glass panes were gone from his windows, but a man was already putting new ones in. Matthew was standing over and directing the efforts of a servant who was sorting through a few last piles of documents laid out on the floor. When I entered, he turned and greeted me with relief.

"Lady Sofia, I am so glad to see you are well. I was worried about you up in Daphne, possibly cut off or even harmed. And I heard about one of the orphanages collapsing. I feel responsible, since it was I who brought you together with the rogue who sold it to you."

"All is as well with me as can be expected. Some children died in that house, and we brought the survivors to Daphne."

He crossed himself. "I will light candles in their memory."

"Well, the wheel of fate is always turning. My orphans in Daphne were all lucky; no one was even hurt. But my home is in ruins."

In short order I told him the rest of my news, and he in turn caught me up with what had happened in Antioch. He had lost nothing in his home beyond a few pieces of crockery and some more windowpanes, easily replaced. The damage in the city overall had been to buildings too old to withstand the shaking. But that was all. By Antioch standards, it was hardly worth mentioning, though that had not stopped looting and panic over food. Matthew was not even aware that anyone had fallen ill, for Antioch is well supplied with clean water from mountain springs. He was shocked that any of my children had gotten sick.

"But," he added, "there is great profit to be made right now by bringing foodstuffs into the city, as people are always afraid after such events and want to lay in extra stores. I was among the first to send agents into the countryside to buy up whatever we could. And of course I straightaway sent several ships to buy food in other cities, including one of yours that happened to be in port. They have already returned, and once again, Lady Sofia, you seem to be in the right place at the right time, for you've already made a huge profit. Plus we have more stores in the warehouse waiting for buyers."

Then he saw my face. "What is the matter?"

"I wanted to distribute food for free to the sufferers, and now I feel useless."

"Well, you are lucky you didn't try to do that: a sure way to start more riots and make enemies of the other merchants! You can still give food to the monasteries and churches and let them be the charitable ones. No one will think ill of you for that."

"Well, then, let it be done!"

"If you feel strongly about this, may I suggest a tenth of your stores? That is in accord with the Scriptures." Matthew looked uneasy.

"Oh well, that will do. No need to look as if I'm about to beggar us both. I will need to take some of it back with me, though. Can you arrange for that and for me to hire stonemasons to help rebuild both the orphanage and the villa?"

"Yes to your stores, but it will be months before anyone will be free to go up to Daphne. Builders are in high demand right now."

That was a disappointment. The thought of living for months in a ruined villa appealed to me not at all.

There was another important task: I sent messengers to Adar al-Mas'udi to find out what might have happened to him, my other Anna, and their family. I was less worried about them now that I knew Antioch had not been badly affected, but still....

At last, having done as much as I could, I returned home, laden with supplies from my own storehouses as well as with poultry and other goods for which I had paid far too much. I also brought Efrem from my first orphanage. He was glad to come and even took along those of his boys who were learning carpentry skills. My menservants had been trying their best to rebuild walls while I was gone, had even saved many small items from the fallen side of the house after clearing away the unsafe rubble, including several books, among them my Papa's wooden book and my recent jottings, and my breviary. A chest had emerged undamaged, and in it were my finery from Venice as well as some good lengths of muslin from al-Mawsil. I was happier about the muslin; it meant I could at least sew clothing for my fifteen new orphans.

Still, our situation was most unsatisfactory. For one thing Sister Constance had left with the nuns while I was gone, and I found Anna huddled beneath one of the shelters, weeping for her Marguerite while she played a game of death and burial. Then it rained one night, and we all awoke sodden and chilled. After another week of clearing rubble and working on the walls, Efrem came to me with a long face.

"Lady, I found another crack in a wall today. It threatens to bring down a new section of the building. To rebuild this house properly will mean tearing it down and starting over, and that will take almost a year. Look around you: the weather may be pleasant today, but do you want the children living outdoors when winter storms come in from the sea? Even that one rain showed how poorly these shelters protect us. I must leave soon, for Mary is carrying another child. She cannot do everything alone.

"And you cannot live like this for much longer. I think you should move into Antioch, at least for now, and wait until the rebuilding can be done properly. The children need more guidance than they're getting here, too. I've had to stop too many quarrels, no one is being properly trained or even looked after, and this setting will just breed more laxity. No one can be happy living among ruins, no matter how hard you try to make it work."

His advice was timely, for I had been feeling more and more discouraged. I sighed. "I know you are right. But what do you suggest we do with all these children?"

"Bring them to Mary and me. We'll find room for them. Older children are always leaving, and soon there will no crowding at all."

He paused, looking somewhat ill at ease. "There is another reason you should move into the city. If you don't, Leo may leave you. He has had enough of cooking in this primitive way, not to mention some of the children stealing from him and vexing him in other ways. They call him Fatty and worse."

Another problem! At least I could approach my cook and ask him what he needed to be happy again, which I did forthwith.

But Leo already had a solution. Scratching his chin and looking over my shoulder as if to see the future written behind me, he said, "Lady Sofia, for some time I've been missing the bustle of city life. This mess we find ourselves in just makes it clearer. I am thinking of returning to Cyprus or at least going to Antioch. I have an idea I hope you will consider. I was thinking about it even before the earthquake happened: I want to open an inn. I've asked Bardas to be my partner, but he says he cannot leave you. But if you saw fit, you could move back into the city and help us get started and be our silent partner, and some of your orphans here could become my apprentices or work in the stable and so forth...."

After that rush of words, he took a deep breath and added, not looking at all as if he meant it, "I'd be glad to take on a few children, hardworking ones, from your other orphanages, too, ones old enough to learn how to cook and serve."

It was such a straightforward and practical proposal that I accepted on the spot. My decision seemed to cheer everyone. It was not until that night, while Anna lay wrapped in my arms and I was looking out of our shelter up at the stars, that I began to realize how deluded I had been over the past weeks. We should have left Daphne straightaway, and none of those illnesses need have occurred. Instead, I could have been seeing after Marguerite right in the hospital—if she had even fallen ill!

And seeing how little other homes in Daphne or even in Antioch had been damaged and how much my villa had been, I could not but feel that the world was indeed alive and speaking to me, just as I had once believed when I was a child. I had forgotten that connection, even living in such an idyllic place, and now I felt it again, but in a different way. The hard blue sky and thick dark forest and haunted-looking ruins of my house suddenly seemed unfriendly and forbidding, as if they were only waiting for me to leave, perhaps even plotting new ways to uproot me.

We would move into the city on the very morrow. With that settled, I fell deeply asleep for the first time since the earthquake.

The move was simplicity itself, although at Anna's insistence we first went to say goodbye to Sister Constance. That turned out to be a trial. I took one of my servants with us bearing food goods, a trio of laying hens, and thick blankets, as I wanted the three nuns to have enough supplies for the winter. There were many embraces shared and tears shed, but we all knew that this was the true moment of parting for us all. My little Marguerite was now dead to this world, no matter what.

On the way down to Antioch, Anna cried until she ran dry of tears.

Efrem took the extra orphans back to the home that belonged to the Hospitallers, and my household stayed overnight at an inn with me.

The very next day, through Matthew of Edessa I found a large, simply furnished, undamaged city house to rent just where the slope up the mountain began—its owners lived in the country and had rarely used it, and since the earthquake they were afraid to return. Within a week, with so little to bring with us and with so much already provided for us, we felt almost at home.

And I heard from my other Anna. Her letter read, "We felt the earthquake and lost a few pots and so forth, but that was all. We count ourselves lucky, as another castle to the south of us, Castle Shaizar, collapsed in past earthquakes more than once. One time the entire family that owned it was killed, and then it was seized for a while by Nizari, and just about everyone fought over it! I want nothing to do with those Nizari again. Maryam writes that they are crawling all over Halab, inciting trouble. They claim the Mongols are a sign of the end of this age and the beginning of the new age and that men must repent and join their cause or be lost for eternity."

After a few stories about her children, she concluded with, "I am sorry to hear that you lost your villa and for all your other troubles, but Allah wills it. I am certain He has a happy plan for you."

That remained to be seen. I was just glad she was alive. Even better, she proposed to visit me with her husband and children in late September, a rare treat for us all. They would stay with distant family in the Muslim quarter for a month, but the real reason they were coming was because she missed me so much that her beloved Adar had consented. I missed her, too, and my little Anna would be glad of playmates nearer her own age.

September arrived, and with it the beginning of cooler weather. Antioch was back to normal, and I found its pace and bustle rather exciting. Leo and I had found a suitable location for his inn right on the bank of the Orontes, perfect for merchants and pilgrims. An abandoned warehouse there had fallen down in the earthquake and the land was for sale, so I snatched it up at a low price and soon had workmen clearing the rubble and building a splendid new inn with all the most recent refinements in style and hospitality.

As soon as it was known that I would pay higher wages than anyone else, I was nearly overwhelmed with willing laborers, including skilled carpenters, masons, and craftsmen. I began to wonder if I had given up on Daphne too soon, but now I was enjoying life here.

Leo and Bardas also sent to Cyprus for another cousin to help them. Her name was Ioanna, a well-built, dark-haired young woman who looked tough enough to handle rowdy guests and handsome enough to please their eyes. Every day more of the construction was done, and I could count on finding her helping somewhere. Indeed, I could measure the progress of the building by the tasks she set herself: sitting in the sun sewing curtains, or sorting through the wares that Leo had ordered, or deciding on the placement of tables and benches with Bardas.

I was feeling more alive than I had in months; and when Anna and Adar arrived, their visit further added to my sense of wellbeing. What a delight it was to have them and their sons with me. The boys, speaking only Arabic and some local dialect, made up for their inability to talk to Anna by throwing themselves into extravagant war play against the hated infidels. She was soon capturing and pretending to behead enemies, not knowing that she herself was the hated infidel. It was a little awkward at first, but Adar passed it off with a laugh.

"There is no real enemy in play, and no harm done!"

I was not so sure, wondered who was teaching the boys such violent sentiments—Adar himself seemed unlikely—but I let it pass, especially as I wanted just to enjoy my friend Anna's company. I left the children to Banjuu and Alexander; since Sister Constance's departure, they had stepped into taking care of Anna quite naturally. Alexander certainly was in his element. We could hear him out in the courtyard behind the house, shouting with the boys and evidently leading expeditions and surprise raids and so forth. Every once in a while, Banjuu's soft voice floated inside, usually warning a shrieking Anna not to get too wild.

But one day I had to see to business. Leaving Anna with my friends, I made my way to the inn, guarded by Golden Thomas, who proudly swaggered along as if he actually knew what he was doing. I had to smile inwardly, happy for the sunshine and for my own fearlessness. How could I once have been so frightened by this world?

Leo and Bardas showed me around the inn, pride imprinted in their every step. Things were going along as well as could be expected, they explained, for there always seemed to be some new delay. Late in the afternoon, and about to leave, I decided to go upstairs and view the newly finished rooms. They smelled of new wood and clean stone, and Ioanna had already arranged the beds and chests.

Thinking to glimpse the Orontes, I opened a back window, which had real panes of glass like Matthew's rooms, thick and round and set into lead. I was surprised to see a man below who looked like Adar's older brother, Mustafa Ibn Husain. He was farther along the wharf, speaking to someone, perhaps a boatman or merchant, but every time anyone walked by, they glanced over suspiciously and finally moved out of sight, apparently into the alley that ran between our inn and the next building.

Following my curiosity—I had not known he had come to Antioch with his brother and sister-in-law—I strolled down the stairs, through the storeroom, and out the back door that led onto the docks to see if it was indeed he. I could hear Bardas and Ioanna in the common room at the front of the inn, moving benches about and quarreling cheerfully. There was no sign of the two men, and I was about to turn back when Mustafa emerged from the shadows and started back, shock written on his face. He frowned and gestured to his companion, and they were suddenly on either side of me, his hand over my mouth. Utterly confused, I tried to back away, but both men gripped my arms. I struggled silently, terrified that they meant to rape me, and then when they made to lift and carry me toward the alley, I thought of kidnap or even murder. Mustafa whispered to his fellow, "No one must know."

Terror, as in the past, lent me strength and clarity. I opened my mouth fully and his hand slid inside it. I bit down hard enough to draw blood, and he cursed and pulled his hand away long enough for me to scream, as long and loud as I could. Back in the inn, Bardas and Leo called my name and I heard the sound of running. I screamed again, was dumped on the ground. I drew my knife and slashed out at a leg that spun around and disappeared, and the men were gone. My servants found me shaking with fright, dizzy with fear, and feeling as if another earthquake had struck.

"What happened?" they both cried at the same time. Bardas picked me up and carried me inside. He sat down on one of the benches with me in his lap and held me while I cried with relief. Ioanna, meanwhile, found water and a towel and wiped my face gently, while Leo brought me watered wine in one of his new goblets and Golden Thomas hovered in the background looking troubled. Once recovered, I told them what had happened. A meaningful glance passed between the men.

"Lady Sofia," Bardas said after a thoughtful pause, "there is much that you never knew about Adar al-Mas'udi's family. But I spent time among the servants when you visited them. It helps to speak a little Arabic in these parts and not to let on that you do. Less said, more learned. I know some things that you do not.

"The fact is that Mustafa Ibn Husain is Nizari. It's not something that many people know; I doubt Anna does, for to her husband's family it is a shameful secret. Anyway, so long as he posed no danger to you—and don't think I've been your man all this time and not seen how you fear them—I had no reason to say anything to you. But now I wish I had!"

I nodded and stood. "Thank you, Bardas. And thank you, Leo. I have no idea what they wanted, and I doubt they had any real plan when they seized me. I need to find out much more about all this! But now I just want to go home. Thomas, be on guard!"

But Leo and Bardas insisted on hiring a litter for me, and nothing happened on our way back. I sent Thomas straightaway to ask Adar al-Mas'udi to come see me about an important family matter and to bring Anna home in the same litter. But even while I was issuing these orders, I was wondering where home might even be.

Adar and Anna arrived the next morning without their children, looking curious but not concerned. After seating them and offering refreshments, I wasted no time with light talk.

"First, Adar, I must ask you if Anna knows about your elder brother Mustafa's ... secret ... faith."

Anna blushed fiercely, and then I realized that not only did she know everything about Mustafa Ibn Husain, but also that Adar knew all about our time in Alamut.

"Yes, there are no secrets between Anna and me. What has happened, Sofia?" Adar asked gently.

I told them everything. Anna looked sick by the end. She came over and embraced me. "I am so sorry, Sofia. Please forgive me! I never knew he would try to harm you. It's all because of me! He and Adar were quarreling one time about Islam, and I got so angry that I told them all about our living in Alamut and your being so important to the Grand Master. He looked disbelieving and I suppose I wanted him to think better of us, so I built you up even more! And he questioned me in a way that frightened me, even though Adar tried to make him stop, and he realized that you and I had escaped. Maybe he wanted to prove his loyalty by taking you back to Alamut."

"Or perhaps," said Adar, "he wanted no witnesses to his being here in the city. He must have known you would tell me. I cannot imagine him wanting to send you to Alamut, since there's a new Grand Master now, one Rukn al-Din. The old Grand Master was murdered by his own men, they say, most likely because he failed to treat successfully with the Mongols. And now Mongol armies are likely to bring the entire eastern branch of that Nizari filth to an end. The only good thing they will have done!"

I had never heard my friend sound so vengeful!

"Well, Rukn al-Din was my pupil as well as the agent of my escape. We have only the kindest feelings for each other. If your brother thinks he can win his favor by kidnapping me, he is mistaken. He might well lose his head for it. Perhaps when you go home, you can tell him that, and that I prize your friendship so highly that I forgive him.

"But despite our shared fear of them, Adar, the Nizari have been a refuge for many scholars fleeing the Mongol advance, including some who are venerated even among the Sunni. And the library at Alamut, I was told, is a wonder unto itself. If the Mongols get hold of the castle, which I highly doubt, they will destroy it as they destroy everything, and they will likely kill the scholars who live there." I was thinking of my former tutor Nasir al-Din, for one. I might have resented him once, but he had not only tutored me, he too had helped me escape. I didn't wish him any kind of harm.

Adar shrugged. "Sometimes to destroy a nest of vipers, one must pull up a rose bush. As you say, the Mongols often destroy everything, and they have already laid waste to several Nizari towns and castles. Alamut itself is probably already under siege. The Great Khan's brother Hulegu leads the campaign, and it is said that he has vowed to destroy the Nizari religion utterly. Rumor has it that many fida'i went to Karakorum in disguise thinking somehow to get close to the Great Khan and kill him, and the Mongols want revenge. Mustafa is sick with worry over Alamut, but he's also mad if he thinks he could have gotten you anywhere near it."

A thought flashed through my mind, illuminating that time at Alamut when the Mahdi and his people had questioned me endlessly. Had the Grand Master used my knowledge to try to penetrate the Mongol hierarchy? I shuddered.

Adar stood up and looked thoughtfully out the window onto my courtyard. "I didn't know my brother was here, but I will find him and stop him from causing you further harm. Meanwhile, may I suggest that your servants keep a watchful eye around your house? I doubt he'll try anything again, but just in case I don't find him first, I will also send one of my men to stand guard outside your walls tonight. He may see Mustafa or his men before I do, and since they know each other my guard will tell them what you told me."

I thanked him and embraced Anna, whose tears had run down her cheeks without let ever since her confession. "There is no shame in trusting your husband, Anna dearest. I forgive you. You needn't cry over it."

The next day Adar sent me a frustratingly simple message: Mustafa would no longer trouble me. And when I asked him about their encounter when next we saw each other, he refused to say anything more.

A few more visits, a few more mock battles in the courtyard, and my friends were gone back to their lives. My Anna was bereft. She had never been given such license before, and she spent many an hour outside with only Sheep and Blade for company, continuing to hack and behead until the play wore thin. It was much quieter after that!

And though Anna and I wrote each other over the next few years, events overtook us all. I never saw my friends—or Mustafa—again.

❧ ⁂ ❧

By the time Adar and Anna left, I had decided that I no longer wanted to stay in Antioch. Of many reasons, there were two in particular: the Mongols were drawing closer, and there were Nizari all over Syria. Having asked Bardas and Leo what else they knew, I learned that, in effect, a Nizari state bordered the principality of Antioch in the south. In truth, other than Mustafa's strange behavior, there was no real reason to fear them. He hated all unbelievers, but I never found out why he had attacked me. If he wanted to do me further harm, perhaps by alerting other Nizari about me, then I wanted to be as far from him as possible.

As for the Mongols: now that Prince Bohemund was related by marriage to King Hetoum, how long would it be before Mongol garrisons began appearing in Antioch?

The only question was where to go, and the only reasonable answer was to Constantinople. I would simply hold my head up high, be a benefactor to the orphanages there, see to it that my daughter was well-protected from any possible gossip, and continue to wait for Lord Joscelin.

The hardest part would be saying goodbye to Bardas and Leo, for they could not abandon their fine new inn. It was almost ready to open and had already drawn much interest. People coming by to stare inside seemed to see it as an act of faith in Antioch's future, while Leo was thrilled to cook as he truly liked—he planned to attract only the wealthiest clients, of which there were plenty passing through the city. My tastes might be refined, but they had been too simple of late. He was already using his kitchen to try new receipts, and the aromas wafting out to the street were better advertisements than anyone crying out their wares in a crowded market.

I asked him to prepare a feast for all my closest servants, for Jonah and Efrem and Mary and for everyone else who served me, to be held the day before the inn was to open. Naturally he thought it was to celebrate our new venture.

The day of the feast, I tried to smile as we seated ourselves at the new, clean trestle tables. Hopefully I wouldn't entirely ruin the party. At the end of a long and excellent meal of many courses that lasted until the sun set, as well as much jesting and song, I finally arose and lifted my goblet of wine. "Please join me in a toast to my partners. God grant them every success."

With many shouts of joy and much applause, everyone rose and toasted with me. But when they were seated again, I had to announce my plan to depart for Constantinople. A general cry of no's arose, but I held up my hands for silence.

"My heart breaks in telling you this now, but I wanted to wait until you were firmly planted here, Leo and Bardas. You both have served me long and well, but a new and promising future awaits you now, and you must not feel obligated to me. I will stay here whenever I visit Antioch, which I plan to do from time to time. You are not entirely rid of me." Both men gave way to tears, but while my throat tightened, I continued.

"The rest of you must decide your futures, too. Alexander, I deeply wish for you and Banjuu to come with me, but I do not demand it. Golden Thomas, I would have you come with me as well." He blushed so deeply that it showed in the candlelight. "Indeed," I looked around at my other servants, all orphans who had chosen to stay with me over the years, "I wish you all might follow me. But this is for you to decide. You are not slaves, and you have all been loyal to me. I will help you find new masters if you wish—unless Leo and Bardas can use you—so please give thought for what you want to do. In a few weeks, I will depart.

"And now let us set the subject aside. It is time for a last round of wine and ale, yes?" Though many people cried yes, I had indeed spoiled the evening, for the last toasts were subdued and the party broke up soon after.

Leo and Bardas walked me to the door, while Ioanna hovered behind them.

"Lady, how can we thank you for all you've done for us? Our hearts are breaking that you will leave us; yet you have made it impossible for me, at least, to follow you. That in itself is a gift, for I would never have been happy in Constantinople," said Leo.

"Well, you are not entirely rid of me," I laughed, wiping away a tear. And I held my hand out to him. He bowed over it and, wiping his own tears, turned back inside. He planned to sleep there overnight with his staff so that they could start early the next day. As I left I looked up at the new sign he and Bardas had just put in place that day: a picture of a smiling lady. They had named their house The Good Lady Inn.

Bardas and my other servants walked me back to my house, though he would return to the inn that night to help the next day. When we parted, he was weeping openly. "Lady, how can I part from you? I know I must, but it crushes my heart even more than it does Leo's. I never expected this."

For the first time I saw his love for me, far beyond that of a faithful servant. How many selfless journeys had he made on my behalf when he could have been married and raising a family of his own?

I embraced him, kissing him on both cheeks. "It will tear out a piece of my heart to leave you behind, but we must accustom ourselves to this turn of events. You know better than anyone how unsafe I feel here and how much happier Anna will be near children of her age and station.

"And there is something else, Bardas," I added on impulse. "It is time you married and started a family, you know, and my making you travel all over the place hasn't helped you. I have your happiness in mind, too."

He laughed and blushed deeply. "Time enough to think of that later."

"You have someone in mind already! Ioanna?"

"Yes, our families have always had an understanding about us, but I could not in all conscience leave you."

"Well, now you must! I will see you married before I leave Antioch!"

So within a few weeks, Bardas and Ioanna were married at a little Orthodox chapel and fêted in the inn, and the day after that, I was on my way to Constantinople. But before my departure, I had spent almost every moment getting my businesses in order: trade ventures and orphanages, the inn, and boys doing copy work, all of which required attention. But like children grown up and moved away, none of them needed me anymore to flourish, so I could leave with a clean if sad heart.

Before I left, though, Sir Reynaud appeared. News of the earthquake had reached his ears, and he had arranged leave with his king just to come see if I needed help, such a kind gesture. He claimed it was on behalf of Basil and Helene; she had just borne another son whom they had daringly named Volodymyr after my father, so Basil could not leave her. Despite that bow to family memory, I doubted Basil would have sent Sir Reynaud or anyone else to see about me. According to Helene's last letter, he was still annoyed with me for not marrying Maffeo Polo and for hiding myself away. The contrast with Sir Reynaud's gallantry was not lost on me.

I took my guest and Anna up to Daphne. He wanted to see the damaged villa, and I wanted to find the nuns in the forest to offer them alms and to see Sister Constance one last time. There had been a hole in our family since she'd left, one that Anna especially felt. Sir Reynaud and our men waited at a little distance out of respect, while Anna and I each embraced her with tears and bade each other farewell.

We were riding back toward Daphne, Anna still sobbing a little and me musing on the future, when Sir Reynaud cut into my thoughts. "Have you thought of deeding your villa to the nuns? Winters can be harsh here, and it may be more hardship than they expect for them to live in the wild when a truly bad one comes along. I know most of the house is in ruins, but now that you've built your inn, I would wager you could get help up here to build it anew."

"What a brilliant idea!" I turned my horse right around and trotted back to their little mud and wattle convent. All three fairly glowed with joy when I told them his idea.

"Yes, it was colder here than we expected last winter, though that is no hindrance. But with a larger convent we could attract more women... We could grow our own food, and devote even more time to prayer instead of to begging! Lady Sofia, how can we thank you?" All three seemed to speak at once. So I left once again, a chorus of thanks in my ears, as lovely a melody as I had ever heard.

ANNO DOMINI 1256-1258

With my final ties to Antioch cut, I took ship accompanied by Sir Reynaud. Now I could begin a new life in Constantinople just as I once had imagined. Truth be told, I was not looking forward to it, even though I would have friends and family there. Assuming that all its citizens felt as Caterina had, and that harsh judgments would be not only my lot but also Anna's if her bastardy were discovered, I could not help worrying. But Sir Reynaud made a quite a pleasant companion—no attempts at courtship—and the time passed quickly. He was a great favorite with Anna, who called him her uncle. He seemed to find her amusing as long as she behaved herself, even played a few games with her like hide-and-go-seek. When he found her, he would swing her up and around, and sometimes tickle her until she screamed with mingled delight and pain. I finally had to ask him to moderate his play, for she was becoming ungovernable. Now that Alexander and Banjuu were her main caretakers, she had grown as wild as she'd been when a little thing.

At least the crew did not seem to mind when she tried to help row or got into mischief below the deck; but then, she was the owner's daughter. Some of the sailors adopted her, even showed her how to tie knots and set ropes, and once they let her climb a rope ladder up to the bottom of the sail, a dream come true for her. I was always terrified for her, but she never fell overboard even if one time she fell a few feet, luckily into the arms of an alert sailor. I rewarded him well, and from then on he was her self-appointed guardian.

We arrived in Constantinople in late October, ahead of the winter storms. It was always a pleasant time of year in the city, less humid than in summer. And to my surprise, even Basil seemed pleased to see me. Having learned that I planned to find a house near him and Helene, he had already arranged everything; so perhaps my thoughts had been too harsh. It was a spacious house around the corner from them that had been occupied by Venetian merchants until recently. The merchants had moved to the city of Soldaia in the Crimea, lured there by new trade opportunities.

There was room on one floor for Alexander and Banjuu, for Golden Thomas, and for my other servants, all of whom had elected to go with me. Another floor was just right for Anna and me, including a bright sunny room that would be a solar where I could work or sew and she could play. There was a good kitchen for the new cook I hired, who was competent if not brilliant, and we even had a fair-sized courtyard with a small stable and garden and room for chickens and a milk cow. We seemed to have everything we needed, including friends. And now, ironically, I had use for my finery from Venice. I was thought most fashionable whenever I went out, even had the feminine pleasure of seeing my garments copied by a few women!

My other servants settled easily into our new life; and when I had no need of them, Alexander and Banjuu in particular often disappeared for entire afternoons to explore the city.

Sir Reynaud threw himself into showing me more of Constantinople, and I saw so many palaces and mansions and churches and chapels and cisterns and forums and towers and gates, most of them ruined, that they all began to run together. The only thing I clearly remember is a sacred icon of Mother Mary and her Holy Son called the Hodegetria, which had always protected the city until the Franks overcame it. Now, ironically, the Venetians had seized its residence, Blachernae church, which was hard by the damaged palace of the same name. He took me inside parts of the palace, which looked as if they had been more camped in than lived in. There were burn marks on the floors where fires had been set. No wonder King Baldwin preferred the other palace.

Sir Reynaud seemed to have found a proper balance when treating with me. His early style of too familiar had been replaced with something like respectful admiration. It was a relief that he finally seemed to understand that I was not open to any wooing.

Helene made opportunities for me to meet new people, and soon I found myself at fêtes and dinners, Holy Day celebrations, colorful jousts held in one of the large forums along the Mese just after Easter, or summer pleasure outings outside the city. Most of my new friends were from prosperous merchant families that owned vast farms and fields with pleasant woods and streams. With such a small population, we were all thrown together quite often, and we endlessly hosted each other. Some of the villas lay far beyond the outer, Theodosian Walls. No one seemed to pay attention to the poorly guarded no man's land that lay just beyond the hills. Basil hosted these people at his villa, too, though I felt ill at ease there the first time. None of the servants were familiar, at least. I never asked, but it was likely that Basil—or Caterina—had turned them all off for letting me escape.

Once in high summer, when the city was unbearably hot and the air so sweltering that everyone felt as if they were dripping endlessly, one of Basil's friends took a group of us on an even more ambitious outing. With many guards, servants, and heavily laden wagons for our provisions, we all rode far beyond the city walls and into the cooler woods where the men could hunt all day. That night we would sleep at our host's nearby villa.

It was most pleasant to escape the city heat, and once the men found a suitable meadow—really more a wide, well-shaded glade with a little stream running through it—we ladies seated ourselves on folding benches or on cushions and spreads. There we idly ate dainty sweetmeats or fruits while we wove flower wreaths and they gossiped. Meanwhile, the men plunged into the forest in search of boar or deer. We could hear their horns blending with the yaps and howls of the dogs. The women laughed, chattered about anyone who was not there—sometimes in quite harsh terms—chaffed each other over little nothings, and wondered whether their men would kill anything. All agreed that if we were to enjoy a proper feast tonight, at least a buck must be killed, and a boar was not entirely out of the question.

I joined in on occasion, but I could never let down my guard, perhaps because I was certain that the others were curious about Anna. Someone had once asked me about her, I had said that she was an orphan I had adopted, and all other questions I turned aside. But I could not help wondering if there was cruel gossip about us, too. This one barrier, subtle though it was, always kept me floating in their world instead of landing solidly. Helene, on the other hand, seemed the happiest I had ever seen her.

And despite my fears for Anna, she never lacked for friends. For the first time in her life, there were children her own age to see almost every day, and she soon learned that she was not the center of the world after all. This was something I had failed to teach her, and as painful as it was to witness some of her tears and rages at first, she learned quickly and turned into a charming, playful child.

In addition to Sir Reynaud, who fairly danced around me attending to my every need whenever he visited, I renewed my friendship with Maffeo Polo. I recalled wryly how Basil had denied that men and women could be friends. How wrong he was! I could trust Maffeo with almost all of my thoughts, he was an able advisor on business matters, and he never renewed his offer of marriage or behaved with the slightest disrespect.

Sir Reynaud was clearly jealous of Maffeo; not only that, he looked down on one whom he regarded as a mere merchant. Maffeo had seen all this before, and he responded with cool amusement and, sometimes, little stabs of wit. At gatherings when he knew Sir Reynaud could overhear us, he would ask me how my courtship was going with such and such a man and then glance over in mock surprise and equally mock friendliness.

In truth, I found all this amusing, too, especially since I did have other admirers. I took care to show no favor to any in particular, of course. Happily, Sir Reynaud was often away with King Baldwin, whose life seemed devoted to trying to raise money and to visiting pilgrimage sites. As far as I could tell, the king did little governing other than to collect taxes on non-Venetians, including Basil and me, and remove anything from the city that he could sell—if that counted as government.

Helene became almost a daily companion. She became pregnant a fourth time—she had miscarried one early on—and was beginning to lose her shape, but she cared nothing for that. It was not something I really wanted to know about my uncle, but she was never shy in telling me about his lusty ways and how much more satisfying he was as a husband than Lord Gilles had been—but then, Lord Gilles had been such a good husband in other ways, if so much older, and so on. She never seemed to tire of her story, only repeated it in different ways.

At least I enjoyed her little children, as well as Cecilia, who looked on me as her special, mysterious, and alluring aunt, although in fact we were cousins.

Thus with so many diversions I made a happy if temporary home in that city of splendor and woe. And if I missed Lord Joscelin, I told no one.

It must have been around May that word reached Constantinople: Alamut had fallen. Its Grand Master, my young once-admirer and liberator, Imam Rukn al-Din, was in Mongol hands, and the Nizari—or Assassins, as the Franks call them—were destroyed. I didn't see how that was possible, since there were still plenty of them in Syria, but that was not my concern. I did wonder what would happen to young Rukn al-Din. What a sorry lot he had been born to. I wondered what he thought of the Mongols, too, with whom he had been so fascinated, and prayed they would not kick him to death in a rolled up carpet.

Alas, I did eventually learn his fate: after being treated like a puppet in Hulegu Khan's ordu and even being allowed to marry a Mongol noblewoman, he was sent off to submit to Mongke Khan in Karakorum and murdered on the way. He was not considered worthy of a royal death. When I heard this, I shed a few tears for that sad doomed boy, whose only desire had been to see the world. In one way he got his wish.

And, along with other scholars and scientists who had been allowed safe passage out of Alamut, his advisor and my teacher, Nasir al-Din al-Tusi, became one of Hulegu Khan's close advisors! I understand that he is building a great astronomical observatory at Hulegu's new capital city. It was he who persuaded Rukn al-Din to surrender. I sometimes wonder if he mourns his Imam's fate, but I will never know.

Banjuu had become pregnant early that year and was delivered of a healthy, screaming daughter in late October. When Alexander was first allowed to hold her, tears came to his eyes. I think it was the first time he realized that he was now a man, with manly responsibilities—not that this kept him from his boyish ways particularly, but he did reveal a new tenderness toward his wife and child that took Banjuu and me by surprise.

The only problem that could have arisen from this birth was that Banjuu would not be able to attend Anna as she had, though Anna was enchanted with her new 'sister', who, to add to the confusion, was named Sofia after me. We must have been quite a sight that winter, all sitting together in the solar: Anna and me at our lessons, Banjuu nursing her curly-haired dark little daughter and singing some cradle song that had been buried in her own childhood and now came back to her when she needed it, and Alexander poking his head around the door every hour to see that all was well and insisting on holding his tiny Sofia as often as he was allowed.

And of course I did what I could for the orphanages in the city, mostly in the form of money and clothing. As a woman I was not really welcome to do more, and since there were far fewer girls than boys in the care of the monks, the caretakers seemed to feel no need for a feminine presence. I was allowed to adopt another pair of girls, but they were both so timid that I gave up trying to encourage them and simply sent them off to work in the kitchen. They seemed happy enough, especially since I gave them a pallet to share. It took them time to get accustomed to it rather than just lying down under a table or on the floor at random!

All in all it was a quiet year, though momentous in many ways that none of us yet realized. I was thirty, middle-aged, but time seemed to have stood still for me. I had one or two gray hairs now and my breasts were no longer so firm, but men still courted me and I still refused them if they grew overbold. Perhaps I did deserve the name of ice queen. I didn't care; my heart was sealed off from love.

It is still hard to explain how or why I kept waiting for Lord Joscelin long after I should have given up hope. Many a disappointed suitor did ask me why. To him I always made some vague excuse, but I had decided that in God's eyes my beloved and I were married and there was no more to think about it. If I learned that he truly had died, then I would be free to remarry, but until then I would stay faithful to him—or at least who I remembered him to be. And I still loved that memory man wholeheartedly: his tenderness to me, his bravery in battle despite his doubts about war, his way of seeing matters clearly, his kindness to my orphans. And his tender passion. I prayed daily to be reunited with him.

Helene brought another son into the world in November. And word reached Constantinople in mid-December that the Mongols were marching toward Baghdad, the capital of Sunni Islam, because the Caliph had refused to submit.

We all felt a general sense of unease, for Baghdad was much like Constantinople or even Kyiv: a symbol, even tarnished and shrunken, of greatness. No Muslims took it seriously as a center for trade or even for leadership, but it was still the center of Islam to the Sunni, and to think that the Mongols might capture and possibly ravage the city was almost unthinkable. Where might they turn next?

Christmas was celebrated in subdued fashion, as Basil was worried about our trade connections and I was simply worried about Mongols getting any closer.

The news reached us in March, along with horrific descriptions of slaughter and burning: Baghdad was indeed taken, and though Christians were spared—evidently Hulegu's wife was Nestorian—at least 90,000 people, almost the entire population, were thought to be killed. I tried not to think of the long lines of captives, the endless beheadings, the piles of corpses, but such images would intrude. And most of the city, which had been a glory of art and culture, was put to the torch, the Caliph was sewn into a sack and trampled to death by horses, and the wealth and knowledge of centuries were seized or destroyed. It was rumored that the Tigris River ran black with the ink of drowned books and dead scholars.

No one with any sense, not even Christians, could believe that such a disaster boded well for anyone, although there were some fools who celebrated in the streets, thinking that Islam would now crash into oblivion and that God had sent the Mongols as deliverers to the Christians. An irony, since the Christians in question were mostly heretics. Gossip said that emirs and sultans and even mayors of cities were streaming into the Mongol camps to pay homage in hopes of their lands being spared. Mongol troops were said to be spreading across Syria, toward Aleppo and Damascus and Egypt. Al-Mawsil was finally swallowed up.

And all the Muslim states, Sunni or Shi'a, truly were 'fainting with fear' now. I heard a story that one terrified ruler who had somehow offended Hulegu came to beg for mercy, presenting a pair of boots with his portrait painted on the soles so that wherever the khan walked, he would be treading on the man's head. Evidently Hulegu was amused and forgave him.

It felt strange to go about my business, to be teaching Anna and visiting my friends, to be writing in my journal, and always to have the same worry on my shoulders as when I had been a child of twelve and about to leave for this very city. My Papa could as little have imagined that Mongols might approach Constantinople as he could have imagined my being captured and enslaved by them while trying to flee. Whenever I thought of my father now, it was without the pangs I had once felt, but I still missed him, especially at times like this when I had no other man I trusted fully to turn to for comfort. How I longed to rest my head against some strong shoulder. Not even Maffeo could offer that.

Of course Basil often discussed various political possibilities before me. Winter blended into spring, Lady Day and 1258 arrived, and spring turned into summer, and many a dinner with him and Helene and our friends turned into debates about what we should do if the Mongols turned against the Greek states—it was known that Nicaea, for instance, was seeking an alliance with Hulegu Khan. This would affect our business, which was his main concern, but mine was that it would also pave the way for a combined Mongol and Nicaean attack on Constantinople. If those envoys to Cyprus knew about me, then Batu Khan must still want revenge and I would find no refuge in this city, either! Interestingly Maffeo Polo, who was often at table with us, thought the Mongols less of a threat than Nicaea by itself.

One warm night in May, he came back to his argument. "What is to keep the emperor from simply marching back in here someday? We know this city is bankrupt. King Baldwin cannot even pay his troops. I would worry more about them than the Mongols. Their armies are mostly far away. The Polo family is already establishing trade ties with Sarai, and now that Batu Khan is dead and Berke Khan has replaced him …"

I heard nothing more for several moments—my heart had nearly stopped with shock. Batu Khan was dead! I was free! I felt like leaping up and dancing on the table, but no one else knew or could understand what this news meant to me.

"Are you feeling faint, Sofia?" Helene asked, breaking my happy spell. "Pour her some more wine, Maffeo; she looks so pale!"

"Oh no, I am sorry, I just got lost in a thought. I am fine."

Maffeo looked at me closely after filling my goblet, and said, "Would you like us to turn to other, perhaps happier matters?"

"No, I am very interested in what you have to say. I believe you were speaking of Berke Khan just now."

"Yes, he is now Khan of the Golden Ordu, or Horde, as we say it. And rumor from the Crimea has it that Hulegu Khan has made a mortal enemy of him by destroying Baghdad."

"Why? Destroying it was customary Mongol practice."

"It's because Berke converted to Islam some time ago, and he feels that Hulegu committed the gravest of sins not only by destroying the city but also by killing the Caliph. I just heard this bit of news today, and it lends further strength to my argument. No doubt there will be civil war among the Mongols soon, which should keep them from our gates." He sat back, looking most satisfied with himself.

Basil grinned. "Well, there go your plans to travel east, Maffeo. You cannot have it both ways, you know." We all laughed, but I saw Maffeo's jaw set a little and wondered if my uncle might be wrong.

That evening was typical. Another time it was Sir Reynaud who held forth—Helene had learned not to invite him at the same time as Maffeo. In fact he mostly agreed with his Venetian rival, but where Maffeo saw trouble if Nicaea were to invade, Sir Reynaud saw liberation.

"I am half Greek, you know. I know it pains you to think of wars and invasions, Basil, for they can certainly be bad for your business unless you know how to use them as opportunities, but this is still a Greek city even after fifty years. You may find yourself glad to be from Rus' and not from a Frankish country, if—nay, when—the city is retaken. I think it's only a matter of time. And I will protect you, too, when that happens, for who knows if anyone with connections to Venice will be safe."

At that moment his eyes strayed to me. His intent was clear to me: my marrying him would seal an unspoken bargain to guard my family's interests. I took a sip of wine, trying to look unconcerned, but a chill swept over me. He smiled benignly around the table, taking no notice of the pall his words had cast on the party.

After Sir Reynaud left, Basil asked to speak with me in private. He spared no breath on idle chat. "Niece, surely you see what the man intends. I have forborne interfering in your life, but now floodwaters seem to be gathering. I beg of you: if he does ask you to marry him, say yes!"

"Well, he has not yet asked me, and tonight was the first sign in over a year that he feels any interest. Let us wait and see … Uncle."

But in succeeding days, Sir Reynaud seemed to be occupied with something besides marriage. He was ever courteous and gallant when we were together, with no trace of his former familiarity, but he was often in that sour, pensive mood I had learned to dread. Not that I had to endure much of it, since I made certain we met only when others were around. Perhaps he was offended. He was clever enough to see through my stratagem; and on top of the teasing he'd had to endure from Maffeo in the past, my latest withdrawal must be a clear message that I was not interested in marrying him, even to ensure my family's safety.

I hoped so. However much I enjoyed his company when he was in a good mood, and no matter that he had been so kind to me in important ways, I could not imagine being married to a man of such fickle moods. He was forever saying something sour or hasty, usually masked as jest. His cynical outlook had shaken me too often, and I wanted none of it. I knew he thought my loyalty to Lord Joscelin was misplaced since he had dropped perplexing and unpleasant hints from time to time, but he would never explain himself. As he had done when speaking of kings Louis and Baldwin, he had simply claimed he was sorry and that he of course respected both Joscelin and me and the love we shared. And then he had stopped speaking of Lord Joscelin at all when he saw it won him no favor.

❧ ⁓ ❧ ⁓ ❧ ⁓ ❧

There was one source of information in Constantinople that was mine alone: John of Epirus. We never saw each other in public; indeed, the one time I sent him an invitation to a feast at my home, he had graciously refused.

His reply had read in part, "We are from different worlds, Lady Sofia, and they do not mix. I think it would be better for us both if we continue to keep our connection hidden. I will always remain loyal to you, for you have treated well with me, and I am always glad to serve your needs."

In recent months with business thriving, I had felt little need of John's services, but with all the unease in the air I decided to write and ask him if he had any news. This must have been early fall, for I remember that the moist heat of summer had passed. His reply had little to say that affected my business concerns, but it did mention that a certain Nogai Khan had been raiding and plundering in Poland. I remembered that name; he was the khan guarding the borders between the Golden Horde and Western

Christendom. It was worrisome, though: did this mean that the Mongols intended a second invasion? Would they soon be at Constantinople's back, ready with some new threat to invade if we did not submit?

I read on and learned that Maffeo had been right. News trickling in from the Black Sea kingdoms was all about war and rumors of war. Berke Khan was indeed furious about the destruction of Baghdad, and rebellion was rife among the Georgians and Armenians against their Mongol over-lords. How Maffeo ever expected to travel east was a mystery to me, but that was not my problem.

Around that time a mad dog bit some poor vagrant in one of the aban-doned parks. He went mad, too, and attacked several people in a market place in the center of the city. I think he tried to bite one man, who struck him down but didn't want to get close enough to kill him outright. The fellow just lay there and screamed and foamed at the mouth, I was told, until he died in agony. There was a general outcry at Constantinople's sordid state, and I heard much more than I wanted to know when Sir Reynaud came to dinner at Basil's. I was there as a matter of course, as Basil always invited me; I think he was ever hopeful that I would allow my suitor to propose to me.

"I led the charge against the vermin, so to speak. Our knights had to hunt down and kill packs of wild dogs and stray cats and even smaller pests if we could snare them. It was not very knightly, I admit, but every-one has been afraid to go outside for fear of being bitten by a mad squirrel! And in the end we turned it into a little hunting adventure." He laughed as if to mock both human fear and animal disease, looked over at my dismay, had the grace to look rueful, and changed the subject. But there was more, I found out later.

I would never have heard about it from Sir Reynaud, but Alexander came to me one evening after supper. Banjuu and I had wondered if he had been exploring the city again—he had so little to do in my household that he often went wandering if his wife and daughter didn't need him. I had never seen him so shaken.

"I was at the market with Cook when we both saw something odd. He wanted to keep shopping, but I went to see what was going on. It looked like a jolly parade at first, with so many knights moving along the road, or at least a public execution, and those can be entertaining. But when I got closer, I saw that most of the people in the parade were helpless beggars and vagrants. King Baldwin's knights were forcing them to march toward the city walls, and Sir Reynaud was leading them. I followed them right out of the city, but most people turned away when they saw the motley procession. I doubt they realized what was happening, but something about it struck me as wrong, and perhaps they felt that way, too.

"I almost regret my nosiness now. As soon as they got far enough from the city walls, Sir Reynaud ordered his knights to herd their prisoners to the edge of a rocky cliff overlooking the water. Then they just hacked every one of them to death and let their bodies fall into the sea! I'm glad he never saw me because I doubt he'd want you to know, my Lady. I never saw such unholy joy written on a man's face before.

"It sickened me, for these poor folk were not criminals! Some of them were children or old men and women! Some were blind or halt, too. To think I was just like them until you rescued me from the streets. But I'm glad I can warn you against him. Perhaps he thought they would go mad and foam at the mouth, too, but I think there is something wrong with his heart or he could not take such pleasure in killing harmless people."

This horrifying story never came to light anywhere else, and I finally decided that those who knew what had happened had either not cared or were afraid to protest—or perhaps they approved. After all, the city was suddenly free from wild animals, there were no more madmen running wild, and most of the beggars who had made going to the market an exercise in tough-heartedness were gone. I imagined that many citizens rejoiced in their new security and never asked themselves how it came about.

For me it was different. First of all I did know, and Sir Reynaud sank so low in my esteem that it was hard for me to greet him with any composure after that. Ironic that it was he who had told me about all the homes for the ill and elderly that had once been supported by royal coffers, but I supposed he thought such idealism was a thing of the past. However, that hardly justified taking pleasure in hurting others.

Still, some good did come out of Alexander's revelation: I decided that since I could not help orphans, I would collect the remaining old and sick and halt and give them homes. It was easy enough to achieve. With so many empty buildings, I simply arranged through Basil to take possession of three in the old Genoese neighborhood. I furnished the homes simply and hired people to gather the needy to occupy them—so few now!—and to see to their wellbeing. Most of the people who ended up there were old and sometimes ill in mind or body, so there was little chance that they would recover. But some took heart and began to work around their new homes, planting vegetable gardens or doing simple repairs and so on. But in truth, while I was glad my project was a success, I had no interest in overseeing it. So I gave that responsibility to Alexander.

He was mightily pleased, as it turned out, and though he and Banjuu continued to live with me, he was gone for hours every day seeing to his wards. He once thanked me for letting him repay his debt of gratitude in such a way. I think he also enjoyed earning money of his own, for at Christmas he came to me with a request that he and Banjuu be allowed to set up their own household in another house they had found near 'his' homes.

"After all, I'm a husband and father now, not a little boy from the streets," he explained. I'll always be grateful to you, Lady, but I cannot feel like a man if I stay living under your roof. It has been a long time since I was truly one of your servants, or it would be different. I can afford to be independent. I hope you understand."

I did, and with a sadness that I didn't show, I agreed to his plan. At least it meant that one more house was being brought back into use rather than being allowed to fall apart. I had never understood why Constantinople's vagrants had not done as I had and simply taken them for themselves, but I suppose someone or other would have thrown them out as unworthy or dangerous or thieving.

ANNO DOMINI 1258-1260

Anna's tenth birthday fell just before Christmas. Though we of course celebrated her name day, this day was also special to me, and I wanted to observe it, too. She was growing into a young beauty, with long coltish legs and a gait to match, and a sense of fun that I had lost when too young. Her hair was red-gold, a blend of Lord Joscelin's and mine, but her green eyes were mine. So I held a little feast in her honor. For the first time, I allowed her to wear her hair crimped and perfumed like a lady's, and it curled most charmingly. She was surrounded by everyone she loved, and at her special request I even allowed her 'uncle' Sir Reynaud to join the festivities, although I used my duties as hostess as an excuse to avoid him. Alexander and Banjuu were there as guests, and Alexander glared at him every time the man wasn't looking. And I looked on with equal disfavor as Sir Reynaud took every opening to jest with Anna and tease her about becoming a woman soon. A chill swept over me. Anna was old enough to consider betrothals; did that make her old enough to think of in other ways? I shook off such dark thoughts. Alexander was leading a very silly parade around the feasting table where Banjuu awaited Anna with a crown of flowers she had made for the celebration, and my daughter called to me to join her.

As a Christmas boon, I completely furnished my young couple's new home, and they moved into it in January. I brought in a tutor who from then on took up Anna's mornings with lessons; I had reached the limit of what I could teach her. He was also given the task of making her into a lady who knew the courtesies and how to sing and dance and play the lute. Such skills had not been part of my upbringing, but they were clearly necessary in this society.

Banjuu visited us with her little Sofia many afternoons, partly to see how Anna was doing, and partly to let me adore my namesake. But with Anna's cousins and friends occupying most of her free time, it was often just as easy for other servants in my household to care for her—mostly to see her safely to the home of one of her friends or, when her friends visited in turn, to make sure that they did not all turn into wild things. Becoming ladies was not always a straightforward path.

Thus it was not as hard to let go of my last two special orphans as I had expected. And now that Anna had friends, I was freed from telling stories about my own childhood—she often forgot to ask—as in another two years I would be entering memory's most dangerous territory.

Losing Alexander and Banjuu was only one of many important changes, though. Worries gathered like storm clouds all through the year and into 1259—and for me, not only worries but also sorrows. I had been right about Prince Bohemund: his father-in-law King Hetoum had persuaded him to submit to the Mongols, and now Antioch was a subject state. This must have happened at the very beginning of 1260, because reports began filtering in by February that both King Hetoum and Prince Bohemund, along with other subject Christian princes and knights and even some Muslim princes, had joined the Mongol armies of one Noyan Kitbuqa and captured Aleppo in late January. Hetoum's reward was a share of the spoils, and I think Bohemund was similarly rewarded with the return of Muslim lands once held by his principality.

Such a bald statement does no justice to this news. It was the end of Maryam, I was certain, for Christians seem to regard it as their holy duty to slaughter Jews when they take a city. I know that many Muslims were killed while Christians were spared: Kitbuqa was Christian. So much for Mongol tolerance of all religions! Throughout that year I tried to find out what had happened to my friend, but it was impossible. The city was soon retaken by Syrian forces and taken back again by Mongols, not just once but over and over, with even more slaughter each time, until Aleppo was little more than a ruin topped by a damaged fortress. I felt sick at heart for months. Though I prayed for Maryam and Rakhel and my trading partners, that was all I could do.

I did learn late that year that many Jews were not killed after all, at least not by Kitbuqa's army. On his orders they were spared, as they had taken refuge in a synagogue. But I never heard from Maryam or any of my trading partners again. I still pray for them, although I suppose it is foolish and dangerous for me to reveal that these days.

Less important to me than the loss of my friends but of great joy to Basil, I lost my trade connections with the city. He had never liked my having my own contacts, especially when they were with Jews, not only because of his low opinions of them but because my connections allowed me to be independent. Now I was entirely dependent on him, and without saying much, he let me know how pleased he was.

Not that I suffered overmuch from loss of wealth, for when one source dries up, merchants always have a new one at the ready. Basil had already become active in the trade between Sarai, the Crimea, and Egypt, where the Mamluk dynasty was now firmly planted and where new boy slaves were always needed for the Egyptian armies. I would have no truck with that, though I may well have benefited from the trade, but I did take interest in my other dealings.

The galleys Basil and I had commissioned with our partners in Venice were now busy all around the Mediterranean, from Constantinople and Antioch to Tunis in northern Africa and the coasts of Spain, so I turned my attention to them. Thus did I discover something that Basil, his merchant friends, and even Maffeo had kept from me; either that or they took it for granted that I already knew. Venice and Genoa were—still are—at war, and we were not only supplying war materials to Venice but we also were most likely trading in slaves there, too. But when I confronted them together at a business meeting in Basil's office, they looked surprised that I would care.

"Well, our profits hardly suffer at all from the war if that's what worries you," Basil responded gruffly. "Our ships always sail under the protection of a Venetian armada. The Genoese try to harry them, but the naval power of Venice is and always will be too much for them. She has several large fleets afloat now that sail in convoys to protect the shipping routes and to capture enemy ships! Not to worry, Sofia!"

"Much good it does them, anyway," laughed Maffeo. "Other than forc-

ing our fleets to pursue them from time to time, they get no benefit at all.
Our ships make a little less profit, but they are rarely captured—we lost
only one in the last three years. We still reap good profits. Our agents
always find the best merchandise at the lowest cost to counterbalance our
expenses for self-defense, and we avoid dealing with middlemen as much
as possible. I think our ships are somewhat of a minor power of the seas."
Both men laughed in a way that made me wonder just what else those
ships were up to.

"Truly, Sofia, your interests are ours, and we take care of them!"

After that I had nothing more to say. Neither man understood my revulsion at slave trafficking or selling weapons, I suspected that our agents
had no scruples whatever, and I also knew my partners would continue
to keep the truth from me. None of our ships' captains would consider
piracy against Genoese shipping anything but an act of war. For all I
knew, they were carrying out raids against Genoese ports—this I found
out later was certainly true!

But I could do nothing. Once I had allowed Basil to take over my
enterprises while I had hid in Daphne, he had gotten his wish without
ever needing to establish official guardianship over me. Now that I was in
Constantinople and enjoying myself more than I had in years, if I wanted
to do anything about it I would have to exert myself in a different direction. I gave up and left everything to my partners.

And having set in motion every possible way of finding out about
Maryam, I turned back to what women were expected to do: overseeing
my household, patronizing my special causes, enjoying the pleasures of
parties and outings, reading my breviary, attending Mass several times
a week, writing in my journal, sewing and embroidering, and most im-
portantly, overseeing Anna's education. I tried not to feel too sad about
my friend as months went by with no word but of more war. Indeed, I
began to pray that she had died sooner rather than later; at least she'd have
avoided all the suffering that must attend all those battles and sieges.

Battles and sieges continued all through 1260. The combined Christian
and Mongol armies did not stop with Aleppo. In late April came the
news that Damascus had opened its gates to the invading armies rather
than suffer as Aleppo had. It was rumored that Noyan Kitbuqa entered
the city with King Hetoum on one side and Prince Bohemund on the
other! Among my friends and family, the opinion was that this alliance

of Christian princes with Mongol barbarians was a danger and a disgrace, for no one trusted a Mongol after Baghdad and Aleppo.

At one dinner with Basil's merchant friends, I learned one of their reasons for feeling the disgrace: one man exclaimed, "Have you heard that this Mongol general spared Jews?"

A babble of outraged talk arose, but though angry retorts rose in my throat like bile, I never allowed them to cross my lips. What use would my arguments be against centuries of ignorance and prejudice? I would be regarded as mad or a heretic, anyway.

"What is good, though," someone added, "is that that our Christian brethren celebrated Mass in the most important mosque in the city and seized or despoiled many other mosques, as is only just." Everyone agreed that this was indeed a great triumph. Well, the great mosque had once been a cathedral, so I could not fault that, but the rest of the damage seemed like dangerous provocation of the nearby Muslim states. Why did no one see that they were planting trouble for the future?

The talk turned elsewhere, to speaking ill of Prince Bohemund. Basil spoke for many when he complained that in exchange for his new lands, the Mongols had forced him to replace the Latin Archbishop with a Greek Patriarch. "I'll warrant that he'll be a pariah among the Catholic kings and princes for some time."

This turned out to be true, and I had to pity a man who worked so hard to protect his little counties. Why Kitbuqa had demanded such a thing was a mystery, especially since the khan was Nestorian—perhaps to stir up trouble. But I understood none of these politics, only that among the Franks the Mongols were finally coming to be seen as a more dangerous adversary than the Muslims; this despite the Mongols' repeated offers to ally with the Christian states against the Syrians and Egyptians. The only takers had been Hetoum and Bohemund. Better an enemy you know than one you don't, I supposed.

Summer drifted by. I spent too much of it avoiding Sir Reynaud as much as I could. I saw that he was not only puzzled but also wounded by my coldness to him, but I did not care.

It was early October when more unsettling news arrived. In early September the Egyptian Mamluks had signed a treaty with Acre—the tiny rump of the lost Kingdom of Jerusalem—that allowed them to pass through their territory in order to fight the Mongols. Indeed, the city leaders had even helped them with weapons and supplies.

The Mamluks' general was a blond, one-eyed Kipchak named Baibars who had helped defeat King Louis in Egypt. He had once been a slave in the Mongol camps and knew their tactics. To everyone's surprise his army fought and crushed Kitbuqa's forces in a great battle at somewhere called Ain Jalut in early September. Kitbuqa was captured and beheaded, but his last words were a threat: Hulegu Khan would return to avenge his death and destroy the Mamluks—and no doubt the other Christian states for aiding them!

On the heels of that came new reports: Damascus had been captured from the Mongols by the Mamluk armies within days of the battle and swallowed up by the growing Egyptian empire.

And what did this mean to me? Only that there would be more wars, battles, and innocents slaughtered, and that all this was creeping nearer to me and my loved ones. I no longer even knew why I thought anyone was innocent. Perhaps we were all so corrupt that we should every one of us be wiped from the face of the earth! Then I would look at Anna or Cecilia or Gilles or little Sofia, or I would think of any of the children I knew or had helped, and my heart rebelled at such hard thoughts.

A part of me did wonder what would have happened had King Louis allied with the Mongols a decade ago. Perhaps he'd have gotten the ruins of Jerusalem to rebuild, while his Mongol allies would have wiped out his Egyptian foes. But what good would have come of that, either, for who is to say that that would not have fed yet another war, and another? It would only have meant that Sir Joscelin and I would be married now and I would have that strong shoulder to lean on that I so desired.

It could not have been long after these events that I held a dinner for my uncle, Helene, and our fellow merchants and their wives. Maffeo Polo was there. He seemed to be in a pensive mood. The talk had come around to the latest news: the Mamluk general Baibars who had triumphed at Ain Jalut had likely had his own Sultan murdered. Certainly he was now Sultan of Egypt.

Maffeo suddenly surprised me—all of us—by saying, "I foresee no good coming of this for any Christian port, for Sultan Baibars hates us all and has since King Louis' war. This so-called treaty with Acre means nothing now that he seeks to expand his empire. I have no doubt that he casts his eyes up and down this coast.

"For that and other reasons, Niccolo and I plan to move to the Crimea soon to seek new markets for our Venetian wares. I see more profit to be made by entering into trade directly with Sarai now rather than continuing to trade along the coast. You never know when Acre or Tyre or some other port city of ours might be Baibars' next target. We already trade with the Golden Horde, and who knows? Niccolo and I may even," he smiled thinly at Basil, "reach the fabled Cathay. The threatened war between Berke and Hulegu has not begun, and I believe we can get far to the east before it starts—if it does."

Remembering how Papa had thought the same about my escaping Kyiv, I cried, "It's not a given that you can avoid such things, you know. It could be very dangerous! Are you certain you want to do this?"

"Indeed I do, Sofia. You know how long Sarai and Cathay have haunted my imagination, and life is always dangerous." I must have shown my unease and disappointment that he was leaving. "I will regret leaving you all, and especially you, my friends from Rus'." He didn't name me, but his eyes sought mine.

"Besides, I am sorry to add, I mistrust the future here. He looked around the table at all my family and friends. "I think you all should consider leaving the city for good. My agents tell me that it is only a matter of time before the Emperor of Nicaea finds a way to take Constantinople and restore Greek rule. I doubt that anyone from Venice will be safe, then.

"Indeed," and he turned to Basil, "I hope you too will heed my counsel, my friend, and remove your entire family to safety. You may be Rus', but you have too many ties to Venice. A better future awaits you in our little Republic of La Serenissima, and I can help by providing new contacts for you. Who knows how a victorious army will treat those who have had dealings with us? I would not want to find out."

After the meal, which ended early since most people had no heart to linger afterwards, Maffeo spoke again with Basil and me in private. "I am sorry I ruined your dinner. I know your daughter and her cousins will be unhappy since they were to perform for us—a lute duet and some singing, yes? Please offer them my regrets.

"But I saw an opening to warn people, and I took it. Many of the men at your table tonight, Sofia, need to be warned, likely several times, before they realize how urgent matters have become. You know how feeble Constantinople is, and Nicaea continues to seek alliances with both the Golden Horde and the Persian Mongols. If his overtures succeed, Emperor Michael Palaeologus might receive aid—meaning armies—from them. I have agents in Acre and other Christian cities across the Levant. They all agree that a serious crisis is brewing.

"One of my contacts, and I will reveal no more than that, has a spy planted with the Mamluks. This Baibars is an even more formidable foe as Sultan of Egypt than he was as a general. Years ago Mongols captured him in the Crimea and sold him to some Syrian lord. I don't know how he became a Mamluk, but he proved on the battlefield that he knows how to use Mongol tactics against them, and he is as ruthless as a tiger. He has vowed revenge on anyone who helped the Mongols before Ain Jalut, and that means that sooner or later Antioch will be imperiled. Indeed, I would hazard that he will try to take Acre, too, despite that treaty, for it lies on his path and must tempt him. At any rate, sooner or later these wars will reach the Mediterranean ports, and we merchants will be forced to find new markets, always a tricky business what with our war with Genoa in the Mediterranean.

"I know I am planning far ahead, but you should do the same. I am deadly serious, Basil: do not delay. You recall what happened to Kyiv. Imagine what the outcome could be here if Mongols help take this city—there will be carnage and nothing left standing!

"And you, Sofia, must persuade him." He bade us farewell, and Basil left with Helene and the disappointed children soon after, looking worried.

I do not know how the others fared that night, but I could not sleep. What should I—we—do? The thought of Antioch falling chilled me, even on this mild night. I had so many connections with the city: all my orphans and their caretakers, Matthew of Edessa, Leo and Bardas and their inn, even the monasteries that took in boys and trained them to produce illuminated manuscripts. I could bring my orphans to Constantinople, perhaps, but I could not see persuading anyone else to leave. And what if Maffeo was wrong, anyway? When I thought on it, what good would it do to take my orphans to a city that might well be under attack itself? I tossed and turned, unable to think of any solution.

And then I thought of my friends Anna and Adar al-Mas'udi, and their family. What would become of them?

I had not felt so utterly alone in a long time. My most trusted advisor was Maffeo himself. Right or wrong, he would be leaving within the month. To whom could I turn after he left?

I finally sat up and knelt before my bedroom shrine. My religion had become a thing of habit, really, and I so missed that feeling of love and even stillness that I had once enjoyed. I had been little more than a child then and full of hope, but so much of it had been destroyed in recent years. I crossed myself and prayed for a while and then just sat.

Well, in a world of war, why not practice a little peace so that it didn't disappear entirely? It seemed natural to follow my old friend Dorje's advice and let my mind meet what was before me. I cannot say I felt more peaceful exactly, or even loved or loving, but I did feel less entrapped by my hopes and fears. And since I could not sleep anyway, I sat in that way until the gray light of morning announced a new day.

◈ ～◉⁄◌ ◔◈◓ ～◌ ◉

That morning after my regular duties were completed, I went to my solar resolved at least to confirm what Maffeo had told us. I wrote three letters: to Adar al-Mas'udi, to Matthew of Edessa, and to John of Epirus. This last letter I sent by Golden Thomas, and he came back with a written reply that provided me less with answers than with even more questions.

Lady Sofia,

In answer to your question, I must, alas, agree with your other advisor. It would be best for you to leave Constantinople as soon as you can, along with your entire family. I cannot say more than that without compromising my sources. As to this business of what will happen with the Egyptians and with Antioch and other port cities, only Our Lord God knows. I can only suggest you let events unfold further before you decide what to do about your interests there.

However, I have some other information that I have wished to share with you for some time. Not knowing whether you might think I was meddling in matters close to your heart, I have refrained from saying anything. And it is not something I can confide in a letter. Since it is related to your questions about both Constantinople's future and yours, now I must come forward. Can we meet in a place where no one knows either of us? A chapel or church, perhaps.

Your servant,

John of Epirus

A strange mixture of gloom and anticipation swelled up. Such a letter coming on the heels of my other fears! I wrote back suggesting we meet at the palace of Botaneiates, a complex of buildings and churches that had once belonged to the Genoese, now mostly abandoned but for a little Benedictine monastic community. Within a day all had been arranged, and I went with a few guards to make offerings at the monastery. I entered the gloom of the empty church and knelt in a side chapel as if to pray before the patron saint of Genoa, George of Cappadocia—an irony, I know, to be praying in the enemy's church. John was already there.

After truly praying for guidance and crossing myself, I arose and John beckoned me to a stall that was completely enclosed. There we held a whispered conversation. Anyone not knowing us might have believed we were lovers at a tryst, what with our heads so close together. I could even smell the perfume in his hair as he spoke into my ear. He wasted no breath on courtesies, though.

"Lady, you must not marry Sir Reynaud."

I withdrew and looked at John in surprise. This was not what I had expected!

"Please listen. Now you can see why I hesitated to come forward, for I doubt you even guessed that I know him, much less that I know he has been, to many eyes, courting you in a lazy way for years. But a time draws nigh when he may finally press a proposal of marriage on you. No doubt he will bring many strong arguments to bear, among them the promise that you and your family will be safe under his protection."

"Yes, he already hinted as much to us all. After that I began avoiding him, and perhaps he cooled toward me as well. And you need not worry. Enough to say that I would never marry him."

"I hope you can stay that course." He paused thoughtfully. "Well, now that I am here, I will continue with my arguments if I may, even if you feel you have no need of them. After all, he continues to mingle in your circle, and he can be very … persuasive.

"He seeks to arm himself against the future. You are wealthy, and his wealth declines. You have only your orphans to care for, easily disposed of, and he has younger brothers who depend on him. He hopes to stay in Constantinople safely despite the fact that he not only serves the Frankish king but also helps to rob the city of its holy relics. And since he is no fool, he is said to see your wealth as a source of his safety: with it he could expand his private militia, one that he has been assembling for some time. It is rumored that he intends to put it at the service of Emperor Michael Palaeologus when he arrives. I know the emperor is gathering his own, much larger army, as well as support from Genoa, and that he's a skilled general. When he seeks to win back Constantinople—and he will succeed—he won't need help from Sir Reynaud!"

I made to speak, but John rushed ahead.

"Wait, Lady, there is more. Sir Reynaud would not be alone in hoping to marry wealth, especially when it is joined with beauty and goodness of heart. And I cannot paint his heart so black as to say I think it holds no feeling for you. But he has secrets, and they are dark." He paused as if searching for the right way to tell me. He took a deep breath and continued.

"I believe, along with many others, that he murdered his father. No doubt the man deserved it—he had just thrown his own wife down some stairs! I know only a little, and that was gleaned from other sources, both men whose word I trust, and I am in the business of trust.

"This much is certain: Sir Reynaud and his uncle brought the pair to Sampson Hospital, claiming that the two had lost their balance at the top of some stairs, that one tried to save the other, but that both had fallen. This story was a thin disguise for what had really happened, and only a man of his uncle's excellent reputation could have hoped it would convince anyone. The lady's neck was broken, yes, but there were bruises old and new—many of them—all over her body. These came to light when it was washed for burial. Such a discovery could not be hushed up, and the talk spread."

"Do you mean Sir Reynaud's uncle the surgeon?"

"Yes!"

I shuddered, thinking of that frail old man, so dedicated to helping others. What a terrible secret to carry in his heart all this time.

"But there is more. Sir Henri's bruises were all new, and the dent in his skull was not from any fall! Everyone said that while his uncle wept wildly, Sir Reynaud shed not a tear; he only looked black with rage.

Then the whispers from the family servants began to spread. All agreed that the eldest son had taken revenge for years of suffering. Beatings are common enough, and every man beats his wife and children a little, for how else can he stay master? But Sir Henri went too far.

"This much good I do know about Sir Reynaud: he worshipped his mother. She was known throughout the city for her gentleness, her piety, and her good deeds. Please understand that I am not blaming him for taking revenge, however ill—or at least rash—it might seem to some eyes.

"But the aftermath was that Sir Reynaud developed a taste for violence. He put it to good use in serving King Baldwin, whose service he entered shortly after this happened, but it does not stop there. His temper is like dry weeds before lightning strikes, ready to burst into flames and consume him and whoever or whatever is nearby. I think his brothers have suffered from it. I know his servants have, and one ended up dead. He now takes pleasure in hurting others, no matter how he tries to hide behind his public love for beauty and art and history.

"And he has secret tastes. More than that I will not say, for I cannot prove these other things I hear whispered about him, although I suppose I could if you wish." I shook my head. "Fair enough. You see why I hesitated to tell you all this. So long as I knew you were offering Sir Reynaud no opening, I saw no reason to say anything, but I think it will not be long before he does propose marriage and in a way that makes you fear refusing him. Please, for the sake of your orphans as well as yourself, do not let him into your life!"

I tried to offer John payment for his information, but he refused it. "This is a gift of friendship, not merely a spy's paid whisperings in secret," he gently chided me. I thanked him, and we parted one at a time without drawing any attention to ourselves.

It took a few weeks to hear back from Matthew of Edessa and Adar. Neither of them could offer anything but their own worries. Anna added a note to Adar's letter. She too had heard about Aleppo; she too was grieved. She wrote, "I am so glad now that I had made peace with Maryam before all these invasions began. Sofia, will we never be free from these terrible Mongols? I can only offer thanks to Allah the Compassionate that you no longer need fear Batu Khan. That was the one good piece of news…." And so on.

She added that her husband was thinking of where they would go if the Mongols advanced toward Antioch, which he had no doubt they would do sooner or later. Their defeat at Baibars' hands meant nothing to him, since General Kitbuqa's forces had been so small. Adar and many of his fellow Muslims were certain that Hulegu would return at any time with much larger forces and try to destroy all Islam.

This I could not credit, considering that the Mongols rest their boot heels on many subject Muslim states already. The only submission they want is to their empire, and many khans are now Muslim, including Berke Khan, who is after all both a grandson of Chinggis and master of the Golden Horde. Berke was already threatening war with his cousin Hulegu over the destruction of Baghdad.

It seemed most ironic that Mongol power was now divided because they had gotten embroiled in the conflict between Islam and Christianity.

The only good to be seen in all this was that more sticks were falling out of the bundle, as my old friend Dorje would have said.

ANNO DOMINI 1261-1262

In late 1260 I decided to follow the Polo brothers' example and leave Constantinople. We had shared a sad parting when they left for the Crimea; it was unlikely that I would ever see them again. I had spent hours with Maffeo the day before they left, sharing as much about the Mongols as I thought would be useful, mostly courtesies of form and speech and, of course, not to touch the threshold of a ger! And for the next month, at every Mass I especially prayed for their success on their journey.

I persuaded Basil to move his household to Venice, too. Maffeo's final words to us had been a plea to leave. "I once boasted about our naval might, my friends, but our fleets cannot be everywhere at once. One day this city will be retaken.

"Well, enough said. Farewell, Lady Sofia. May you find happiness with your husband when he returns…." I had blushed and nodded, tears in my eyes.

The most immediate reason to leave, however, was Sir Reynaud. One morning in late January, he arrived at my house without warning, accompanied by several armed knights instead of his usual retinue. He insisted on seeing me.

I glanced out the solar window onto the courtyard when a servant brought me this news. Perhaps it was only because of what I now knew about him, but I felt uneasy about the way those men hovered in the courtyard. Usually he brought only a few attendants who would head for the kitchen to get something hot to drink on a chill day such as this. But these bold looking men stood outside the door into the hall as if on guard.

I met Sir Reynaud in the main hall, having told my own guards and menservants to stay close at hand and having sent one out a side door to call on Basil for a few of his guards. I tried not to let my disquiet show, however, when I greeted my unwanted guest as courteously as I could, seated him in the chair of honor, and placed myself on a bench just far away enough from him that it would not offend. Having called for dried fruits and wine mixed with water as a further gesture of hospitality and exchanged a few meaningless pleasantries, I could ask with some calm, "And to what do I owe this surprise visit?"

He looked at me keenly. "I hear that you think to leave Constantinople, Lady Sofia. And with not one word to me, your oldest and most fervent admirer? I am wounded to the quick!" He tried to smile. "I know I have somehow offended you. That has been clear for months. But to cut me out of your counsels entirely in such an important matter as this seems most unkind, most unlike you."

"I am sorry for any hurt I caused you, Sir Reynaud. But Maffeo Polo has agents all over the Levant. There is much you may not know, or perhaps you do." The knight's expression revealed only impatience. "At any rate he has learned much that alarms him and affects us all. He has persuaded my entire family to leave. He had no thought for his own gain."

Sir Reynaud flushed as if I had insulted him, which perhaps I had. Sometimes truthful words slip out awry. Trying to soften them, I added, "I don't mean to imply that you....

"Also, I thought my uncle had told you. Besides, my thoughts are only now being formed; nothing firm has been decided."

Sir Reynaud looked as if a weight had lifted from his heart, but mine sank. In seeking merely to be well mannered, I had opened the wrong door.

"In that case, setting aside whatever your merchant friend has told you," he said contemptuously, "there is time for you to consider my offer. I know it would be in best form for me to approach your uncle first, or perhaps I should say again, but having learned to doubt your heart, I come to you instead with my own heart a-tremble." I held up my hands to ward off his words, but he plunged ahead.

"Sofia, you cannot be unaware of my love and esteem for you. Many a time I have wished to press my suit, but honor held me back. I respected your hopes—your hopeless dreams as I saw them—that you and Sir Joscelin would be reunited someday. But it's been years with no word from him. Your daughter has almost grown to womanhood without a father. Her bastardy," here my mouth fell open in astonishment, "has never been a hindrance to my regard for you both.

"Oh, did you think I didn't know?" He could not suppress the self-satisfied look that slipped across his face. "I assure you I have guarded your secret ever since I learned it, even laughed off gossip about your widowhood, your betrothal, and above all, her suspect birth. Your secret has been safe with me. We all have them, and yours is, so to speak, born entirely from love."

"I don't know what makes you think such gossip is true—"

"Basil let something slip a few months ago. When I questioned him closely, he denied it, but he also eagerly encouraged me to seek your hand in marriage. It was shortly before the Polo brothers left, and my guess is that he straightaway realized you now had only one serious suitor, one who could help him and preserve your good name."

At that moment I could have wrung my uncle's neck!

"I see. Well, I thank you for your tact, Sir Reynaud, both now and in the past. But you must see that this is the reason I cannot marry until I have proof that Lord Joscelin is dead. My heart says he is not. As Aristotle says, 'Love is a single soul inhabiting two bodies,' and so it is with us. I love Sir Joscelin still. And only Anna's true father can free her of the taint of being born outside wedlock."

"Does that matter so much to you, that she be freed from 'taint' in this sinful world? Bastardy is not as uncommon as you think, especially among the nobility." He paused thoughtfully. "Of course, it has always been different for men than for women, but since no one knows about Anna … at least for now…."

I stiffened. "What do you mean?"

"Only this, my dear heart: that I now formally seek your hand in marriage. I am no fool. I know you have doubts, perhaps have heard gossip about me—ah, I see from your face that I have hit the mark—but I will make you an admirable husband, one who will protect your interests and guard your wellbeing with all the power at my disposal. Why rip your life here apart on the chance that Nicaea or some other petty Greek kingdom might seize Constantinople? Even if it does, you'll be safe with me, for in addition to being half Greek, I have a plan that will ensure I am still welcome here!

"As to your attachment to Sir Joscelin, I think it is time for you to know the full truth about him." I had no idea how to react to this bold statement. Sir Reynaud drew out the moment by pouring himself some more wine and speaking thoughtfully.

"I knew him well for several weeks. We became fast friends in a short time because we shared two great loves: of brawls and of women. While I was there, many a night we got drunk together and found a fight. Many a morning found us in some bawd's bed—and once it was both of us at the same time on her! Or one of us and two of them apiece, it never really mattered. Such secrets never stay buried forever, and many know his; he is not held as high in others' esteem as he is in yours!

"To be fair I must add that he was grievously unhappy, and he seemed careless of his life or what he did with it. I, on the other hand, conducted myself voluptuously solely for pleasure. I doubt he told you any of this, so am I not the more honest with the woman I hope to take to wife? All such youthful wild behavior is now long past for me, but who knows about him—if he even lives? And henceforth I want you and you only in my bed, nor will I ever stray from you once we marry."

I stood. "I have heard enough, Sir Reynaud. Please go now. Such revelations make me ill. They reveal a small spirit in you that confirms I am right in refusing you."

Sir Reynaud's face went white, then red. He stood, too. "You think to dismiss me so easily? I have shown you I know your worst secret, shown you what a loose-living man your so-called beloved really is, confessed my own follies, and still you try to dismiss me out of hand? It won't do, Sofia. I have the power to destroy your reputation! You have no choice but to marry me or be ruined among your friends here."

"All the more reason to leave Constantinople, then! Again I say, please go!"

In answer, Sir Reynaud strode to me, seized me in his arms, and forced a kiss on me, his tongue almost thrust down my throat and one hand tearing at my gown!

"Stop! Help!" I cried as soon as he let go a little.

"Shut up and enjoy yourself," he muttered. He tried to kiss me again and I struggled so mightily that my gown ripped at the back and fell off my shoulders.

That seemed to drive him to frenzy, for he threw me down to the floor would have fallen on me had I not screamed so loudly that he jumped back. Seeing my horror and fear threw him from blind lust into blind rage, for instead of continuing his rape, he began screaming obscenities at me while he seized and hurled everything at me that came to hand: books, a candlestick that missed by a hair, and the jug of wine, which drenched me in sticky, blood-red sweetness.

I screamed again as loudly as I could, and three of my servants rushed into the room, threw him to the floor, and pinned him down. He was shouting curses at them, calling to his knights to come to his aid, but one of my servants had prudently barred the front door. I heard Basil's men arriving, and outside came shouts and the clash and scrape of sword on sword.

"Enough!" I cried. "Pick Sir Reynaud up and escort him and his other men out. They are none of them welcome here anymore."

My men marched him to the door. When they opened it, Basil's and Sir Reynaud's men were hard at it with fists and knives. I shouted loud enough to deafen the angels, "Stop! Enough!" Everyone was so startled that they froze in place. Luckily no one was badly hurt, and Sir Reynaud stalked off with his men, livid and shaking but in control of himself again. There were no farewells.

Nor did I ever see or hear directly from him again. To this day, though, I pity him, another sad, twisted soul so burdened with dark secrets that they overtook all his good qualities. My own sins seem small in comparison. At least he had never been as demented as Qabul, or so I still hope for the sake of what was good in him: his love for his mother, his city, and his kindnesses to me. Even though his murders of those innocents were unforgivable, they surely came from some warped notion of protecting his city. And I still cannot believe he meant only to use me.

At least his revelations explained his early attempts at familiarity with me. Had he mistaken me for some kind of harlot? If what he said about his capers with Sir Joscelin was true—even if it was not—perhaps he had thought to share me, too. I can only offer thanks that I would never have married him.

His misconduct to me was what convinced Basil that we all should leave Constantinople. It took only a few days for ugly rumors to spread in that small world, although I doubt Sir Reynaud's reputation gained anything by his foul mouthing to our mutual friends. When his friends taxed Basil with the story, now swollen with lies in which my orphanages were entirely peopled by my bastards, he made certain that they also knew how he had violated my hospitality, attacked me, and been thrown from my home by our combined guards.

He always ended my defense with, "And can you believe anything such a man says? No, his story is a patchwork of deceit to cover his own filthy behavior. He wanted her wealth, and when she refused his offer of marriage he tried to rape her! Had she not mistrusted his good intentions and called for my aid before admitting him to her house, he might have done it and thereby forced her to marry him. Now he seeks to destroy her reputation out of simple spite. Who will you believe: a man who sells the city's soul or a virtuous woman who supports orphans and the elderly and ill?"

Thus he managed to avoid the question of Anna's bastardy—and redeem himself in my eyes, for I was enraged with him at first for revealing my secret to anyone. I had taxed him mightily after Sir Reynaud's attack, and I'm sure his vigorous defense arose from guilt as much as self interest.

For once I was not sorry to see Anna fall ill with a cold so that she was kept from her friends for two weeks, long enough for the scandal to wither away. Happily for me, some other juicy rumor quickly replaced it. She never gave any sign of hearing about me from her friends before we left, for which I thanked God.

But I was left with new doubts about my beloved. Had Sir Reynaud thought to estrange me from Sir Joscelin by lying about him, or was there some truth to his so-called confessions? My beloved had never made a secret of his brawling as a youth and of his passionate nature. But the kind of lasciviousness Sir Reynaud spoke of seemed beyond belief.

I felt sick at heart. What if I was waiting for someone as wanting in … I knew not what … as Sir Reynaud was? Argamon and Batu Khan both seemed simple in their demands compared to Sir Reynaud's mad romps. Was I an innocent or overly proper? Not according to Caterina's priest with his long list of carnal sins. But at heart, beyond sin or excess, I only knew I didn't want to think about Lord Joscelin holding anyone in his arms but me.

And recalling his tenderness and loyalty and bravery, not to mention the high esteem his king felt for him, I decided I simply must maintain my faith in him until he was proven to be either dead or too much a stranger for me to continue loving him. The latter possibility was almost as chilling as the former, for it compromised not only my future but also Anna's.

A falsehood spread as truth is a cancer that can multiply and stick and rot. And told again and again to others, it spreads further until everyone believes the deceit while truth lies bleeding and forgotten. This was clear from the cold reception I was receiving at people's homes, for Sir Reynaud had embroidered his spiteful stories about me in the wickedest way.

At least Helene was a good friend to me during that time. She knew how wounding the gossip was, and she claimed to be glad to abandon such a poisoned atmosphere even though she was leaving her home and the many friends she had made there. It was a hard time for her to be dealing with such a move, for she was growing big with her next child.

We left a few days before Lady Day, as delay could be bad for her health. The unhappy feelings Sir Reynaud had caused, the packing, the sad farewells to the friends who refused to leave the city and who kept their faith with me, the especially sad farewells to Alexander and Banjuu and little Sofia, and the journey to Venice in winter all added to my sense of not merely loss but of impending doom, a feeling I could not shake off for the first week or so. We scarcely welcomed 1261, as we were already far from land and there was no priest to offer Mass. It took almost two months to reach Venice's lagoon because we had to stop so often at islands to wait out storms. Even Anna, my fearless sailor, did not much enjoy this journey.

We tottered ashore to lashings of rain and wind so heavy that all of us who could ran to the cover of the nearest porticos. It was a cold, miserable gondola ride to the Greek fondaco, and much of our baggage did not arrive until the next day. How strange it seemed to have no Banjuu or Alexander—no Marguerite!—to help us, but at least Fotis and Irene and Golden Thomas were still with us, among our other servants. All were all well trained, and soon they had us settled into our rooms. The next step would be to find a home.

This I left to Basil. For several days we were virtual prisoners of the weather, for a high tide combined with the nasty storm turned the lowest parts of the city into swamps. And this was not even the worst of storms: our host at the inn assured me that it was not a true Acqua Alta, as the Venetians call them. Those bring terrible flooding to the islands—the last time, some twenty years earlier, the water had risen higher than a man, he said, and entire villages on the little islands were swept away. He had been a boy, but he remembered it all too clearly.

But then the sun came out, and the city seemed to open her arms in welcome. Anna was enchanted to be back in Venice and eager to sample all its pleasures—excepting the sugarplum that had made her sick last time. That Sunday we returned to the Cathedral of St. Mark for Mass. By happy accident, we met the eldest Polo brother, his wife Agnesina, and his little nephew and namesake Marco. As we left, having accepted an offer to dine with them the next night, Anna caught sight of three new columns placed near the Doge's ceremonial entrance to the church.

"Where do those square pillars and that odd short red one come from? And look at that: four men clustered together like they want to kiss each other. Are those all from Constantinople, too?"

Marco the Elder laughed. "The four men are—they are a group of Roman emperors—tetrarchs—offering each other the embrace of peace, and we proudly keep them here in safety. But the pillars are all new prizes from Acre: the square ones are columns of St. John. One of our war fleets won a great battle in the harbor there and seized them from the Genoese. And may it teach them a lesson—they think to rival us, but that is absurd. We have the strongest navy on earth!"

"Beware of hubris, husband," his wife cautioned.

Happily, the topic of war did not arise when we all met the next day for dinner. It was a jolly party with several more guests invited, too much food and drink, and it ended with music and spur-of-the-moment dancing. Since Agnesina disliked dancing because of her gout, I danced with her husband. We both enjoyed it so much that we became quite friendly in a short time. It was pleasant to be admired safely by an older man, as by unspoken agreement we set limits: no lighthearted banter that could cause problems later ever crossed my lips, and he was far too serious and devout to even think of insulting his wife by offering me idle flattery!

I spent time with her, too, recalling everything I could about her brothers-in-law's doings in Constantinople. She was most grateful, as little Marco had never met his father. Now she could tell him more about Niccolo, for letters from either Polo brother were rare.

By mid-May we were settled into our new lives. No ugly rumors followed us there, and the sweet spring acted as a balm to my spirit. Happy friendships sprang up so easily, beginning with the Polo family—one visit led to another and to new acquaintances. And I had a good friend already in Beatrice Falieri, who straightaway adopted both Helene and me and brought us into her circle of friends.

Basil and Helene and I had decided to settle together, and he had found a newly built Ca' right on the Grand Canal. It was much like the Greek fondaco where we had been staying, though it boasted not only an entrance from the water but also a grand façade on the opposite courtyard wall facing a street that led to the local church and market. The Ca' had first floor and mezzanino rooms below ours partly for storage and partly for other families to rent. These became our servants' quarters, and the large courtyard offered an outdoor set of stairs leading up to the main halls. One of these halls was quite large, with fancifully painted walls. Other rooms on that floor were for our bedrooms and private sitting areas, and some even boasted fireplaces. The topmost story was a rooftop loggia, which turned out to be most refreshing during the sultry summer months that were creeping up on us.

Basil and Helene and I set about furnishing the main hall with not one but three master chairs; with many beautifully carved chests, benches, barrel chairs, and tables that could be set up for dining; and with tall candle sconces. We ladies saw to it that all was artfully arranged around the room. We also decorated our more private rooms with great canopied and curtained feather beds, carven chests, rich window curtains, and more, including the few pieces of embroidery I had managed to salvage from Daphne after the earthquake. There was room to spare for everyone and everything, while the garden and orchard in the yard were perfect for lively children.

Helene's next child was born in June, another boy whom she named Claudio. What a collection of names her children had: to name every child, some of whom I am sorry to say died in childhood, would be to burden my story. She loved—loves—them all, and I love them, too, even the ones I will never meet.

A new life, a fresh start. I could only rarely keep in touch with my people in the Levant, but at least there seemed to be no immediate threat against Antioch. The various wars scarcely seemed to touch us in that city of beauty and light and gaiety. I continued doing as I had done before, but with a lighter heart: opening another orphanage and a home for the elderly and ill and finding more manuscripts from Constantinople to copy and sell, some scholarly and some more humble, like the famous Tale of the Two-blooded Border Lord. Even though there is too much war in it for my taste, the poetry is elegant and reminds me a little of the Lay of Igor's Host, my beloved Rus' epic.

I even found time for quiet evenings with Anna, who still loved my stories and once again insisted on her monthly allotment.

And a few books I gave away later to a very great man, of whom I will now write.

In early July he came to Venice briefly to oversee the setting-up of a new monastic school for Dominican monks. I lack the details. He was a doctor of sorts—of the soul—named Friar Thomas Aquinas, and he was and is known as one of the greatest philosophers and theologians of the century. On this rare visit, I had the good fortune to meet him at the home of a merchant whose entire family loved books and learning just as I did. We were not seated near each other—such a thing in the presence of his great chastity and almost aversion of women was not to be—but I did overhear some of his conversation. It was conducted in Latin, happily, and seemed to me to make much sense. Too many theologians seem to despise God's world and His creatures, but he spoke differently. I remember him saying, "How can we find our way to Him except by honoring what He has provided for us: our senses?" If the man's girth was anything to go by, he did not despise the sense of taste!

He spoke with feeling of Aristotle and the great influence this ancient genius was having on his thought. It came as a surprise to me that the friar and his fellow scholars knew much about Plato and even Socrates but not about Plato's great pupil. Clearly Friar Thomas found Aristotle's philosophy a refreshing challenge to current thought, though he thought his translations were tainted by dualism: he knew them only in Arabic translations.

I asked a neighbor who replied with surprise, "Well, some Greek philosophy was never lost to western scholars—I think Plato—but until recently, Aristotle's works were."

I thought for a moment about the whims of fate and time. While uncountable treasures of classical Greek writings had been destroyed in Constantinople in 1204, I owned several manuscripts of Aristotle's works in Greek as well as a few by other greats like Plato and Pythagoras and the great historian Diogenes Laërtius. Some of these texts John of Epirus had found for me, hidden in the city by those who did not despise learning as most Franks seemed to, some came from Nicaea or even Trebizond, and some had been sent to me by Adar al-Mas'udi.

A brilliant thought struck me: I could have copies made for this special man and send them to him!

The evening came to a sudden halt, however, when Doctor, or as he preferred, Friar Thomas stopped in the middle of a sentence. His face became suffused with joy, and he sat immobile for such a long time that his host gently removed his knife from his grip for fear it might fall onto his other hand and slice it! And when the spell or ecstasy was over, the saintly man only said, "I regret it very much, but I must leave you. An inspired line of thought has come to me, and I must not lose it." Everyone hastily stood, and the friar departed to a waiting gondola, escorted by his puzzled host. Soon we all offered our goodbyes and I left with my escort, Marco Polo the Elder.

My courteous companion, whose wife hated going anywhere, had soon become my virtual guardian—and adviser as well. Happily, his wife liked me and even encouraged this arrangement. I had become a sort of aunt to their ward, Marco Polo the Younger, who was a charming blend of both parents and a sad reminder of Niccolo's lost Juliana. And whenever Marco the Elder received letters from the traveling brothers, which was rare, he shared the news with me. Thus I knew that they had reached the city of Soldaia in the Crimea and were considering traveling eastward to a city I knew of from my slave days, called Bokhara.

The next morning I made arrangements for all of my copies of Aristotle to be copied by a reliable scribe and his apprentices. It had to be done quickly, for I had no idea how long Friar Thomas would be staying. And later that week after Mass, my scholarly friend who had hosted the great man was able to approach the Friar and offer him the manuscripts on my behalf. I stood some distance away, hoping he might acknowledge me, and so he did. Indeed, he even came up and gave me his blessing for what he described as a most wonderful gift.

In parting he added, "I will send them to my faithful translator William, as I speak no Greek. I hope to find fresh inspiration in these writings."

I felt absurdly pleased. And I saw him again one morning when I had gone to the cathedral to pray before my favorite statue of Holy Mother Mary. He happened to be at prayer there, too, and we left at the same time.

He actually remembered me and stopped to speak to me, a most gracious gesture for one who had neither interest in nor respect for women in general. "I saw you praying before the Blessed Virgin. Is she your patron?"

"Yes, I confide in her as if to my own mother, who was lost to me when I was very young. And I ask her to watch over those I love, though some of them may no longer even live. How she must have loved her son! I feel that love coming from God through her sometimes, and it always gives me new courage."

"Well spoken, daughter. I know few women who were born into our faith who are as devout as you are, yet I hear you are a convert. Very good, very good." I blushed, he blessed me, and we parted company. As a way of expressing my appreciation, I arranged for the rest of my collection to be copied and sent to him as each was completed. Before he departed a few weeks later, I received back a very kind letter of thanks from one of his attendant monks.

With such happy events, most of them much more worldly, I almost forgot my empty, cobwebbed heart.

Over the next few months, what with overseeing all my projects small and large and ensuring that Anna's education was proceeding apace, I discovered I was actually enjoying myself much more than I ever had in sad, mutilated Constantinople. Helene and I explored the city together whenever she felt up to walking. She seemed always to be pregnant or recovering from her latest birthing, and it was quite a project to get her out of the house, what with all the servants and guards she insisted on taking. She preferred our little garden.

But once she had overcome her sluggishness, we both liked the quiet gondola rides, the lovely rippling reflections of elegant buildings, the sense of serenity that would steal over us, and even the sweet smelling little posies we buried our noses in. On occasion I could persuade her to explore some small quarter of the city that could only be reached by pontoon or wooden bridges. It was so quiet away from the city's hub. There were many districts, considering how small Venice is, and I think we saw them all. We would often stop to rest and pray in some local chapel, which was always adorned with lovely fittings, mosaics, and statuary.

There I sometimes heard that strange music with its achingly lovely harmonies; prayer went on night and day. I had learned it was called Gregorian chanting. Sometimes I would lose myself in the music, remembering earlier quiet times when I had ridden out with Q'ing-ling into the quiet forest in Hungary. The feeling of peace felt just the same.

During the hot, sultry summer we all delighted in outings to some cooler spot, perhaps on one of the islands that dotted the lagoon or in a woodland glade on the mainland. I had mostly mastered Veneziano and begun to learn Italian. I kept abreast as best I could with my interests in Antioch and was thinking of making the long journey to see to them next spring after the seas settled down—I'd had enough of storms aboard a ship—but this plan never came to fruition.

One morning in early autumn, Anna and I were out walking with our servants. I loved going to the Piazza San Marco and the Piazzetta, partly because they were so large; in general, large spaces were not something Venice could boast. I caught sight of two somehow-familiar faces across the Piazzetta, but they were walking briskly toward a crowd that was gathering to witness an execution between the two pillars—no gambling that day. They disappeared behind a knot of people while I hurried Anna past the grim parade of soldiers and prisoners. I had never understood why it was entertaining to watch someone die horribly. But those young men's faces haunted me. Where had I seen them before? I thought on it off and on for the rest of the day, teased by some lost memory, but to no avail.

And that night, for the first time in years, I had a dream.

Alas, it was in tatters by the time I awoke, but one thing I did remember: Anna's spirit friends Sheep and Blade were sitting with one of the youths I had glimpsed. Anna's spirit friends must be a clue to something lost to my waking memory.

The next morning I stopped her on impulse as she was about to leave for the schoolroom with Gilles and Cecilia—Cecilia's last year, as she was now betrothed to a wealthy merchant whose eye she had caught at church. Anna had been teasing Gilles about something but she turned back, a laugh on her lips.

"Anna, you may wonder why I ask this, but do you still see your spirit friends?"

She looked surprised. "Not since we left Constantinople. I said good-bye to them at the docks as we left. They said they wouldn't be welcome in my new world. Oh, and my ghost father ... yes, I remember! There was one summer when he appeared to me often in Daphne, but I've seen nothing of him since then. He said he would send his men for us. But playing with spirits is for babies, anyway."

I kissed her on her forehead—when had she grown so tall?—and sent her on her way. And then I sat down and thought about my dream, but when I tried to reenter it, it dissolved like mist, leaving me feeling like I was sitting on a nail-studded Mongol saddle again, unable to rest until I had divined who they were and how I knew them. I gave up and went about my day.

After hours of mild unease, it came to me while I wasn't thinking about it. It was not Sheep and Blade but Anna's ghost father that provided the missing link. One of the young men had been but a youth when I last saw him, someone I had only met for a few hours: Philippe, Lord Joscelin's new squire. And the other was Lord Joscelin's other squire, Hugh! I had never seen them together, never even wondered where Hugh had gone, and them being together was as much what had confused me as their being years older.

My heart almost stopped, and tears sprang to my eyes. I thanked Almighty God, Christ our Savior, Holy Mother Mary, and all the saints in one breath. I would somehow find them both; and with any luck at all, they would either lead me to my beloved or confirm his death. Either way, I would finally be free.

Of course such a search is easy to put into motion but not to finish swiftly. I began by telling Helene. We straightaway sent Golden Thomas and Fotis to inquire at every inn and fondaco in the city. After an endless-to-me hunt of two days, including to outlying areas, they returned with the disappointing news that there were no Frankish knights to be found, and no young men named Hugh or Philippe. They must be staying in a private home.

Or else they were not who I thought they were.

The next morning I awoke wondering what I could do next: encamp between the Piazza San Marco and the Piazzetta and hover about until one of them, perhaps even Lord Joscelin himself, walked past? I could scarcely wish for another execution to draw them out. But what if they or perhaps Lord Joscelin himself were on the point of leaving or had already left? I fairly wrung my hands with frustration, paced back and forth for the entire morning, and finally went to my uncle. His resources were greater than mine, his connections of longer standing, and he of all people would want my unmarried state resolved one way or another. He had once even admitted that my loyalty must forgive much in my choice.

I found Basil checking some stored goods on the ground floor of our Ca'. He listened thoughtfully, a frown on his face, and looked at me intently. "Niece, I will gladly join your search. While I've never thought you wise in remaining faithful to a ghost," I almost shivered when he used Anna's word, "thus it is. Truly, I would see your heart at rest."

After several moments' thought, he said, "I wonder: were these men even wearing Lord Joscelin's colors?"

I searched my memory carefully, grateful that knightly colors were so bold and easy to recognize. Sir Joscelin's shield lying in a corner of the room at Castle Sa'amar where he had lain ill: its colors had been red and blue diagonal bands with a lion and a fleur-de-lis above and a little castle below. "Yes, both men were—red and blue bands on a slant!"

"So it is likely that they are who you think and that they are still your lord's men. That is a good start. The next question is where they might be staying and where this pair would be going when you saw him."

"They seemed in no hurry, and I took it as granted that they were there to witness the execution, but I suppose they might be on an errand for Lord Joscelin...."

"Perhaps they were just stopping there on their way to somewhere else ... like the docks! Sofia, when you want to know what ships have arrived the day before, you go to the docks to reach the customhouse. Might your Lord Joscelin be sending his men to ask after you or your ships?"

"Well, it's unlikely, for how would he know I have any? But at least that gives us a place to start looking."

"And I, in the meantime, will set inquiries into motion among my contacts.

"As well, have you thought of the hospitals scattered around the city? Some are run by monastic orders like the Benedictines, but at least one is funded by the city. And then there are some small ones funded by confraternities that have just twelve beds, one for each apostle."

It would have been easy to abandon such an enormous project, but instead I felt new hope. That very day I sent out Thomas once more, first to the customs house at the wharf, and then to the public hospital. I reasoned that if my beloved were here, he might be ill or poor or both. In mid-afternoon Thomas returned from his errand with a little good news.

"The customs master remembered just such a pair of men. They were asking after ships that might be sailing to Antioch or Constantinople soon, as their master wished to send letters to each city with a reliable captain. But he had no idea where they might be staying. And then I went to the Benedictine hospital, but there was no one like Lord Joscelin there now, though he might have stayed there once. I gave a monk the description you gave me, and he said it sounds like the same man, though older. But he left a month ago after recovering from a fever." It was little enough, but I felt a swell of hope. Was it too much of a miracle that Lord Joscelin had been here all this time, or that he might still be?

"Lady, I would like to go out again to search. Perhaps your Lord Joscelin removed to a different hospital or to a private home. Think it no trial. All of us who serve you want you to find him. I came to you after he left, but that makes me all the more eager to see the man you waited for all these years."

I assented, and Thomas departed on his own quest. And after thinking on what to do next, I wrote a letter and sealed it, addressing it to the two young men and their master. This I sent by another servant to the customs master, along with a silver grosso, which was valuable enough to ensure it would reach their hands. I told him to promise the customs man another one once it was delivered.

There was nothing more to do that day but wait for what would unfold. I scarcely slept that night.

The next morning Thomas left to look in yet another part of the city. But I felt too impatient to wait, so Helene sent Fotis back to the docks to see if those two men had returned to the customhouse and received the letter. I then went to work with Anna on her lessons. He soon returned, so excited and breathless and clearly upset that he could barely speak.

"Calm down, Fotis," I said, trying to sound calm, "take your time." In truth I was almost beside myself with anxiety, fearing that Lord Joscelin had died or left, but when Fotis could talk, his news was not about him.

Finally, he said, "Constantinople is fallen, Lady Sofia! A ship arrived this morning with the news. There was such a crowd that I could not get close to the docks. All I know is that it is in the hands of the Nicaeans and that most Venetians fled with nothing but the clothes on their backs and that some starved to death and others were lost at sea. This ship came on to bring the news. No one has any idea what kind of revenge is being taken against those who remain, but houses and storage sheds and wharves were set ablaze, and women and children were left standing in the streets weeping and terrified." Fotis burst into tears, and all thought of Lord Joscelin vanished.

Helene and Irene had come into the room and heard most of this, and Irene started to cry, too. She and her brother put their arms around each other, but Helene shooed them out of the room, saying, "Go cry elsewhere."

I heard them outside the door, Irene weeping, "Lost children, just like we were!"

I was aghast. No one had expected this quite so soon. I crossed myself and prayed for them all, especially the women and children, for why would they be spared?

"Mama," Anna cried, "is this why you wanted us to leave? One of my friends told me it was because you were a bad woman. I pinched her and told her I would never speak to her again, and then I sent her home."

"Really? You never told me this before."

"Well, you were gone out at the time, and I didn't believe her anyway. But what does this news mean? You can tell me. I'm old enough now, almost eleven."

"As yet, no one knows, but I fear for many of our friends in Constantinople."

She came up to me and put her arms around my waist. "I'm afraid, too. I don't like all this fighting. Why should it be this way? Why doesn't God stop it all?"

I stroked her hair. "I don't know, my darling. I don't know."

Helene left the room to tell Basil, tears on her own cheeks. Outside, shouts and weeping seemed to spread like a flood. I decided that the best thing would be simply to await further news. "I think we should try to continue our tasks. It will help settle our minds."

Helene and Cecelia soon joined us in what I still thought of as the solar. "Basil and his eldest son left for the docks to find out more, so we will soon hear exactly what happened," she announced.

There was nothing else to do but to try to behave as if all was normal. But we were too uneasy to do much—our needlework kept falling from our hands, and none of the children could think straight enough to follow their lessons.

The thing about Venice is that there is little noise of comings and goings. The most you are likely to hear is gondola rowers calling greetings or warnings to each other. With no clatter or whinny of horses, there is often no way to hear when someone comes to your home. And because Venice is a safe city, there is little need for more than a guard or two at your doors. So when we heard noise out in the courtyard, we all thought it was Basil returned from his mission. Cecelia looked out the window to see and said, "No, it is not Father. There are strangers down below."

Helene nodded. "No doubt Basil has sent a messenger to tell us what is happening. I'd not be surprised if he comes home quite late. There will no doubt be meetings with his—your—partners to decide what to do." She had glanced at me while speaking. "Sofia, would you go downstairs to learn the news? I'm happier to stay here with my little ones and Nurse."

Hope and fear played on every face, even our children's, for they had all left many friends behind in that faraway city. Down I went to the main hall, trailed by Anna and Gilles and Cecilia and her brother Paolo; they were as eager to hear what was happening as I was. But when we arrived, no one was there. I went to the main door and looked out. On the stairs leading up to it, our guards stood uncertainly. One saw me and came up to me. "Strangers, Lady, seeking admittance. But with Master Basil gone…."

"Well, unless they offer you some threat, let whoever it is up. They may have news."

I went back into the hall and stood, surrounded by young ones. A tall, graying-haired stranger resembling my lost Papa entered first, Hugh and Philippe behind him. He stopped as if turned to stone and cried, "Sofia!"

I beheld a ghost: the ghost of Lord Joscelin.

Had young Gilles and Paolo not rushed forward to support me, I might have fallen. Lord Joscelin rushed forward and took me in his arms, set me down on the nearest chest, and knelt beside me, tears streaming down his cheeks. Anna tried to push him aside to get to me, but when he looked up at her, she gasped and stepped back.

After I had taken a deep breath and my sight had cleared, I stood, as did he. Neither of us could move for an eternity. We just stared at each other. How haggard he looked. His beard was gray, his hair was streaked with white, and his gray eyes seemed much more deeply set in their sockets. An unfamiliar scar ran down his left cheek. But it was still he.

A kind of madness seized me. I slapped him as hard as I could, burst into tears, and fell into his arms. "Never, never, never leave me again, do you hear? Never!"

After a stunned moment, he slowly wrapped his arms around me and held me and let me weep, murmuring nothings into my hair. At last we stood apart.

"Come this way to a more private hall, my lord. Anna, you come as well. Everyone else, go to your mother upstairs. Tell her that Lord Joscelin is found. She will want to welcome him, but tell her to give us time alone first. And see to his men's needs: food and drink." I nodded to Hugh and Philippe, one no longer so young and the other now fully grown.

With eyes as round as wheels, the young ones all clattered back up the stairs while I led Lord Joscelin and Anna into a side hall. I used the short time to gather my thoughts as best I could. My beloved, for so he still was, led me to another chest and sat down beside me.

Anna stood before us, staring at him. "You are the ghost I saw," she said.

Lord Joscelin stared back and then looked a question at me. "This is your daughter, Anna. And Anna, this is Lord Joscelin of Braissac, your father."

He looked at his daughter gravely. "I used to pray to the angel I saw hovering over your mother's shoulder. That must have been you. I asked her to protect your mother and shower my love on her, especially when— but there will be time now for each of us to share our memories."

A rumble of voices on the stairs and the door was thrust open. There stood Basil looking confused, a little angry. "Who is this?" he demanded.

"Uncle Basil, may I present Lord Joscelin, who has somehow found me."

My beloved rose and offered a courtly bow that Basil did not return. "Found her, did you? And about time! My servants have wasted the past two days looking for you, and you appear right in the midst of a crisis!

"Well," he said in a softer voice, looking at our tear-streaked faces, it is a happy day for you, Sofia. The rest can wait." And he strode forward and clapped Lord Joscelin on the back. All is forgiven and forgotten, is it? I hope so; we should arrange the wedding as soon as possible and finally remove the taint of Anna's bastardy."

Basil's unguarded tongue was too much. I shouted, "Do you see who is in the room with us? Get out and leave us alone!"

Anna looked stricken and, when he saw her, so did my uncle.

"I am sorry, Sofia. I never meant to cause harm ..."

"Then listen to Sofia and leave," said Lord Joscelin sternly. "She is and has always been the wife of my heart! And Anna is my daughter, dear to me from the moment she was conceived." And he drew Anna into the circle of his embrace.

It was a glorious moment for me: the three of us united, finally, as a family, facing one who had never really forgiven me for bearing a child out of wedlock.

Helene appeared at the door and, seeing Lord Joscelin and Anna and me, burst into tears and held out her hands in welcome. "At last! I knew you would come someday!" I almost laughed after all the attempts she had made to get me married to someone else.

"Lady Helene, what are you doing here?" Lord Joscelin looked as dazed as if a falling branch had struck him.

"I—I am remarried ... to Sofia's uncle, Basil Petrovich."

"Please, Basil and Helene," I cried, "leave us alone for now. We can sort out everyone's stories later."

Basil turned red with irritation and Helene blushed. "Of course, Sofia. Come, Basil, she is right. Give them a chance to be together. We are not needed right now, and I want to find out what you've learned about Constantinople!"

Lord Joscelin looked surprised and Basil made some growling protests, but Helene took his arm and he allowed himself to be led from the room.

My beloved turned back to me. "For days we have been trying to find a galley to send a letter to you in Constantinople. That is how I got yours

201 ♣ Rebecca Hazell

early this morning. And now I hear cries and wails that it has fallen, and I can only thank our Merciful Lord that I found you at last, here and out of danger!"

I nodded and tried to gather my thoughts. "I have so many questions. Did you ever receive any of my other letters? And where did you disappear to? After that disaster of a campaign, I searched for you in Acre, in Antioch, among all the ports of Outremer, in Constantinople. I even approached King Louis and Queen Marguerite in Acre—"

"Wait! One question at a time, please! And I have my own for you, my love. But first of all, please let me look at my beautiful daughter. Anna? Is that your name?" He offered his hand to her.

But Anna, still looking stricken, had backed away from both of us when he had released her. "Stay away from me!" she shouted. "You made my mother into a whore! I'm not an orphan; I am a bastard just like my friend said!"

She looked at me. "And you betrayed me, Mama!" Sobs poured from her chest like water from a burst dam. "You are a bad woman!"

My heart threatened to rip open, but now was not the time. "Oh, Anna, my dearest, don't listen to Basil. He has a hurtful tongue. He doesn't understand. And soon your father and I will make everything all right with the Church and with anyone who dares try to hurt you. My only aim was always to protect you from slander and lies."

I reached out to her, but she eluded me and ran from the room. My happy reunion collapsed into nightmare.

"Please, I must see to her."

I ran after my daughter and called to her before she could run upstairs. "Anna, stop it and come here! That is an order!" She heard the steel in my voice, the voice that I had rarely used with her but which she knew to obey. She unwillingly turned back and came to me.

"Shame on you! Never ever speak to me like that again!" She hung her head, tears still streaming down her cheeks. In a softer tone, I added, "You know that any other mother would strike her daughter for such words, but I will not. I know that to find your father in this way is as much a shock to you as it is to me, so I forgive you. Basil should have his cruel, foolish tongue cut out!" Anna looked up at me in shock, for I had never said anything so harsh in her hearing about anyone, ever.

"Oh, I don't mean it, but everything is happening at once," and I burst into tears, too. We wrapped our arms around each other and wept for who knows how long. After what must have seemed an eternity to him, Lord Joscelin opened the door. I looked over and saw puzzlement written on his face.

"Come back with me, Anna, and let us sort through things together. I want only for you and your father to love each other as much as I love both of you, and it won't happen with us standing out here with servants spying on us."

I turned toward a slightly open door. "Don't think I don't see you there!" A flurry of movement, and our discomfited servants fled.

I took Anna's hand and, smiling through my tears at my beloved, led her back into the room. "Let us begin again. Anna, I ask you to rejoice with me, for at last here is your father, who must share some deep bond with you if you were able to see each other when I could only worry. Lord Joscelin, I think you are right: this is the angel who came to comfort me when I stood in peril of losing everything else that mattered to me." And I took his hand and put hers in it.

He looked down at her gravely and said, "I would never hurt your mother or you. I have braved many dangers to find you both, though I never knew that you were part of what I sought. Daughter, I swear on everything that is holy never to let harm come your way again as long as I am able to defend you and your mother."

Anna looked up at him in mingled hope and disbelief. "How can you make such a promise after being gone all my life? What if you go away again?"

"That will not happen if I have anything to say about it," I laughed shakily. And Lord Joscelin put one arm around me and another around Anna.

For the first time, outer noises intruded on our ears. From the streets and alleys and canals came shouts, weeping, curses and oaths, running feet, church bells pealing, the cry repeated endlessly, "Constantinople has fallen!"

I looked up at Lord Joscelin. "What happened? Do you know?"

"I know only that Constantinople is in the hands of the Nicaeans— whether by battle or stratagem I cannot say."

"Well, Basil may know more, but right now I have no desire to speak to him about anything! I want to hear about you and learn the answers to my many questions, more than I can ask in one day."

Lord Joscelin snorted. "Constantinople fallen: what an irony, and on this of all days! I would have sent letters there for nothing.

"Well, let us start with the question of how I found you. In fact, you found me. My squire Philippe came to the docks early this morning, as he or Hugh have done daily for the past few weeks, to see if they could find a ship to carry us or at least my letters to Constantinople or Antioch so that I could once again look for you. Beyond that, I had written letters to send to every other place I thought you might be, and was trying to send them with any reliable captain willing to take them. Instead, Philippe found your letter waiting for us. He hastened back to me, I read it and learned where you were staying, and I rushed out to find you. I have been ill, Sofia, and I am still recovering at a Ca' I leased.

"After all the endless fighting, the imprisonments, all the other trials I have undergone, and the misery of never hearing from you, to have you here where I never dreamed of finding you is nothing short of a miracle. I swear by Saint Christopher to build a rest house for travelers here in Venice to thank him for carrying us safely to each other."

His arm trembled around us, his tears mingled with ours as he kissed our cheeks, our hair. Ann looked up at him with a strange expression— perhaps awe that he was there and doubt that he could be.

A guilty-looking servant knocked timidly on the door and, after I admitted him, asked if we were joining the rest of the family for dinner. It seemed that only a few moments had passed. After looking at each other and without needing to speak, we wiped our tears, smiled, and repaired to the main hall. Everything was laid out, and Basil, Helene, and the elder children were waiting, trying not to look too curious or eager. It was a quiet repast, with many covert glances shooting along the table from all directions—especially from Basil—toward Lord Joscelin. I scarcely heeded them. My beloved was back, and my heart was too full for me to eat more than a few bites. I did not want to miss a single moment of having him beside me.

Anna, too, seemed just as eager to take in every detail of his person. And he had changed, but not in essence: his features were still strongly modeled, his eyes serious and, it seemed, an even deeper gray as they took in each of us in turn. He seemed well enough dressed, but the hollows in his cheeks and that new scar bespoke many sufferings.

Finally Basil spoke. "Sofia and Anna, I did you both wrong. Please forgive my over-hasty words. I promise to make them up to you. Lord Joscelin, I wonder if we might speak privately later, perhaps after this meal."

Joscelin gravely nodded. "Yes, sometime today, but first my wife and daughter need me. Perhaps we could wait until tonight?"

Helene spoke. "I too would like a chance to speak with you … about Lord Gilles, and what you might know about his last months of life, how he—" She could say no more, just sat looking teary-eyed and sad. She cast such a glance of guilt and woe at me that it came to me: even now she felt blameworthy for having remarried. After all, I had kept my loyalty to my beloved alive, never married when I could have, and I had been obligated by nothing but love.

"That, too," my beloved said.

Another silence fell. He cleared his throat. "I think I should share most of my story now, for clearly everyone wants to hear it." We all nodded, even the other children, who seemed agog at the fact that this stranger had claimed their cousin-aunt as his wife. Unless Helene had told them something, which would be against my express wish, they knew little or nothing about my life and Anna's birth.

"As you all know, I was a member of King Louis' expedition to rescue Jerusalem." The boys' eyes straightaway lit up with excitement. Holy war! Bravery! Heroism! Stirring images must be crossing their young minds. "Things went awry from almost the beginning. I do not know if you received any of my letters, Sofia …"

"I received seven letters, and I have them still, much worn and cherished."

"I wrote you two dozen or more, knowing they might miscarry, and some I never sent, not knowing how to find you."

"So you have been looking for me, too!"

"Indeed I have."

"I wrote a reply to your first three, but then there was nothing. The others I received were together. The last one was from Acre, and by the time I got it I was sure you would be by my side within days. I waited for you to come to me. That was ten years ago, and then you never—and I—but now I must hear your story from beginning to end!"

He looked at me with such dismay that he could not muster words at first. "Praise God you waited. When I first saw Anna, I thought at first that you had married another man, and I was crushed!

"Well, there was more than one reason for my disappearance, including pirates—but I will speak of everything in its place. First, I must tell you a little about the war and my part in it, for it explains much of what happened later."

"Yes," cried Basil's sons, far more eager for tales of battle and bravery and even pirates than I was.

But suddenly I felt almost unbearably happy. I had been right about pirates—which meant that in truth I had never truly lost touch with my beloved. Now all I needed was for him to clear himself of the sins others had laid at his door, and everything I had lost would be restored to me; everything, that is, but youth.

Joscelin looked at the boys with amused cynicism. "By now you must all know the outlines of that disaster." Everyone nodded. "I will spare the ladies the worst particulars. Perhaps I can tell you men another time. Suffice it to say that our armies suffered as much from bad strategy as from heat stroke, bad water, bad food, Greek fire, and plague as it ever did from battle. I wrote to you, Sofia, about the king's younger brother Robert of Artois, his poor judgment and his absurd influence over King Louis. Did you receive that letter?"

"Yes."

"Well, he led us all to ruin. There was a secret ford revealed to us—"

"Yes," cried Helene, my husband's last letter spoke of it!"

"Ah. Well, Count Robert and his men, along with Templar knights, were entrusted with crossing that ford and surprising the enemy. Which they did: they charged into the enemy camp and killed the Egyptian general in his bath." The boys laughed aloud at this while the girls blushed and twittered like sparrows.

"But Robert disobeyed his brother's—his king's!—orders to wait for the main army to arrive. He and his army pursued the fleeing Egyptians into Mansourah, expecting to kill and despoil. Instead, everyone in the city defended themselves from the balconies above. Worse, elite troops called Mamluks were stationed there, and once the alarm was raised, they attacked, killing almost all of our knights and fatally weakening the rest of our army. Had I fought in that battle, I would be dead, and for nothing but the ruin of my beloved king!" The girls fell silent, the men and boys looked horrified.

"After the rout at Mansourah, we won two great battles, but it was not enough. Two Saracen armies entrapped us between them. We were hopelessly outnumbered. I now see that when you are defending your native soil, you have the will to fight all the harder. When faith in God—and we must credit the Saracens with that—meets love of what is yours, He raises your arm with double strength. So it was with them. So we were doubly outnumbered, for we had only faith in God. Our chivalrous hearts counted for little."

I looked over at the men and boys. All were as rapt as if a spell had been laid on them, while I merely felt sick at the thought of such waste of life, such terrible suffering, and for what? For some idea that still made no sense me!

"So there we were, trapped in our camps and awaiting supplies and relief that never came, when plague struck. It was mostly caused by the terrible heat and the decay in our water—it was tainted by corpses of slain soldiers, but men still ate whatever they could fish from it and even drank the water. I lost my young pages and my squire that way, Sofia, to my everlasting regret. They got so thirsty one day that without my knowing they went down to the river and drank their fill, only to die in agony."

I shuddered, tears filled my eyes, and I could say nothing.

"My king was sorely stricken by dysentery, but I was among those who were spared the worst of it, for I at least ordered my men to boil what little water we had, just as my old friend Adar al-Mas'udi had taught me to do—and those of my servitors who obeyed me never fell ill with dysentery. I wish I could have persuaded King Louis to do the same, but his physician was set against it. And despite his own illness, the king was always going through the camps to speak to the sick and dying, to offer them solace and comfort. It did not aid his recovery.

"I often went with him, though I was unwell from bad food or lack of it, and I will always remember how he never lost either faith or kindness during that dark time...."

He stopped speaking aloud to follow some memory. And I thought of my last meeting with the king. He might be a kind man and brave, but he was still, to my eyes, blinded by his fixed ideas.

"We finally tried to retreat to Damietta by both land and river. Despite our entreaties, King Louis refused to board a galley, though he was gravely ill. He preferred to suffer just as his men did, and he was among the last to leave, though he could scarcely stay on his horse. Lord Gilles and I were nearby but not with him, and it was then that hails of Saracen arrows struck down my friend of so many years. He had lost his shield, and I was not quick enough. I was wounded, too, but not badly.

"Lady Helene, I tried to carry Gilles out with me, but his wounds were mortal, and … I will say no more. He died with Christ in his heart, and now he rests in Paradise, for that is guaranteed by his sacrifice." Helene burst into tears. Basil and young Gilles looked most serious, but it was I who went to her and put my arms around her. She clung to me and sobbed until she regained control of herself. Finally I returned to my seat and Joscelin continued.

"By that I was separated from my king. Only Marshal Geoffrey of Sargines was with him at the last, and I did not see where he took him. I was sore pressed to escape at all, but Hugh and Philippe and I fought our way back to the retreating troops, looking for the king. Everywhere was slaughter and carnage.

"The next day we received word that Lord Geoffrey had taken him to a village where a Frankish couple living there took him in, so there our reduced forces went to help guard him with our bodies and lives. But Hugh and Philippe I sent on to Damietta, disguised in Bedouin clothing, for I saw no reason for them to die, too. I hoped they would be able to get word to you, Sofia. They and a few others escaped under cover of night. I had given them the last of my supplies and monies, as I had no hope for myself. And at least something might yet have been saved and the king liberated, for our little army banded around the village to protect him, and there were envoys and talk of a truce. By then I was one of those waiting by our king's side, unsure whether he would live another hour but determined to fight to the death for him.

"Alas, somewhere in the ranks, some fool of a sergeant called out in panic that the king had ordered us to surrender. Weapons fell, men were taken, some killed on the spot.

"We who were with the king were all seized and bound with him and treated most roughly, excepting the king. They brought us to the new sultan, who did not know whether to kill us or ransom us. Again my king showed what a valiant and honorable man he is, for he refused to make any false promises when asked about ransom; he would only pay what monies were his, and that only with his queen's consent. In the end the sultan accepted the return of Damietta and a huge ransom that he forgave part of, since he was so impressed with King Louis' dignity.

"However, all still nearly came to naught, for after we were taken down to the sultan's camp on galleys and were waiting to see what would come next, a great stir arose in the camp. We saw many soldiers take horse for Damietta and thought it had already fallen to the Egyptians, but soon all became clear: the sultan's men were being lured away by a ruse, for his tents were invaded, a wooden tower that was part of his quarters was assailed and set on fire, and he was slain by his own men before our eyes when he fled, bleeding, right into the river!

"One of the murderers cut out the slain sultan's heart and brought it to King Louis where he stood on the galley watching all these horrors. The man's hand was dripping with his own sovereign's blood, and he asked the king what he would pay for the heart of his enemy! I was on a different boat from my king, but the dragoman who was with us and who had been translating for us was listening and told us everything he could hear. King Louis just stood there in grim silence, and finally the man went away still clutching his bloody relic.

"Now it seemed that the rebels might kill us after all and that we would soon be in Paradise together, for straightaway the boats filled with Saracens.

"However, instead of beheading us as we expected, they shoved us into the galley's hold where we spent a miserable and hopeless night. But with a new day came unexpected hope: the troops had raised a new sultan, and he sent for us all and assured our king that the previous sultan was the culprit of much mischief and never trustworthy. The same ransom agreement was made, and after much pain and hardship that I will leave out, at last we were sent down to Damietta. There, as you may know, good Queen Marguerite herself counted out the first ransom monies before she took ship for Acre.

"Also in Damietta, to my great surprise I found Hugh and Philippe waiting for me with supplies, of which there were few left in the city. What a terrible scene—too many had to be left behind, including the wives and children of the dead soldiers, and all the wounded—but we three were put in one of the queen's galleys and through God's grace arrived in Acre not too long after she did. I will always be as beholden to her as I am to my king!

"But when King Louis arrived in Acre, he was, alas, still far from well, and so was I. I lingered on there for more days than I could count, seeking to serve him when I could and trying to regain my own strength. All my remaining wealth soon disappeared, so I sent Philippe to Braissac with letters seeking enough monies to travel again. Then I prayed and waited. It would take months for him to return. I also sent enquiries to Rome to learn whether my first marriage had been annulled. And I wrote several more letters to you." Basil shifted at that moment. I glanced over at him and saw him flush. It came to me: he—or perhaps Caterina—had never given me some of those early letters!

"When you did not reply, Sofia, my heart was wrung with anguish, for I refused to believe you were dead. I could only pray you had not abandoned me for some other man and that your silence only meant that my letters had gone astray. It was a stormier year than usual, and shipwrecks were all too common." I looked up at him and shook my head, unable to speak.

"Meanwhile, I had to borrow from the Templars to survive. By the time Philippe returned, I was a familiar face to their clerks, and much of the wealth he brought me was already owed! I paid all my debts, and then I decided I could wait no more. So I went to my king and begged to be released to seek you out. With his permission and blessings, I wrote you that I was coming. To think that was over ten years ago! I knew I could come to you with a clean heart, Sofia, for not only was the marriage annulled but Ysabel had taken the veil." I took his hand and held it against my cheek.

He paused, looking down at me for so long and with such love that the others finally shifted and Basil murmured in impatience. Lord Joscelin lifted his eyes and gazed around at his host and hostess in turn. "Believe me, had I known what Sofia was suffering, I'd have left Acre straightaway, no matter what, and likely we would have been reunited long ago. But hindsight is always the clearest sight. And I accept all blame for causing her harm—though I can hardly regret the result!" He smiled at Anna, who blushed and looked down.

Basil made a kind of growl of approval. "I see you are as fair-spoken a knight as my niece said. Do continue."

My beloved nodded. "So, along with a few other knights, my men and I took ship on a Genoese vessel bound for Limassol and then Constantinople. It was early autumn by then, and we expected no trouble since we were with a convoy of ships. Instead, a violent storm blew our flotilla apart. Once the winds died down, our galley was lost and becalmed in the middle of the sea. Our captain decided we should try to go east—something about the clouds. His oarsmen rowed manfully, and soon thereafter the wind did pick up and we did sight what we thought was an island.

"But fate was against us. That island was more clouds. They brought another storm that tossed our ship about like a child's toy, and the ship foundered. Most of those aboard drowned, but after floating for hours clinging to wreckage, Hugh and Philippe and I, along with a few others, were cast ashore on what we took for an island. We were barely alive by then, but a few fisher folk found us the next day when they came out to collect whatever spoils were left from the shipwreck and to dispose of corpses. Us they took in and nursed back to health.

"For weeks I was too ill to even ask where we were—I had broken ribs and my Egyptian fever returned, so I was the last to recover—but when I did, I had to laugh. We were not on an island at all. We were only a few miles from the Latin city of Beyrout. I had little left to offer but my last silver coins to our hosts—an old man and his wife who had agreed to take us in—but at least I could offer them thanks in Arabic, which was pleasing to their ears. I am still amazed that they didn't simply kill us outright, but they were good people and good Muslims, uninterested in war and killing.

"It was spring of 1251 before we left. Someone in the village took us to the city, and once again I had to borrow monies from the Templars and once again wait, for Hugh this time, to travel to Braissac to raise further monies. So I sent you one more letter, praying that this time I might receive a reply. I even dreamt in my heart that you would magically find me in Beyrout! But again I got no answer.

"Hugh finally returned with news that my mother demanded my return, for my little barony was struggling mightily and there was little more to wring from it. I had to make a hard decision: I must return home. I owed that to my patrimony and to my mother and brothers and sisters.

"And so I did. It must have been the right decision because for once nothing stood in my way other than the passage of time. We found a ship bound for Venice, arrived after a quiet crossing, found another galley that took us to Marseilles, and from there I went home.

"But I still sought you, Sofia, if only from afar. I sent Hugh to find you, but …Well, Sir Hugh, you can tell this part of things."

Hugh, who had been more interested in his meal than the story, blushed and paused before beginning. "You seemed to have disappeared, Lady Sofia. I went first to Constantinople and asked around at the docks for your uncle. I called him Vasily the Rus', so that took time to sort out, and then it took awhile to find out where he lived. But," he turned to Basil, "when I went there, you were not at home. Your guards refused to tell me anything, though from something one of them let slip, it was clear that Lady Sofia had been there at one time and that there was some ill will toward some of her servants."

Basil and I exchanged grim smiles, but by now all had been forgiven. Why spoil the evening with our old grudges? I did recognize the irony, though: it would seem that Leo's spiced wine had been both the means of my rescue and the partial cause of my long separation from my beloved!

"I tried to trace you around the city, thinking you might have set up a separate household, but no one seemed to have heard of you. From there I set out for Antioch, but again, no one knew anything about you. I of course asked after you at your orphanage, but no one knew, or at least would say, where you were now living. The usual caretakers were not there or surely they'd have known me. The youth in charge seemed most suspicious of me when I said I had sought you in Constantinople, was surly and rude, and gave me dark looks. He even warned me not to return or there would be trouble!

"I also looked for Lady Helene, but she too had vanished. So my lord's plan to have me escort you back to Braissac came to naught, and I had to return to him with only disappointment to report."

Had Hugh been mistaken for a henchman of Basil's sent to find me? Good God, I myself had made it impossible for Joscelin to follow my trail!

Joscelin picked up the story's thread again. "Once I had returned home, there was no hope of leaving anytime soon. My mother was overwhelmed, and my family needed me. There was simply too much to do: turn off a scoundrel of a bailiff and find a trustworthy man and younger, more reliable stewards; repair our castle, which was falling into ruin; find new, dependable tenants for the farmlands that had been allowed to fall into disuse; see to it that the fields were drained, dams and channels were brought back into use; even buy new livestock. I also had to scrape together dowries for two of my sisters and then see them married. It took more than four years, each an eternity, before I could leave. Ironically, had you been there, Sofia, my life would have been a joy, for working on my own demesne spoke to me in a way that war, even for my beloved king, never has.

"Well, never mind. At first I wrote you every month, but once Hugh returned with no news, I had no idea where to send my letters. I kept them, though, and they await you back in Braissac.

"It was early in 1256 when I finally left. I was determined to track you down. I took only Philippe, leaving Hugh to be a strong arm for Braissac. We arrived in Marseilles and took passage in a convoy of Genoese vessels. We got as far as the Port of Hadrian on the Italian peninsula and were headed into the Mediterranean when Venetian war ships attacked us. Most of the Genoese ships guarding our flotilla were scattered, so our captain ordered his sailors to flee. He knew of a safe harbor to wait out the battle, and a storm was brewing. All seemed to be well; we found a snug bay with a narrow entrance, protected by rocky hills on three sides. There we waited until both battle and tempest had moved on.

"The next morning several of the crew went over to a fisherman's camp they knew of, thinking to return with fish and fresh water from the stream there. But when they didn't return by sundown, our captain grew uneasy and decided that we would depart at sunrise the next day. It was too late. Our sailors must have found not fishermen but corsairs—in this case Dalmatian. They infest that area like lice. It was our ill luck that they were encamped there at the time. They had killed our men, but not before finding out about us, and they were waiting for us outside the bay. Being rested and strong, they beset the ship and slew almost everyone aboard, though one man jumped overboard and swam to shore. He had become a friend of mine while on the voyage, and I had often spoken about you. It gave him pleasure to hear my description of you, your hair and eyes and perfect beauty. I still wonder if he escaped. And it is possible. He was running toward the forest when I last saw him."

"This may amaze you, but that I think I know!" I cried. "One of Basil's business partners spoke with him! He was on a Genoese fishing boat that was captured and brought here. He had to pay a ransom before the Venetians would release him." Joscelin smiled grimly. "He also spoke of knights defending his ship, and he mentioned you!" A thought struck me. Could it have been his friend calling to me when I had left Venice that last time; had he somehow known it was I? I dared not voice my thought. It seemed too fantastic.

"So he may have reached home, God willing. I am glad.

"Well, I was not quite so lucky. The ship caught on fire. I was trying to defend the other passengers when something hard hit me from behind and down I went, into blackness. When I awoke, I was bound hand and foot and my captors were rowing away from the burning ship. Another two knights and my good Philippe had also survived. We were brought back to the corsairs' camp, where we were enslaved and treated most roughly. Because I spoke a little Greek, I was able to tell them that they should hold us for ransom. But while the leader thought he might do that, he decided first to use us to row his galley—he thought using noble knights as galley slaves would be most entertaining, and profitable, as we were so much stronger than most men!

"However, on a whim he left Philippe on a beach near the Port of Hadrian, promising to slit my throat if my squire did not appear at the same spot on the same day next year loaded with ransom monies. I had no doubt that Philippe and I would never meet again in this life, and I only prayed that he could find a new life back home. I regretted not knighting him, too, for it would have been only right. Nor did I understand his unswerving loyalty to me, but that I will tell of in its place!"

Down the table, Philippe turned red and bowed. He looked quite handsome right then. Cecelia was staring at him in wonder, and when he looked up their eyes met briefly.

"I sometimes think it a miracle that I lived as long as I did on that wretched ship. Only my prayers to your guardian angel kept me alive, I think. And to imagine that the angel I prayed to was actually flesh and blood! I think our Lord will forgive me for my error, for you still seem like an angel to me, Anna—or a gift from God." Although she turned fiery red and ducked her head, I caught her little smile.

"And I heard your prayers," she murmured. "I often tried to tell Mama about my ghost father, but she always looked so afraid that I never pressed. And then when I was so sick, you came to me and I did tell her all about you! Remember, Mama?" Anna looked over at me eagerly and I nodded. "So, what happened next?"

"Well, a year passed, and by then the corsair captain had forgotten about the ransom and would have cared nothing had he remembered—I got this scar from him, and for no reason but his bad temper." Joscelin pointed to the mark on his face. "He had come to prize us knights for our strength.

Three more years went by, I grew thin and wretched, and the other knights died of fever.

"Finally I decided that I no longer cared if I lived or died, but that I would row no more. I feigned the same fever, and my masters threw me overboard to drown as they always did with slaves. By God's will a spar from some lost ship was floating nearby in the water, and I used my last ounce of strength to swim to it. I clung to it out of some impossible desire to live, and here came God's punishment for the wicked: a huge flotilla of Venetian warships guarding several merchant ships appeared on the horizon. They saw the pirates, gave chase, and destroyed both of their galleys and killed everyone aboard. I prayed for the poor galley slaves who had done nothing to deserve their terrible fates, but at least they were freed from a cruel life.

"After the battle someone saw me off in the distance. I might have become target practice, but I hailed the captain in three different languages and he sent a boat out for me. By then I was so chilled that I truly did catch a fever. I was brought back to Venice, taken in by the Benedictine hospital, nursed back to health by Greek physicians, and clapped into the Doge's prison until I could pay a large ransom!" I trembled inwardly—perhaps it had not been his friend after all; perhaps I had foreseen—and fore-heard—that my lord would one day be imprisoned there!

"That was when I sent a message back to Braissac for the last time, and it was only a few weeks ago that both Hugh and Philippe arrived and freed me. Philippe, bless him, had actually returned to that beach and waited for me in a nearby village for a month before returning to Braissac without me. He was ashamed to go to his own home, though he might have with honor since I could easily have been dead. But he kept faith with me, and in Braissac he stayed until Hugh and he received my message. How strange life is!

"Needless to say, when they arrived, straightaway I knighted him." I looked over at Sir Philippe, and he smiled most charmingly. "And then I began sending one or both of them to the harbor to seek passage yet again to Constantinople, or barring that, letters to you. By Almighty God and Saint Christopher, I feel I have paid the debt of all my misdeeds ten times over by now, but I have been rewarded beyond my happiest dreams in finding you today, so easily, when I might have missed you once again, Sofia." And he boldly leaned over and kissed me on the mouth.

By the end of his story, there were tears in all our eyes, even Basil's, a little. Surely after such sufferings and setbacks as my lord had endured, no one could doubt his fidelity to me!

We spent the afternoon—the entire family—sharing our stories with my beloved. He had much more to tell, too: details, mostly, and how memories of our times together had kept him alive in the darkest times. Again and again we marveled at how some letters could go astray and others so easily reach their destination, not to mention all the coincidences and near misses that had kept us apart when we were searching for each other.

At the same time, having to share my Joscelin with others made me more and more impatient. I wanted time alone with him! Alas, over the course of the afternoon I began to understand that time alone with him was what I might rarely get from now on, for there would always be more people involved than us two.

Watching how Basil kept his gaze on him, I could see that he still harbored doubts, about what I couldn't say, until I realized what my marriage would mean to our partnership. Basil and he would have to come to terms—literally—for once we were married, Lord Joscelin would own my shares. I had paid less and less attention to business matters, but there would need to be some serious sorting out of who owned what and likely some difficult bargaining. All that would take time. My uncle was probably already thinking of all this—doubtless those were among his urgent questions—and he could not be pleased to let go of all the wealth that he had been using as he saw fit.

And I would suddenly be dependent solely on my husband. Well, surely it would not be so different from being dependent on Basil....

The evening arrived all too quickly. Finally, with shadows creeping over the city and shrine lights beginning to glimmer here and there, my beloved took his leave, having also taken supper with us. He had gracefully put off his private meeting with Basil, pleading his frail health. As I lay in bed that night, I set my earlier thoughts aside, especially as they were not central to my heart. I was more concerned for Anna, whose world had been turned upside down this afternoon.

Indeed, she had come to my room to say goodnight and lingered on, many questions still clearly on her mind. So I had let her ask whatever she wished and tried to answer as honestly as I could. By the time we bade each other sweet sleep, at the very least she saw that I was no "bad woman", only a flawed one, who had waited so long for my beloved that I had almost dried up for lack of him.

"You know, Mama," she'd said at one point, "your cheeks are pinker and your smile brighter than I've ever seen, even since coming here. You seem so happy." She sighed. "I hope my father won't take you entirely away from me."

And this was what I pondered as I sought that sweet sleep: how to navigate a new and entirely uncharted course into a life with a husband and child and, hopefully, more children in the future. It would not be here in Venice but in a new and entirely unfamiliar country; that was certain. Yet another leap into the unknown!

I remembered that sense of doom I had felt when we were sailing for Venice, and as if a rain cloud had risen from nowhere to cover a bright noon sky, it settled on me again, threatening to blot out the sun of my great happiness. I shook off the feeling, chiding myself for spoiling my own joy with vague fears for the future. Had I not surmounted worse obstacles not once but several times? I would be starting a new life, yes, but this time with the two people I loved more than myself. It would all work out somehow, step by step. I turned over and fell asleep making wedding plans.

The next two months were a chaos of activity. There were not only the making and constant changing of plans for our wedding and departure; there was the question of what had happened in Constantinople and to our friends who had stayed behind. Each day more ships arrived with bits of news, and one bore two letters from John of Epirus, written about a month apart but sent at the same time. Here is part of the first one:

Lady Sofia,

May God's blessings shower upon you. I hope this missive finds you in good health and spirits. I am in both. I imagine you have heard of the fall of Constantinople, as the Latins would have it. I see it as my city's liberation! It was taken not by force but by stealth, and neither Emperor Michael nor King Baldwin were even here. Of course the false king fled west, no doubt to beg at yet more courts. Many Latins and Venetians fled the city, too, for rumors flew like birds of ill omen, predicting terrible retributions to be exacted. Now preparations go forward for a great triumphal entry of the true emperor. I hope he will not be too shocked at what he finds here …

I have made a few plans to ensure my future welfare, and I will try to protect your interests and your people, including your servants Alexander and Banjuu …

I breathed a little easier on reading this news. But the next letter gave me even better news. Most of the worst rumors had proven inaccurate or false. As John put it:

The great triumphal entry was humble and full of shock indeed, for the city is, as you know, a disaster. I doubt any of the sovereigns of the Greek states knew how far it had fallen in fifty-seven years of slavery to the Latins. The Blachernae palace was too ruined by fire damage on the floors and the like for our sovereign to think of living there—and the Bukoleon bears the taint of its previous occupant—so Emperor Michael VIII Palaeologus, as he is now entitled to call himself, must make do with a lesser but unharmed palace. What barbarians those Latins were and are! I am so glad to be rid of them, never to have to serve their wicked whims again.

But other than burning a few homes and warehouses at first, we Greeks were most tolerant to those who remained, and so is the Emperor. The Venetians were punished very little. Some fifty of the greediest merchants were blinded and their noses were cut off, a mild enough punishment, but there were no mass executions. Emperor Michael wants to reestablish what has been lost, not to exact revenge.

He even allowed some to stay, though many people, Latin and Venetian alike, daily lose their homes to the Genoese who now flock to the city. Genoese merchant warriors played a vital role when Constantinople was retaken. They lured the Venetian fleet away from the city, and they got the reward they asked for. If they do not want to settle in the city itself, they now have their own, much safer enclave across the Golden Horn.

Hubris indeed, I thought, remembering Marco Polo the Elder's boast and Maffeo's warning: no one can be everywhere, controlling everything! But there was more.

You may also be interested to learn that Emperor Michael is allying himself with both the northern and southern branches of the Mongols and that there is much trade already building up between their territories and our great city, slaves being the staple goods. Mongol traders bring them here, and then we ship the boys to Egypt, which seems to need more and more slave soldiers. I wonder about the size of the army this Sultan Baibars is building and what he plans to use it for.

While I was not happy to hear about the slave trade and was certain that Basil would find a way to dip his oar into it, I also realized that my private worries had been for nothing. I had to laugh at myself a little—there would be no Mongol threat to Byzantium after all! That worry was now far, far behind me, and at long last I dismissed my fears. I straightaway sent a letter to John, thanking him for looking after Alexander and Banjuu and their little daughter.

And early the next year when I was almost ready to leave Venice, I received a final letter from him; it ended another chapter in my life.

My good Lady,

I have many pieces of news to share. One piece may bring you joy, though knowing your tender heart, perhaps not. Sir Reynaud was not greeted with the open arms he expected. The new emperor had no use for his Frankish knights and banished them, but not before meting out the same punishment to him as to the Venetians. He was blinded and his nose was cut off for selling holy relics and also for killing innocents. Like several others, he recently died of his wounds.

But I did see to the welfare of your former servants Alexander and Banjuu. They and little Sofia are safe and well, though their homes had to be moved to make way for Genoese families. I put my service to my true Emperor to good use, and he personally undertook to support them and their wards. He wants to recreate the heaven on earth that guided his predecessors, and what better way to do it than to support such good works as theirs?

Over the months that followed, we also heard from those friends who had survived, some of whom arrived in Venice with little more than the clothes they were wearing. We took two families in for a while and helped them begin life anew. They were certainly surprised to find Lord Joscelin there! My myth of betrothal had turned out to be true after all.

And to my surprise, at least, by the next year all the surviving Venetian merchants were invited back! Their wealth and expertise were sorely needed if the city was to be rebuilt. Basil, of course, was delighted. Since he was already doing business in Nicaea, once communications were easy again he contacted his old agents, including John of Epirus, who simply picked up the threads of his own trade—selling reliable information—and our business interests in Constantinople soon throve again. John was now free to reveal that all along he had been a spy for Nicaea, and he had been well rewarded for his contributions. He was a happy and very rich man.

But in truth I paid only as much attention to these events as was necessary. At long last the wedding I would be attending would be my own, and I made the most of it. I had gowns made for myself and for Anna and Cecilia and Helene, as well as wedding garments for all the men and boys. There were so many other arrangements to be made, too—thank heaven I was not responsible for them all—including permission from the Church to marry and a special dispensation for Lord Joscelin to remarry. His sin was actually seen as greater than mine and required a heavy penance that he would not speak of but which made him look as if he had been attacked by fleas, for he was forever scratching when he thought no one was looking. He also arranged with the local priest to perform the ceremony before his small chapel.

Once the notice had been posted on the chapel door, Helen and I plunged into plans for decorating the church and our Ca', where the wedding feast would be held. It would be rather modest, given the unusual circumstances, but there was no doubt that Anna would no longer be a bastard in the eyes of the Church or of the world. Lord Joscelin had seen to that!

I'd have been happy every moment but for the fact that I saw so little of him and never alone. It seemed that the custom was to keep us apart as much as possible. Certainly when we were together, my relatives watched our every move! It drove me wild because I still had private questions I needed answered, particularly about Sir Reynaud's accusations. When our family learned the news of Sir Reynaud's death, I had looked search-ingly at Lord Joscelin to see how he reacted.

And react he had. "I knew him once! We met in Ascalon when I was waiting to ransom Lord Amaury. We became friends for a little while after he helped me fend off some ruffians in a bar who taunted Robert about his manhood. So Reynaud was knighted! He was a strange man, but I am sorry to hear about his death."

That was all he said, but of course it set me to wondering whether Sir Reynaud had told me more of the truth than my beloved had, or less. On the one hand I no longer cared, but on the other hand I hated the idea of secrets dividing us.

The biggest worry, however, was Anna. While she enjoyed being fitted for new garments and wanted to help with decorations and so forth, whenever her father took my hand or told me how much he loved me, a shadow was sure to pass across her face.

I like to think that Joscelin would have noticed, too, but he was not only wrapped up in wedding preparations but also in the inevitable haggling over how my partnership with Basil was to be dissolved—as was I. My uncle first tried to persuade Joscelin that everything should be kept as it was, but that was clearly not a workable plan. My betrothed was a noble landowner, not a merchant; and even if he had been interested in trade, he lived too far away to be an effective partner. Indeed, I sometimes noted a certain haughtiness in his manner toward my uncle.

And as I had foreseen, once Basil had admitted defeat he wanted to give away as little as possible. But armed with all the documents and agree-ments we had drawn up in Antioch under the careful eye of Matthew of Edessa, Joscelin and I ensured that all was slowly sorted out, including a codicil to the new agreement that gave me some power over the monies myself. I greeted that part with relief and gratitude. And since my shares in our business made me enormously wealthy, Basil could at least comfort himself on not needing to provide me with a dowry!

This brings me back to Anna, for she and I also had some sorting out to do. I would come upon her sometimes sitting by herself in the loggia, her hands idle and her gaze empty. Usually I would send her off on some task, but finally I stopped and asked what the matter was.

"Oh, Mama, everything! You never give me lessons or tell me stories of your past anymore, and I wonder if I will ever hear them again. Now I must share you with my new father, and I don't like it! When he's here, he has eyes only for you and you for him. I keep telling myself it's only because of the wedding and Constantinople and making plans to move and so on, but I'm going to lose all my cousins and my friends when we move. I lost some of them already because they died in Constantinople, and they were so young, like me … and I'm so afraid!"

Now, I know that most parents would respond harshly to such notions, but Anna had been my lodestone for so long. How could I dismiss her fears? After all, she had already gone through as many changes in her life as I had, and she was much younger. I simply enfolded her in my arms and let her cry.

I was suddenly reminded of being in the Mongol camps and how my friend, the old monk Dorje, had comforted me after I had lost my beloved Lady Q'ing-ling. How he had valued kindness! I had learned that much from him, that and the practice of peace.

That thought gave me an idea. After her tears had passed, I said, "Anna, I want to teach you something right now, something that you can add to your prayers each day. I sometimes forget to do it, but I always find it gives me strength when I remember. It's called the practice of peace, and it does bring a more peaceful mind."

Her eyes brightened. "I would like to learn that!"

So, as best as I could remember, I taught her the practice just as Dorje had taught me. At first Anna laughed. "This is too simple. I'm always doing this anyway."

"Well, try it when you aren't 'doing this anyway,' when you are upset, for instance, and see what happens." In fact, after that I began doing it more, too!

That night when Lord Joscelin arrived for supper—he at least broke bread with us every day—I had an inspiration. "Anna and Paolo, would you perform a duet for us? Gilles and Cecilia, you could join in, too. You haven't performed for us since Lord Joscelin arrived, and I miss our musical evenings."

The young ones hastily sent for their lutes and the sheets of music they had notated themselves, and we were treated to a delightful if not perfectly tuneful evening of music and song. Indeed, at one point Basil and Helene suggested we adults dance, and so we did, laughing and gay, and even Philippe and Cecilia took a turn with each other at one point. Finally, Helene excused herself to see to her babies.

I think that evening did much to bring Anna and Joscelin closer. When he praised her performance, she smiled and bade him goodnight with grave courtesy as she and the others followed Helene out to go to bed. Little did I think that this evening was bringing others closer as well.

Around this time I received an unexpected letter from Friar Thomas Aquinas. It was written by one of his monks, but he had likely dictated it and he had signed it. It contained thanks for the help I had given him. My translations of Aristotle had contained interesting differences from those he already possessed, and he was being led to new discoveries of great import to Church theology.

Underlying the thanks I got the feeling that he might not mind my sending him the works of even more Greek—or even Muslim—scholars, so I took a few hours to sort through my collection and selected several that I thought he might find useful. I sent for the same scribe to copy them all out, asking him to use only his best apprentices to work with him and to finish as quickly as possible. When he understood that they were for the great doctor of souls, he was eager to begin, feeling that this work was sure to please God.

And, in a spirit of inquiry, I included a description of that practice of peace. Dorje was pagan, after all, but so was Aristotle. If the good doctor disapproved of this practice, I was sure he would write back and say so, and I would do it no more.

When the copies were finally finished, I sent them off by courier to the good friar's monastery with a humble message of goodwill and a request for his blessings.

Joscelin was quite impressed when he saw the large package I had assembled. "This is a gift of great value to the Angelic Doctor, as he was called when I knew him in Paris. He was often invited to dine with King Louis."

"Oh, so you know him."

"Not to speak to, but I often served my king at dinner when he was there. One time the strangest thing happened. Friar Thomas fell silent while the talk flowed around him. Suddenly he struck the table with his fist, which startled us all, I assure you, and cried, 'That argument disposes of the Manicheans!'

"My king saw that something important had happened. He sent me for writing materials, and Friar Thomas was able to write down his logic and thus preserve it."

"Something like that happened when I first saw him, too. His must be a very great intellect!"

Writing Friar Aquinas also inspired me to send word to the caretakers of my remaining orphanages, to let them know my happy news and to assure them that my support for them was unwavering. I also asked Efrem to let Bardas and Leo know how happy I was. And I invited several of my young scribes to come live in Venice, where they would find work aplenty.

A few weeks later I received a warm letter of thanks from one of Friar Thomas' secretaries, but it would be another two years before I received a full answer. And since there was nothing in it about that peace practice, I decided I could continue doing it.

⸎ ⸎⸎⸎ ⸎⸎ ⸎

We wed in late November. It was snowing lightly, making every surface look as if sugar had been grated over it. I bathed and washed my hair and dried it before the fire, a maidservant bound it back in elaborate coils and perfumed me all over, and Helene painted my face with too much color. Then she helped me dress. As she had, I felt odd wearing blue, so I had chosen a pale green samite with a lining of deeper green silk for my gown and a sheer veil of gold, trimmed in the same dark silk and attached with a wreath of leaves, as of course there were no flowers in bloom. She even made me wear the blue ribbon around my knee! We would be wrapped in warm mantles, anyway, so not much of my face or my finery would show.

Last of all I put on the necklace and earrings that Joscelin had given me so many years ago in anticipation of our wedding.

Lord Joscelin, Basil, and Sirs Hugh and Philippe awaited us before the chapel along with a crowd of curious onlookers. Word had spread quickly if the many poor men in the crowd meant anything. We listened to the priest's short sermon on the sacred meaning of marriage and exchanged vows before its entrance, and the priest blessed the marriage ring. Joscelin, having first slipped the ring on my first three fingers in turn, slid it firmly onto my fourth, the wedding finger. We turned, he gave a bag of pennies to Hugh to give to the poor, and then he turned to me and declared what my dower would be should he die—it was beyond generous—and we were led inside to celebrate the wedding Mass. Both Lord Joscelin and I shed a few tears, and I heard happy sobs from Helene.

When I looked around before we knelt before the altar, red candles glowing, even Basil seemed moved. Anna just looked stunned, though she was dressed beautifully, her hair was crimped becomingly, and so on—all things she liked. I let the words of the Mass flow into me and prayed for blessings to descend on our marriage while the wedding veil was draped over us both, but part of me was numb with surprise that after all these years, nothing had happened to prevent our being wed.

After the Mass and more vows taken, another sermon, prayers, and further blessings, we were married. Joscelin stood and received the Kiss of Peace from the priest, helped me rise, and we faced our family and friends for the first time as man and wife.

An inner silence drowned out the sound of hurrahs and clapping that I know must have filled the air. I don't know what I had expected to feel, but in a certain way it all seemed so ordinary. Here I was, married at last to the man I loved, with both my daughter and me cleansed of our tainted past, so why was I not ecstatic?

But the moment passed. Our relatives and friends accompanied us back home accompanied by a jolly group of musicians who played a special wedding march for us, while all around us were noise and laughter and happy glances. I looked up at Joscelin, who was holding my hand, and he smiled down at me. I caught a glimpse of Papa in his smile, and I smiled back. My beloved was rapidly recovering from his fever, and even his stride seemed more vigorous that day.

And tonight after the feasting, I would lie beside him, this time truly as his spouse, for the first time in twelve years—one for each apostle, I mildly jested to myself.

In truth, I remember little about the wedding feast: except for no sanglier, it was much like Helene's and Basil's. My uncle had spared no expense, and everyone in Venice seemed to be at it, from the Polo and Falieri families and the people we had known in Constantinople to every trading partner he knew, including a few I had never met! I heard laughter and caught significant looks cast our way, but no one seemed other than curious. Behind our backs, judging must be going on, too, but not at the feast at least. Basil had provided too much food and wine for anyone to mar the day with gossip. And here came the special cake and then the race out of the main hall as the unmarried men tried to collect my ribbon—Joscelin laughingly protected me from outright assault—and then the procession to the marriage chamber—my room and now ours, even to his sword and shield leaning in one corner—seeds flying everywhere, and even swallowing a sip of the sweet-sour Bride's Broth before Joscelin forced everyone out.

My last glimpse was of Anna, looking most forlorn before Paolo and Gilles swept her off to celebrate more. I was glad I had thought to ask them to take care of her.

Sounds of retreating feet, more music, shouts, and laughter echoed from the main hall. Joscelin locked the door and turned to me. At last I was alone with my beloved. I stepped forward, expecting him to sweep me into my arms, and mine were already opened to him, but he instead stopped and knelt before me. Burying his face in my gown, a move that set me afire with passion, he was silent for many moments. I put my hands on his shoulders and tried to pull him further into me, my body nakedly aflame. But he drew back and looked up at me with tears in his eyes.

"What is it, my lord?" I asked. The silence drew as taut as a bowstring before it is released.

Finally he said, "Sofia, I am utterly unworthy of you. I must now confess all my sins before you, as I already have before God. This is part of the penance that was exacted of me in exchange for forgiveness. I am, despite the annulment, an adulterer for lying with you when I did. Please do not hate me, for though I am now cleansed of sin, this and my many other sins stand between us like ghosts of the dead, haunting my past and our future."

I began to tremble. This was not what I wanted on my wedding night, and the dread I had tried to drown for the past few months resurfaced, bloated even further for having been submerged for so long.

"Cannot you disobey your priest a little and lie with me first? It has been so long since you held me in your arms."

Joscelin shook his head. "As soon as I disrobe, you will see what I undertook for your sake, and you will ask why. And I will be forced to tell you, anyway." He sighed and set me on the only chair in the room.

"Not even after Yolande's death and my penance for it was I freed from the terrible bondage of lust. Even on my way to the Holy Land, expecting to die, I was ensnared by it more than once, and I lay with camp followers or whores from time to time. In Ascalon before the battle where I was captured, there were new opportunities among the noble ladies, most of them married. Remembering Yolande, I never seduced any of them, though they tried to seduce me. I turned down offers, Sofia! I swear, I never touched anyone of high birth.

"But there were others … I had my way with more than one maidservant, and two I got pregnant almost at the same time. And I did see to it that each woman was cared for during her lying-in. I also sent them both monies to raise my bastards.

"But when one of the women died some thirteen years ago or more, I sent for both children and brought them to your orphanage. You never knew that in private I endowed your orphanage well, for I wanted them to be no burden to you. I knew they would be raised properly there, but I lied to you when I brought them. You will likely remember them: Rotrou and Agnes. I have often wondered what happened to them." He fell silent.

My heart had been sinking rapidly during this confession, and now I was stricken to the core. It would seem that my worst fears were all being confirmed.

Finally I spoke. "I guessed as much. Rotrou has taken the tonsure and is an accomplished scribe in his monastery. Agnes is a maidservant to a wealthy family. They are both in Antioch." All this I recited with a leaden heart.

"Joscelin, it breaks my heart that I am right about this, for many people, including my uncle and his first wife, told me much evil gossip about you. It always seemed so at odds with what I knew of you: your chaste behavior with me, your other confessions so humbly offered, and especially King Louis' high esteem for you. I have wrestled with these and other slanders for over a decade, and hearing that they are not slander after all is hard to bear on such a night as this."

A moan escaped from Joscelin, and he buried his face in his hands. "I have done such wrong. I cannot even ask you to forgive me—this is what the priest told me I must do, and I even argued with him, told him my penance was too ill, for it needlessly punishes you, too. But he was adamant, and he was right twice over."

"Is there more?" I asked after a long silence.

"No, nothing after that. Once I went to a brothel with Sir Reynaud, but nothing happened. It came about after that first brawl when we fought side by side for my brother Robert. I spent a few more nights of drinking with him. Then Robert left, and I fell into a pit of despair. Nothing was going right, and after being imprisoned and so ill-treated, I had even lost interest in women. After one night of heavy drinking, I told Reynaud this, and that I no longer cared about living or dying, and he led me to that place before I knew what he was about. We were inside when I realized what it was—boys and girls as well as women—but no pleasure lay there for me. He tried to make me stay, kept going on about all the delights of the flesh I had never tried—well, no need to tell you about that. I turned and left, for the first time thinking myself such an innocent!

"The next time I saw him, he offered me his regrets. He said he had been too full of wine to know what he'd been about, but I'd had enough of getting drunk with him. It was becoming more humiliating to wake up with an aching head than it was to be begging all over town for loans for Lord Amaury! I never sought out Sir Reynaud's company again. And soon after that, he left and help came for me. You know the rest."

It was like the sun coming out at midnight. Suddenly, forgiving Joscelin for Agnes and Rotrou seemed easy. Sir Reynaud had simply lied! "And you have reformed since then? There were no other women in these past years?"

"None. No woman could tempt me until I met you. You reawakened me, Sofia, body and heart and soul. I have been faithful to you and to my every memory of you since then. Those memories kept me alive."

"Even with maidservants and the like?" To rate menials so low nipped at my conscience.

"Yes, even with them." We both smiled, shyly.

"Well, then, I do forgive you, my lord. I have loved you from the moment I met you, and now that we are wed, I will always be sure of you. And never again, I hope, will we need to rely on letters that might go astray! What an ill fate to be kept apart for so long and to suffer so because of them!

"You see, I wrote to you about Agnes and Rotrou and all the other nasty bits of gossip that came my way, but after I had lost all notion of where to look for you, the worst of all happened. Though I had thought Sir Reynaud was my friend, he tried to force a proposal of marriage on me and in doing so slandered you to me. He told me that you and he had done all the things he wanted you to do with him—and he left nothing to my imagination! And then he tried to rape me to force me to wed him—

"Good God, he did? And after spewing such filth into your ears? It's lucky for him he's dead already, for I'd have found him and cut his heart out!"

"I think he must have envied you and your command over yourself— envied you and over time come to hate you when I stayed so loyal to your memory.

"I wonder if he had always wanted to take me from you, for his first addresses to me were overly familiar. He had no respect for your brother, either, called him a Ganymede, whatever that meant."

Joscelin flushed. "I know what he meant by it. And he was probably right. A man with his tastes would know, for I have kept back more than I told you, things he said that matter nothing now. I doubt he told you everything he liked to do, or you would understand as well. It's not un-common, but ..."

A man with secret tastes. I shuddered, remembering how he used to smile and jest with all Anna's cousins, boy and girl alike, and how he liked children 'in their place'—Anna! His games with her aboard the ship! What might have happened to her if I had married him? But Sir Reynaud was gone, just as Qabul was. Ironic how much alike they were, considering how cultured the one had been while the other had been such a brute.

"How can I ever make up to you for all this: your lost years, all the abuses and slights and slanders you endured, having to raise Anna alone?"

"Well, they were not entirely unhappy. I had her to comfort me."

"Yes, she is the fair lily that grew from the muddy pond, a phrase I once heard somewhere. We must think on what future will be best for her."

"Well, now I would like to put all memories aside, and all thoughts of the future!"

And while music floated into the room, I finally removed my wreath and veil and turned so that Joscelin could unbind my hair and unlace the back of my gown. He slowly undressed me, once again with praise on his lips. He kissed my breasts, each in turn, though they were no longer young and firm but marked by pregnancy. He caressed my belly and flanks, praising them though they too were marked. His hand slid to my secret spot, and when I almost swooned he carried me to the bed and wrapped me in the down covers, for the only heat in the room was mine! The fire in the fireplace had dwindled to almost nothing. Joscelin went to it and added more wood.

And then he slowly undressed, too, almost as if he was shy or wanted to hide something. When he removed the last of his clothing, a strange, stiff, hairy-looking shirt, I saw what he was hiding: his entire torso was raw and inflamed. Now I understood: this was a hair shirt and was part of his penance. I burst into tears.

"Do not cry; I deserve it more than I deserve you, my love," he said, slipping under the covers with me. I only have to wear it for a year."

"Wait, I will find you some salve," I cried.

"No, I need nothing but you to heal me." And he drew me into his embrace.

I need say no more about that, for this is the secret that lies between not only man and woman but, finally for me, between husband and wife. Suffice it to say that the long wait was worth every moment, and it made the consummation of our love all the sweeter.

It must have been very near dawn when we finally burned out our immediate passion for each other. Joscelin had gotten out of bed to revive the last embers of the fire when he turned back to me, a log still in his hand, and said, queerly, "Do you see what I see, Sofia?" I climbed out, shivering, to stand by his side.

He had set his log down and was pointing at the low fire. The bark had fallen away in places on the foremost log, and outlined in flame was one word spelled out in the most perfect script: CARITAS. It was the old Latin word for the generosity of a loving heart, one of the three great Christian virtues. At first we could not move. We looked at it, at each other, at it, again and again.

"God forgives us, Sofia," Joscelin said at last.

And something made me answer, "Perhaps He did long ago, and we are the ones who must forgive ourselves."

Another silence until he said in a solemn voice, "I see guidance in it, too. Before I went on Lord Amaury's campaign, many churchmen who traveled with the troops urged us to kill without mercy in this life because God wanted us to save our enemies' souls. Somehow their deaths would purge us both, and the Almighty would raise us up and save us from perdition. I never saw how, but I was young and desperate to save my soul.

"But does this one word not reflect our Savior's message more clearly? When Christ spoke of fire and a sword, he never said we must live with those in our hearts or hands. He offered us his body to redeem us from our own brute natures, and we can offer the same caritas in His name."

I could only agree with him, but I said nothing.

"You are turning to ice." He went back to the bed and swept off the covers, brought them back and sat me down before the fire. He wrapped us both in them, and there we sat, entwined in each other's arms, until finally the other logs split and sank, and the fire died, leaving only the one log, that word still clear upon it. The room grew cold, but we had each other. Gradually the room grew lighter, and another miracle occurred: the sun rose as it always had, casting a rosy glow across us. We arose to face our new life together. After dressing in leisurely fashion, we entered the main hall for breakfast, hand in hand.

What do you tell others when you have witnessed a miracle? I tried to tell Helene, even showed her the log in the fireplace, but she straightaway shook her head. "Someone must have carved the word into a tree trunk."

"But look how it follows the grain of the tree bark. Don't people carve words sideways across the bark so that you can read them straight on? Otherwise you have to tilt your head. And I've never seen holy words carved into trees, either."

She shrugged dismissively.

"But even if you are right," and I knew she wasn't, "it is a miracle that this happened on my wedding night. And the log could easily have been tilted in another direction or been at the back of the fireplace."

She grew a bit peevish. "Well, best not to share your 'miracle' with anyone else. People don't like it when there's a real-life mystery! That's for saints and the scriptures, not for us ordinary sinners.

"Enough about that: what was it like last night? Was he worth the wait?"

I had once asked Batu Khan almost the same question on the first night he had bedded me, me so drunk I could hardly hold my head up and Argamon parted from me forever. So, since it was no use forcing Helene to believe what she didn't want to believe, I laughed and said yes, and we wondered together about whether my wedding night had been as satisfying as hers had been.

"I expect you to be carrying soon," she jested.

I went along with her and jested in kind, feeling the power of the miracle fade. I would certainly never mention it to Basil or to Joscelin's men or the other children, but after breakfast I took Anna to see it. We got there just in time, as the maidservant had come in ready to sweep out the fireplace and set a new fire. I sent her on to the next room and pointed out the word. Anna, at least, was gratifyingly convinced. Just then Lord Joscelin returned to the room, and the three of us stared at the log until the maid timidly knocked on the door and asked permission to finish her task. We all moved away, feeling a little foolish.

"Well, from now on 'caritas' must remain in our hearts, for it cannot not last in a fireplace," Anna sighed.

SPRING TO SUMMER
ANNO DOMINI 1262

We spent the winter and all of the spring in Venice, though Philippe returned to Braissac in March. Not only Lord Joscelin but also Philippe and Hugh had become part of our family circle, especially Philippe, for he was of high birth as well as being a charming young man. We celebrated Saint Anne's feast day just before Anna turned eleven, and Joscelin was foremost in showering her with gifts after we returned from Mass, some quite silly that made her laugh. Christmas was especially cheerful that year, too, with a splendid Mass in the Cathedral and much feasting for the many holy and mock-holy days that followed.

I had not been wrong in trusting Joscelin with my love, for he was as kind and thoughtful to us all as I had remembered. He became a great favorite with his adoptive nieces and nephews—indeed, the boys looked up to him as something of a deity. Basil came to like him, too, though there would always be a little reserve between them. No matter that princely blood ran in our veins; we also had lucre in them, especially my uncle!

Joscelin and I were welcomed as a couple in our Venetian circles, too, though I am sure there were lingering doubts about Anna and her father. He was rather grave at first, but as he came to see that there was no shame in mingling with the merchant nobility of the city, he revealed another side to his nature, a sense of wry humor, that endeared him to my friends and made them indifferent to our past. It had been many years since he'd had opportunity to use his social graces, but those he had, too, in abundance. He had, after all, served a great king. I caught more than one envious glance cast at the two of us, by husbands and wives who had never achieved more than dim affection for each other and who could see that we shared so much more.

Our plans to leave were not forming quickly, but the weather would not improve enough for us all to travel until April. And by then there was another reason to wait. I only realized after January had passed without a moon cycle: the telltale sickness and sore breasts had meant nothing to me at first and I had ignored them, but when I realized what they truly meant, I was thrilled. Helene realized she was pregnant again, too, and from about the same time—perhaps, she jested, even the same night! Ever since Joscelin had wed me, Basil had clearly been inspired by memories of their own wedding night, she told me, smiling secretively.

Another child! Truth be told, I was also terrified, for I was no longer young. But Lord Joscelin laughed when he learned the news and listened to my fears. "What joy! And though childbirth is always a dangerous time for a woman, it happens every day. My mother bore twelve children. She was well over forty when my youngest sister was born. You will meet her soon.

"And Sofia, you will always be young to me. You have lost not one whit of your bloom: you are a ripe peach of a woman instead of a little peach blossom. Give me the fruit any day!" And, to the horror of a passing servant, he swept me into his arms and twirled me, set me down, and kissed me on the mouth and then on my breasts!

The sickness was not nearly as strong as with Anna, and for the next few months I was happier than I had ever been in my life. Joscelin and Anna seemed to be united in their love of me, and that shared love seemed to be budding into a cautious affection for each other. Plus Philippe was an entertaining guest, liked by all, and Hugh added stately gravity to every occasion.

Not all was perfect harmony, however. As time passed it became ever clearer that Philippe and Cecilia were beginning to like each other very much. At fifteen, she was turning into a lovely young woman with less of a nose than her mother's but with her finely arched brows. And her hair was the rich red-gold of her father.

I thought it a shame that she was already betrothed to another man, for no one but Basil liked his choice of husband for her. In my imagination she and Philippe would have become affianced and then gone to Occitaine with us. How lovely it would have been for Anna, too. Basil would have been unhappy at losing his daughter to a foreigner, but I tended to regard his feelings with about as much respect as he did mine.

Cecilia's fiancé often visited: a widower some twenty years her senior named Venerio Tiepolo who was related to yet another line of Doges. He had a bit of a paunch and a ham-handed way about him, and he always spoke as though he alone had any thoughts worth thinking, which thoughts he liked to share at length. Every time he came around, Cecilia seemed to wither.

The irony was that Philippe truly would be an excellent match. In time he would become lord of a wealthy barony not far from Braissac. Watching the three of them together was always a bit painful: Philippe looked like a dog whose owner had denied him his bone, Cecilia was scarcely able to conceal her dislike of the one and her delight in the other, and Venerio inevitably held forth on his favorite subject, wealth and how cleverly he amassed it at others' expense.

One mild and sunny afternoon, Anna and I were sitting on the loggia with our extended family, all of us ladies at our embroidery or sewing and Paolo and Gilles at their Latin—though Anna kept intruding to correct them, much to Paolo's annoyance! I was past the morning sickness and enjoying the day, the company, and life in general. As the sun grew low, Venerio, Basil, and Basil's two eldest sons came upstairs from the ground floor office where they had no doubt hatched some new scheme to enrich themselves. The rest of us greeted them with varying degrees of warmth.

Philippe had been sitting by Cecilia's side, the two whispering together and laughing now and then. At a glare from Lord Joscelin, he gracefully if reluctantly removed himself to another bench. Nearby, Anna's lute leaned against the wall. Philippe had a lovely singing voice, so he persuaded my daughter to play for us while he sang.

Meanwhile Venerio had taken Philippe's place and Cecilia's hand. She looked away while he caressed it. So there was Philippe on the one hand, singing a love song clearly directed at Cecilia, and Venerio on the other, holding forth about all the money he had shaved off a recent contract on some goods like nails or goatskins! Finally Cecilia excused herself, pleading a headache. Philippe's song came to a quavering end and Anna began another, but his heart was clearly not in his singing anymore. When it ended, he too excused himself and left the loggia.

Sensing that something could go wrong, I followed him inside. With shadows rising in every room, I strode from one hall to another but found no sign of either Cecilia or Philippe. Nor were they in the room I still called a solar or on the rooftop, but while up there I caught some movement under the fruit trees. I went back down and out to the top of the outside stairs, and there they were, half hidden among the trees, kissing while he fondled one of her breasts!

"Philippe! Come here!" I called. "Quickly, both of you!"

They looked up, startled, and he hastily stepped away from her. Cecilia's hair had come unbound, and she lingered to set it aright, but Philippe obeyed, looking most shamefaced for a man of twenty-two.

"How long has this been going on?"

Cecilia joined us on the stairs, looking more defiant than ashamed. "Forever, for he is the only man I will ever love! I am a sacrifice to greed," she declared. And, as if in imitation of some passion play, she clasped her hands to her breast and looked up at the sky. "Mother Mary and all the saints, please spare me from the clutches of evil."

I had to laugh. "Well, Venerio isn't so much evil as he is puffed up with self-importance. And if you're really so unhappy, then you must speak with your father. I will go with you if you wish. No date has been set for the wedding, so perhaps it's not too late to withdraw gracefully from the betrothal. Philippe, I do take it that you want to marry her, not just seduce her."

His whole face turned red, and stumbling on his words, he cried, "Of course I—but what about Basil—and Lord Joscelin—and how—" and he sputtered to a stop, looking past me.

I felt more than saw a shadow loom up behind me. Two shadows, to be exact: Basil's and Venerio's. I had no idea what they had heard, but I turned and said brightly, "I found Philippe comforting Cecilia in the garden and am just bringing them inside. Come along, both of you. Cecilia, you must lie down for a while to rest your head. I'll bring you a cool cloth in a moment."

"Yes, aunt," she murmured gratefully. But when she tried to pass by the two men, Basil seized her by both her hair and arm so hard that she cried out. His face was purple with rage.

"You little strumpet. I'll see you to your room, and you won't come out until you're married!"

He started to drag her away, she screamed, Philippe cried out and rushed past me, and I hastily moved aside. Suddenly the world was spinning, steps were rushing up at me, and my arm-hip-belly-shoulder-head hit something almost all at once, and so hard that I thought I would die. Instead, sweet blackness rose up and blotted out even the pain. The last thing I heard was, "Her baby!"

⸙

Sharp pains in my belly woke me. At first I thought I was back in the Mongol camps again, being kicked by soldiers. But I was in my bed. My left arm was in a splint, and there was a poultice of some sort wrapped onto my forehead, which was hurting as much as it had when I had survived the Bedouin attack all those years ago. Helene was with me, as were two strangers: one, Helene's midwife, was stuffing towels between my legs and the other, a monk by his attire, was carrying something away wrapped in a bloody towel and handing it to someone outside the room.

"Don't move," Helene cried when I tried to sit up. "You're still bleeding! And your head ... You are lucky to be alive, Sofia! But...." she turned her head away and began to weep.

"Not my baby?"

She nodded. "He came out too soon—you were struck in the belly—he is dead."

A low moan rose from my heart into my mouth. It turned into a wail, a door flew open, and Joscelin suddenly beside me. Ignoring everyone's protests, he slid his arms around me, cradled and comforted me as best he could.

After my first wave of tears had ebbed a little, he stroked my hair and murmured, "But you live, Sofia. You lay almost lifeless for over a day. Basil himself went for the best surgeon in Venice. This is Arsenios Doukas, a

Benedictine monk who works in their hospital. And he brought his best physician with him."

"Yes, I bound your broken arm and looked at your head," added the surgeon monk. "You are very lucky, Lady Sofia. You hit your head straight on, so though you have a terrible bruise and swelling, those will pass with the arnica poultices. When you began to miscarry, Lady Helene sent for me again, and for her midwife to help me. We delivered your stillborn son; the pain is what woke you."

The midwife spoke up. "Brother, now I can safely say that her bleeding has stopped."

"Good," and he turned to me. "You will not die as long as your people follow my instructions. Boiled water, and lots of it, for cleaning you and keeping childbed fever at bay."

The midwife nodded agreement.

But all these words flowed past me like water. A son.

Leaning against my husband, I wept, though not even tears could express my feelings. He stroked my hair and croaked, "We can try again, my love. Another will come to us."

The surgeon cleared his throat unhappily. "Perhaps, my lord, but you must prepare yourself for another possibility. Only time will reveal whether she can still bear children." I looked up at Joscelin in dismay. He had turned white, and I knew why: without a son to carry on his line, his family would lose all their holdings. And that was unthinkable.

"As for you, my lord, out you must go. There is nothing more for you to do but let her sleep and heal."

Joscelin slowly released me and dragged himself to the door. "I will be close by."

"He spent the night outside your door last night, and he'd have been in here with you if the surgeon had allowed it," Helene said. "Here, drink some of this. The physician left it for you." She helped me drink the mixture. But after a few sips, I tasted the opium and turned away. No comfort could come from that, only dreams that might hurt as much as my head and heart. I just lay there with tears streaming onto my pillow, wishing I could sink into the ground and vanish forever.

Just before the medicine did sink me, though merely into troubled sleep, I remembered Philippe and Cecilia. Anguish seized my heart. Philippe would blame himself and Cecilia would be punished, and their lives would be haunted by sorrow.

At my insistence I spent that night in Joscelin's arms, hurting everywhere and so miserable that I could not sleep except in snatches. Not even the opium drink that was forced on me despite my protests could stop my heart from aching even more than my head. I doubt my beloved slept, either, for every time I looked over at him, his eyes were open and tears were on his cheeks. At one point when I had drifted to sleep and then awakened with a start, he whispered, "Fear not. I am here." He could not know how that echoed another man's words—those of my former Mongol master Argamon—but here at least I could trust the man who spoke them.

For the next week I lay abed. From what I could gather from Anna, who mostly wept the one time she was allowed to visit me, Philippe had been banished to an inn until Lord Joscelin could deal with him, and Cecilia was locked in her room. Joscelin and Basil were not on good terms, though they were united in condemning Philippe. Finally Anna dried her tears and told me another side of the tale: hers.

"At least my father was less harsh about Cecilia than my uncle. He says she is merely young and foolish, but that just made Uncle Basil angrier. I feel sorry for everyone! Especially because Cecilia confided in me, and I am on her side to the bitter end! Uncle Basil cares only for wealth and connections. How can he love Aunt Helene so much and be so blind to his own daughter?

"Meanwhile, he keeps trying to soothe Venerio's ruffled feathers. I cannot understand why he bothers. I never saw such a puffed up old cock. A few weeks ago just as I came into the big hall, everyone but them was looking out the window to see the Doge sail by, and he kissed her and tried to run his hands over her. I saw how frightened she looked. When he saw me, he took his hands off her like he'd been burnt, so I knew he was doing wrong. I ran up to her and claimed I had a great need for her to join me up in the rooftop loggia and got her away from him.

"But I did wrong, too, Mama. I see it now. The truth was that Philippe was waiting for her, and I had come down to bring her to him. Not even a fool could miss how in love they are, and I wanted to help, and after what I'd just seen it seemed only right to get her away from that Venerio. Philippe and Cecilia had never met in secret before, I think, I hope, for she was most surprised. If I hadn't tried to help, then and whenever they wanted to pass letters to each other or … and now they are in terrible trouble." She began to sob again.

Helene came in then, chided her for disturbing me, and led her away. Anna cast me such a stricken glance as she left that I realized I must do something soon.

But in truth I was in no condition to offer her any comfort. My head still hurt—those nasty headaches from the time of the Bedouin raid seemed to have returned—and the rest of me was still sore. But it made me impatient to get better. My baby was lost, but there were still other people who needed my aid, including Anna.

I fell asleep only to dream of a mountain that I must climb but which kept crumbling under my feet at every step, until I was climbing on all fours and panting like a weary animal. And when I looked up, there were Anna and Cecilia and all my orphans on the highest peak, trapped by terror, and calling to me to come to their aid. I raced faster and faster, and the mountain crumbled just as fast, until it looked as if I would never reach the top. Worst, I had no idea how to save them, and I was all alone.

The dream finally woke me up, and there was Joscelin beside me, stroking my hair from my sweat-drenched face.

I seemed to take forever to heal. My head hurt without let, and even when my body had mostly recovered, I could only walk as far as a chair before I had to sit down and rest. But I had plenty of time to think. At last I spoke with Joscelin. "I cannot lie abed when there is such trouble in the house. Nor do I want Philippe blaming himself or being blamed for my fall."

Joscelin looked surprised. "But he was—"

"No, he was trying to protect the girl he loved. To my mind, Basil was the real wrongdoer for hurting his daughter! Sometimes it is hard to imagine that he and my father were brothers. It seems so ironic: Papa was the gentle one, who died fighting to protect Rus', while Basil, surrounded by peace and prosperity, is violent toward his own flesh and blood!"

My husband absently stroked my hair while he thought about what I had said. "It is certainly a different view, and I doubt that others will see things your way. But knowing you, I expect you have a plan." He smiled ruefully.

"Well, yes, if you approve, I do." He smiled more fully. "I would like Basil and all three young people to come together, here. I hope that if it comes out right, poor Cecilia, who truly is the sacrifice to greed, may yet be liberated."

At this Joscelin laughed aloud. "Always seeking to help someone, my love! Well, I will see to it, but only if you agree to return to bed right now."

I was glad to do that, and my husband took his leave. However, it took most of the morning to discover where Philippe had gone. Hugh finally found him in a tavern, already drunk and weepy, though it was still early in the day. Before bringing him back to the Ca', he had to take him back to his room, clean him up, and wait for him to get sober enough to present himself. So the gathering did not take place until the late afternoon. Helene had fed me broth and tried to give me more of that opium drink to help me sleep, but I would have none of it. I wanted my wits about me. Finally, I heard my family approach my room. Basil almost bellowed in fury at seeing Philippe waiting outside my door.

"Why is he here? I gave orders he was never to be admitted again!"

I heard my beloved's voice answering quietly. "Be patient, Basil, and you will see. Your niece summoned him for a reason. You owe her this much after all she's been through." Joscelin led them in and took his place, arms crossed, by my side.

Golden light was pouring into the room, gilding the wall paintings and making them seem more alive than I was. It also shone on four very unhappy faces. "Basil, Philippe, Cecilia, and Anna, Lord Joscelin asked you to come to me for a good reason," I began. "First, I know you all have felt bad since my fall. It has been a hard time for every one of us—"

A babble of voices cried out sympathy, regrets, self-blame, and even, in Basil's case, self-justification. I held up my one good hand to my aching head. Perhaps it was too soon to be doing this. But the voices stopped as suddenly as they had begun when Joscelin boomed out, "Shut up, all of you, and listen!"

Once I could think again, I said, "I want you all to hear me out. First of all, Philippe, you did very wrong in bringing Anna into this. She has confessed her guilt, but it is time for you to confess yours, for you were suborning an innocent and using her love for Cecilia to benefit yourself."

He hung his head. "I am entirely at fault in this and in so many other ways. Love for Cecilia blinded me, but it is no excuse. Please, all of you, and especially Anna and Lord Joscelin, accept my deepest regrets for bringing Anna into this disaster." He fell on his knees. "But I know there is more. I beg your forgiveness, Lady Sofia, for nearly causing your death and for causing you to lose your son, and I beg for yours, Basil Petrovich, for abusing your hospitality, and yours, Cecilia, for leading you astray." He was so pathetic and charming at the same time that Cecilia burst into tears and threw herself on her knees next to him!

Basil reached out to seize her, but he checked himself when Joscelin stepped forward protectively. My uncle was so dark with rage that I feared he might burst.

"Please, everyone, listen to me," I said in my most commanding voice. Alas, I was so weak that it sounded more like a wheeze. "I have more to say. Basil, I know how angry you are with Cecilia, and indeed it was foolish and wrong of her to carry on with Philippe behind your back. But you are as much to blame as Philippe for my falling down the stairs."

"Me!"

"Yes, for Philippe was only rushing to save the girl he loved from your wrath. As Anna says, why do you love your own daughter so little that you would sacrifice her to your greed? Look at how you love Helene. Would you sacrifice her in that way? You have turned into such a worshipper of Mammon that it blinds you and makes you cruel—the jolly uncle I once knew has been lost for years! Now I begin to fear for your salvation! We have wealth aplenty, and yet you are never satisfied.

"Cecilia is much too young for Venerio, and it matters not what his connections are: he is a venal man, ruled as much by lust as by money. He has done things to Cecilia behind our backs, things Anna had to witness, that were as wrong as anything Philippe did! Venerio will be a terrible husband to her and a poor partner to you—just listen to the way he talks of cheating others and think on what kind of loyalty he might show you!"

Basil visibly struggled with himself, but he heard me. He crossed his arms and looked down, still red with rage.

Silence fell in the room. I doubt any of those four had expected me to speak so bluntly to my uncle, though it was what we all thought of him.

How I wanted to go back to sleep by then! But I had to finish it all first.

"What is more, if you will listen to one who has everyone's interests at heart, I have a suggestion to rid you of Venerio without his pride being wounded further. You will claim you want nothing more to do with Cecilia and plan to put her in a convent up north. Then when Lord Joscelin and I leave for the Languedoc, we will take her with us."

"No!" both Philippe and Cecilia cried.

"Well, it's most unlikely you will end up there, but until we leave, you must certainly behave more chastely. That will be easier when Philippe goes, which he must do straightaway. He should return to Braissac and await Lord Joscelin and you, if his desire to marry you is sincere. Certainly his remaining in Venice does no one any good."

"But I do want to marry her! She is my life, my heart, my—"

"Enough!" Lord Joscelin cut in. "You weary us all with your troubadour tongue, and Lady Sofia has more to say."

"Yes, there is one more thing. Basil, I must answer to myself for my fall as much as you or Philippe must answer to me, for it was I who made the misstep that led to it. Philippe bears the blame of a hasty heart, you of a greedy one, and me of being too willing to help young love blossom. It is my weakness, always to try to help."

"Well, at least you see your own flaws," Basil muttered.

I sighed. "Yes, I do. Now I ask you all to leave me and to think on what I have said. I need to rest, for all this talking has wearied me to the bone. We can meet again later, perhaps tomorrow morning."

Basil still looked angry, but also a little shamefaced. He nodded and left. Philippe helped Cecilia to stand before bowing to his lord. "With your permission, Lord Joscelin, I will do as Lady Sofia says. Her heart is so caring and generous that it puts us all to shame. If Basil Petrovich agrees to her plan, I will be in Braissac awaiting my beloved. If not, I will at least no longer be living like a shadow and drinking away my means."

Joscelin replied, "You are indeed fortunate. I think Sofia sees things too generously sometimes. You cost me an hcir as well as nearly killing her! I was tempted to beat you myself, but you served me so well in the past that I could not do it. Yes, you should go, but I will help you make the travel arrangements. There is business you can do on my behalf, so you needn't feel as though you're of no worth in this sorry affair.

"Now, Sofia, you can rest with an easy heart. It is up to the others to sort out all the details. Come, Philippe." My beloved husband planted a warm kiss on my lips and left.

At the door Philippe turned and bowed to me. "Thank you for all your kindness, Lady Sofia. If ever you need my sword arm, it is yours."

With both heart and mind more at ease than it had been for days, I drifted into the first good sleep I'd had since my fall, and the next day I awoke with new hope in my heart. I would recover, I would bear not one but many more sons—and daughters—for my husband, and I would pick up the threads of my new life very soon.

Of course once everyone had agreed to my plan, it must be executed, which took time. A few days later Basil came to me to announce that he had succeeded in disentangling Cecilia from the betrothal, at least for now, while keeping on Venerio's good side.

"When I first approached him, he still wanted Cecilia despite his humiliation in front of you all. He claimed he was impatient to hold the wedding as soon as possible, especially because right after all this happened, I had promised him a larger dowry—he let that slip! That was when I began to see your point of view, Sofia: he is venal! But I told him that my daughter was now in open rebellion. He'd had a rebellious son and he had disinherited him, so I appealed to his memory and cautioned him that he wanted no wife who would defy him as his son had, that Cecilia must be brought under control first. That made him pause, and only then did I add that I wanted to send her away to a convent until she submits to my will."

Basil smiled grimly. "And it is true that she has been a mighty slippery maiden lately, and most disrespectful to me and even Helene.

"I said nothing about Joscelin and you, though. I knew that Venerio would see no reason why Sir Joscelin of all men should take her north. After all, it was his knight who stirred up this hornet's nest.

"Now I just have to come up with a way to break off the betrothal entirely without offending him. We will claim that Cecilia has fallen ill with a disfiguring disease!"

I shuddered and crossed myself. "Don't say such things!"

"Oh, so it's fine to lie about putting her into a convent but not to invent a disease? Come, Sofia, who's not being jolly now?" Basil laughed and took his leave.

Shortly thereafter Joscelin looked in on me. "Time to take a walk. You haven't been outside in days, Sofia, and it is warm enough to sit outside for a while. The April sun will do you good. And if walking to the loggia tires you, I will carry you and set you by the balcony so that you can watch the boats pass by."

And he did: he lifted me lightly and took me to a bench outside, and it was indeed a pleasure to be there, with the water sparkling on the Grand Canal and the sun gently warming us. I had felt cut off from the life of our family, too, so when Paolo and Gilles came out to play backgammon, and Helene arrived with her entourage of nursemaids and children, and Anna and Cecilia joined us, I was happier than I had imagined I could ever be again. I fell asleep half-cradled in Joscelin's arms and dreamt that I was sitting beside a murmuring brook that spoke the names of everyone I loved.

Not until early May did I feel well enough to travel. By then things had sorted themselves out between Venerio and Basil. When the man realized how long it might be before he could get his hands on Cecilia's dowry, he decided that their betrothal was not for him, anyway. It seemed that his shady dealings had caught up with him and that he owed money to his backers for goods that were unaccounted for, goods that he had actually offered to sell to Basil before they disappeared. He graciously admitted defeat in the arena of love and promptly transferred his affections to a recently widowed and very wealthy relative of his.

I think even Basil rejoiced, for he'd have lost both profit and pride had he paid Venerio for goods that were not the man's to sell. We left shortly after the festival of Pentecost, which was an occasion for worship, piety, holy processions, and extravagant feasting. The night before our party left, we held a farewell feast, and one of his toasts was to me for leading him out of trouble. "And if he turns honest someday, we can still do business together!" We all laughed, but as much at him as at his jest.

The next morning witnessed a sad parting, though. Not only Cecilia but Paolo and Gilles were to accompany us: Paolo was to seek new trade connections at some seasonal fair in a county bound to Francia called Champagne, while Gilles was to be Lord Joscelin's squire. The boy would serve him on the journey north and thus begin his training as a baron in his own right.

Gilles was thrilled, as Paolo had always been the friendliest of his stepbrothers. Now that he was shooting up like a spring weed, they were even the same height, and the two of them together could hold their own against any persecutions the older brothers might bother to think up—not that either needed to worry about that these days, for the eldest brothers were now partners with their father and too busy to bother with the younger boys. And I think it made Gilles happier to leave than he would otherwise have been, since it was unlikely he would see his mother more than once every few years.

Needless to say, of us all Helene was the most desolated. She was entering late pregnancy, and she had her youngest children still about her—and Basil's two eldest sons—but Gilles was her last link with her dead husband. I suspected that Basil was secretly happy to send the boy off for that very reason.

But answering Helene's tearful cries to keep her boy, Joscelin had argued that it was necessary, for Lord Gilles had left holdings in Francia that needed their master. Stewards could not have served Gilles from afar for this long and not gotten up to mischief. The boy must become a strong knight and then offer homage to King Louis for his lands. Joscelin promised her that he would bring him up to be a proper, and tough, Frankish lord.

I was thrilled to have so many young people coming with me, and not only for Anna's sake but for my own. I had not fully recovered from the shock of losing my son, and I would still awaken some mornings to find my pillow wet with tears. Surely the presence of so many lively young people would cheer my heart and give me more to do as well.

On the other hand, I would be so far from Helene, and my orphans would be lost to me forever along with Alexander and Banjuu and Bardas and Leo and Anna and Adar, just as surely as Q'ing-ling or Perijam or Maryam were. It was only as we were embracing and saying our tearful farewells that I had to admit to myself that once I had married Lord

Joscelin, everything had changed for me forever. I was to enter his world and leave mine entirely behind.

Again that sense of dread arose, but what more could happen to me after all I had already endured? I had no idea, but I crossed myself and whispered a prayer for everyone's safety. If I had learned one thing in life, it was that nothing is certain.

We parted with many tears and promises to visit every few years. And Helene, at least, did have an excuse to come to us, to see her son knighted and more, so there was hope for the future. Still, she had been my best friend, almost my sister, for years. Now I would never again enjoy her easy companionship any time I needed it. That realization broke off a piece of my heart and carried it away, never to return.

She even offered to send Fotis and Irene with us on our journey. Fotis was good at everything, and Irene would serve Anna and me. They could continue as Paolo's servants when he returned to Venice the following spring. It seemed such a happy arrangement.

Our motley assemblage of trade goods, baggage, servants, children, knights, and husband and wife departed from Venice, possibly never to return, for only God knows our fates. We were on barges that are also used for carrying goods inland to Vicenza, a sort of sister city to Venice from what I could make out. At Basil's insistence we must go there first, where I was to find his agent, who would take charge of various goods my uncle was sending him.

The journey took all day, but I saw little of the countryside because it was so warm and sultry that I fell asleep. My dreams reflected what I had seen before my eyes closed: a gentle-looking land, green with fields of corn or with vines just beginning to ripen, softly rolling tree-covered hills, a pale mountain range rising in the distance, peasants laboring here and there, villas nestled among cypress trees, a fortified castle every once in a while. All seemed at peace.

The late sun invaded my makeshift umbrella on the barge and woke me in time to see Vicenza looming up before us. Walls with towers surround it, and many more towers rise up inside it, which is surely why it is called the city of a thousand towers.

We arrived as the sun was setting, just in time to enter the city gates before they were closed. The town guards challenged us at first, but on finding out who we were, they courteously escorted us to meet their mayor, who is called the Podestà. Sometimes it is very pleasant to have good connections, and Lord Joscelin made the most of Basil's, with the result that we all stayed in the Podestà's palace, a grand Venetian-style building with porticos and loggias and spacious halls and bedrooms. It is set along one side of the central piazza, near which rears a squat military tower. That evening over an abundant supper, the mayor told us a little about the city.

"Things are not always so peaceful here. Heresy is only held in check by our saintly bishop, Bartholomew of Vicenza …" That name caught my attention; it was familiar to me. I finally placed it after some thought: he had traveled to Cyprus with King Louis, one of many dignitaries, "… and has been bishop in several cities. Thanks to him our new cathedral boasts a thorn from the Crown of Thorns, a gift from King Louis himself!" So what Sir Reynaud had told me about false relics might have been wrong … "The good bishop even founded a monastic military order to fight heresy and disorder in Lombardy. I wish they would do the same here! The homes of our greatest families are fortified against each other, since there is almost constant war between them; and beyond that, we are forever warring with other cities. One cannot really blame any of us after that vicious Ezzelino da Romano did so much damage, not only to our homes and lands but to our loyalties!"

Our host was especially full of glee over the fall of this tyrant Ezzelino, who had ruled not only Vicenza but also other cities for the Holy Roman Emperor Frederick, a king whose name had never meant much to me. These Romans and Franks and Germans and Italians all had hopelessly intertwined histories. But truth be told, I was not very interested. It all sounded so complex and mean-spirited, and it had nothing to do with me. But I politely listened to him and Joscelin and his other guests carry on about some political party called Guelphs, who seemed to support the Pope, and how glad they were to be free of Ezzelino and his Ghibellines, who favored the Holy Roman Empire and were thought to be heretics, perhaps Cathar, perhaps something else. I gathered from the conversation that heresy was rife in northern Italy.

Not caring about any of these politics, I wanted only to retire early to rest. When I was able to excuse myself along with a handful of other wives, the men were debating the battle strategy of the allied armies that had recently defeated Ezzelino and led to his death, a battle they were certain would be celebrated everywhere a thousand years hence.

I fell asleep after seeing my brood to bed and only awoke when my husband joined me. "I didn't mean to waken you, love, but it was worth staying on. We talked about the fastest and safest travel routes, and tomorrow I will hire more guards." I kissed him and fitted my body to his. I didn't want to think about unsafe travel, and soon, enfolded in his passionate embrace, I did not need to.

Early the next morning, Paolo and Gilles took the short walk with me to the house and place of business of Basil's agent. He lived on one side of the busy market square that was bounded in part by the palace where we were staying. This piazza differed little from the smaller ones in Venice, and the buildings could have come from there, too. But of course instead of water, there were streets and horses and carts rumbling on cobblestones, and much noise of booths being set up and people already calling out the merits of their wares.

I conducted my uncle's business for him, the youths by my side looking on with interest at all the documents and seals and signatures that went with it. Paolo regarded this as part of what he need to know, so I explained everything to him as I went, but Gilles was more interested in the fact that Lord Joscelin still let me conduct such affairs at all. It brought home to me how lucky I was to have a husband and uncle who granted me such independence!

We came away with one of the merchant's servants, who was to collect the goods we had brought, plus, to Paolo's delight, a commenda agreement, a kind of blind partnership, which Paolo was to be responsible for handling, as well as letters of credit for use in this Champagne fair he was to attend. It was his first adult foray into the world of trade, and he could not be more proud. Gilles looked a little envious when he saw Paolo strutting and crowing, but his was to be a different lot. His turn would come.

By the time we met up with Joscelin and Sir Hugh and the others, they had hired a dozen stout pike men and two men with crossbows to go with us. Just knowing there might be danger made me feel uneasy.

But as it turned out, thanks to my brood of four, our journey to the west coast of the Italies was remarkably free of trouble and full of lively times, song, and good cheer. And having joined a large caravan of fellow travelers, including several merchants, we were safe enough, though our group would swell in numbers one week and dwindle away the next. It was often almost like a parade, with standard bearers and sometimes musicians or at least drummers marching ahead of the procession, followed by the richest and most self-important merchants riding mares, while their servants and menials followed them leading assorted beasts of burden. Guards surrounded us all.

When it rained one day, I learned why no one used carts when we passed one mired in the mud. I pitied the poor horses, straining to pull away from the bite of their owner's whip, but there was nothing I could do and I was the only one to see a problem. People simply did not seem to see the whipping or to hear the man's furious curses or his horses bellowing. I suddenly recalled travel in one of the great Mongol ordus: they had been indifferent to other people's pain, but they cared for their horses above all. Indeed, a slave was more likely to be mistreated than an animal.

Every day we passed through lovely countryside: meadows or hills dotted with fortified manors. They looked so innocent sitting sleepily in the sun, while around them peasants toiled in golden fields or tended blossoming orchards. I sometimes heard the song of thousands of invisible bees. At times dark cypresses lined up like soldiers upon the hills, glowing as if from within when the sun was behind them.

Once we saw a band of knights and foot soldiers leaving one of the larger castles, heading off for somewhere. Luckily they did not come our way! It seemed a sin that so many wars had been fought there. Traces of recent conflicts, mostly in the form of ruined castles, scarred the soft landscape, though at least there were no piles of bones. Hills and valleys, little towns and large cities alike were walled and guarded zealously, but we had papers of introduction that were as effective as any Mongol paize.

I scarcely remember the names of all those cities. Verona, I remember, had many towers and the ruins of an old Roman amphitheater. That tyrant Ezzelino had come from there, as had a martyred saint named Peter of Verona. We went to the cathedral there to pray, and I learned about this saint, who had been sent to inquire into heresy and converted people with his mercy, his humility, and his clear teachings. He had been murdered by Cathari, which set me against them straightaway.

After we had left the city and were traveling past meadows, fields, and olive orchards, Joscelin suddenly remarked, "Ezzelino! Such blood lies on that man's hands, Sofia. To punish Padua for resisting him, he had 11,000 captive citizens slaughtered on that empty meadow to our left! Now no one wants to plant there. Imagine such pitiless slaughter!"

"No, thank you. I've seen slaughter like that, and even imagining it makes me feel ill. Besides, try imagining millions killed and you'll get an idea of what we were spared when the Mongols turned back from your kingdoms."

We rode in silence while I stared glumly away from the meadow he had pointed out, now greenly lazing in the sun. But unbidden images came to me, of blood and screams and wails, of dismembered bodies and vacant-eyed severed heads. Was I wrong not to want to think about such things anymore? I would rather simply venerate the sainted Peter the Martyr, but perhaps that was cowardice.

Finally I turned to Joscelin, who was riding beside me looking pensive. "I am sorry, my lord. I seem not to be myself these days. All I want is peace and a simple life with you. No more wars."

He took one of my hands and kissed it on the palm. "I thought perhaps you were expecting again. I remember you were a little sharp last February when your morning sickness bothered you."

I sighed. "No, I think not. But perhaps soon...." He looked a little disappointed.

We stopped overnight at a city called Cremona, which also dates back to ancient Roman times. It was built in what I was coming to recognize as an Italian Roman style, and it too was embroiled in the same divisions as in Verona and Vicenza and, had I realized it at the time, even Venice to some degree. It had something to do with each city regarding itself and the lands around it as sovereign but acting together in some kind of league against their particular enemy, Emperor or Pope. Their choice seemed to depend on which was the nearer threat, Empire or Papacy. And religious divisions seemed to mirror these enmities. That was as much as I cared to know.

However, as we passed through the city's heart, we did stop our train to allow the young people to stare at a great tower being built of bricks. The workers stopped briefly and stared back, but one of the overseers came over and bowed to us. One of our guards asked him what they were building, and he translated for us.

"It will be a great tower. When it is complete, it will be the tallest tower in the world."

"And ask him when he expects it will be completed," said Joscelin.

"Oh," he translated after a brief discussion, "only another fifty years or so. The overseer says they have been working on it for over thirty, and that his father was the overseer before him. He boasts that it will be the finest tower in the world when it is done, though he won't live to see it. It is a matter of civic pride, he says." The overseer looked quite pleased.

We moved on, me pondering how some people are so happy to build something fine for a future whose fruits they will never reap, while others, like this Ezzelino, are content to destroy and ravage what isn't theirs just to fill their own purses and bellies and satisfy their greed for power—and, I suppose, in his case to satisfy his outright cruelty!

As Lady Q'ing-ling had said all those years ago, that seemed to be the way of the world, though I still failed to see why.

One afternoon we passed through another old Roman city, Piacenza, whose name means peaceful place. It was set in a river valley that was as softly beautiful as every other region we had passed. We arrived on a holy day, and the streets were thronged with people following a procession led by a bishop, his chanting priests, and acolytes waving censers. Some of the citizens were carrying a beautifully adorned statue of Holy Mother Mary through the streets, but I never learned what the occasion was. The holy men and the statue all looked so beautiful, and you could feel how much awe they aroused in everyone's hearts. It was as though all our minds were briefly one and at peace. After the procession had passed and we could make our way to our inn, Joscelin spoke thoughtfully.

"It is an irony: the first Holy War was proclaimed here, in a city whose name means peace. And heresy thrives here, I am told, from want of good relations with the Church and her vicars. Politics plays a role, too, as it seems to in all these places."

"I remember that when you first described the Occitaine to me, you said that the more beautiful and peaceful a place seems on the surface, the more people fight over it. I suppose that holds true for religion, too."

He nodded.

In another city we went through—thank God we didn't need to stay there—we just missed witnessing a hanging. Still-twitching, foul-smelling corpses were swaying in the breeze as we rode past the gibbets. The young people all stopped their gaiety and stared as we passed through the thinning crowd. Then Gilles spotted a man selling sweets and called out for us to stop and buy something. The corpses were forgotten, for which I

was glad, but I did ask Joscelin why twenty men and three boys—I counted them—would be hanged all at once.

"Treason, I suspect. They all looked like low class citizens; from their
stench they were probably dyers, the types who try to stir up trouble over
working hours or wages. They should have been glad they had skills and
useful work."

His response surprised me. "But what if their masters were cruel or
unreasonable? Did they have no rights?"

Joscelin looked at me in surprise. "What rights would the lowborn
even need?" His reply silenced me, but then he continued thoughtfully.
"Well, lower class people have some. And they are much freer than their
country cousins. If they were merely peasants, there would be taxes to pay
and work obligations to their lord that they are free of in the city. And
they can seek a new master if they're unhappy."

"It surprises me, my lord, to hear you speak so unfeelingly about these
men and boys when you feel so strongly about protecting your villagers at
home."

My husband looked taken aback. "Well, I suppose the difference is that
my villagers are mine. I know them and I want them content. But I am
older now, too, Sofia. I see some things more clearly than I did when I was
in the Holy Land. Being responsible for the welfare of my barony gave
me a different perspective, a larger one."

Though I wanted to say more, I held my tongue. Lord Joscelin was
patient with what he termed my overly generous heart, and it would not
do to quarrel over some poor corpses. However, I did call Golden Thomas
forward and gave him some coins.

"Give those to the priest standing there, the one praying near the hanged
men. Tell him it is for their widows and bereaved mothers."

Joscelin held his tongue, but he did not look well pleased.

AUTUMN
ANNO DOMINI 1262

After less than a month of easy travel, most of it pleasant, we reached Genoa in late July under a sun that felt as if it might cook us all. There we met with a little cooling breeze from the sea, though the sea smell of wharves mingled with even less pleasant odors. Genoa is another bustling maritime city, very ancient according to Joscelin, who had been there before. It is as beautiful as Venice and for the same reasons: riches robbed from others. Though the city is set among hills and surrounded by orchards or fields of corn, it seems like a marble dream, at least until you reach the docks, where warehouses compete with fortified palaces and the stench casts a pall over the lovely buildings. A lighthouse with three crenellated towers sits on a hill overlooking the city, and a fire burns there day and night to guide the galleys and warships into harbor.

There were plenty of battleships, too, for the war with Venice was still going strong, and for all I know may still be. I was rather surprised that we were admitted so easily, but being Rus' and not Venetian gave Basil an advantage. He even had contacts there. And when I thought on it, I realized that Franks like Lord Joscelin would of course be welcome in the city, as King Louis' war had added to Genoese wealth. The king's armies had sailed in their ships, not in Venetian ones.

Lord Joscelin took us to an inn run by the Knights Hospitallers. I stayed with my weary wards while he paid off our guards and went out with Hugh to arrange our passage on a ship leaving for King Louis' port of Aigues Mortes. It seems a rather frightening name, for it means Dead Waters. That business done, they came back for us and we strolled along the wharf idly looking at whatever caught our fancy, which was much, for warehouses and markets line the street that runs along the docks. It was our first day in weeks where we weren't traveling.

South of the main docks is a lovely central piazza where stands a fabulous new palace, very busy with men going in and out. It seemed new and sparkling compared with the heavy stone or dull pink marble of older buildings around the open court.

"I heard about this from Basil just before we left," my husband exclaimed. "The Palazzo San Giorgio. He told me to find it and see what it looks like, though I scarcely expected it to be finished already."

I looked at it curiously. "Why, the statues and decorations on the front look familiar! How can that be, and why would Basil care?"

"Well, apart from its practical and very commercial uses, it represents Genoa's triumph over Venice in Constantinople. Emperor Michael Palaeologus tore down the Venetian embassy there and gave the materials and works of art in it to Genoa as a reward for her help in retaking the city. You probably passed the embassy and never knew what it was. This palazzo is intended to be the political heart of the city, totally independent of the clergy, quite a daring innovation. It was built by some powerful nobleman with ambitions."

"Oh, I see. It certainly must have been built in a great hurry! This adds to the bad blood between the cities, I suppose."

Joscelin smiled grimly in answer. "There is bad blood within Genoa itself. I will take you to this building's local rival next. "Come this way. We should pray for a safe journey before we leave."

So next we visited the palazzo's bitter rival, the cathedral, which is dedicated to San Lorenzo, an early Christian deacon martyred in Rome. It is one of many fine churches in the city. There are three black-and-white striped, pillared portals on the front, most impressive, and sculptors were hard at work on some stone carvings around the entry that tell stories of the Virgin Mary. Entering was like crossing a border, for suddenly I saw that the Roman or even Greek style was giving way to something quite different from what I was accustomed to, though I saw much more like it later in Francia and the Languedoc. The space is enormous and austere compared with San Marco or Hagia Sofia, but there are also some fabulous holy treasures inside: sacred art, some of it carved of ivory; chalices of gold or silver; jewel-studded crucifixes; and much more.

I asked Joscelin how such a collection of beautiful and holy things had come together, and he laughed softly. "Seized from others, my dear, from around the Mediterranean. It is a sign that God favors them, or so men say."

"And what do you say?"

"I prefer to say nothing. It is better to keep one's thoughts to oneself in such matters.

"However, before you get too upset about where all this comes from, I would like to tell you and our young ones the legend of San Lorenzo."

I nodded agreement and waved to my wards to join us. We stopped in the middle aisle of the nave while he spoke to us all like a guide.

"When San Lorenzo was being tortured by the Romans on a heated gridiron, he supposedly said, 'This side of me is cooked. Turn me over and have a bite!' This is why he is the patron saint of butchers, roasters, and jesters."

Everyone laughed, and so did he, though we drew some disapproving stares from passing pilgrims.

"He had been the protector of the Holy Chalice of Christ, which was said to be carved of emerald. Before his arrest he is thought to have sent it back to a monastery in his native Spain for safekeeping, where it resides to this day. Except that this cathedral claims to possess it, too, and far be it from me to determine the truth of the matter."

He led us up to where the sacred chalice was displayed in a kind of treasury room similar to the one in San Marco. It was a wide, green, many-sided bowl that seemed a little oddly shaped for a drinking cup; and while it was green, it was not carved of emerald. Even if I had given up the life of a merchant, I still knew my gems!

But there was so much else that was so fine, so full of piety and transfiguring faith, that I would have loved to spend an entire day there in prayer. Reliquaries abounded, including one I was not allowed to see: a chained marble box holding the ashes of Saint John the Baptist, which was kept in a special chapel that women were not allowed to enter but for one day a year, and that day was not the day.

Lord Joscelin went in, however, along with the boys, to pray for a safe journey for us all, as mariners had done for centuries, while we women prayed standing outside it. I was reminded of my departure from Kyiv so many years ago when we had all prayed for a safe journey. I had certainly not expected what had followed—all of my companions lost, being captured and enslaved by Argamon, Papa likely killed in battle, my escape from Batu Khan's ordu and near imprisonment in Iran … discovering love and loss at Castle Sa'amar … building my own life in different places, different cities. But now I was setting foot onto a new route in my life's journey. My prayers were especially heartfelt.

The next day after searching long and hard, Joscelin located his Genoese shipmate and they were reunited, both of them surprised and happy that the other was still alive and well. My husband brought me to meet him, and I had to endure many high-flown praises of my beauty and grace, well knowing that I was now in middle age and no longer the beauty I had once been. My remaining memory of that city is of a huge feast his friend held in honor of their friendship. It was the first time I saw Joscelin drunk—and rowdy, too. Though his jollity was well earned after all he and his friend had undergone, this new side of him gave me pause. What else about him did I not know?

But not even the delightful songs a troubadour performed for us could keep me from my bed, and I left early, already half asleep, haunted by a plaintive love song that reminded me of a similar song I'd heard in Iran, for it featured a nightingale longing for a rose. At least there was no double meaning hidden in it, no Nizari plotting harm while intending good.

I awoke at dawn the next day, snug in Lord Joscelin's embrace. We were soon on our way to the docks where a new style of square-sailed galley awaited us. This ship was fitted with a castle at the front for protection, and my lord and I were given space in a largish cabin that sat below it. That was a sign of the captain's respect for us, as it was also where he lived. The others had to make do with spaces below the deck.

Luckily the journey did not take long, for the ship was crowded with people from all walks of life. I kept a strict watch on my girls, as some of the rougher men behaved quite rudely to them, trying to pinch them—even Anna—or steal kisses. It gave me something to do, since that vague sense of unease arose once more.

I tried to explain it away by reminding myself that I missed Helene and her children, not to mention all my other well-loved friends scattered over half a continent, most of whom I would never see again. And an unknown future approaching me with every sweep of the oars and every gust of wind in the sails seemed reason enough to feel a little faint-hearted. But then Lord Joscelin would come up beside me and put his arm about my waist, and all would be well again.

Anna was somehow troubled, too. She had seemed to enjoy the journey to Genoa, though sometimes she kept to herself more than usual. I thought I understood. This change in her life must seem especially hard after all the traveling and resettling she had already done. One night after seeing to all my young wards' comfort and ensuring they were well-protected by our guards, I was turning to leave when I realized she was trying to choke back tears. I sat down beside her on her pallet and put my arms around her.

"What is it, dearest?"

She turned her head away and began to weep in earnest. "You go into a bright and happy future, Mama, but what will become of me? Cecilia will marry Philippe, and Gilles will go north and claim his inheritance, and I will be alone. I will miss them both, especially Gilles—he's like my brother!" She let out an especially loud sob.

"And I keep trying to love my father as I should, but he stole you from me! I cannot help myself: I am angry! I am so sorry, and I try to be a good daughter to you both, but …"

I clasped her close to my bosom. "I cannot tell you how to feel, nor do I judge you. You are the best of daughters, and I cherish you. You will find new friends to love and who will love you, too, and perhaps a new grandmother in Lord Joscelin's mother, someone who will pet and spoil you just as a grandmother should. At the same time, it is only right and good that you should miss your old friends. I miss mine, too."

"But what will happen when I am old enough to marry? I think my father already wants to get rid of me, for I see him looking at me now as if he's trying to decide something. I think he'll want me to marry as soon as he can find someone to take me away from you! I'm afraid, Mama!"

"He's said nothing to me about marrying you to anyone. He wouldn't do such a thing without my knowledge and consent—and yours! No doubt someday there will be a man just right for you, who will give you the same joy as my husband gives me. And I promise you this, my darling: I will never make you marry someone you cannot love, nor will your father.

He knows what a love match is, after all."

Anna wiped her tears and pushed away from me a little. "You are right, Mama. I'm acting like a silly child, am I not?"

I laughed softly, released her from my embrace, and sat up. "Only a little. We all have fears, dear one, and I am glad you share yours with me. You know you can come to me at any time."

"I know, and I am glad, too. Good night, Mama."

"Good night, my sweet. Rest well. We arrive tomorrow, I am told."

I went back to the curtained-off area of the cabin where Lord Joscelin was already stretched out on our pallet. He awoke long enough to put his arms around me, but I lay awake looking at his profile in the near dark. Had Anna seen something in him that I had missed? Or was she worrying needlessly? That feeling of dread settled on me like a bad habit, and it took most of the night to find sleep.

The next afternoon we arrived at Aigues Mortes, a dismal port town enlarged by King Louis solely to transport soldiers and goods for his holy war. It was surrounded by a specially dug lagoon for Louis' ships, smelly marshes, and a passage from a river called the Rhône that led to the sea, also Louis' work. It was clear why it had been given such a dreary name. Two round towers stood guard over it, one quite tall and with an oddly rounded parapet, which I suppose had been built as a lookout, though there was little to look at beyond flat marshes, an old church, and a square named after the king. From the busy and fishy-smelling market we passed through to get to our inn, I gathered that most people lived off the sea.

We spent the night at a hostel filled with pilgrims—this seemed to be the other reason for the city's existence, since not only warriors but ordinary people were forever leaving for or arriving from the Holy Land—and the next morning we returned to the docks to take ship for yet another port, which Joscelin called Narbonne, very ancient and once Roman. He stopped briefly at the customs house to post a letter to his mother, and we were on our way. I saw him tucking another letter into his pouch, which must have awaited his arrival. I hoped it was good news.

After we set sail following the coastline, some strange and, to my eyes, wondrous sights greeted us: thrice we saw scattered herds, twice of wild horses and once of a kind of cattle. Both horses and kine were completely different from what I knew, both in size and coloring. I guessed they were wild because no fences kept them in. They were fascinating. Were these breeds common throughout this new world I was entering? The horses were small and white with gray legs, though all the smallest were black. The cattle were equally undersized. Down the railing, one of the crew-members was pointing them out to Gilles and saying something, and later I overheard Gilles telling Anna in a voice of superior knowledge that the horses were born black but turned white when they were fully grown.

"So," I said, joining my husband at the railing and thinking he might mention the letter, "are those horses and cattle like the ones in your lands?"

He laughed. "No, both are ancient breeds that you can only find here in the south. Not good for much, really, so the people hereabouts let them run wild."

"And what happens when we reach Narbonne?"

"I plan to take you all home first, to my castle, to leave Cecelia there. Sir Philippe's mother is, according to a letter that awaited me at the customs house, already planning the wedding. She and my mother are great friends and eager as can be to meet the young bride. Although of course, foremost is Mother's desire to meet you!" I hadn't realized how ill at ease I was about that letter, for I had feared it might be a summons from King Louis. Joscelin had written him from Venice some months ago, and I was dreading the response. Despite the king's promise, what if he tried to drag my husband into another war after all? Or, equally horrible, perhaps my husband's letter had told the truth about Anna, and Louis had banished him.

A few days later, we reached Narbonne, a port that seems ever in danger of turning into an inland city, as it sits by another river called the Aude, brown and full of silt. Men on barges and banks were hard at work dredging out muck from it to keep it flowing properly. But after so much travel by sea, I was glad to stay there a few days while Joscelin made arrangements for our travel onward. There were Roman ruins to gape at, including the remains of an ancient road, and a lively market to visit.

I also noticed that the Star of David was sewn to the clothing of many men, and veiled women, too, but no one seemed to treat these Jews with the disrespect they too often received elsewhere. A chance remark to Lord Joscelin revealed that Narbonne is a center of learning for those of the Jewish faith; many great scholars moved there from Baghdad several hundred years ago.

And in the market, I found an odd book quite by chance. It had some-how found its way there and was buried in a pile of oddments like scraps of brocade. I discovered it while lazily examining the scraps. The owner of the booth only knew that it came from the Archbishop's palace and that the book celebrated love and quoted the legendary—to anyone from Narbonne—Ermengarde, a Viscountess of Narbonne. She had lived sev-eral decades ago. A book about love: that lured me into buying it! Oddly enough, it was written by a cleric and was a collection of epigrams by queens and princesses and this Ermengarde. Its title was 'A Treatise on Courtly Love.'

I took it back to our inn and began to read it, and was thus engaged when Joscelin returned from his errands. He laughed when I showed it to him. "Why, this contains many of the same wise writings by the great Queen Eleanor of Aquitaine that I read in my youth. I once wrote you about her. Do you remember? In the letter I had thought would be my last farewell to you."

"How could I forget? I will read it with that much more eagerness."

But to my disappointment, while the book praised the power of love to ennoble the heart, its author also described women in the harshest of terms. And my own beloved must have misunderstood its message, for while it claimed to guide some youth named Walter in loving a lady from afar, I got the feeling she was married. The reward for his loyalty was un-clear. Was it to end in an adulterous liaison? Or did it purify the heartbro-ken lover and inspire him to great deeds? No wonder Joscelin had once had such wild ideas about loving me! At least he had outgrown them in the past twelve years. I hoped so, since the book claimed that true love could never happen in marriage.

Worse was the advice on how to seduce women of low degree: it amounted to rape! I hoped it had not guided Joscelin into his follies with women. I finally set the book aside in disgust.

When he was finished with his preparations for our journey, Joscelin had hired an even larger number of guards than we had used in Italy, as well as a pair of young knights who had been on board ship with us and who were heading north to a tournament to try their fortunes. I gathered that it was from winning prizes at tourneys that many landless knights, younger sons like them, survived.

Joscelin had also bought horses for us that he called palfreys, as well as mules for our goods. We needed an extra mule already, for Paolo had been at work while aboard, trading a small packet of cloves for heavy hemp rope. I had to hold my tongue, for the trade seemed most impractical to me, but Paolo had to learn sometime.

One evening Joscelin came back to the inn with a great slab of honeycomb. After the family supper in our private room, shouts and laughter drifting up the stairs from the alehouse, he brought it out and passed dripping chunks around the table. "Try this, everyone, and tell me if it is not the best honey you ever tasted!" We were all of us, especially the boys, soon sticky from the palest, most delicate-tasting honey any of us had ever eaten. Not even the hearty honey of Rus' could compare.

"The hives are set up in the hills near fields of rosemary, and the bees harvest the pollen almost entirely from their flowers. It's unbelievably expensive!"

Expensive it might be, but it was worth every penny. I noticed Paolo's ears pricking up, and the next day he came back from the market with Golden Thomas staggering behind him carrying a pair of huge flat boxes. "I found more honey, Paolo cried, "and I made sure that each comb is most carefully wrapped and boxed. This is ichor itself, and I will make a fortune at the Champagne fair when I get there!" I laughed: no blood of the gods ran in his veins, only the blood of a merchant.

On our journey to Braissac, we took a roundabout route in order to avoid areas of Occitaine that were still almost in a state of war. We often traveled by barge up or down rivers, depending on which way the current flowed. The lands we passed were unfailingly beautiful, surrounded by trees and greenery, often with steep, craggy hills rising in the distance. I especially loved the willows along the rivers, the way they trailed their long leafy fingers in the water. The river men used barges with poles to keep us moving when the way lay upstream. Often we left the rivers and made our way over the passes of steep mountains—mere hills by Caucasus standards—clad at their bases with fine trees but often with recently ruined castles perched atop them.

So many people seemed on the move, too. Some were simply peasants bringing foodstuffs or wares to market, their simple carts pulled by sturdy horses laden with amulets and jingling bells and the like to ward off evil. Some were the usual merchants. And many were pilgrims, men and women alike, following some route of faith, their hats adorned with shells and medals to show where they had been. Most of them seemed filled with joy or with holy awe, though a few were lame or blind and were led by a companion. I especially pitied the blind folk, who could not rejoice in their lovely surroundings.

But despite all the beauty, there was also almost a smell of fear in the air, as though unhappy ghosts haunted the ruins we passed. But the living seemed afraid, too. Every once in awhile we would pass men or women whose cloaks bore a yellow cross sewn on the back, and sometimes on the front as well. I supposed they belonged to some mendicant order, though they were treated with scant respect by our guards; indeed, many of these people seemed to radiate an odd mixture of fear and defiance.

Still others, who seemed to cringe at our approach, wore strange hats or imamahs; yellow patches were sewn onto their garments, too. They also wore one legging or sleeve too short or too long. When I first saw them at a distance, I took them to be clowns or jesters, but then we passed close enough to see that the patches were usually Stars of David. So the men with the tall funnel-like hats and the women and children with odd-length sleeves were Jewish. Were the others Muslim? I could not make out their patches—maybe crescent moons?

Whenever we passed them, especially the Jews, people in our cavalcade would spit and even throw rocks at them. I caught Gilles at it and forbade him to do it again, which put him in a foul mood and raised some eyebrows among our companions.

On the other hand, the clergy often seemed to receive scant respect, too. One time I remember in particular. We had been travelling with a richly attired deacon and his retinue at one point and had passed some peasants on the road. They stood aside, but without a hint of reverence. After we passed, I glanced back and one was glaring at the deacon and making a crude gesture. He saw me and quickly turned away.

After a few such mysterious encounters, I finally asked my husband what it all meant, from the ruins to the strange way people behaved to the patched people to the odd burnt smell in the air. I had begun to feel that sense of dread more and more, too, especially since he too seemed to feel some grim emotion.

"Well, most men hate Jews and barely tolerate them," he answered. "They must wear those patches and the odd clothing so we know who we are. Now, don't utter a word of outrage; that is just how things are here, and you will quickly make yourself an outcast if you start to defend them. Nor will you be able to help them. They can always convert to Christianity, but they choose not to, so they must take what comes their way."

Well, I was outraged, but he was right. This was not my world, and after all, I had had to learn not to hate them myself. Not everyone was blessed with a friend like Maryam or been helped by someone like her son, who had been so kind to Lady Q'ing-ling when she was dying; nor had they ever received the generous hospitality I had experienced in Aleppo.

But Joscelin had moved on, so I dropped my thought. "The ruins are of Cathar castles. You are not imagining the stench; I too smell it. Heretics have been burned here recently. My king wants to wipe them out; they are treasonable as well as lost to the Church. He supports the work of the Popes, who have for years been sending Dominican monks to inquire into the faith of anyone suspected of heresy—or of harboring heretics, just as bad to his eyes."

"And to yours?"

"Well, I see why he does it, but I regret his means. When Saint Dominic first began preaching among the heretics, it was as a poor monk with no pretense to the glitter and pomp of the many Churchmen who seemed too worldly and vain and grasping. He tried to bring the true word of God and to explain Christ's sacrifice to those benighted by the strange ideas preached by those they called Perfecti—like that old hermit my father once knew. But they would not listen, and some fifty years ago when someone killed a Papal envoy—no one knows who the murderer was, but the Cathari were blamed—the Pope declared a holy war against the heretics.

"That was when those Normans came down and seized our lands. You recall my telling you about this before, yes?" I nodded. "But the heresy smolders on, and so an Inquisition was created to find and destroy those who preach falsity. Heretics are now handed over to the state to be burned so that no blood is shed, for that would be unchristian."

I shuddered. "Burning is a terrible way to die, though."

"Yes, it is. And the Inquisition has brought ruin on my beloved Occitaine. I shudder inwardly."

"But what are Perfecti?"

"Well, I doubt there are any left hereabouts, but they were men, and sometimes women, who committed themselves to a life of simplicity, kindness, poverty, chastity, and so forth. They preached their doctrine to those too angry with the worldliness of the Church or too oppressed by their lives to see how pernicious it is."

"But those virtues sound quite Christian to me—it is shocking that with such ideals they would kill anyone—but then I suppose devout Christians kill each other in worldly wars, not to mention killing infidels."

"True enough, but you must understand that their ideals are where the similarity ends. I know little of their doctrine, only that it is utterly at odds with the message Christ brought us: they actually deny that he brought salvation through his sacrifice! From what my father told me, they think the world is divided between two warring gods, one all-good and spiritual, and the other Satan himself: physical, corrupt, and completely evil. They even deny the power of our One Almighty God! They think this world is the domain of Satan and that spirit is somehow trapped in flesh."

It sounded like Manichaeism to me. I had learned a little about that religion in Iran. But all I said to him was, "What folly! How can spirit be trapped in flesh and even know of its own existence except through what only flesh can feel? Does not a heart ache with love or pity, does not an eye tell us where evil things lie so we can avoid them and go to the good?"

"So you can see how dangerous these people are."

"Not really. Folly always reveals itself sooner or later. Should not these Dominicans continue to preach the good news rather than declare war on people?"

"Not when they will not listen. Besides, as I say, it is also about politics. The southern nobles chafe under the yoke of Francia and choose to support anyone who will resist crown and church—and that is treason by any definition. I may regret it, but I also see the good that King Louis has done, good that could spread here, too, were there not such resistance to Francia. It is too late to fight what has happened; better to look to that good and go on."

I fell silent. My heart was racing and a lump had formed in my throat. Hypocrites and liars could easily wear the outer garb of Christianity, behave and speak in all the right ways all their lives, and still be heretics or even rebels in their hearts with no one suspecting them. These inquisitors might well miss them while destroying many innocents! And two kinds of poison would spread: suspicion and fear, as well as a taint on the souls of the executioners.

Besides, this was the man who had once spoken so feelingly about what had happened in Braissac and Bezier. Where was that man now?

The mountains and ripe fields suddenly seemed tarnished with blood. The sun shone down on peasants mowing fields for fall planting, but the hiss of their scythes sounded sinister; we passed a meadow aglow with sunflowers and another almost blue with rosemary, abuzz with bees and smelling sweetly of honey, but their scent was sickly; a group of young men, clerics by their tonsures, passed us laughing, but their laughter hid threat; pilgrims with holy medals on their hats stopped to watch us pass, but they seemed to glare at us darkly.

I wanted to weep for pity and horror, but instead I turned away and sought out the young people, who were playing a guessing game. That helped but little, for it reminded me of my first journey down the Dnieper when my beloved tutor Alexander would play guessing games with me to while away the time. Now he was gone to dust, and I was on another journey that was equally laden with dark possibilities. After all, I myself might be considered a heretic for practicing peace!

Perhaps people were right and this world was naught but a vale of tears.

I sighed. In what way did such dark thoughts help anyone? I sat down with my young wards and tried to drown my gloom by listening to the boys tease the girls, mostly Cecelia, about her upcoming nuptials. Though their talk was surprisingly bawdy, at least they were still innocent of the unsparing cruelty some people are capable of.

❧ ⚬⚭⚬ ❧

We paused at a fortified castle called Carcassonne to rest for a week while Lord Joscelin arranged the next stage of our journey. He found another party of merchants we could join in a few days, plus a new set of armed guards. It seemed odd that he had to hire more and more guards, but I supposed he was being cautious after all his misadventures.

I liked the castle at first, which was surrounded by a great stone wall with elegant towers and crenellations; an old town and castle stood nearby that we never visited. Some of the city towers were topped by windmills, which seemed most playful, although there was an air of serious purpose to the place, and much praying in the chapels and cathedral at all hours.

There was also a new village just across a river outside the walls. It turned out that King Louis' men had built it. It is a novel kind of settlement called a bastide, which is the model for resettling Catholic peasants loyal to the Crown. They share good-sized plots of farmland and yet are taxed as town dwellers. Very clever: loyalty to God and Francia, all in one place and simple to govern. As far as I could tell, though, the villagers who came into Carcassonne to buy or sell wares seemed happy enough in their new homes. I thought it was because they were no longer at war there, though I was soon to lose that illusion.

One day as we were leaving the church after morning Mass, some unseen person began to scream horribly. The sound came from everywhere and nowhere. I had not heard anything like it since escaping the Mongols, and my hair stood on end. I looked around, seeking to find whoever was in such pain and rush to help him. Surely he had suffered a terrible fall or the like. But all around me, people were ducking their heads and looking down at the ground, leaving their conversations and hurrying away.

I turned to my husband and was about to ask what was going on, but he gripped my arm so tightly that it hurt, and whispered, "Say nothing on pain of arrest! I will tell you later." He released me, and I followed, rubbing my arm and remembering a time when Argamon had hurt me even worse—or so I claimed to myself. I remembered Anna and Cecelia behind us, and I turned to see them both white with shock. I slowed down to take their hands, as much for my comfort as for theirs. The boys followed along in silence for once, shock and confusion written on their faces as well.

When we arrived at our lodging, Joscelin led us all into our private room and shut the door. Speaking softly, he said, "I am sorry if I hurt you, Sofia, but believe me when I say that much worse hurt could have come from saying anything right then."

"What is all this about? Why did no one go to aid whoever was screaming? And why did you hurt me?"

He sighed. "The Inquisition is stationed here, and that screaming came from the Bishop's Tower near the cathedral. They were torturing a heretic."

Anna and I both cried out in protest, but he waved his arms in alarm and said, "Softly, softly if you please. You endanger us all!"

"What is this inquisition, then?" asked Anna. "And what kind of bishop tortures people?"

Paolo put on a knowing expression, crossed his arms, and leaned against a table, but Gilles looked mystified and Cecelia just looked afraid.

Joscelin began pacing back and forth, clearly pondering what to say. "I see that Paolo and Cecelia know, but I will just say this much to you all. Some years ago the Pope called a holy war against all heretics, including the Cathari, who were everywhere in Occitaine. The French king sent lords south from Francia and Normandy, and their armies invaded our homeland in the name of the Church.

"They did destroy the Cathari leadership, but they did not stop there. They also seized many innocent nobles' lands. You will recall my telling you about this part, Sofia. It was in the midst of this terrible war that my father offered fealty to the king as a way to protect our lands from the kind of destruction all of you have already witnessed, if you were using your eyes. You must take what I say most seriously, or you will never be safe! And I would protect you young ones, my wife, and my lands from harm, for it takes little for the Inquisition to set its dogs on anyone, and then your lands and goods are seized, your home is burned, and everything left goes to the Church!

"This very castle was a Cathar refuge before it was taken. But when its count came out to parley under a flag of truce, he was seized and imprisoned in his own underground prison where he soon died. Rumor had it that he died not of dysentery, as his jailors claimed, but of something far more sinister. So you see: anything can happen to any of us, of any rank, even now.

"Especially now, in fact, since after the wars were over the heresy did not die. There are many simple folk who still cling to wrong, even heretical beliefs. After seeing the destruction wrought on their homes and lands and masters in the name of the Church, many plain folk converted to various twisted versions of religion.

"That is why with my king's aid, the Inquisition was set up to root out any remaining heresy. Its inquisitors are Dominicans, once pledged to educate both clerics and laymen alike. But nowadays they have free rein to compel confessions in any way they see fit. Some genuinely want to see those who wandered from the true faith to return to it, and they treat people mildly if they are found guilty. But others gladly use torture.

"The wars may have ended years ago, but the fear remains. You all must be careful with your words and," turning to me, "with your deeds."

It was a somber group of young people who left the room after this chilling account. I felt the same, and Joscelin and I barely spoke to each other for the rest of that day.

We left early the next morning, and no one regretted it. Over the next week, I kept feeling that same sick dread, but now it was worse, for it was mixed with pity and shock. Clearly no one truly felt at ease in the land whose name had once stood for "yes", for delight, for troubadour song and the delights of dance. Not even my husband, who was friend of the king, felt safe!

On we went, along slow-moving rivers, over sere mountain passes where ruins of Cathar castles perched high above us, and past pretty Roman-looking villages surrounded by ripening fields and orchards. We stayed in several towns large and small, each with its church standing over it like a sentinel for faith, or in monasteries where I was always surprised by the wealth and splendor of the chapels.

Although the stained glass windows were luminous and the gold candlesticks glowed, the altar cloths of silk were heavy with embroidery, and the statues emanating holiness were awe-inspiring, so much adornment did sometimes seem ostentatious. I had thought monastics would turn away from such worldly distractions, but most of the monks we saw were rather worldly themselves. Or perhaps we ate better than the ordinary monks did, since we always dined with the abbot. We—and they—ate well indeed. I could not put my finger on it, but the difference between many of these holy men and the nuns Marguerite had joined was most striking: a kind of ease and lack of spiritual seriousness.

We joined and left several caravans, mostly of merchants. We were all amused to see that, just as in Italy, they had standard bearers walking before them and musicians performing, clearly as much to proclaim their importance as to entertain. Paolo announced his intention to command just such a display for himself when the time came. We also rode a few miles in the well-guarded train of an archbishop, who was elegantly attired and riding on a white ass decked out with red and gold trappings.

We worshipped in a dozen or more churches that boasted special relics.

Thanks to Sir Reynaud, I supposed, I had become quite cynical about the value of relics, but I saw far too much credulity about these, not only among the peasants but on the part of priests, too. I cannot tell you how many cloths I met with that had covered Christ's face, including one with a woven border that spelled out "Allah is Great" in Arabic! That one I could not resist asking the priest about.

"A hundred years ago a pious count brought it back from the Holy Land. He donated a great sum to the Church for the honor of bringing it here. There are many false cloths, so do not be fooled if you see them elsewhere! We have the only true one. It was hidden for safekeeping for centuries, and then it was miraculously discovered in a nearby cave just before Sir Bohemund arrived in Jerusalem. A pious priest there who feared for its safety offered it to him." This priest would have gone on in great detail, but I saw Joscelin looking impatient to go so I thanked him and kept my lips sealed.

Outside my husband spoke. "And why did you ask about that cloth, my lady?

"Because there was Arabic lettering woven into the border, and I could read it. It said 'Allah is Great,' so it could not possibly date from the time of Christ. But I also could not bear to disappoint the priest. It clearly meant much to him."

"I see. Well, you behaved wisely, my love. As you might guess, this is not a country where you can safely question any church's relics, even unsound ones. But make no mistake: some are very real, and they are known to work miracles."

I bowed my head and reminded myself: was not it a miracle that my beloved and I had found each other, that we had witnessed a miracle together on our wedding night? It was almost as if a curse had been lifted since then, for so much good had happened—excepting my fall and miscarriage. And who knew? Perhaps there was reason why I had miscarried. I sighed. I still grieved for my lost son.

But once again I felt my faith being tested. I had adopted a new religion and was following it to the best of my ability, and I was always moved by the sacred beauty of the churches where we worshiped as we made our way north. Sometimes while praying I felt as if God was by my very side, whispering 'caritas' in my ear. But also, I was older. I had long ago lost my youthful passion to seek the right path to God, and until now it had seemed enough to act as a good Christian should and, as Lady Q'ing-ling had once counseled, not to worry so much about what to believe.

Now, however, I saw I was in a world where one's beliefs meant the difference between survival and fiery death. It might be wise to have my breviary in hand every day, and to see to it that my young wards understood that they must guard their thoughts carefully against anything the Church deemed heresy.

They all laughed at me when I brought the subject up at supper one night. "We were raised good Catholics, and so we remain," Paolo assured me. "You and my father are the ones who were ever in question, Aunt, and you are the most devout of us all! Lord Joscelin scared us in Carcassonne, but when we spoke of it later, we all realized that we are in no danger."

Joscelin looked sour but only said, "Well, you have been warned." And I dropped the matter entirely.

The day finally arrived. We had said goodbye to our last companions and reached my lord's barony. It was a warm late summer day of golden hay fields and sweet lavender, vineyards and blooming roses, firethorn bushes, and orchards heavy with ripening fruit. In harmony with melodious birdsong was another kind of music, of uncountable bees harvesting their nectar. How soft the valleys seemed: the sound of the watermills along the river grinding the peasants' corn for bread, the hills above them alarmingly craggy, some with caves that might hide anything in their depths. My dark mood had passed, and I wondered if I might explore them if that were allowed—my new role as chatelaine had yet to unfold. But it held promise, not threat, and everyone seemed happy.

Sir Hugh had gone ahead the day before to let Lord Joscelin's mother know that we were almost there, and we were greeted almost as returning heroes. We passed through a small, well-kept village that had been decorated for the occasion with bunches of flowers tied here and there, and a welcome party awaited us at the foot of the craggy hill on which Braissac castle perched.

Hugh and Philippe were standing near the front of a crowd of well-wishers, Philippe beaming with delight. A gray-bearded, nobly dressed man and two older ladies stood side-by-side well in front of everyone. I was briefly reminded of Q'ing-ling and her rival Har Nuteng, but these ladies were holding hands. One stood close to the man, so the couple must be Sir Philippe's parents.

I had guessed aright, for my husband's eyes were only for the other woman: Lady Alianore, as I learned to call her. She was frail looking and tiny, her head swathed in a wimple that made her look nun-like, and her attire simple but cut of rich gray cloth. Her cheeks were red as apples, and her toothless smile was as broad as could be without cutting her face in half. I liked her straightaway. Half a step behind but almost next to her was a thin, elderly priest who was narrow-faced, smiling just as broadly, and leaning on a cane.

Sir Philippe actually wept with joy when my husband bade him come forward and help Cecelia dismount. He chastely kissed her hand in greeting and led her to his mother to be formally welcomed. Cecelia seemed overpowered, too, for now the reality must strike: she was bound to a foreign man in a foreign country, likely never again to see her father or her stepmother. It was hard to tell whether her tears were of joy or fright, or perhaps both. At least she spoke enough of the speech of Francia to greet her mother-in-law properly; I had seen to that on the journey.

Meanwhile Lord Joscelin had swung off his horse and helped Anna and me down from our mounts. But when Lady Alianore came forward to greet us, some heavy-set, rustic-looking man suddenly rushed forward close behind her, looking as if he might burst with the importance of the occasion, and nearly knocked her into her son's arms. Joscelin embraced his mother heartily, kissing her at least three times on each cheek, and then turned and took my hand, bringing me face to face with her.

Before she could say a word, the rustic man, whom I later learned was the bailiff, came up to me, bowed, and with a face flushed as red as fire-thorn berries, offered me a gift of flowers bunched together and almost crushed by his grip. I thanked him, but he was already backing away, wincing from a poke in the ribs and a severe stare from his mistress and my husband.

Now that the bailiff was out of the way, my mother-in-law embraced both Anna and me as though we had always known each other, crushing the flowers further. "At last I meet my beautiful daughter and grand-daughter," she cried. "I hope we will come to know and love each other well."

Anna and I both murmured our thanks, and that lurking dread which had followed me on this journey dissolved into happiness. It truly felt like coming home.

Now we were presented to Philippe's parents, Lord Guillaume and Lady Agnes of Saijac. They seemed delighted with their son's choice of bride and were already making much of her. Perhaps, all this time, I had simply been afraid of the welcome that might await us all.

As the tonsured old priest bowed to me, Joscelin said "This is our priest, Father Pierre, one of so many Pierres in this county, who serves my castle and village." Father Pierre stepped forward, and we bowed as he made the sign of blessing over each of us.

The village elders were there, too, all dressed in their finest shirts and much-washed leggings. And behind them stood the entire population of the village as well as peasant families from farther afield, all arrayed in their best and looking thrilled to be there, to see the new foreign chatelaine, and perhaps to get away from the drudgery of daily work for awhile.

Leaving the peasants and villagers behind, our party walked up the short winding road to the castle of Braissac. Happy chatter surrounded me, but I simply wanted to soak in my surroundings. I would have been content simply to follow my husband and new mother up the hill, watching as they happily talked about this and that. But Father Pierre appeared by my side, a man as chatty as Dorje had been, though the likeness ended there.

The priest, whose limp and cane made walking very slow, wanted to know all about the churches we had visited, what relics we had prayed before, and whether we had seen any heretics.

"They are everywhere, you know. Half the people with yellow crosses on their clothing are unrepentant in their hearts."

"Oh, so that is what those crosses meant. I thought it was some lay or mendicant order of the church."

Father Pierre laughed in surprise. "Why, did your husband not tell you?"

I shook my head. "I never thought to ask."

He shrugged. "No harm done, at any rate."

We walked along in silence, me pondering my error. But he suddenly began again. "Sometimes I think Mother Church should take more interest in helping all sinners understand the true faith, not just heretics. I believe even the heretics would return to our fold if we only had enough educated priests to do God's work properly! And ordinary people would benefit so much, too. Thank God for the sainted Dominic, for his order is producing educated monks and priests as fast as they can in order to undo the terrible damage this heresy has wrought here in Occitaine, even here in this little village. Do you know about that?"

I nodded and added, "Yes, Lord Joscelin told me about it. It must have been terrible.

"Speaking of the Dominicans, I have met one of their order: Friar Thomas Aquinas."

I thought the poor man might faint. "You have met the Angelic Doctor himself? Oh, what an honor! Please tell me all about it."

I did so, though I had to be brief, as we were now passing through the castle gates and into the courtyard.

While listening to the priest with part of my mind, I had also been noting the place where I would spend the rest of my life. The castle itself is much like so many others we had passed on the way: about the same size as our country palace outside Kyiv, though memory might be playing me tricks. It sits in harmony with its hill, is more or less rectangular, has round towers at three corners and an older, squared one at the fourth, and has an arched entrance that leads into a spacious courtyard. Though it boasts heavy ironbound gates and arrow slits, there is no moat or drawbridge, and inside the walls it feels more like a home than a fort.

It seemed that everyone who lived or worked in the castle was present that day, dressed in their best or at least cleanest garments and excited to see their lord's new wife. From what I could tell, and later I was proven right, the ground level of the towers was devoted to storage of various kinds, since barrels and boxes and casks sat outside an open door as if ready to be moved inside. There were stables at one end of the yard and a kennel with various breeds of dog all barking madly; and to my delight, at the other end was a little enclosed orchard and garden full of vegetables and flowers with the gate thrown open as if in welcome. Various outbuildings that I could not identify sat near or against the near wall. I would likely need to learn their purpose soon, not to mention finding out who all these smiling and gaping people were.

Lady Alianore led us straight from the yard into a modest hall that looked to be very old—it had floors of beaten earth, shuttered windows thrown open to the sun, a few simple embroidered wall hangings, a built-in basin for washing hands, and doors leading to side rooms. We followed her up some stone stairs into the main building, which I had already learned to call the donjon, and entered a high-ceilinged, much larger, and most gracious hall with more embroidered hangings on the walls, including the Braissac banner; tall windows fitted with small round panes of greenish-hued glass; and a dais at one end.

The room was set for a feast, with trestle tables before the dais covered in snow-white cloths set together to make three sides of a rectangle. Long benches sat along them, the ones nearest the dais being covered in bright Oriental carpets. Completing the rectangle, the long head table on the dais was also adorned with fine carpets and fresh flowers, and several chairs sat behind it. Servants were moving about, putting finishing touches on the preparations for what promised to be an enormous feast.

The floor was of wood, though I could hardly see it for all the fragrant herbs and grasses strewn on it—the aromas of mint, lavender, and rose petals rose up and mingled delightfully as we tread on them. This custom, too, reminded me of my lost home in Rus'. And best of all, the floor was clean! We had stayed at inns where rushes had been strewn over leavings and bones so old that it felt like I was walking over a fetid swamp instead of a floor.

My mother-in-law suddenly stopped halfway across the room. Removing a ring of keys from her belt and handing the jangling lot to me, she said, "I just remembered! These are yours now. You are henceforth the chatelaine of this castle." I was somewhat taken aback, as I'd hoped to defer my new duties until I understood them, but I bowed and took them, fastening them to my own belt. "What a weight is lifted from me," she smiled, and I understood what she meant: several keys were large and heavy!

"And I hope to carry that weight just as you would wish, to learn from you how to do things properly here."

She smiled, looking most gratified. "As you wish, daughter.

"Olivier," she called in a surprisingly strong voice, "where are you? Bring out the wine for our guests. They should be here soon, and I must show my son and his family their rooms." A plump, middle-aged man with thinning hair scuttled into the room from a door at the far end of the hall, a pair of servants behind him bearing trays of cups and jugs of wine.

Having bidden the rest of our party to take their ease, she led Joscelin, Anna, and me out of the hall and up a spiral staircase to a room that was so spacious that its huge curtained bed at the far end seemed dwarfed. Gaily painted chests and plastered walls with bright murals relieved the gloom, painted hangings warmed other walls, and a fire burned in the great fireplace near the bed, though the day was warm. But then, the room was surprisingly cool, and there was no glass in the windows. Only wooden shutters would protect the room from the cold at night. And it might be very cold in the winter. I resolved to ask my husband about adding glass windows up here as well, for it would be my solar as well as our bedroom.

Our servants soon came in behind us and began unpacking our baggage. Joscelin disappeared back down the stairs murmuring something about greeting the guests who were due to arrive.

Leading us toward an adjoining room, Lady Alianore pointed out a locked chest in passing. "That is the spice cupboard, and one of your small keys opens it."

"Oh, I am reminded, Lady Alianore: I have a gift for you." I signed to Anna to join us, and she pulled a fat package out of the silken pocket hanging from her belt.

"Here, Lady Grandmother Alianore. Oh, I mean Grandmother Lady!"

Lady Alianore laughed with amusement, opened it, and exclaimed with delight; in the package lay several packets of different spices. "Oh thank you; saffron, too! You could not have chosen a more delightful gift, my dears. I think the best thing to do is to put them away right now. Here, Anna, you do the honors."

That done, she announced, "Now, come this way, my darlings."

The room next to ours was also most pleasant. "Here is where maid-servants and small children once slept, so I imagine you would like your daughter and her maids to stay here. I had it cleaned and beautified just for you."

I looked at Anna, who nodded slightly. "Yes, please," I answered. "She only has the one maid here, Irene. My other women servants would also stay in this room? Is that how it is done?"

"No need to ask my permission for what to do; it is entirely up to you how you wish to use these rooms. I am so glad to be able to hand over all responsibility to you at last. I am a tired old woman now, and my only wish is to retire as soon as I can to the convent that stands just over that hill." She led me to a window to look out. "See, you can just make out its chapel tower."

"I hope you will not hurry away. We have only met and you speak of leaving. I truly will be depending on you to teach me what I should do and how to do it."

She smiled. "You are not to worry; I will. Now, I am sure you would like to wash your faces and put on your finery, for we have a great feast planned, in case you could not guess." We all laughed. "When you are ready, just come downstairs, and if there is time, I will show you more."

With Irene's help and that of another maidservant, Anna and I quickly washed as much of ourselves as we could with a basin and jug of water before donning our best gowns. I wondered if they would seem outlandish, since Lady Alianore's attire was so simple compared to our colorful Venetian silks and velvets and various chains and jewels.

We descended the stairs back into the Great Hall, where Joscelin, with the help of Philippe and Hugh, was entertaining several men who had arrived while we were upstairs. We found Lady Alianore amidst a group of young women, who all turned, stared, and said with one breath, "Ah." I think they were referring to our clothing, which was much admired by them all. It turned out that they were my new sisters—four of them—and after being presented to them and straightaway mixing up their names in my mind, I followed the lady to the servants' end of the hall, where doors were hidden by a pair of carven wood screens.

"I suppose I am too eager to pass on my duties to you, but as you expressed a desire to learn about them, I will present your excellent steward to you, thanks to my son, who—here he is, waiting to meet you! This is Pierre le Brun, so named to distinguish him from all the other Pierres!"

Pierre, who must have been named for his brown hair, had been hovering by one of the screens, and now he came forward and bowed to me. He was so thin and knobby that he could have been made of wood, and when he humbly stepped back, he even walked in a wooden way.

"Oh well, as long as we're here, I may as well at least show you the buttery and the pantry. Come this way," and Lady Alianore led us around the screen into a sort of hall with a room on either side, one full of butts and bottles of wine or ale, and the other a kind of pantry lined with cupboards that servants were quickly filling with covered trays. "Olivier is the butler and Martin oversees the pantry. Olivier, Martin, where have you disappeared to now?"

In darted two menservants, one of whom I had last seen hurrying into the hall followed by servants and wines. They both bowed.

"So why are you lagging about? We begin our feast in an hour, there's much to do. Tomorrow I will bring the new mistress of the castle around to meet everyone, but for now I want her to myself."

The men bowed again, though I noted they exchanged wry smiles with each other, and vanished into another room, perhaps the kitchen.

To me she said, "And here in the pantry you see the cupboards where we keep the trays of food before they are brought into the hall. And if you look through that door you'll see our cellar, where we store everything safely. There's a trap door that leads into another cellar below, very practical. All in all, it is a very well set up castle, I think you'll find.

"But what am I thinking? I am so atwitter from having my son and my new daughter and granddaughter here! You should be meeting the rest of your new family and our guests!"

As we entered the Great Hall yet again, Lord Joscelin called out, "Mother, I will see you shortly. For now, I would see to my own duties. I am leaving my trusty knights Hugh and Philippe to do the honors."

He came up, kissed all three of us, and left with a bow to his family and guests. Someone called out, "I know where you go: to see how your hounds and falcons fare!"

We all laughed, but at that moment I glimpsed what life might be like in the years to come, not so different from life in my country palace near Kyiv. And would my husband be gone often, as Papa had been? Well, no time for that silly worry! I put on a smile for all the family and guests who were arriving every minute.

The rest of that day was devoted to feasting, to music and dance, and to games. We were joined not only by all of Joscelin's brothers and sisters and their wives, husbands, children, chaplains, and knights, but also by those nearby barons and their families and retinues who were friendly to us. Their names faded as quickly as they were told to me.

The hall, which had seemed so cool and spacious, grew hot and close from so many bodies crammed around the tables. And the bounty set before us was almost overwhelming: so many courses, so many meats and fish and birds and pies and mustards and pickles and fruits and sallats and sweets! Everyone was stuffed, but by dint of eating slowly, we survived the afternoon.

My new sisters seemed very happy to know me, and I began to make sense of names and relations, though I made a few mistakes, called a boy by his father's name and the like, all of which was greeted with teasing and hilarity.

From a chance remark I had overheard before the feast began, I knew that there were some present who were not so friendly to each other and who had nonetheless been invited. But everyone behaved with decorum, so I set aside any concerns about some sudden drunken brawl. I might have to worry about that sort of thing later, but I was confident: had I not already dealt with such problems in handy fashion when just a girl in Papa's palace?

What a day! Jongleurs performed tricks and acted out stories all afternoon, and our neighbors' ready teasing and wit, much of it bawdy, filled any gaps. I had not witnessed anything like it since leaving Constantinople. I had expected more solemnity here, because in Cyprus people had restrained their tongues. Now I realized that people there were following King Louis' example.

There was even a music gallery above the servants' entry, a legacy of troubadour times, where a quartet of musicians sawed away on a stringed instrument that Joscelin told me was called a viele, beat rhythms on a tambour, strummed a harp, or blew heartily if not perfectly on a hautboy. After the meal when the tables had been removed, there was dancing with great vigor and jollity and, in my case, with the right partner. I did not regret shredding my shoes this time! Indeed, when we all joined in ring dances, some of the caroles were the very tunes I had once danced to long ago with Sir Reynaud at Helene's wedding. And watching Anna dancing cheerily with Gilles made me realize that she was almost grown, which led to thoughts about Cecelia.

Philippe's mother and father would be leaving late that evening, taking their son and new daughter with them, so I knew that a sad parting awaited us, but what was the use of anticipating sorrow? This was a time for gladness and learning how to belong to a new family. Loneliness was just an old habit that I could abandon, I assured myself as I let the endless jesting and storytelling wash over me.

The evening ended, to my surprise, with a song my husband had composed just for me. I had never heard him sing before, and he was most expressive. Or perhaps I was biased. Here it is.

> *No maid however young and fair,*
> *Or blue her eye or gold her hair,*
> *Or soft her blush or light her step*
> *Can ever hope to compare*
> *With the charms of my Sofia.*
>
> *Most true and trusting is my love,*
> *In all her deeds the peaceful dove.*
> *With sweet kisses and caress*
> *From me all pain she doth remove*
> *With hand and heart, my dear Sofia.*
>
> *I vow to be faithful and true,*
> *To shield and always comfort you.*
> *I would die before I fail*
> *In all ways to love and honor you,*
> *My darling peach, Sofia.*

His song made us all laugh and weep at the same time, and though it may not be as memorable as the Lay of Igor's Host, I treasure it far more—indeed, the only other song ever written for me I still regard as stupid.

But at day's end the party broke up. Those who lived close enough went home by the light of an almost-full moon, while the rest were found rooms for the night. The men could look forward to good sport on the morrow, for Lord Joscelin was to lead them in a hunt in his own forest.

Last to leave were Lord and Lady Saijac. Our parting with Cecelia was indeed sad, though the distress of leaving us was softened for my young cousin, as Lord Saijac had invited Paolo to accompany her to her new home and to stay on for the few weeks leading up to the wedding. She and Anna and I bade each other goodbye in the courtyard, our faces wet with tears, but Paolo, who regarded this short trip as but another adventure, made such silly remarks that we all had to laugh in the end. They rode off, Philippe by Cecelia's side staring at her as if moon-struck.

And so to bed with a head full of wine and a belly full of food.

I awoke far too early the next morning to the sound of chapel bells. How my head ached! Lord Joscelin groaned and put his hands over his eyes, but then he kissed me, threw back the covers, took off his night cap, poured cold water into our basin, washed, and hastily dressed. I followed suit; and after waking Anna and getting her ready, we joined the entire family and our remaining guests for daily Mass in a little chapel that opened off the lower hall.

Afterwards we broke our fast with bread, wine, and ale before the men went off to hunt. Every moment seemed new and fresh to me, and even my aching head could not hinder the joy that rushed through my entire body.

Lady Alianore and the remaining ladies and their daughters joined Anna and me in my new solar, where we all pulled out our embroideries and spindles and so forth. One of them had brought a lute and sang to us, and several ladies joined in the refrain. I was pleased to hear much admiration and curiosity expressed not only over my fashionable garments but also about the new wall hangings and screens I brought out, which were from Venice, full of gold threads and adorned with my own special stitches learned from Lady Q'ing-ling and Perijam. Soon I was obliged to stop my own work and teach them to my new friends, a task I took on with pleasure. I had worked hard to master the Langue d'Oc and was delighted to use it at last.

At one point at Lady Alianore's invitation, the musicians appeared, and a few women even danced with each other amidst much laughter and jesting. After the musicians left, we continued on with our work in leisurely and lively fashion, for the teasing and laughter never stopped. My sisters-in-law were the best at riddles and word play, and I came to like them as much as I already liked their mother: Marie, Blanche, Agnes, and Alainne, whose ages must range from twenty to thirty-five.

We ladies had dinner together, with yet more music and song, and that evening we supped with our lords on cheese, wine, venison pie, and small birds caught that afternoon, everyone being most gracious and full of high spirits. And again there was music and dancing and, for those with tired feet, games of dice.

The next day, however, our last guest departed. After breakfast Lady Alianore took me by the hand and began to teach me my new role.

I spent the next few days in a haze of work: meeting daily with the steward, Pierre le Brun, and with the bailiff of crushed flower fame, who was called Alard; and with a host of other servants, all of whose names, duties, locations, schedules, and so forth I must learn. I made sure Anna was learning alongside me, which was not her idea of pleasure, but she would need to know these things soon enough. By the end of the week, I had pretty much mastered where everything was, if not everyone's names, and so had she.

It was a delight to see her and her new grandmother together. I think the old lady was happy to have a pretty young face to look at and a bright young mind to teach now that her daughters were all married and gone. And Anna, as always, loved attention.

I was happy in my mother-in-law, too. She was rather abrupt at times and not always organized, but when at her best she was gracious and kind to her many servants, knew the names of everyone's children, sent gifts of fruit from our orchard to the sick along with her special medicinal syrup, and generally made herself loved. And she was unfailingly kind to me, happy to answer all my questions, and full of praise when I did something right.

I saw little of my husband except at morning Mass, at meals, and at night. He was busy with his own duties. But I might catch sight of him in the distance, sometimes with his daytime cap tied around his chin, looking most domestic. It always made me smile to see my warrior thus arrayed, so different from how I had first known him.

We had been following this routine for a few days when one night Joscelin said to me as we climbed into the giant bed and he pulled the curtains around us, "I saw you hard at work today, my love."

"Yet I rarely see you, dearest. I wonder what you do with your time."

He leaned his head on his arm and looked at me closely. "Would you really like to know?"

"Not only that but to see where you go! Then in my mind I can fill in some of the lost years I spent without you."

"Well, then, tomorrow I will steal you from my mother and show you whatever you wish. Would you like that?"

I would indeed, and I showed him my gratitude that night not only in word but also in deed. We sank into happy if exhausted slumber.

The next day he took me with him wherever he went, apparently most amused that a wife would want to know what her husband did with his days. It turned out that many of his duties were the same as my Papa's had been and that they were parallel with mine: he first met with Pierre le Brun to go over the castle's and lands' accounts and to decide if anything was to be done that day with the fields, forest, meadows, villages, and so forth under his authority, and much more; and since I was there, a surprised Pierre was also required to go over my household accounts right then as well. After that, Joscelin conferred with his marshal, Sir Bègue, an elderly knight I had seen only once, at the feast, who oversaw a small but loyal and doughty band of knights and who was training Sir Hugh to take his place soon.

At my request Joscelin took me down to the courtyard and interrupted their combat exercises to present me to them. He gave a speech about protecting his beloved wife with their lives that moved a few men to tears. They behaved like awkward children when I stepped forward to meet each man, not knowing whether to bow or to advance and kiss my hand or both; a few bumped into each other trying to do me honor. I kept a straight face through it all.

Gilles was among them that day, for he had rapidly progressed from serving as a page at our table, which was too silly and always sent Anna into fits of laughter, to being a squire in the stables. He looked well and reasonably happy, given that his soft life was now behind him forever.

Then we saw the bailiff Alard, who was my husband's link to the peasants and villagers and their needs, as well as to what tasks were or were not actually being accomplished on Braissac lands. I gathered that the peasants owed Braissac labor as well as taxes and that Alard was not very popular; in addition to being self-important, he also collected said taxes!

Joscelin even took me riding that afternoon. As we left the castle and passed through the modest village, everyone who saw us dropped what they were doing and ran to do us homage. We saw shepherds up in the fields and the stone hut where they lived, baked their own bread, and wove wool from the sheep they had sheared. We passed farmers stacking hay, a man fishing in our pond for the very fish that would be served at our table that night, and so much more.

In the afternoon Joscelin took me back along the road we had taken into Braissac, pointing out and naming special rocks or streams or stands of wood, each with its own story, until we reached a steep path that led up to the caves I had seen and wondered about. We had to leave our mounts and climb the final hundred feet or so, to the very cave where the Cathar Perfect had lived.

"Here is where all our troubles started," my husband solemnly announced, "and here, God willing, is where they end." And he took me into his arms.

We did not return until nearly sunset, and I saw Lady Alianore studying me as her son kissed me chastely on the cheek before leading our horses off to the stables.

Anna rushed up. "Where have you been, Mama? I have been with Grandmama all day, and we missed you—though we had such fun! She taught me a new game, and I wanted to teach it to you, but I couldn't find you anywhere—"

"That is enough chatter, Granddaughter. Let your mother go up to her room and prepare for supper. Clearly she has been out riding, and that is enough for you to know."

And I swear the good lady winked at me!

That night as we prepared for bed, Joscelin said, "So now you know what Mother and I did for those four long years! And to think how hard she worked by herself after Father and brother died! I know I'm a very lucky man. Even if I had to replace a few dishonest men when I returned home that first time, Braissac is blessed with as good a set of servants— and villagers and peasants—as anyone could ask, don't you think?"

"Yes," I murmured, hoping he would soon put his arms around me once again. My entire body was still on fire from that afternoon.

Instead he added musingly, "I thank God and our Savior that all my knights adore Mother so. Not that long ago she was quite a beauty, and I think a few of the older men were in love with her. Lucky for me, since after my brother died they all held my demesne in safety, as much for her as for me. Many a chatelaine came to a bad end if her husband left for war while she had to manage alone for many years."

"What do you mean?"

"Oh, some wives had dishonest or disloyal servitors. Worse, sometimes servants or greedy neighbors even raped or murdered a woman to get at her husband's wealth or lands. And if she had children at home, they killed them, too. That is why I work hard to be a good master to them all, to reward their loyalty, why I shower them with generous gifts of clothing and monies. And my knights take pride that I train them constantly.

"But enough of that talk. I have other uses for this night." And he ended the conversation as I wished, with a deep kiss and more.

While I was always ready for the delights of the night, I was also taken aback by his story. It reminded me that there were unforeseen dangers everywhere in this land of warmth and beauty.

I was soon left to do business with Pierre le Brun on my own. Lady Alianore had gladly put more and more responsibilities into my hands so that she could go to the chapel and pray or go to the convent to visit the abbess, who was happily making arrangements for her to join it early the next year. I suspected that the lady's dower monies from her dead husband were already trickling out in that direction.

Pierre le Brun was and is a gentle soul, dedicated to his work and clearly grateful to be serving in such a good household. When he went over the household and kitchen accounts with me, he felt it his duty to keep a tight rein on the cook's and butler's and baker's desires to present bounteous meals. Knowing his bent, I also listened to Olivier and Martin and my cook when deciding how much wine or ale to bring out for each meal and when to buy more wine; what meat to slaughter, how much of it to salt or smoke or to eat straightaway; how much bread would be needed; how much milk should go to butter or cheese; what receipts to use and which spices I should dispense for them; even when more mustard or vinegar must be prepared.

And though Pierre would have preferred me not to involve myself directly with them, I personally saw the baker, the laundresses, and a myriad of other servants every day. This was for my own benefit, for only then could I feel in touch with the daily activities in my new home. And it gave me such joy to have charge of such a large household on behalf of the man

I loved so well.

Friar Pierre often visited me, as he was so impressed that I would know a great man like Friar Aquinas. We became quite friendly, and through him I learned much about the life of the peasants and villagers of the barony. He was a good priest, tried to offer sermons once a month, and took a personal interest in everyone, for he remembered the bad days of goods seized and heretics burned, along with their houses. He wanted no more terrors visited on his flock.

I asked him about his lameness. "I broke my leg one day when I fell from a balky mule down into a steep ravine," he said in a matter of fact voice. "I am lucky to be alive, but it added to my parishioners' sympathy for me. I was bringing a basket of food to a large, very poor family whose man was dying, so they see it as a kind of sacrifice for them." He paused. "The Lord God always has a purpose behind his actions; because of that, now they trust me and the true word of the Church."

I was touched by this man's devotion. I wanted to believe that the Church's every word was true, too.

And after supper, always a modestly festive occasion, my husband and I would finally repair to the solar alone. We truly were alone: our servants never stayed in our room with us. This was at my request, for I had never gotten over being surrounded by people day and night when I was Argamon's slave. And every night in Braissac, a world away from that dark time, he took me in his arms and made sweet love to me. Afterwards, both of us drowsy with work and love, he would ask me about my day and I would ask about his.

I suppose all of this may sound very domestic and humble, but I reveled in my new life just because of those qualities. They spoke, nay sang, of quiet peace and simple joy.

The only thing to briefly mar that time was that I discovered quite by accident that not all the women servants were free. I had passed the same raggedly dressed woman with dark graying hair several times before I realized I had never learned her name or position. Finally I stopped her in the courtyard to ask who she was, and I learned more than that her name was May: I learned she was Lord Joscelin's half sister! I questioned her closely, but she had little to tell. She was much surprised by my interest.

"I was brought up here, I work hard, my mother is dead, and since my father Lord Braissac died my lot grows worse, since Lady Alianore was always displeased about his lying with my mother. Probably because she was a Muslim infidel, as am I—your Christ never showed me any particular mercy! But what do I care? I am fed, I have a bed, I like working, and I have the prayers my mother taught me. I do them when I can."

"Do you not long for freedom? And my husband is your half brother. That makes us sisters!"

She looked aghast. "No, we are not. I mean … Well, I don't know what I mean, but things just are as they are. Freedom means nothing to me. I only long sometimes for a little more rest."

I went to Joscelin that very afternoon ready to do battle, but when I broached the subject, he merely looked surprised. "I have no objection to freeing her; indeed, I had forgotten about Gallega and her daughter. Gallega was a Muslim slave and she raised her children in her faith, so there was no thought of freeing them, either. I think her sons all died or were sold, but certainly I can free this woman."

"You don't even know her name, do you?" I was not quite ready to let go of my outrage.

"Now don't be hasty; let me think. I have been away awhile, you know," he answered mildly.

I blushed beet red. "I'm sorry."

"Oh, I remember: May, because she was born in May. She's older than I am. I had nothing to do with her after leaving the monastery and then moving to Francia." He paused thoughtfully. "You know, I have a trusty tenant, a farmer whose wife died a few months ago. Do you think I should marry May to him? It would be a boon to them both, I think."

"I have no idea. She is Muslim. Would that not be an objection for both of them?"

"Well, let us see, my beloved firebrand."

Oh that all problems could be solved so easily.

Time flowed swiftly, and with the day drawing near we began preparing for Philippe's and Cecelia's wedding, which would be held before the chapel in Saijac castle. The day before we were to leave, a messenger arrived with a letter for Lord Joscelin; I assumed it was something to do with the wedding and thought no more of it. And he said nothing to me that day or the next when our family went over to Saijac, followed by an army of servants bearing gifts, mostly from me. Lady Alianore, Anna, Sir Hugh, and I traded jests and witticisms, but Joscelin seemed to be in a thoughtful mood. Only when called upon did he come out of his musings and join in our banter.

The wedding was lovely, the feast splendid. I cried, for now that I was married I could afford the luxury of tears. But also with Cecelia's wedding came the realization that, God willing, Anna would be a bride within the next few years. Philippe's parents had already invited her to stay and be trained as a future wife, an offer I had gratefully but firmly refused. But in truth the time would soon come when I must say goodbye to my beloved child. My heart sank a little, and all I could do was pray that she would live as near me as Lady Alianore's daughters did. I wondered if there were any suitable young men among Lord Joscelin's neighbors.

We returned home the next morning with Paolo, Fotis, and Irene. At some point, the brother and sister would return to Venice with their young master and rejoin Helene's service. My husband still seemed pensive, and when I asked him why, he smiled ruefully.

"I've been trying to find the right time to tell you some news, my love. I had thought to stay home for good, but I received a letter from my king a few days ago summoning me north to his court in Paris. He still plans to return to the Holy Land to battle for Christianity—no, no, do not look so aghast! He has no intention of taking me again, but he does want my advice, especially since I now know so much about pirates and so forth, things that interest him and might affect his strategy. He invites you to accompany me as well. I decided this summons could wait until after the wedding.

"My real question is what to do with Anna and Paolo and Gilles. I think of bringing them with us, too. I know Paolo and Gilles would like that, for once my duties are fulfilled, I could shape my journey to pass through Troyes for Paolo to go to one of its fairs and to Caudeaux to show Gilles his fief. But what about our daughter? Would she want to stay behind, perhaps with Cecelia to continue her training in household arts, or would she want to go with us? She is a bit of a mystery to me, you know. I often find her looking at me with something like dread or mistrust—"

I burst into laughter. "She thinks you want to marry her off as soon as you can so you won't have to share me!"

Joscelin smiled but did not join in my laughter as I'd have wished. "Well, she must be somewhat of a mind reader. I have been considering her future, though she is still too young to wed yet. But I am responsible for her, though I have no idea how to proceed. I decided to let the question settle itself sometime in the future."

"I do hope you mean to include me in such a matter!"

"Of course, but it is too soon. When she grows older, we can come back to it and put our heads together. If there's one thing I know, it's to respect your wishes whenever I can!"

I smiled and took his hand. He kissed mine and we rode on, both of us much happier. How exciting: I would be traveling to Paris, a true capital city, and not ruined like Constantinople! I was most curious to visit it after Sir Reynaud had spoken of it with such wry humor. How long ago that life seemed to me now; how far away were the troubles and politics of Constantinople or the Saracens or Nizari or Mongols, and how peaceful my new life was.

Lady Alianore was not well pleased when she heard the news, though. "Good God, when will the king have done with you? Now I will have to go back to all the duties I passed onto Sofia. And she was doing so well, too!"

I blushed and bowed a little. She was not to know that other than learning so many new names and titles for all the servants, managing everything was not much different from what I had done in Rus' or Antioch or anywhere else I had lived. All that had changed was that I followed different hours; ate a little differently; was relearning the joys of music, song, and dance; and was actually far less distracted in dealing with my duties than was she. Clearly all those years of managing everything alone had taken their toll on her. I understood her hunger for the cloister.

My husband answered bleakly, "It is not like the old days, Mother, when ours was an independent barony. If the king seeks my counsel, I am bound by law to go to him. But not to worry; the longest he can keep me there is forty days. And I'll likely be home much sooner than that."

When Anna learned of our proposed journey at supper that night, she felt as I did, for she was accustomed to travel and mostly enjoyed it. She too had heard of Paris; she too wanted to see it for herself. Her first question was, "Can we sail there?" Joscelin nearly spilt his wine trying to choke back laughter.

Gilles was delighted, too, because he would finally see his county, be knighted early by the king himself and no longer have to do stable work, and begin to take on his duties as Vicomte of Caudeaux—he would outrank Joscelin then. All he knew so far was that it was a small but rich county somewhere south of Paris and north of us and that his father's stewards had held it for him for over a decade. Who knew what he would find?

And when Paolo heard about our plans, he was surely the most delighted of us all, for on our way home we would pass through Troyes in time for the autumn trade fair. At last he would be able to sell his honey and all the other trinkets and trade goods he'd been collecting for the past two months, not to mention extend his family business into the profitable wool industry.

We were also to travel through Lord Joscelin's fief, for he was responsible for two other castles, more farmland and villages, several manors, various fishponds and woodlots, the forest dedicated to deer and boar, a mill, tolls, and much more. In terms of land and rents, the only true wealth in his eyes, he was far wealthier than Papa had been.

And evidently my trader-tainted wealth had been responsible for a recent increase in his holdings, for he had just purchased the right of fief from an old widowed count who lived a few miles and a county away and who had no living offspring. With the king's consent, Joscelin would inherit it, but he wanted to visit it now and speak further with its lord. And when the time came, Joscelin would become a count and outrank Gilles! It made me laugh inwardly, for such rankings meant little to me, who had once been a princess and then fallen into slavery. Everything could reverse and even vanish in an instant. I also had to smile that my naïve plan to buy land in the Occitaine had come to fruition in an unexpected way.

And May was given her freedom and a husband all at the same time. It took some gentle argument on my part before Lady Alianore would agree to part with her. To her discredit in my eyes, her reason was clearly spite against May's mother. But I finally persuaded her that it was best to have no reminders of her dead husband's past behavior to spoil her memories of the man she held dear.

When I was able to tell May the news shortly before we left for Paris, she was astonished, delighted, afraid, and determined to be a good wife. She met her husband-to-be for the first time when he came to the castle to take her to his home. He was a sturdily built man with so much beard I could scarcely see his face, and he seemed quite pleased with his new bride. He had already promised to let her practice her religion as she saw fit, but I took him aside before he lifted her onto his mule and insisted he make another promise: never to beat her. He was much surprised, but he solemnly agreed.

September was already upon us and the first harvest was coming in when we travelers gathered in the courtyard to depart. Lady Alianore wept as she embraced her son. "I know not why, but I feel as if I am saying goodbye forever."

Joscelin encircled her in his arms as if she was his child. "You must not fret, Mother, for I'll be home before you know it. Look for me in two months. We will celebrate Christmas together." She tried to smile.

Anna and I embraced her as well. The Lady suddenly seemed so frail. I was reminded of Q'ing-ling in her decline, though age and not illness had weakened my mother-in-law. How much Lady Alianore had endured, and all she wanted now was to rest. A wave of resentment toward King Louis washed over me.

At least she had Sir Hugh and good servitors to help her. I acknowledged Hugh's salute as my husband lifted me into my saddle. "Take good care of Lady Alianore for us," I called. "She is my mother now." He bowed and nodded. What a strong and good man he had become. Did he ever miss his England?

Out the gates we went, and once more I had that feeling of things repeating themselves: leaving Papa's palace, leaving Kyiv, leaving Antioch, Constantinople, Venice, even leaving Qazvin. I did not count escaping the Mongols or Alamut as leaving home, but there too I had left behind people I cared about even now, like Rukn Al-Din.

I had to remind myself that I was not leaving my new home forever, only for a short while, because gray dread threatened me yet again. I firmly set it aside and motioned to Anna to ride beside me. I was astride the gentle palfrey Joscelin had found me at the beginning of our journey in Occitaine, which I had named Pax, and Anna was riding hers, which she had jestingly named Gilles, much to her friend's annoyance.

For the next week or so, we traveled through a smiling land: past fields being harvested, each marked off by hedges or ditches and splashed along the edges with firethorn bushes; through small villages where everyone came out to greet their lord and to speak with him in person about their grievances; and over his toll roads and bridges where he noted what work would be needed for the next spring. We stayed in his modest manor houses, hosted by the local steward and his wife. Each house had been cleaned and adorned with garlands just for us, just as the meals were abundant in our honor. It almost felt like a pageant, a feast of new faces, new sights, even new dishes for which I asked and received the receipts. I had not expected to enjoy myself so much.

Anna and the boys were as happy as I was, for this part of our adventure seemed so gentle, so empty of the constant threat that had seemed to hang over us on the journey to Braissac. We saw fewer and fewer yellow crosses, the priests and chaplains we met seemed to be well liked by their parishioners, and my occasional sense of dread slowly dissolved.

We stopped briefly at Gilles' barony, where he was greeted with much pomp and good cheer. Joscelin's fears had not been realized because, we found out from the steward, King Louis himself had undertaken to keep it safe and prosperous for the future baron in memory of his loyal knight, Sir Gilles I. It was much like Joscelin's, only differing in the terrain, so I will write no more about it. We left, feeling a certain relief about our young Gilles' future, while he made much of himself in friendly rivalry with Paolo. Anna started calling her horse Sir Gilles just to tease him.

Within another week, blessed by good weather and surrounded by a land turning from green to gold and which grew gentler the farther north we went, we were in Francia and approaching Paris. With every mile you could somehow feel the presence of the city growing as we traveled over soft hills; through forests of oak, birch, and willow; and past farms and fields where peasants were harvesting their earthy riches. Finally the city loomed up before us, girdled by massive pale walls with battlements whose round towers were set at exact distances from each other. The walls were pierced by several fortified gates and were crowned with many church towers and spires reaching into the sky. I was reminded a little of Carcassonne.

Having entered by bridge over a moat, we found ourselves on a paved street wide enough for two wagons, which led straight ahead over a low hill disguised by buildings crammed together. Paris was nothing like Antioch or even Constantinople, but it was certainly busy. Our guards had to force a path along the street past creaking carts and through noisy milling crowds of people, many of them young men whose tonsures proclaimed them as clerics but whose garb proclaimed them to be from all over Christendom. The side walkway was lined with shops and booths, many of them on the first floor of two- or three-story houses. Butchers, pastry vendors, grocers, fortune tellers, bird sellers, barbers, shoemakers, hat makers, wine sellers, whores and more vied for attention, each with their own call that was repeated almost endlessly until someone stopped to do business with them.

Underfoot were the stinking remains of chamber pots; men or boys herded cattle or goats to mysterious destinations; and sturdy women balanced baskets of what looked like laundry or fruit or bread on their heads, skillfully avoiding dangers from above, below, and around them. A group of women dressed like nuns hurried into a house to avoid a naughty youth who was following them, calling out his love. A man staggered by bearing a heavy water sack and whistling through his teeth. A whore, little more than a child, was leading a young man dressed in what looked like a monk's garb into a side alley. I was more or less used to big cities, but the clatter and commotion of Paris outdid them all.

It took me a while to understand why: under the noise of commerce was a kind of deep buzz: of excitement, of drama, of debate, which came from those young men! They were gathered at street corners or strolling down the street with arms linked, avoiding the sudden spills of ordure dumped from above by chambermaids; or crowded around a room open to the street. When we passed these odd rooms, there was always someone dressed in clerical attire talking inside. The youths even stood jammed together in stairways, while an invisible voice boomed out from above. Some of them could not be older than twelve or thirteen.

Farther along came song and the sounds of lutes and tambourines played with more fervor than harmony: as we passed the source of all this noise, a tavern, I looked in and saw yet more young clerics playing instruments, swigging cups of liquor, groping at the maidservants, and generally behaving like any other man in a tavern. The muddy side streets were unpaved, and the stench that came from some of them was appalling. A man carrying a heavy sack stumbled out of one lane and was nearly run over by a well-dressed man on horseback. The sack split, spilling chunks of coal everywhere. I looked back to see the angry charcoal carrier take up a clod of coal and hurl it at the man's back before bending over to pick up his fallen load. The horseman turned back, furious, but what happened next was lost in the crowd.

My wards were as fascinated by everything as I was. Paolo cried, "Oh, of course! These youths are students, and the men doing all the talking are their professors. Paris is almost as famous for its great universities as are the ones in Italy, but I never thought it would be like this. I thought there would be schoolrooms in the monasteries or the churches, not on the streets as though the lecturers are shopkeepers."

Indeed, alongside the shops, all along the Grand Rue, for such was its name, were places of learning. I caught snatches of sentences here and there, always spoken in Latin.

My husband laughed. "Yes, a new theory for sale on every corner! All this has grown quite a bit since my last visit. But these teachers must be lesser scholars. I do think there are standards that must be met for true academics; but as for these fellows, I don't know."

The crowds of young men grew thicker, the noise of competing lecturers turned into a waterfall of words. Every available space seemed filled with students, from lecture room to pastry shop to cheese monger and, of course, ale house. And cats were everywhere, often black, cleverly stealing a fish from a fishmonger or racing across a street without once being stepped on, or leaping onto a passing wagon and riding along looking self-satisfied. It was all I could do to keep track of what my husband was saying!

"We are actually in the heart of the Latin Quarter now, so called because that is the language everyone can speak, no matter where they come from in Christendom. Look down that street; see all the young men sitting on bales of hay around the lecturer? They are rich enough to afford seating while their fellow students must stand. Of course not everyone approves of this new public style of teaching, not to mention the way subjects are taught. And too many youths who come here are poor, have nowhere to live, and would just as soon get drunk and brawl as attend to their lessons." He laughed. "I admit to joining a few tavern fights just for the fun of it when I was still a young and angry squire.

"Some students wander about from city to city seeking knowledge, or at least good wine, song, and loose women. Many write satires criticizing the excesses of the Church or they compose bawdy songs—at least they used to: the Goliards. Some cities think them a pestilence, since they sometimes foment riots among the real students, but that kind of fighting I always avoided as treasonous.

"And then there are thieves, not only of purses but of knowledge, who pose as students and poison everyone's minds against learning altogether."

We passed one entire building that seemed devoted to teaching, with the murmur of lectures floating down from many open windows. "Ah, that must be the university called the Sorbonne, founded by the king's confessor. It is quite new, but I hear it is already as excellent as the Cathedral School of Notre Dame. You can find the greatest teachers here and in a few places like the Cathedral School, where things are set up properly. Friar Thomas Aquinas teaches in Paris sometimes, or he used to, but the days of quiet learning and strict discipline are gone, for this kind of education is more and more out of the hands of the clergy."

"How can that be?" Anna asked.

"It mostly goes back to a scholar named Peter Abelard, who was notorious for several reasons—but look! We are almost there!"

I'd have loved to hear more about this notorious man—indeed, to hop off Pax and join some lecture at random just for the joy of it, the atmosphere of learning was so full of energy and excitement—but Joscelin was pointing ahead.

"See there? The Petit Châtelet lies straight ahead over the River Seine, guarding the Île de la Cité, which is one of two islands lying right in the heart of Paris."

We were approaching a broad river spanned by a wide stone bridge— the Petit Pont, as I later learned to call it—but you could scarcely tell where street ended and bridge began, for here too were more buildings, more people, more shops, more students, more noise, more bustle! Nothing Petit about it! Ahead stood a stone fortress with a guard gate standing open under it; this seemed to mark the end of the bridge. We passed from light into the dimness of a tunnel, and back into light.

Joscelin seemed to be in his element, for I had rarely seen him so animated. "This island is where a Roman fort used to stand in ancient times, and here Saint Genevieve rallied her fellow Parisians to defy the Huns—

she is the city's patron saint. Centuries later Normans and other barbarians sacked the town but could never breach the fort here on the island, and now it is where my king lives." We were entering a great public square full of people of all ages, many of them also students. There seemed to be some kind of market, too, with everyone jostling to reach not only foodstuffs but also books. How I wished I could stop there, too. Such riches of learning offered to everyone! I had never seen anything like it before—it must once have been like this in Constantinople! We passed on.

"Look, Sofia, to your left behind those battlements are the Royal Palais de la Cité and the offices of government and so forth, and the Saint Chapelle, where we will mostly celebrate Mass while we are here."

The Saint Chapelle—Sir Reynaud had mentioned it …

"… And to your far right stands the Cathedral of Notre Dame with its school. See how high the cathedral's spires reach? And over there, between palace and cathedral, is the Hotel-Dieu, the oldest hospital in Paris."

A magnificent cathedral stood to our right beside another huge square, while to our left the roofs and upper floors of a stone palace were visible behind their protective walls. The square itself seemed to be an open-air market devoted to pigs, kept closely penned, and to pork products. Sir Reynaud's tale of the pig running loose in the cathedral now made sense to me, and I laughed inwardly. Indeed, I felt a bubble of happy anticipation rising in my chest as we rode on.

But it was the cathedral that commanded my attention above all else: it was amazing, not only for its height and beauty but also because I had never before seen flying buttresses. These are like slender decorated wings of stone that swoop out from the sides of the building and drop down to join the earth. But as I was to learn, they are not decoration. The cathedral has such thin and soaring walls that these buttresses are needed to keep it from tumbling down! The entire structure is a marvel of balance and harmony. I fell in love with it on the spot.

In addition to the pointed arches and splendid stained glass windows, and sacred carvings and statues that adorn its facade, its upper heights are also decorated with fanciful stone figures called gargoyles that serve as both guardians and spouts to drain off rainwater. And other figures called grotesques simply sit and stare down at you as if to warn you to go to Mass or be swallowed up by some demon from hell. It would have been more frightening, though, had they not been so playfully carved.

I stray from my story, I know, yet it was a wonder; and more await-ed inside the cathedral. We would often attend Mass there, usually on Sundays or special holy days, and I must mention the statues of Holy Mother Mary and the Christ child and of the saints; the glowing rose window, which had only recently been completed; the golden light of hundreds of candles, the rich altar, and so much more. It brought me back to Kyiv, at least in spirit.

Ahead of us loomed the walls of the palace, crenellated and embel-lished by towers, with soldiers standing on guard at intervals. You would think the king had something to fear from his own people, but perhaps this complex had been built long ago when Paris was much smaller and likely more vulnerable. I was not to learn until later that King Louis was responsible for this added security.

Guards saluted Lord Joscelin at the entrance, and having offered the proper papers and password, my husband led us all inside to a huge court-yard that reminded me somewhat of Braissac, though on a grand scale. To one side through an open gate in one wall I glimpsed orchards and gardens with pleasant walking paths. To another side were so many build-ings that I could assign no use to them, but they certainly drew many people in and spat as many out, some looking business-like, others look-ing happy, and still others looking dejected. I decided these must be the government buildings, but they resembled nothing like the ones in Kyiv or Constantinople, so I gave up trying to make sense of them. There were also the usual stables and outbuildings; those I recognized, at least.

We dismounted, our horses and baggage were taken in different direc-tions, and a steward greeted us and led us into the palace proper and up to our rooms in one of the round corner towers. He and Lord Joscelin seemed to know each other, and they spoke in friendly fashion while the rest of us continued to stare out of each window we passed. The spiral stairs twisted up and up, each revealing some new vista. It seemed that our party was to reside on different floors, as Gilles and Paolo and Thomas were directed with their servants to a round room below Joscelin's and mine.

We had entered our room, spacious enough, with a good-sized chest and with a fire already burning, and the steward had begun to say, "My lord, the king and queen command your presence and that of your wife tonight after supper," but I was suddenly unable to listen or to care.

There stood Anna, unsure which way to turn. It was not only that she did not know where she was to stay, but also she had realized before I had that the king and queen would know nothing about her and her past. I suddenly wished that neither of us had come, for she would surely be exposed to blame and gossip of the worst sort! I knew how that felt; that horrible Yolande, who had briefly been married to Joscelin, had treated me thus. No wonder I had felt such dread.

"… And your young women can stay in this side room." Well, at least one problem was taken care of, but what about the deeper issue?

When the steward had left and Anna gone off with our maids, I quickly spoke to Joscelin. "My love, it never entered my head until now, but Anna might have difficulties here. After all, you are well known, and our marriage is so recent that they cannot miss that our daughter was born out of wedlock. Even if you can smooth everything over with the king, talk and perhaps mockery might shadow her everywhere she goes."

Joscelin smiled in just the way that made me love him. "Well, the king and queen already know, for I wrote about both of you right after we found each other again, and again when we married, so they have had time to forgive us. I've come to think that sometimes forgiveness is easier to find than permission! I believe you will find that any gossip about Anna or us will meet with no favor here at court, for you both are shielded by royal favor."

I had to sigh with relief. "I wish I had known that before. I think it explains why I kept feeling that I would be caught somehow and punished wrongly. After all, I have done such penance for my sin, and so have you. I would not have Anna suffer for what we did."

"And she will not, nor must you give into dread or other whims. Perhaps they stem from another cause…?" I understood what he meant, but I could not say yea or nay, for I never knew when to expect my moon cycles. He looked disappointed when I shook my head, but only said, "Well, now we must dress for supper and our audience with their majesties. I will see to the boys, too, and then I'll escort you all to the Great Hall. It is almost like coming home to be here again. Look down from this window; you can see the yard where I first met King Louis as a boy and where we learned the arts of war together."

Below was a courtyard set up for martial games where several young men were engaged in mock battle of various sorts: tilting at a kind of whirling, wide-armed wooden statue or crossing swords or throwing javelins, all under the watchful eyes of several older men. It looked as if one pair of boys was enduring a scold, and I had to smile at their long faces.

So we dressed and went down, and Joscelin greeted almost everyone we passed, and a few times he even stopped and presented Anna and the boys and me to his special friends. I looked for censure in their faces but only saw friendly interest, and my tight heart began to loosen. Perhaps this visit would work out after all.

And so it did until the very end. I had a wonderful time in Paris, beginning at supper that very night. It was an odd gathering: our family was all seated almost halfway down one of the long tables but above the salt, as they say; the king and queen and their family sat at the dais; and all the other courtiers were seated by rank above or below us.

But at the far end opposite the king was the motliest assortment of men and women I had ever seen. Clearly they were all desperately poor, and the nobles of the lowest rank who had to sit near them almost visibly held their collective noses, for you could smell them even where we sat. Joscelin saw me staring covertly at them and leaned over to whisper to me while offering me a dainty piece of meat.

"Every night the king invites beggars to sup at table with him, and anything left over from their meal is served to him. More is handed out every day to a hundred poor men. It is cautionary to us all, though clearly not valued by everyone. I think the fear the paupers raise in people's hearts makes it hard for them to appreciate the king's generosity. On the other hand, all Paris loves him for it."

Watching those hungry people stuffing themselves with wine and bread and meat recalled to me other occasions of feasting and hunger: that terrible journey to the Mongol camps when we captives all went hungry; or even Ramadan, when people fasted during the day and feasted at night. I wished I could think of something wise to observe about it all, but my mind was blank. I was no longer as softhearted as I had once been, though my husband might think me far too tender still, but my appetite was certainly ruined. I admit it: I was not eager to join King Louis in supping on another's leftovers, especially when they had been pawed over by such dirty, hungry people. As it was, there would be little enough left for him, but a few pious—or perhaps ambitious—nobles could be seen here and there, abstaining from their meat in order to follow his example.

To my surprise, after that somewhat painful supper, rather than attending on the king and queen as I had expected, we all repaired to the king's newly built Saint Chapelle for evening Mass, as the entire court was expected to be there. The king and queen entered from a private door behind and above us all, making quite an impression on me. They looked most reverent and regal standing up there amongst their family and close advisors.

During Mass, to quell my dread over the coming audience, I looked around curiously between prayers and genuflections and during the sermon, but it was hard to see much in candlelight beyond painted and decorated walls and pillars. Over the altar is a kind of canopy, and over it sits the special repository for the king's reliquaries, one holding a piece of the True Cross and the other the Crown of Thorns. Was it real or had Sir Reynaud had just been cynical? After all, he had never said he'd seen inside the reliquary.

Behind me, Paolo, who rejoiced in such absurdities, whispered to Gilles and Anna, "Did you know that that are also two other great portions of the Crown of Thorns already in Paris? I hear there are enough thorns among them and already given away to various kings and archbishops across Christendom that the original crown must have been like a helmet towering two feet over our Savior's head." The three of them had to stifle their laughter, especially when Joscelin looked around and frowned at them.

After Mass finally came our audience with the king and queen. I expected many courtiers and ladies would be there, listening in and hearing what I hoped they would never hear, but to my relief we were granted a private interview. Indeed, the king and queen graciously welcomed us and summoned us forward. King Louis had regained his health, though he did not seem robust anymore. Queen Marguerite had also aged, though she remained lovely in a faded sort of way—but I too had faded, no matter what my husband said.

"Come closer, my friend," the king reached out a hand. Joscelin strode forth, knelt, and kissed it. But when he stood, so did the king, who gave him a hearty embrace that reminded me of Qacha and Argamon, although the only resemblance was the love that each man felt for the other. So this was why Joscelin was so faithful to Louis! They truly were friends, and to be readmitted to royal favor must mean so much to him.

Meanwhile, the queen drew me to her side for a private conversation. "Let them have their time for sharing memories of war and battles. I want to speak with you about something else."

Now I would receive the chastisement that surely awaited me. And in fact her face was most serious. She began with, "You did sin gravely, you know."

I bowed my head. "I know, my lady, and I have confessed and done a year's penance for it, and then over ten years more in essence."

She smiled. "Yes, but that is good. The Church forgives you, and so do I." I felt a tightness between my shoulder blades easing as she spoke. It was one thing for Joscelin to tell me—and why had he not said so before tonight?—and another to hear her say this directly to me.

"I do understand the love you and Lord Joscelin share, you know, for I love my king and husband in just the same way. We used to have to meet in secret on the stairs between our apartments, his mother was so jealous of me. It was sad, for she was a great lady, but her one weakness was her son and the power she held through him—and over him. She never saw that I could scarcely replace her in his affections. He never listens to me as he did to her! And, though I deplore your rashness, I admire your loyalty to your beloved for so many years. I imagine how hard it must have been for you to go to Acre to seek him when you bore such a painful secret in your breast."

I bowed my head. "Yes, harder than I could ever express, even to him."

"Well, Christ our Lord taught us forgiveness, and all that is in the past. Your daughter is no longer under a shadow, and you will bring her with you tomorrow to attend me."

I scarcely remember what else we spoke of; clearly the meeting had been meant to heal old wounds, and I was forced to credit the king's reputation as a good and fair man, no matter what I thought of his notions of holy war.

The next morning I saw Saint Chapelle in daylight and was almost overwhelmed. I had been to many beautiful churches and grand cathedrals, but this was the most special of them all. It was both intimate and spacious, like entering a sacred realm where everywhere you looked was beauty, from the walls painted with royal motifs to the canopy over the holy relics to the many-colored glowing light pouring down like blessings through the tall stained glass windows. Here the only feelings possible were awe and reverence, and I pitied Sir Reynaud for never having seen it finished before he died. He might not have shared my reverence toward God, and he might be tainted by many sins, but he would have loved the beauty of this most Holy Chapel. It also put me in mind of the way the emperors in Constantinople had their own entrances to Hagia Sofia, as if to elevate themselves above mere mortals. I wondered if the deposed King Baldwin had given King Louis the idea.

After Mass I was able, finally, to bring Anna to meet Queen Marguerite, who took special pains to make her feel welcome and to nip any gossip in the bud. The great favor she showed both of us was surely enough to satisfy everyone, or so I prayed. Happily, the king forbade that kind of talk as ungodly.

"Come here, my dear," she said to Anna as we joined the other ladies-in-waiting at their tasks. We had brought pieces to embroider and were pulling them out from our bags. "Show me your embroidery; I so rarely see stitches like those."

Anna stepped forward with the shy elegance of a deer, bowed gracefully, and handed her piece to the queen. "Lovely. I see your mother has taught you those interesting stitches from the Orient. Will this be for your private use? I recall her making purses for her two little servant girls so long ago."

"You must mean Banjuu, who got married and lives in Constantinople now. She and her husband run a home for elderly poor people. And Marguerite took the veil and became Sister Constance. I loved them both well, and I still miss them. But no, this is a cloth for the altar at the Convent of the Holy Mother near Braissac."

The queen smiled at her and then at me. I had learned my lesson, and we both knew it. I had insisted Anna bring the altar cloth she was working for her grandmother's convent instead of the belt she was sewing for herself.

Anna and I often waited on Queen Marguerite after that, since Joscelin usually disappeared each morning, sometimes directly after morning

Mass. He often did not reappear until the evening meal. But under the queen's protective eye, Anna and I met and, in my case, became friendly again with the queen's ladies-in-waiting, some of whom are even younger than Anna.

I particularly became friends with a woman whom I had known only slightly on Cyprus: Lady Heloise, who had been widowed during the war in Egypt and had escaped Damietta with the queen. We shared a common history, for there were few ladies like her left at court. She was older than I was, but her graying hair was styled in the latest fashion and her gowns were of as elegant a cut as the young women's. She had decided but humorous opinions, and she was always cheerful and full of chat.

That first morning she had beckoned me to sit beside her. "I am so glad to learn that Lord Joscelin escaped the clutches of that horrible young woman. She was so mean-spirited toward you."

I was glad to know there was sympathy for my cause, but alas, straightaway she began asking me various questions about my life since Cyprus. Those I answered most carefully, and happily she did not ask me about Anna.

When it came my turn to ask her about her life, she said, "I was born and raised in Paris, was married at fourteen to an important lord, the Comte du Melun, and until going to Damietta I had never traveled anywhere but to his county southeast of Paris. That disaster made me glad to return home for good!" We both laughed ruefully, and the talk turned to other things.

She must have spoken kindly of me to the others after we left that morning, because from then on I was always greeted with kindness and respect by the other ladies; and their welcome extended to Anna, who soon had her own circle of friends her own age. It was a pleasure to see my daughter in the garden playing ball with the other maidens, for the queen often led us down into it to stroll about on sunny days. The last roses were in bloom, the air was fragrant, and the world was golden with autumn.

Of course we did not attend the queen every day. Sometimes she was elsewhere, and then Anna and I could go out wandering with the boys, although Gilles would soon be entering the king's service and his days would no longer be free. He and Paolo had already begun exploring Paris. Fotis and Golden Thomas were always with them, and they could hold their own: at thirteen Gilles was already a tall, strapping youth with wavy brown hair and a continual smile, while Paolo was as thin as a beanpole with a nose like the prow of a galley. He was already a man if purpose counted for anything. He had soon learned his way around the city, and in addition to several ells of Paris-woven cloth, he had begun buying a vast array of gewgaws from various stands in anticipation of the great trade fair in Troyes that we were to attend.

Every time we went out, they had something they wanted to show us, starting with the central areas of Paris, which turned out to be much smaller than I had first supposed. I hated going off the main thorough-fares, but the boys wanted Anna and me to see everything, so we once even went down a dirty lane so narrow that we could only pass in single file. The houses leaned toward each other from above, their roofs almost touching. Nasty, but how the young people loved it!

However, to reward me for my bravery, Gilles insisted that they take us out riding, too. Paolo was less interested, but then he was a poor rider, having never needed to learn horsemanship in Constantinople or Venice. To the north and west, I discovered, there is much empty land protected by those massive walls; they await the city's growth. This gift of foresight came from a great king called Philippe Auguste, and it was but one of many good things he did for the city, like having its main streets paved. He had also established a large market called Les Halles, which we visited several times at Paolo's insistence. It has buildings and walls and gates and, according to my young guide, guards to protect it at night.

A community of merchants takes up most of the Right Bank, as it is called, with docks on the Seine and many boats unloading or loading there or passing under the Grand Pont or the Pont a Change bridges. I was a little overwhelmed at first; only Antioch compared with its noise and variety, and the bridges were crammed with shops before you even reached the market! But Antioch was so Oriental and ancient seeming and elegant compared to this rough, rowdy, youthful world.

I soon favored going over the Pont a Change whenever we went to Les Halles, as it was lined with jewelers' and money changers' booths. After seeking out the best, I finally ordered and later received four fine enam-eled rings, one for Lady Alianore, one for Joscelin, one for Anna, and one for myself. I also bought some fine silver plate for Braissac, some slender pouring vessels, and an enameled necklace, this also for myself.

I could also have bought crystal and glassware, but the workmanship was inferior to what I could find in Venice. I began to plan what I would ask Paolo to send me once he had returned to Venice, for it would be fitting for the Lord of Braissac to demonstrate his wealth and hospitality with the best pieces I could find.

I bought fine gold and silver wire, too, some of which I used for adornment on a pair of gowns to wear at court. I could not keep wearing my Venetian attire, for it was too different from the styles in Paris. But I also bought some gold leaf to send as an offering to the abbey at Saint Denis, which we were to visit. And I wanted to commission an illuminated copy of the Holy Scriptures to send to the convent near Braissac. That seemed a fine gift for Lady Alianore to take with her when she left us for the holy life.

Now, the reason I disliked the Grand Pont is this: though it is as lined with buildings and shops as is the Petit Pont and you can buy the most charming song birds and other delights along it, the area stinks of blood and urine, since it lies near the butchers' and tanners' and dyers' quarter. Besides, it is guarded by a sinister-looking castle called the Grand Châtelet that is used to house prisoners among other things, so perhaps that is why I felt such revulsion at first seeing it. We hurried by it every time we went over the bridge.

But to tell of Les Halles is to risk being thought a spinner of fairy tales. I had thought the Left Bank and the Latin Quarter and even the Right Bank were busy, but this great covered market was of an entirely different order. There are two fine large buildings, but both are always so crowded that it is hard to get past all the vendors and their customers. Everywhere I looked, men were buying or selling fine silks, wools and linens, varieties of corn and fresh bread and vegetables, flocks of chickens to be slaughtered and brought to inn or home, cattle and geese and even rare animals like monkeys—I had finally learned what to call the little hairy man-creatures—and so much more. Each vendor had his own cries; each tried to out-shout his neighbor.

Paolo had to shout to me to be heard as we passed a booth devoted solely to honey and beeswax. "I was at first most tempted to try to sell my honey here, but when I approached that man, he laughed in my face. I cannot sell anything here at all, since I am not a member of a guild. How I wish I could find a business partner here, too."

The poor boy: he was fairly itching to begin his new career. I shouted back, "We'll do our best to get to the autumn fair at Troyes. Surely Lord Joscelin will be done with these meetings soon."

"I hope so. I tire of waiting, no matter how much I enjoy this city. There is only Gilles to keep me company, and he is a silly boy who only wants to become a great lord—as if owning land ever made anyone great!"

I said something pacific and we soon left, Anna having bought some trinkets for herself and Irene. Irene was so grateful that I was put in mind of my lost slave girl Kateryna with her ill-fated bear skin, or more recently, Banjuu and Marguerite and their matching clothing. I still thought of them as my girls, and I still missed them.

For such a small city, there was always something new and delightful to discover in Paris, from the varieties of plums you could buy right from a farmer's cart to the best cheeses you ever tasted brought straight in from the country, and from scented oil created just for you to a fur-trimmed pair of gloves to silk fringes for a gown—all of which I did buy! And the street cries! One called out for you to buy his pigeons, another to buy salted or fresh fish. You could get chestnuts from Lombardy or raisins from Outremer, not to mention delicious breads and pastries. Street hawkers offered little waffles and cakes and wafers or pies filled with fruit or meat, and I often sat at supper picking daintily at my food, having eaten my fill of something much tastier than what you got at King Louis' table. I must have looked so saintly!

Nor did I stop with treats and finery: what a collection of books I found for sale in the Parvis, as the plaza before Notre Dame Cathedral is called. Some books were poor copies of Aristotle and other Greek and Roman philosophers, clearly meant for the students who jostled each other—and me—to find some coveted text. But many types I had never seen before. I bought a book called Le Roman de la Rose that I later regretted as too flowery, long-winded, and silly; and another that contained proverbs, some of which were taken from the Holy Scriptures and some of which must be folk wisdom.

One proverb that I came across could have served as my motto: 'My homeland is where I graze, not where I was born'. I also found a book of herbal remedies and a delightful collection of animal tales, which Joscelin called fabliaux when I showed them to him. And I found an entire book called Roman de Renard that centered on a cunning fox called Renard. Anna and I began reading these books aloud to each other whenever we had time. It helped us both master the speech of Francia further, for many were written in that language and not in Latin.

One day, overriding Paolo's desire to visit the market yet again, Gilles insisted that we take our horses out into the fields and woods to the west of Les Halles. We followed the city walls, and where they met the river we saw the towers of some big square castle outside them. It looked quite daunting and at the same time rather strange, sitting beyond the city like that. And on the opposite bank there was another castle built right into the city walls. I got Gilles to ask some passerby what they were for, and the man stopped to explain. From his tone of voice, he clearly thought we were woefully ignorant, as I suppose we were.

"The one past the walls is the Louvre. King Philippe Augustus had it built with his own money to protect the Right Bank in case we are ever invaded again. The castle built into the walls is the Hôtel de Nesle, which some noble or other owns. But Philippe Auguste built the guard tower on it—see, the tallest of those towers? It also protects us, God willing."

We thanked him and went on our way, me pondering the acts of kings. Of course Philippe had also gone on a holy war, but he came home when he saw that his domain and his health to guard it were both at risk. That meant much to me. I admired his practicality over King Louis' relentless idealism. It might be the duty of every Christian king to take up the cross, but there had been so little point to Louis' disastrous invasion. I still could scarcely credit that he intended to go again. Crossing myself, I silently prayed for all those who had suffered or would suffer in wars, including my king.

"What is it now, Aunt? You are always praying about something," Gilles teased.

"Never you mind," I smiled. We rode on.

We went to the market in front of Notre Dame as well, which was only held once weekly and was the only place you could buy pork. While I had seen every other kind of farm animal roaming the streets of Paris, I had never seen a single pig anywhere but here. I eventually found out why: Philippe Auguste had lost his son when the prince's horse shied at an errant pig and the youth fell and died. After that the grieving king decreed that no pig could run free in the city and that only this one market could sell pork, and then only once a week. The few live pigs that are brought in for slaughter are vigilantly guarded to keep them from escaping. Sir Reynaud's story took on an entirely new aspect after this, for the vendor responsible for the pig that got into the cathedral must have suffered serious fines or even imprisonment for his carelessness.

We also visited the Hotel-Dieu, which is more than a hospital; it also provides housing for students. This was what drew us there, for Paolo had finally found some new companions: young scholars who lived there and who were eager to meet a lady-in-waiting to the queen. We first gathered outside the Hotel where Paolo presented them to me. We just looked inside some of the rooms devoted to the sick. The conditions were as appalling as Sir Reynaud had said, though there were at least beds, and nuns were tending to people. I caught a whiff of dirt and body odor that sent me reeling back outside, though the smell followed me. It was then that I realized: not only were the patients not very clean, neither were our student hosts. They were, so to speak, dirt rich!

I learned much from that visit, though. The boys we met were surprisingly respectful, though I saw the eldest one eyeing Anna's dark-haired servant Irene with admiration as they led us to what they called their college, a house where many students lived and cooked together. They showed us into their room, where four beds, little more than piles of hay, were crowded into a tiny space. An equally tiny table with a stool and one candle was all they had for their studies. It was stacked with the few books they were required to read; I supposed they shared them.

Almost everyone in the college soon crammed into the room to gape at the ladies. Then it turned out that we were expected to dine with them, for they produced bowls and cups and a loaf of the coarsest, most crumbly bread I had ever seen! A pair of students left for a little while, and while they were gone I listened to the others talk, realizing slowly that they were anticipating this meal as a great feast, for there would be meat. The young men returned at the almost same time, one staggering in with a full jug of ale and the other with a large, steaming bowl of pea soup!

The 'cook' made a very pretty speech of welcome, and I thanked him as courteously as I could but, I said, "I must refrain from eating the soup and drinking the ale, as I have taken a certain vow about food and drink."

No one thought anything of this, for people were forever taking vows to atone for an ill deed or to ask for special blessings, but my reason was different. If these young scholars could afford no more than bread and ale and some dried peas, it would be wrong to take food from their mouths.

Poor fellows: that soup was thinner than a Mongol stew. Anna I allowed a small portion, and she and the youths all set about eating. She set down her bowl after one sip, though, whispering to me, "There's no meat in it, just a ham hock!"

I'm afraid she was overheard by her nearest neighbor, Irene's admirer— he had managed to sit next to her—a young giant whose name seemed to be Welf. "Meat? Certainly there is meat in it, but not much. Until my father sends me more money, all I can afford is a ham hock. But meat is unheard of for many a student. Beets, a few onions and peas and beans are good enough for us. Even candles are a luxury for most."

Anna blushed, and then blushed even deeper when he added, "But while I am well-off, being the son of a baron, even the poorest student is wealthy in spirit because we gain knowledge. I myself have traveled across Christendom seeking it. I've studied at the University of Oxford, which is not far from my original home, and at the University of Bologna, and at the University of Palencia, in Spain, though none can equal Paris! Some day I may become an archbishop or even a cardinal for my pains, and then all my troubles will be repaid with good!"

"Yes," another jested, "you can rob everyone with taxes and eat well and wear fine garments! I'm sure your uncle the bishop will see to that."

They all laughed, even Welf. "Yes, and save souls all at the same time! But on the other hand, I might marry." He looked at Irene significantly, and I realized that because she was dressed so finely, he had no idea she was not of his station.

It took me a little while, listening to their slurping, burping, witticisms, laughter, and occasional questions about what life at court was like, to realize that these young men, ranging in age from thirteen to twenty-seven, were all from the same land as Sir Hugh, an island called England.

"Yes," said Welf, when I asked, "we belong to what they call the English nation. There are three more: the French, the Norman, and the Picard, each with its own colleges in their particular quarter of the city. No nation gets along with the others, so we English go everywhere together, eat at the same inns, sit together at classes, and so forth. You should hear what they say of us, that we English are drunkards and that we have tails, and besides that they lump us in with the Swedes and Danes and even the Germans.

"Well, what we say in return is that the French are too proud—"

"Not to mention all weak and soft and womanish," one fellow cut in.

"And the Normans are always trying to act all stiff and strong—"

"Not to mention how boastful they are!" By this time all the students were laughing, Gilles and Paolo joining in, while Anna and I smiled politely. It seemed like some special boy's game, perhaps entitled Insult.

"And don't forget," Welf continued in a sort of sing-song voice,

"Picards are traitors and fair-weather friends,

"Lombards are greedy and spiteful.

"Romans want to overthrow all rule—"

"And they bite their nails," someone chimed in.

"And the Germans are gluttonous and mad."

Now everyone was roaring with laughter, and in a moment they were all singing a bawdy song that I really didn't want Anna to hear. I stood, and they stopped, but it still took some time before I could persuade my boys that it was time to leave, for they'd have been happy to stay, as would Fotis and Golden Thomas. Likely Gilles and Paolo would have ended up spending all their money on their friends at a tavern and, if the songs meant anything, at a brothel. So much for the chastity of clerics!

Welf courteously offered to guide us all back to the king's palace, but I made equally courteous refusals. His admiration for Irene set up warning signals through my entire body. She had ripened into a young woman, and I was not only her mistress but also her protector. If he wanted to propose marriage, I would approve; but if his ambitions were as he claimed, that seemed unlikely. As soon as he found out she wasn't of noble blood, his admiration might turn into seduction if it were allowed to flower. That treatise on love came back to me: beyond fearing she might be raped, which was foremost, I suspected that King Louis would not be pleased to hear of any slips of morality amongst his courtiers or their households. I wanted no scandal surrounding her that might cast a shadow on us.

Outside, Anna seemed mightily disappointed that we had to leave so suddenly, and she asked me why.

"I thought their songs unseemly for a young maiden's ears, Anna, especially a young noblewoman's."

Anna seemed torn between laughter and tears. "I am no milk babe, Mother. I did live around animals growing up, you know, so I heard nothing new. Besides, I hear you and Father almost every night!"

I was shocked into silence and then into remembering that my child was growing up. She would be twelve this December, and my moment of decision was almost upon me. Would I tell her my full story? Clearly the violence of it might come as a shock, but then perhaps she could draw some life lessons from it as well. Tomorrow I would go order a blank book and finish my story; there would be so much to sort through, since I would still leave nothing out. She would not need to hear most of it yet, so I had time to decide what to tell her.

And I vowed to be quieter in my lovemaking with Joscelin from then on, and to ask him to be quieter, too.

Near the end of September, we paid a sad farewell to Paolo. One morning he approached Joscelin after Mass and announced that if he delayed any longer, he feared he would miss the best goods at the Fair of Saint-Ayoul at Provins. That in turn would render his visit to the Cold Fair in Troyes in November meaningless, and he had made commitments for various goods to Basil's partners back in Venice. There were other fairs he wanted to visit on the way home, too. He must leave.

So, armed with guards and accompanied by Fotis, he had set off.

The day they left, Irene cried bitterly at losing her brother, and I was almost tempted to send her with him just to get her away from that Welf, who kept sending her notes that she would dutifully hand over to me. But she'd only have been in the way, especially since Fotis seemed so happy to be off to a new adventure with his master. After all, Paolo would stop by Braissac on his way home, so it would only be a short separation.

Welf continued to be a problem, however. Whenever we went out, he seemed to appear from nowhere, to find ways to fall behind with Irene. She had never received attentions from any man before this, was all pretty blushes and artless response. I am sure he found it both entertaining and enticing.

Finally, having sent Irene with Anna to wander in the palace gardens, I summoned him through Gilles. I wanted to speak with him alone.

At least Welf's manners were good. He bowed creditably on entering the solar and spoke courteously, "Greetings, my Lady. How can I serve you?"

"I want to speak with you about my servant Irene." He barely masked his surprise. "Yes, she is our maidservant, an orphan without any protector but me. I feel it my duty to ask you outright what your intentions toward her are. Though she is no lady, I would never let her come to harm through some idle dalliance of yours. So, sir, what are they?"

Welf considered long before he spoke. "It was only right of you to guard your maid's honor. I did not know … I mistakenly assumed that she was one of your … cousins or the like. You being too young to be her mother, of course." He smiled winningly, but I did not smile back.

"I suppose, then, that I must withdraw my attentions. I was halfway to asking her to marry me, but it would never do to marry a maidservant. My father would disinherit me." He sighed. "Irene is a lovely maiden, and she deserves a good man. But you were right in putting a stop to my courtship. I promise never to write her or follow her again." He bowed most correctly and left. I could tell that he was wounded, though, and I regretted it. But the fear of him learning about Irene from Gilles and then finding a way to seduce her was stronger.

I never told Irene about Welf's visit, and I made Gilles promise not to tell, either. She was surprised by the sudden disappearance, then saddened, then fretted for a week or two, then seemed to forget. She mentioned him to me only once. "I suppose Welf's father forced him back to England. He must have gotten tired of spending money on his son when a parish has been waiting for Welf for the past few months. He just wasn't sure he wanted to go, but the decision must have been made for him."

I flinched a little inwardly, but only a little.

At the end of September, the entire court rode out well past the city's northern gates to the Abbey of Saint Denis to celebrate Michaelmas, to pray, and to give alms. King Louis, I was forced to admit, is a most generous and pious king. Our diminished family went as well, stopping by the Saint Lazare Hospital to give alms. It is for lepers, so we did not go inside; indeed, we stayed upwind, for people were afraid the disease might jump the walls. Oddly, bakers make up a great number of the members of this grim and sad community, which the king now supports along with numerous other hospitals and their inmates inside and around Paris.

We cheered up again after leaving it. Lady Heloise rode beside me, happy to explain any questions I had, which of course were many.

"The abbey is named after the patron saint of Francia. He was a missionary and the Bishop of Paris, and he was beheaded by the evil Roman governor of the city, who was of course a pagan. That hill we are passing, happily for my story and your mind's eye, is where he was martyred. In his honor it was thereafter called Mons Martyrum, but we call it Montmartre nowadays.

"It is said that Saint Denis rose up after his execution, picked up his head, and walked a thousand feet before falling again. That is where a pilgrimage shrine was later founded, but the abbey that bears his name lies farther to the north. You will soon see that it is quite beautiful and also very special, for it is where all the kings of Francia have been buried since it was built. The king, I hear, intends to commission effigies to lie over each tomb, even of the earliest kings of Francia, like Clovis and Pepin. I find it very moving, and you must as well; do you take my meaning?"

I nodded.

"And there is a Benedictine monastery there, too, which is quite old. I expect the king and his inner court will visit its abbot and sup with him. We might not even return tonight, and the lesser members of the court like you and me will all repair to a nearby inn—

"Oh, look, they are already setting up for the October fair. I wonder if we can stop at it on the way home. One farmer always sells the richest cream you ever tasted. Not that I use it for eating: it also works wonders on the skin." Just like Mongol women! As we passed, I saw many men and a few women setting up booths and stalls and even a few solid buildings. The aroma of roasting meat drifted across our path.

Lady Heloise was right about the abbey. After we had celebrated Mass, and the king and a few of his family and intimates had gone to visit the abbot, she kindly took Anna and Gilles and me all around the basilica, as the church is called. It is the first so-called Gothic or French style church ever built. It has the same flying buttresses, but doubled, and they give it airiness and grace on the outside. And its odd crenellated parapet, more suited to a castle than to a church, and its single tower instead of the two on the Cathedral of Notre Dame, add to its special charm.

Inside, your eyes are drawn up and up, dazzled by repeating pointed arches and rows of pillars, and hovering above all, wondrous stained glass windows that seem as much windows into heaven as my long-ago icons once had. A round rose window as they call it, also of stained glass, stands above the central door into the basilica and casts more jewels of light into the space. The entire church is breathtaking. I had no need to feign how moved I was.

The crypt below with its many tombs made me feel most solemn. It was a good reminder that death comes to us all. As I looked at them, a shiver ran over my entire body. But Gilles and Anna were in a silly mood. When he thought no one was looking, he lay on the floor between two tombs and posed, hands crossed on his chest, as if dead. Anna had the grace to be scandalized by that, or perhaps she just realized that I was watching. She whispered something to him and they went back up into the church proper, trying not to laugh.

We spent the night at a large inn while the king and a few favorites, Joscelin among them, stayed in the abbey as guests. I'd have missed him hugely, but Gilles came to the room Anna and I shared and cheered us up. He had sought us out to while away the time, since he was not invited to stay at the abbey. Gilles had met some of the squires he would be training with and regaled us with stories about possible friends and rivals among these boys of the haut nobility, some of whom were haughty indeed. As usual, he made us laugh by acting out their silly pretensions. I realized how much I would miss him when the time came to leave him with the king's trainers.

After Mass the next morning, we all joined the cavalcade back to Paris, and I caught a glimpse of Joscelin among the honor guard surrounding King Louis. Lady Heloise rode with us again, amusing us with stories of her life at court. I liked her better and better, for her tales were full of wit and humor, and at the same time they taught me much about the French way of seeing life.

The fair was not yet open, but she and several other ladies did fall back to buy trinkets and, yes, cream, which the vendors were glad to sell them. I made the mistake of following behind. They were already returning, and I should have gone with them then, but a tent surrounded by colorful banners depicting odd-looking symbols drew me onward. I thought just to look at them quickly and then to return to ask Heloise what they meant, but a woman dressed in motley came out when I rode up and began urging me inside her tent to have my fortune told. When I refused, a gang of hard-looking men suddenly surrounded me.

They probably had never heard a lady scream, but scream I did, and several knights in our company were soon bearing down on the ruffians, laying about and quickly rescuing me. This was shaming enough, but the king and queen heard the noise and were staring at me as I rode back, red-faced, to join their train. Lord Joscelin rode back to see me, looking stern. At least he began with, "Are you all right?" I nodded, looking down, unable to meet his eye. But then he added, "Don't do anything foolish like that again. King Louis marked it, and you especially offended him by seeking out a fortune teller!"

I was about to explain, but he goaded his horse back toward the front of the procession. I was left with nothing but shakiness and shame. At least Lady Heloise was a comfort: not only did she listen to what had really happened, her quelling looks at the other ladies likely spared me some back-biting and teasing.

Back in the city, I had to face my husband that night, but before he took me to task I was able to quietly tell him what had really happened and vow never to fall into such an error of judgment again. He, at least, forgave me, and we went to bed happy.

More days of waiting passed, both on the queen and for Lord Joscelin to finish his conferences with the king. She had of course chided me gently about my visiting a fortuneteller until I had explained what had really happened. After that she seemed to take a special kindly interest not only in me but also Anna. I think it is because she had been brought to Francia as a bride when she was thirteen, and she knew what it is like to live far from your first home and to know so little about your new world.

With Paolo no longer there urging us to go to the market, I was sometimes able to talk Gilles and Anna into going over to the Latin Quarter, where I could listen in on some master or watch the young men debating. This kind of debate was something I had never seen before, and I was surprised that it was tolerated, given what was going on in the Occitaine. A fellow might begin his argument by denying the Holy Trinity and then proceed to debate with his opponent until it was proven that the Trinity did indeed exist! I heard many such arguments, but no one seemed to take seriously the heresies they debated.

Indeed, these exercises seemed designed more to teach one how to think and argue logically than to learn anything in particular. One night when I mentioned what I had seen that day, Joscelin told me that they are based on the logic of Aristotle and that this style of debate was started by that notorious Peter Abelard. After I had begged him to say more about him, he told me the entire story.

"Although he was a cleric, he also deliberately seduced a lovely student of his named Heloise. She was half his age, which made it even worse. They married in secret, and he fathered a child whom they named Astrolabe of all things, but he was cruelly punished: castrated by her irate uncle's henchmen. The lovers ended up in different convents, he in the abbey at Saint Denis—yes the very one we visited not long ago! They wrote to each other until the end of their lives, and their sad story is famous across the Pays de Francia.

"And now you know as much as I do."

And he began kissing me in a way that made me forget those other lovers.

Later, though, I remembered Heloise and felt a pang of pity for her, who seemed doomed to follow the whims of the men in her life. And I wondered what had become of Astrolabe, whose story was never made part of theirs. I learned later that he took the tonsure, too.

I began to be more interested in listening to snatches of lectures, even from the streets, than in attending the queen. I wished I could go inside the actual university buildings, but they were not open to women. There I'd have heard regular lectures, mostly on theology, but also on law and medicine and what are called the liberal arts, which is the kind of study I mostly heard in the streets.

Joscelin had said in passing that all students are required to begin their studies based on an ancient system that I recognized at once as the one devised by Al-Farabi. My tutor at Alamut had used it with me: first the Trivium of grammar, dialectics and rhetoric, which teach one how to see the way language is built, to think logically, to speak eloquently, to use syllogisms, and to discover the flaws in an argument. Then they progress to the Quadrivium: arithmetic, geometry, music, and astronomy, which includes astrology! Since it is included in the Quadrivium, I had to wonder why King Louis holds it in such low esteem as more fortune-telling; it had been accurate for me, if frightening. Anyway, all seven studies are the basis for the later, more complex higher studies.

In listening to some of the lectures, many of which were taught in verse for easy memorization, I felt almost as if my old teacher, Nasir al-

Din, stood beside me. How ironic: so much learning had flowed into the Islamic countries that had overrun Byzantium, and only then did it travel here via the Frankish states of Outremer, probably because the Franks had destroyed so much of it in Constantinople!

Despite my desire to spend all my time listening and learning, I did have to put in regular appearances at court or be thought very rude. And sometimes I was glad to be there, for the king and queen often entertained distinguished visitors whose conversations I enjoyed hearing. In the evenings at supper, Joscelin and I were seated just close enough to hear them.

Friar Thomas Aquinas himself came to Paris and was dining with the king one evening. Everyone was especially quiet at table that night out of respect for their venerable guest, so it was easy to hear their conversation, which compared heresy with other religions, particularly Islam and Judaism. The good Friar won my heart at first, for he spoke out in a ringing manner that, "It is wrong for a Christian to try to convert someone to his religion, Jew or Muslim, even if our religion is the best and truest. The Holy Synod in Toledo commands us not to, for no one can be forced to believe something, and no one can be saved against their will."

The king murmured something in response, but all I could hear was the answer.

"No, that does not mean I love the Jews. They practice usury, which should be stopped wherever it is found; not only that, whatever was taken from a Christian should be returned and the Jew be heavily fined!" This rejoinder took me aback, for in truth, from the noble merchants of Venice and its rivals to the money changers of Paris to the Templars with their far-flung banks, Christians found plenty of ways to practice usury; they just called it by different names. But what he said next truly shocked me.

"As for heretics, they began as Christians and so they should end as Christians. They deserve to be banished, not only from the Church by excommunication, but also from this world by execution. They corrupt the faith, just as forgers corrupt money, but they are much worse. Since forgers and the like are swiftly executed, so should be heretics. Especially since the Church is merciful: she gives every apostate two admonitions and allows him to repent. But after that, there is no choice but to excommunicate the malefactor and deliver him to the civil authorities to be put to death by fire."

I turned to my husband and spoke, I thought, softly. "But what about the cruelty of burning someone alive? Why not imprison these poor souls? Surely if they are treated with Christian love, they will repent."

What I had not expected was that at that moment, as sometimes happens even in a large group, no one else was speaking at that moment, and my voice carried across the room as if borne by an evil wind. All eyes turned to me. I blushed redder than fire and looked down.

From the king's table came Friar Aquinas' voice. "I know you, do I not? Yes, you are Lady Sofia, who sent me all those wonderful translations of Aristotle." Friar Aquinas was smiling benignly when I looked up in surprise. "I never forget a face.

"But to answer your question, which clearly comes from a tender heart, it is a long-held custom to burn traitors at the stake, and heresy is treason both to Church and to king. Perhaps you can look at it as a purification of the body, as some do, or if you wish you can see it as the best way to divide body from soul so that at the Resurrection no heretics will be present.

"But most heretics do repent and are spared—we seek to save souls, not to make men suffer. They may lose worldly goods or be required to wear the yellow cross, but such punishments are mild compared to the tortures of hell."

All I could do was say thank you and bow. I could feel my husband beside me, radiating rage at me. I sat through the rest of the meal without eating a bite and at the Mass afterwards could only think about what the good friar had said about the Resurrection. It made no sense to me. Criminals of all sorts, some of whom had never been caught, would certainly be resurrected at the end, too. Why would any earthly authority try to sort out heretics' bodies from the rest when God already knew everyone, and especially their hearts?

That night when we returned from Mass, Joscelin had scarcely sent Anna and the women to their room when he turned on me, his face disfigured by fury, and slapped me so suddenly that I fell hard against the bedpost.

"Never, never speak up before the king and his counselors like that again," he cried, while I slowly stood, rubbing my cheek and my back. "You had no right! And you were beyond lucky that Friar Aquinas knew you and understood your motives or you might have been arrested!"

I turned away from him in silence, undressed in silence, and went to bed in silence, facing away from him. He paced for several minutes before joining me in bed. I felt a soft touch on my shoulder, but I pulled away.

"Sofia, I never meant to strike you so hard. I am sorry, but believe me, it was the only way I could make you understand how serious your misstep could have been for us all. I might have lost the king's favor, you the queen's. We'd have been under constant suspicion, and all that I have tried to build at Braissac for us swept away with little or no warning."

"Well, you have lost my favor, instead," I managed to say, my throat was so strangled with hurt. Who was this stranger I had married? I knew he had the right to beat me and that a slap was mild by comparison, but that meant nothing to one who had only been struck once before in her entire life, and then by a Mongol barbarian. But after tonight I could not deny the truth: these Franks and Normans could be every bit as barbaric as any Mongol. And I had spent so much time misguidedly hating my captors!

To Joscelin all I could say was, "Never, ever strike me again. It is the one thing I can never endure from any man."

I felt him turn away from me, then, and that was when the tears came. I doubt either of us slept that night.

The next morning on the way to the queen's solar, Anna whispered, "Mama, you must learn to hold your tongue! Even I can see how wrong it was of you to intrude on the king's conversation like that. Please, if you value the good things that have come to us, never endanger us with such talk ever again."

I was struck dumb. I could not even rebuke her for her pert words, for I knew them to be true. But it also grieved me that even my own daughter would not take my part.

The Queen smiled at me when we entered and bowed to her, but she took no particular notice of me after that, which was as much as I could have hoped for. Those ladies in waiting who had arrived before us cast curious and not entirely friendly glances my way, and even those maidens with whom Anna was friendly made no effort to draw her near them. We received the same treatment from those who entered later.

Only Heloise seemed indifferent to convention. She was among the latecomers, and strode over to sit by me, exclaiming, "Well, you certainly surprised us all last night, Lady Sofia. What made you speak up like that?"

"I had no intention of speaking up; what I said was meant for my husband's ears alone, but the room fell silent at that moment, and my worst habit, that of seeking to understand, was revealed to all. I probably do have too tender a heart, but burning people seems so unlike what Christ preached on the mountain, so unlike the Golden Rule.

"But I am foreign-born, and no heretics were burned in my homeland, though I once witnessed a man burn to death by accident. It was beyond horrible. So perhaps that is why the thought of it strikes me so deeply."

"Well, that is enough said about that," the queen said in a voice of finality. "Sofia, you meant well, but as someone unused to our ways, it would be best for you not to comment on what you do not understand."

"Yes, my queen," I said softly. "And thank you."

I suppose my humility touched something in the hearts of most of the ladies, for from then on I was made welcome enough, while Anna was again included by her group of friends.

So when I saw my husband again that night, I had to speak, hard though it was to humble myself. "My lord, I suppose I am but a weak foreign woman. I will never speak out like that again." He smiled and stepped forward as if to embrace me, but I stepped back with hands held before me.

"But I meant it when I told you never to strike me again. I am no dumb animal that needs blows to guide it. I have it on excellent authority that my mind is as good as a man's."

Joscelin looked sour and did not reply. We undressed and climbed into bed, the same distance between us as the night before.

Late that night when I thought he had fallen asleep, I got up, wrapped a quilt around myself, and went to stare out the window at the training ground. I had waited so long for my dream of marital happiness; but had I sold my birthright for a mess of pottage? "Where has caritas gone?" I whispered.

A moment later, Joscelin's voice came from behind me. "It is here, in my arms, Sofia. I never wanted to marry a dumb animal. And I can hardly fault you for what I love in you. I love you so much. I promise: I will never strike you again." And he picked me up and carried me back to bed.

MID-AUTUMN TO WINTER
ANNO DOMINI 1262

We left Paris in mid-October. Lady Alianore had sent a message that she was ill and sorely needed her son to return. The time the king could keep Joscelin there was almost up anyway, so he was able to gain permission to go. He bade his king goodbye with a clean heart.

It was hard to say goodbye to Gilles, though. We all tried to behave gladly for him during our final days together, knowing that a bright future lay ahead of him. But we would all miss him grievously.

The day of our departure came; Gilles was to move to new quarters and a new life that very day. He claimed it was but another great adventure, but there were as many tears in his eyes as in everyone else's when we bade each other farewell. Anna especially wept, gave him a little scarf she had embroidered, and looked back waving farewell until we were through the gate. She was losing her childhood playmate, and only God knew when any of us would meet again.

Once we were outside Paris, it was clear that autumn had arrived, a fact hidden by the bustle of city life. The fields had been harvested and leaves on the trees were turning every color of gold and red and brown, and there was a mild nip in the air even on sunny days. Mostly it rained, though, deepening the gloom I felt. The distance between Joscelin and even Anna and myself had grown for me, a feeling of heartbreak compounded by their lack of understanding and the way they seemed to have drawn closer to each other, apparently over my ill advised words.

But perhaps it was simply that my husband was worried about his mother, and she was sad to leave her friend behind.

Both of my sovereigns had forgiven me for my errors, at least. I had spent my last days in the city recovering their goodwill. Having repeatedly begged for an audience with them both, I was at last granted a few minutes, during which time I had spoken feelingly of my regrets over what I called my foolish, intrusive words. I had also asked if I might make up for my error by contributing to one of King Louis' hospitals, perhaps the one for fallen women or the one for the blind. He had revealed a sense of humor over that, and graciously and smilingly accepted the heavy purse of gold I had offered him. So, given that I had recovered both royal favor and presumably my family's affections, I could not fathom why I felt so heart-weary. The farther we traveled, the more that familiar dread crept over me. I put it down to my own worry over my mother-in-law.

The journey seemed to take forever, and we were all eager to be home; yet when we were almost there, we turned aside. I now wish I had followed my instinct and asked to go straight to Braissac, but Joscelin had some business to do on the king's behalf, and he made it clear that he expected me to go him. Given the fragile state of our feelings toward each other, and knowing he was as impatient as I was to be back, I did not ask.

Our destination was a town called Cahors, south of Braissac by several miles. It is a pretty town, sited by a river that surrounds it on three sides, and it boasts a wonderful black wine, which we drank too much of that night.

It is also one of the centers of the Inquisition.

There was a sense of simmering outrage among the people there, a feeling of men looking over their shoulders, of not meeting each other's eyes, even on the part of the loyal Catholics. Many had seen their friends and neighbors go through a kind of hell of being questioned without knowing what they were accused of doing; many had been called upon to testify about—possibly against—those selfsame friends and neighbors, seen property seized or burned and people condemned to prison or at least to wearing the yellow cross for a number of years. A few had been condemned to the stake. All this Joscelin told me, along with a warning to say nothing, a command I gladly obeyed. I decided that the reason he took me there was to show me how much danger I had directed our way.

We stayed overnight, and I was not sorry to say goodbye to the town, no matter how delicious its wine.

Heading home, we had traveled but a few miles when a cry came from one of the guards at the front of our caravan. We stopped abruptly. Because of heavy rain, I had pulled my hood far over my head, so when I looked up, squinting through the downpour, I saw little beyond someone who looked like a priest flitting in the woods to my left and then vanishing. He was mostly a smear of blue. I wondered what order the priest belonged to, having never seen a blue cassock before, and what he was doing there. To this day I doubt anyone else even saw him, for they were all staring at something on the road ahead.

I motioned Anna and Irene and the other servants to stay behind, nudged my palfrey forward, and stopped in horror. Joscelin and his men had dismounted and blocked much of the sight, but I saw enough: bodies lay strewn on the road in spreading pools of rain-dappled pink.

They had clearly been the victims of robbers. Almost everything moveable had been stripped off most of them, for they were naked, and bloody. Joscelin sent a few of his hired knights out to see if they could find any trace of the bandits, while Anna and Irene and I stood shivering under a dripping oak tree. The remaining guards checked each of the fallen, looking for survivors.

It was a terrible task, achieved all too quickly. Of the eight people there, only a young woman, who looked to be about sixteen, had survived. She had been cut on the scalp and was bleeding freely, but her wound was not actually serious. However, she seemed out of her wits, and no amount of questioning could get her to make sense.

A few of our guards dragged the bloody corpses to the side of the road and made a makeshift shelter for them, hopefully enough to protect them from wild beasts. It seemed especially terrible that such folk had been attacked, for it was clear from their calloused hands and bent bodies that they had been humble people of small means. That might be why they had tried to travel without any guards.

The rain and mud defeated the search party, and they were soon back. After conferring with my husband, two men rode off. Joscelin came to me where I stood over the girl, trying to protect her from the rain with my cloak.

"I have sent men to the next town to find someone to come gather the bodies for burial." I nodded dumbly. Anna and Irene were huddled together under a nearby tree, sobbing. His men soon rejoined us, followed by somber peasants with hoes and picks. They began to collect the bodies.

"There is nothing to do but go on," my husband finally said. "One of my knights will carry the girl before him to the next village."

With our progress slowed to what seemed like a crawl, it took almost all day to reach the settlement, the last before Braissac. We'd have been home already had this terrible thing not happened. Everyone was chilled to the bone, and Irene had begun shivering and sneezing violently. Indeed, we were all troubled, not only over the deaths of those people but at the thought of robbers. At least there was a warm fire and hot drink and food at the homely inn where we put up for the night. We could not persuade the young woman we had rescued to take more than a few sips of water, so I sent her to bed and set a servant woman to watch over her.

We awoke the next morning to sun streaming into our room. Soon after breakfast several of the village elders appeared, drawn by the news of bandits and murders. While Joscelin spoke with them in hopes of finding out who the victims were, I took Anna and Irene to see the injured girl. She was still asleep. That seemed a good sign, and we left quietly.

"What will happen to the poor girl?" Anna looked near tears.

"I don't know. Perhaps we can arrange for her to stay here in the inn until she recovers. It would not do for her to travel further, and we must get home to your grandmother."

"You don't intend to take her with us, then. It somehow seems so heartless. We are now responsible for her, are we not? That is what you always taught me."

"Yes, but we are even more responsible to get back to Lady Alianore, who is ill and longs to see us. And until this maiden tells us who she is, we have no way of knowing who or where her people are. She may have friends or relatives nearby who can care for her."

As it turned out, Joscelin had already asked about the girl, but no one in the village knew her. As these towns are so small, and so few people leave them except to go to a neighboring fair, that was not surprising. What eased our minds was that he had already arranged with the innkeeper to take the girl on, a handful of copper deniers sealing the bargain. The man assured us that he would send word to Braissac once he found out who she was. He thought it would not take long; he would send her back to her home, well protected, after she recovered, or keep her on as a servant if that did not work out. We could leave with clean hearts.

We arrived in Braissac late that day. "Oh my dears," Lady Alianore cried when we entered the hall where she had been sitting forlornly on a bench. She was looking frail, but she was no longer ill. "I was sure I'd not be alive to greet you, and now I know not whom to embrace first! I am so glad to be proven wrong about my forebodings!" And she burst into tears. With such embracing, such commotion as the servants hastened to welcome us back and serve us a late supper, and such happy emotion, the disaster of the previous day faded. How glad I was to be back. How my mother-in-law delighted in the gifts I had brought her, especially the gold leaf for the convent, how happy we were to be together again!

However, Irene was not well. By bedtime, she was too feverish to help Anna undress, and I sent her straight to bed in a separate room with strict orders to rest as long as she needed.

The next few days were spent preparing for the feast of Saint Martin, which was also to be a celebration. All of Joscelin's family and neighbors would be joining us, including Cecelia, Philippe, and his parents and kin. Lady Alianore gracefully and gratefully put all the planning and organizing into my hands.

I'd have enjoyed every minute of that but for Irene. What had seemed like a cold had traveled to her chest, and her cough was sounding worse and worse. She seemed to grow paler and weaker by the day. I kept slipping away from my duties to see how she was doing, bringing her broth or little tidbits to give her strength, and making sure she was warm enough. Anna, too, was worried, and kept pressing little gifts on me to give her because I forbade her to come into the sick room. Finally Joscelin sent for both the physician and the local surgeon to bleed her. Both men offered little hope that Irene would recover.

Anna was left at the mercy of terror and confusion, and I often came upon her kneeling in the little entryway chapel, deep in prayer before the crucifix. She had come to depend on Irene on the journey here. Now it looked more and more as if my daughter might lose yet another beloved servant.

I took to nursing Irene myself for a great part of each day, but to no avail. She gave up the ghost on November 8, Anno Domini 1262, having received the Viaticum from Father Pierre. And just before she died, she looked up at me and asked, "Will you send word to Welf?" It was a knife in my heart.

"Of course, my dear." She smiled and closed her eyes. An hour later, she was gone.

Anna and I were crushed by grief. How I regretted not sending Irene with Fotis as she had begged me to let her do, or even letting Welf court her a little longer, for now the joys of love were beyond her reach forever.

Anna simply could not believe that another of her favorite servants had died. "I feel as if I am cursed," she wept while the shrouded corpse was carried off to the chapel for a funeral Mass.

I took her into my arms and held her and tried to soothe her. Someday, I prayed, she would understand that sorrow is a sign of a loving heart.

All during the Feast of Saint Martin and the jollity that accompanied it—people wanted to eat heartily in preparation for Advent—I put on a face of welcome, but in my heart I was desolated. I could endlessly tell myself that I had done what I could for Irene and that death comes to us all as God wills, but my heart was weighed down by how easily we can all pass into death without warning. Whenever I had a chance, I went to the chapel to pray for her soul, sometimes forgetting the passage of time. Anna was often beside me.

Advent began, and I gladly fasted even more than was required. And I did send word to Welf, who wrote back that he too felt infinite regret. He had truly loved her, called himself a coward for not following his heart instead of convention. Now he planned to travel back to England, and to be much more serious about his calling to the Church.

Shortly afterwards, the owner of the inn where we had left the injured girl sent a message to Joscelin asking him to come get her, that she was recovered, but that she had no living relatives and no home—such was as much as he could get out of her. She was not able, or perhaps willing, to work for him.

It seemed like this might be the answer to my prayers: I could train her to serve Anna and me. While affection for her new servant might not blossom right away, at least the pain of losing Irene would be blunted a little.

Sir Hugh went for the girl, and they arrived in Braissac on a chill, gray day at the end of November. Her name was Grazide, though she was unwilling to tell us much more than that. She won Anna's heart straight-away by telling us she was an orphan. Her aunt and uncle, the last of her living relatives, had been among the slain. She was as thin as a piece of straw, homely and simple. Within a few days of trying to train her as a maidservant, I gave up and sent her to the kitchen where she was assigned to turn the spit for roasting meats. It was a disappointment, but perhaps Grazide would at least start eating properly under Cook's direction. She seemed to be able to live on air.

And now my story draws to its close. I will now send the parts I recently wrote to the bishop as my final penance, for the rest of it he already knows.

But there is more to my story that the bishop will never see, and I wrote it for you, Anna, for you need to know. It was late afternoon and surely no more than ten days after Grazide arrived. I was crossing the courtyard when ghastly screaming burst from the kitchen. Thinking a fire had started, I ran straight there where a frightful sight greeted me. Cook had fled somewhere, as had all his assistants but one: Grazide. She was face down on the floor, still screaming, her skirts over her head, surrounded by four soldiers. Two held her down, a third had unloosed his breeches and was having at her, while a third stood looking on and laughing!

I must have screamed, too, for I recall a look of surprise on the men's faces. I seized the closest thing to hand, a spit, and rushed toward them, waving it wildly and shouting at them to stop.

The laughing soldier stepped forward and grabbed the spit from my hand, looking both amused and annoyed. "Go away, lady, or risk harm. What we do is nothing to you or even to the wench. After all, these heretics claim you cannot sin below the waist!"

"Heretics? What you do is a sin against Our Savior and the Lord God and Holy Mother Mary all together! Get out of my home!"

He frowned and his voice grew hard. "It is just as much a sin to protect a heretic as to be one, or perhaps you are one, too?"

"I see no heretic, just a terrified girl!"

I remember little after that, only that Lady Alianore rushed into the room with Anna close behind, put a hand to her heart, and fainted, that I called to Anna to get her father, and that I myself was dragged away along with Grazide. Joscelin's knights were nowhere to be seen.

Where the soldiers first took us, I know not to this day. We were thrown into a cart with five other people, all peasants, none of whom I knew; and before Joscelin could be found, we were on the road, my villagers standing at the edge of the hamlet staring with their mouths agape, me crying out for help, and Grazide sobbing without let. Finally she ran out of tears and I out of hope that shouting could do anything. All I could do now was to pray and not lose my head. Surely Joscelin would be coming after me straightaway.

I know now that he was just leaving a woodlot far from the castle, where he and his steward had been deciding something humble like what trees to cut down next. Certainly by the time he got back to the castle and learned what had happened, events had overtaken me.

We were not brought far that first day, as it soon grew dark. When we stopped, we prisoners were locked up in a barn somewhere. We all agreed to huddle together, as we'd have frozen to death singly, but we still shivered all night. No one felt like speaking. At one point I drifted into a desperate dream that muddled up my rape at the Dnieper, the Bedouin attack, and Sir Reynaud's assault on me, but I was startled awake by the sound of horses arriving and men dismounting. Torchlight flared between the cracks in the barn door.

Shouts rang outside and were met with raised voices from within the house where our captors were staying. I thought I heard Lord Joscelin, but I could not be sure. After a small eternity everything grew quiet. I kept expecting the barn door to open and my husband to sweep me into his arms and tell me it was all a mistake. Instead, the same angry voices came clear again, a door slammed, the sound of hoofbeats faded away, and the most desolate of silences was all that remained.

The next morning we were taken to a castle and crowded into the bottom room of a stone tower where several other frightened, half-frozen people were already imprisoned. It was cold and damp, and with no windows it was unbelievably dark. There were no blankets, not even straw for beds, and we were given only coarse, crumbly black bread and cold water.

Rats ran by and sometimes over us.

I now know we were put underground at the tower's base, below the level of the moat. I had nothing to say to the other prisoners, and they spoke nothing to me. But I had something to say to Grazide. When we had finished our bread, I mustered my courage to ask the hard question.

"Grazide, are you a heretic as the soldiers claim?"

"No, I am not. The Catholic Church is the heretic, the fortress of Satan, and I curse the day you and your knights came and took me away! I could have died in peace, but you had to come and think you were saving me."

That seemed to open floodgates of speech, to each other at least, and I soon learned that I was the only Catholic there. "You are a Good Christian, too?" ... "Where did they catch you?" ... And, "Who betrayed us?"

Slowly I pieced together the reason why we were all there—or at least why they were. An exiled Perfect had secretly returned from Lombardy and wandered from village to village offering to take anyone back with him who wished to go. A few had decided to follow him, including Grazide and her family. Each had set out from their respective villages, following paths they thought were known only to themselves. The victims had arrived at the very place where they had all died; those who came late turned around and raced back home.

Everyone in the group kept trying to find someone to blame, but they all agreed that Satan was behind the bad timing and bad luck that had pursued them at every turn. First the robbers and those murders; then men from the village where we had left Grazide had set out to find and fight bandits and instead had come upon a gathering of the surviving heretics praying with the Perfect. That must have been the man in the blue cassock I had glimpsed. All were arrested, and worst of all, some traitors had straightaway saved their skins by exposing their fellows. People from several villages were arrested as well, and now here they all were.

As for Grazide, she and the murdered people had not identified as heretics at first, hence the delay in arresting her. Evidently her refusing to eat was what had finally drawn suspicion onto her head. Word had gotten out, and the local priest had sent for soldiers to arrest her. Her fellow prisoners commiserated with her but also praised her willingness to starve herself to death, a noble deed. I remembered how I had once thought that the

Manicheans should have done the same, but it had seemed so foolish to me, yet here were people willing to abandon life for … I knew not what.

For much of the night until exhaustion overtook us all, people murmured together. "We must summon our faith" … "To be burned at the stake is no great sacrifice for eternal freedom from this life of hell…." "Did you hear about Brother Thomas? He came to a bad end" … "You mean?" … "Yes!" … "Do you know who he lay with?" … "Does it matter? He broke his vow of celibacy and now he is cast out and must do penance" … "Well, that is why being burned is better, if even a Perfect cannot fight against the desires Satan plants in him …"

Me they despised and refused to speak with, nor did I speak with them. I now realized the danger I had fallen into and could do nothing but sit and shiver with fear and cold. I felt as if I'd been swallowed whole by despair. Here was my dread brought to life; here were my darkest fears, my deepest loneliness I their starkest form. In the past I had faced doom and death, but what frightened me most this time was not my own fate but that of Anna, Joscelin, Lady Alianore, and Braissac. For all I knew, the worst had happened: all of them arrested and taken to some other castle, Braissac seized, and each of us soon to be condemned to prison, the stake, or at the very least to the disgrace of the yellow cross.

After four so-called meals, the only way we had to count, the door swung open, a torch was thrust in, and a guard motioned to everyone but me to come out.

And then my own version of hell began again. I sat alone in the dark and tried to pray or at least practice peace. But all I could do was worry about my family and try to imagine what else I could have done for Grazide but try to stop the rape. And would the fact that we had tried to help her on the road be counted against us? These and other thoughts chased round and round in my head until it felt as if they had worn a groove in it.

A solitary meal passed before the other prisoners returned. The little amount of light cast by their guards' torch as they came in the door showed a group of shaken and terrified people. A fog of despair followed them into the cell and seemed to make the darkness all the darker. Then the guard motioned to me to come out.

It was the last time I saw any of my fellow prisoners.

Another man was being taken from a small cell as we passed it. His guards joined mine, thrusting us both before them, clearly taking us to the same place. I stared at him covertly. He was thin, short and frowning, perhaps forty, tonsured like a monk or priest, and wearing that blue cassock I had glimpsed on the road. Knowing no better, I'd have thought him a member of some Catholic order like the Franciscans or Dominicans. His face was brown from sun and creased from outdoor work, so I assumed he was a peasant.

We were led up from the tower along a spiral staircase and out to a battlement walkway that allowed glimpses of high rocky hills and a few villages. Below me in the courtyard, people were coming and going and behaving just as my people did at Braissac, apparently unaware of what their towers were being used for. I had no idea where we were. At the end of the walkway, we were made to stop before a large double door leading into a square tower. Our guards had said nothing to either of us since taking us out of the cells.

Now that we were side by side, the Cathar Perfect, for so he was, looked over at me. "I do not know you, lady. Are you one of us?"

"No! But I tried to save my servant girl from being raped by soldiers in my own home, and for that I am arrested. I didn't know she was a heretic."

He snorted and looked down at his tightly bound hands. Without looking at me, he softly said, "That would have been Grazide. I was giving her the Consolamentum when your party arrived. Had you not tried to save her, she would be in Heaven with God right now. But you tried to do a good deed, so listen to me: it is not too late to be freed into the truth. Do you know any of your Scriptures? The Gospel of Saint John?"

"Of course, by heart."

"There is the proof of the true religion: "And the Word was made flesh and dwelt among us. Christ was never born from corrupt human flesh.""

He had no time to say more, for the doors opened and our respective guards shoved us each inside. The Perfect began reciting the Lord's Prayer loudly until one of his guards struck him across the face.

By then I was no longer paying him much attention. Before us was a bishop, Dominican by his habit. He had set his miter aside in favor of a snug cap. Both that and his garment were lined and trimmed in fur. He was sitting at a table looking at some papers, while two clerks with their cowls pulled over their heads for comfort sat on either side of him. The rest of the room was empty, but a fire blazed in a large hearth, providing the first hint of warmth I had felt in a small eternity.

My fellow prisoner was shoved forward while I was signed to stand by the door.

The bishop looked up. "You are the so-called Perfect calling himself Timothy?"

My fellow prisoner nodded.

"And you consider yourself to be what is wrongly called a Good Christian, known to the Holy Roman Catholic Church as a Cathar heretic?"

"Your church is that of Satan, and you are the heretics, you greedy, self-righteous mockery of a bishop! Look at you, all trimmed in fur and velvets, all—"

"Silence!" the bishop roared. "You are only required to answer my questions. Anything else you say will only make things worse for you."

Timothy crossed his arms and glared at the bishop.

There was further questioning, and though the Perfect answered honestly, sealing his fate so far as I could tell, he never lost an opportunity to accuse and insult the bishop, the Church, and anyone else with a faith contrary to his own. But nothing the man said could make the cold-eyed inquisitor even change his expression. The bishop behaved as if nothing more could be expected of such a lost soul. At the last he gave the heretic the three opportunities to recant that Friar Aquinas had mentioned, but Timothy the Perfect was happy to scorn them and to cry out his allegiance to his Cathar faith.

It took perhaps an hour in total, and the verdict was no surprise: Timothy the Perfect was condemned and ordered to be given over to the secular authority, the baron of this castle, whose men would burn him and the others at the stake.

Timothy had refused to identify any but his fellow prisoners as Cathari, and they had evidently already confessed. Though nothing direct was said, it was clear to me that he would be tortured until he revealed the names of more of his kind—or of anyone else he could think of.

I had to pity him, and to be grateful as well, for as he was led out he turned to me and cried, "You see what monsters they are, woman. Repent of your false religion and you will join me in heaven shortly, never to return to this earthly hell."

I replied with equal force, "I am no heretic. I merely made the mistake of trying to help one of God's creatures. I know nothing of your faith, nor do I want to learn."

I spoke knowing full well that the bishop was listening. I was being honest as far as I went, but I also suspected that if I were to be examined closely, my faith would as little resemble the Catholic religion as Timothy's did.

The Cathar was led away.

I stood and waited, but the bishop seemed to be in no hurry to examine me, for he first looked over what the clerks had written down, taking his time and ordering corrections that he wanted made before the official documents were written and placed in the Inquisition records.

Finally he looked over at me. "Why was she brought here at the same time?"

One of my guards looked bewildered. "Father, I thought you said—"

"Never mind what you thought I said! You are dismissed. Wait outside."

My faceless guards disappeared—that is to say, I have no recollection whatever of their faces or figures, I was in such a state of terror—and I was left alone.

"Come forward, woman."

I had learned from the Nizari Grand Master how to hold my tongue, not to mention having recently seen how dangerous it was not to, so I stood silently and let the man look me over. However, I did look at him in return. Timothy was right. The bishop's robes were gray as they ought to be, but they were made of velvet, and the fur that trimmed his velvet hat and robe was ermine. In addition to a heavy woven gold band adorned with crosses that wrapped around his shoulders and hung down the front of his robes, he wore several gold rings, one of which boasted a large ruby.

"What is your name?"

"Lady Sofia of Braissac, recently wed to the Lord Joscelin, Baron of Braissac." I had had plenty of time to think through what I might be able to do to protect my husband and family. Being newly wed might put some distance between my husband and me and my apparent crime.

"And do you consider yourself to be what is wrongly called a Good Christian, known to the Holy Roman Catholic Church as a Cathar?"

"No. I consider myself to be a humble daughter of the Holy Roman

Catholic Church. I am no heretic. I have learned just now, in this very room, that one of the vows a Cathar takes is never to lie. I would be lying and betraying that false faith if I told you I was a good Catholic when I was not."

The bishop looked at me sternly. "So you deny that you are a Cathar heretic."

"Yes, Father. While I am always ready to have my understanding corrected and may have fallen into error out of ignorance, it was not done as a heretic but as one newly converted to the Catholic faith."

"Explain yourself."

I realized I had been drawn out farther than I had intended, but now there was nothing to do but to go on. And perhaps my forthrightness would prove to be in my favor.

"I was born in the faraway country of Rus', which followed the Greek Orthodox Church until it was destroyed by Mongol invaders. Much later while in the Holy Land, I lived as a refugee in a Hospitaller convent. That was when I converted to the Holy Roman Catholic Church. All this I can prove, and I can provide many witnesses, none of whom are heretics or even under suspicion of heresy."

"You speak boldly, especially for a woman. Is this the character of your people?"

"No, Father, it is my personal failing."

The bishop stroked his cheeks. "So why are you even here if you are innocent?"

I took a deep breath. "When on our way home from the service of King Louis," the king's name being another weapon in my arsenal, "my husband and our people came upon a scene of robbery and murder. Only one person was left alive, a girl of perhaps sixteen, whom I now know is a heretic named Grazide. We took her to the nearest town and paid for her care, and when she recovered from her wounds we brought her to Braissac since she said she was without family or home. We put her to work in the kitchen, since she was too simple or perhaps stubborn to do more than that.

"A few days ago, I heard wild screams from the kitchen and ran to see, thinking fire had broken out. Instead, I found four soldiers who had chased all the kitchen servants away, seized Grazide, and were abusing and raping her." This description at least made the bishop raise his eyebrows, although I could not tell whether he too was horrified or whether he was surprised that I was.

"I saw only a terrified girl, Father, not a person of this or that faith. I had no idea she was a Cathar. At worst, I am guilty of hastiness in trying to defend a helpless woman. I was but a good Samaritan."

"My, my, what a nimble tongue you have, Lady Sofia. Well, we will certainly look into what proofs you can offer. Meanwhile, we will at least put you in better quarters."

I bowed, feeling much lighter hearted than I had when I'd entered. Perhaps this nightmare would soon be over. "May I beg a boon from you, Father? It will help you as well as me if I am allowed to write to my husband and let him know where I am so that he can bring proofs to you. He will come forward and clear my name. He must be frantic with worry by now, as will be the other members of my family."

"We are not made of stone, Lady. I grant your request. I will have writing materials sent to your room."

I was taken to a higher room in the same tower; this one had a window, a cot and thin blanket, and a chair and table. Some time later a guard brought me a sharpened quill pen, paper and ink, and I wrote to my husband. I pleaded that he assist the person who brought him my letter in all ways, to provide the proofs my inquisitor wanted, and to come personally and vouch for me. The man took the letter and the pen and ink and left me alone again.

I spent untold weeks alone in that tower, visited by no one but the guard who brought me meager meals. There was little to see from my one window, as it faced out toward the countryside, which was hilly and dusted with snow. Indeed, it snowed a little almost every day, so I usually kept the shutters closed and endured the dark. There was no fire, and I had to walk briskly around the room, wrapped in my cloak and that blanket, in order not to freeze.

At least the bread was a little better, and I was allowed wine and some onions, but I had little appetite. Since I was not allowed very much time to eat, I took to hoarding bits of bread to save for later, for hunger would overtake me at the oddest hours. After the first few days, I realized with sinking heart that I might be there for a long time, so I began keeping count of its passage by breaking off a short piece of straw each morning and laying it beside the lengthening line of its fellows under my cot. Sundays I knew from the chapel bells and the sounds of worship that floated up from below.

With nothing else to do but pray, I did, and I was always on my knees when the guard brought me food. And I always crossed myself properly before standing, hoping my gesture would not be lost on him. Finally I asked if I might be allowed a crucifix and paternoster beads, and my request was granted. But my next request, that I be allowed to attend Mass, was not.

"We don't want the likes of you twisting things around. Lots of heretics attend Mass and think they fool us. But the bishop is no fool: they may not tell lies aloud, but they act them out."

"A lie is a lie, and I don't speak them or act them," I said quietly, taking the crucifix and reverently placing it on the table so that it rested upright against the wall.

But I knew I was lying.

I knew there had been deep faults to my faith since I was small. My father's priest Father Kliment had repeatedly told me so. Everyone else had revered him as extraordinarily wise because of his years at Mount Athos, a place so holy that women are not allowed on it, and he had never married after returning home. But I had always resented him. Although he taught me that God is the all-powerful, all-seeing, all-loving Creator, he never seemed loving. Instead of drawing goodness out of me as Papa and Baba Liubyna did, if I got into mischief he warned me of God's wrath and scorned me as a daughter of Eve. But no one else thought me wicked, and mostly treated me with affection if not respect.

As for being a woman, it had always seemed to me that without Eve we could not know good deeds from evil. When I was about ten, I'd finally asked the priest why God had put a tree with forbidden fruit into the Garden of Eden at all. If He was all-powerful, He surely could have kept Satan out of the garden. And if He was all-loving, why did He allow Eve to taste the fruit, be frail, and tempt Adam; and why had he allowed Adam to succumb to temptation and then punish them? Since God was all-seeing, He knew what would happen and could have stopped her, so He must have wanted her and Adam to know good from evil. He could even have offered them this fruit that would show them how to serve Him better.

Father Kliment's face had turned almost black! He seized me and thrust me onto my knees, shouting at me to beg for God's mercy and threatening me with damnation if I did not banish the demons hidden in my heart. He raved about blasphemy and the fires and agonies of Hell, while I huddled at his feet weeping with terror. But he never truly answered me; and later when other questions arose, I never turned to him for guidance!

Indeed, after that dreadful day I began to wonder why I must simply accept his word, especially about what Hell was like. Had he been there? How did I know he was right if he was relying on someone else's word, and they on someone else's, back and back in time? Had any ordinary person since Christ ever died and come back to life to tell about Hell? And if they had been in Hell, could they be trustworthy? I had even pored over all the Scriptures to discover what our Savior had said: Genesis and Exodus; Matthew, Mark, John; the Gospel of Mary and The Sofia of Jesus Christ; Saint Paul's Letters to the Romans and John's Revelation; the Psalm of David, and many prayers. The rest were sermons by the patriarchs of Rus'. And although Christ talked about judgment and Hell, nowhere did He describe it.

So how did I—or anyone—know anything for certain?

That question had frightened me so much that I had to touch and name my face and arms and chest and legs. I even looked in my polished steel mirror, but all I saw was a cloudy image. My fear spread. I began touching and naming buildings and animals and plants and trees to make sure they were there. But when I went up to Alexander and patted him on the back and he asked what I was doing and I told him, he just smiled in his gentle way. "You just know," he said, bending down to look me in the eyes and taking my hands in his. "That is God's gift. Perhaps you should trust your senses more and your imagination less."

He had calmed me because his love for me pierced through my fear. And when I tried his advice, I did just seem to know. And the world did seem trustworthy. Trees never turned into arms or arms into birds, and Alexander was always my kind and gentle tutor. Even the angelic world was almost tangible, and I certainly had seen both the common spirits and my friends Sheep and Blade. Soon life flowed back into its usual channels, and I fell back into my usual ways.

Of course I had still felt uneasy about damnation, and I tried to be good, but fear of Hell stopped no one else: other princes, our knights, and the boyars hurt the weak and innocent; our servants pilfered things; merchants cheated their customers. So why should I, who meant no harm, worry overmuch? Deep inside, deeper than my childish fears, I felt close to God because His creation was so glorious. And until my time among the Mongols, I had always trusted that His love was a greater version of my family's love for me.

But now, alone in the dark, I had no idea about God or Satan or anything else in this world. I had become a cipher, and the church to which I had converted had turned against me for doing my Christian duty.

One day I awoke to chapel bells pealing extravagantly and long; Christmas must have arrived. I knelt and prayed to the Holy Trinity and then to Mother Mary herself for deliverance, not only for myself but also for all those I loved. Enough time had passed for Joscelin to have come here by now and to have brought witnesses or proofs or whatever was required. Where was he?

Each day after that, my heart shrank into itself, just as my body was growing thinner. I began to feel ill each morning and then to vomit. Who knew what illness I had? Perhaps I should simply surrender to death and free my husband and the rest of my family. Perhaps he had come to the same conclusion and had abandoned me.

I finally took to my bed all day and could not eat more than a morsel of food at a time. I lacked the energy even to save some for later. I lost count of the days and took to sleeping as much as I could, too weary even to walk around the room anymore.

When I was at last brought before the bishop again, I had to be held up in order to walk. My hair and body were unwashed, my clothes were wrinkled and dirty, and I knew I stank. I must have presented quite a contrast to the well-dressed, hearty-looking bishop.

"Well," he began without ado, "are you ready to confess your heresy?"

"Father, I am no heretic."

"Tell me what you do believe, then."

I recited the Nicene Creed in a mere whisper, but I made sure that I emphasized the Filioque as I spoke.

And then I fainted.

For many days I was brought to the tower and questioned. At least I was being fed better, for they gave me warm soup and a little meat, and I was provided with makings for what would be a small fire if I wanted to keep it alight, which I did. I pulled my cot over to the fireplace and spent many solitary hours feeding that little flame. It seemed as if the days were beginning to grow longer and perhaps a little warmer, but nothing else changed.

Around the same time that the food improved, my journals appeared on the bishop's table. Another bishop had joined the one I was grown familiar with. He had his own table and clerks beside him, and he sat closer to the fire. I took that as a sign that he was the senior of the two. On seeing the books, a surge of hope washed over me. I cried, "Is my husband here to take me home?"

The new Inquisitor just stared at me and said, holding up the wood-covered book Papa had given me, "Explain this infernal book to me, you red-haired witch. Is it a Cathar bible written in Satan's script? Or is it how you call on him in your dark rites? I cannot make out these strange symbols that are mixed in with Greek letters. And what are these vertical lines of writing at the end of the book if not evil spells?" It seemed that I was no longer simply suspected of heresy, but also of witchcraft, perhaps because of my red hair.

"No," I cried, now more angry than terrified. "That book was given to me by my father, who was a prince of Rus', when he sent me away from my home to what he thought would be freedom. It was my journal, and most of it is written in the Rus' alphabet, called Cyrillic after a missionary monk who brought my people the word of Christ long ago. He also gave us the written word and he devised new letters for it to suit our speech. After I was captured and enslaved by Mongols, I knew Papa was lost to me forever, so I sometimes used it as a journal and then as a copybook when I was learning the Uigur way of writing."

"Go ahead, then. Read, and we will see," said the new Inquisitor. He pointed out the page before grasping his heavy gold crucifix, which hung from an equally heavy chain, and holding it up toward me as though to ward off evil.

I began. "The man sits, the man sat, the man runs, the man ran. The boy sits—"

"Stop!" I looked over. From his expression, this bishop seemed to think

I was mocking him.

"Bring me the book. I will hold it up to you and you will read whatever I point to. That will keep you from casting a spell on anyone."

I spent the rest of that morning reading parts of the book aloud and at random.

After that ill start, I was made to return every day but Sunday. Eventually, along with being made to read Papa's book to him, the new bishop wormed my entire life story from me. He even got out of me the parts I was ashamed of, like tricking my uncle in order to best him after I had escaped from him.

How frustrating it was to witness this bishop's slow acceptance of who I was, like watching a long-drawn-out spring thaw. When he had finished with my Papa's book, he gave it to one of his clerks, who took it over to the fire and tossed it in. I stared at it stupidly, too tired and ill to grieve. With it gone, all my links with my past were burned to ash.

"Just to be sure," the senior bishop smiled. There was no hint of warmth in his face.

At least when he started in on the book that Joscelin had given me, he could read it for himself. With increasing surprise, he turned page after page. "This only repeats what you wrote in that first book. Why did you write it?"

"I don't remember.... Perhaps I wanted to remember my life properly...." Finally I summoned my last reserve of strength and stood as straight as I could. "No, I felt compelled to recall my past, for though I endured many sufferings, with the bad came much good, like learning the many faces of holy love. Such lessons brought me to convert to the Roman Catholic faith, to which I will always remain true."

"You need not work so hard to convince me. The other heretics did that when I questioned them separately. Every one of them abused you and cursed you for saving that peasant girl. She had received what they think of as last rites, the Consolamentum, and she was the angriest of all with you, for putting her into your kitchen and breaking her will. She had vowed not to eat again until she was dead.

"I suppose you will be glad to learn that they are all now in the hands of the civil authorities, and that in a few days they will burn at the stake while you are saved. Still, I must examine your books most carefully. I see signs of great errors in your faith, but whether they are deep enough to condemn you...." He shrugged.

I did my best not to reveal what I felt, suspecting that any sign of compassion or weakness for the others would be my undoing, but in my heart I prayed for their souls.

"When I have read everything you have written, I will come to my decision."

He took another two weeks. During that time, the heretics were all burned in the castle courtyard. From my tower I could hear their screamed prayers and cries of agony; they seemed to last all morning. Among them would be poor Grazide. She had not realized the death by starvation that she had sought; surely it would have been easier. Mercifully the screaming soon stopped, at least, even if the stench of burning flesh grew stronger. My guess, my prayer, was that everyone had fainted from pain. But that sickening smell lingered in the air for days afterwards.

That night I startled awake from uneasy dreams—or I believed I was awake. It seemed as if there was a glow in the room coming from nowhere, and then I realized that someone was sitting on the chair by the little table. It was Dorje, my old monk friend. He grew brighter and brighter, and he was smiling at me. I heard him speak, though his lips never moved. "Remember: terrible beauty, terrible purity, and terrible compassion. You are never only what you think." He faded, and so did the glow, but I felt deeply comforted. Somehow I could continue on despite the hell I was in; my feelings of abandonment and fear and despair could neither destroy nor define me.

The next morning when I awoke, I don't know how or why, but I was certain he had died and that he had found me across death's barriers to offer me comfort in my darkest time.

ANNO DOMINI 1263

It was January the 25th, Anno Domini 1262, when I was brought for a final time to the tower. By then my clothes had begun to resemble sackcloth, they were so dirty, and my skin was caked with the grease of two months without soap. I must have stunk worse than any Mongol. The room was strangely empty, yet it was also the fullest it had ever been, for although the lesser bishop and his clerks were gone, my husband was standing before the senior bishop.

At first I thought it meant that he too was falsely accused, but when he turned at the sound of the door opening, I saw no fear, only relief and perhaps anger, and then perhaps repugnance at my sorry looks. Beyond him, the bishop looked as sour as if he had sucked on a lemon.

I fell to my knees and burst into tears, and Joscelin was beside me in an instant, lifting me in his arms and carrying me before the bishop. I rested in his arms as a child would with its father, while the inquisitor pronounced final judgment on me.

"Lady Sofia of Braissac, you are hereby acquitted of all charges of heresy and of any suspicion of witchcraft." After a pause, he added, "You are most fortunate in your friends." I heard the acid edge in his voice.

I wept all the harder on hearing this news, but the bishop went on. "However, in reading your journals I have discovered many errors in your understanding, though in compensation not in your heart. You are beyond fortunate, for they are all faults that can be righted by proper instruction. So my sentence is two-fold; indeed, I might say three-fold. First I command you to make amends for all your past sins and transgressions by undertaking a pilgrimage. Our good King Louis suggests that Rocamadour would be the best place, and I am compelled to agree, especially as you are now in ill health and not fit to travel far. That city lies fairly near Braissac.

"Next, for you to learn rightly the true path to salvation you will need a proper priest and confessor. Your local priest, Father Pierre?" He looked at my husband, who nodded, "He is not qualified. So Lord Joscelin will soon be receiving into his household a member of our order to guide you and watch over your soul.

"But my third command, or perhaps wish, is that you finish your story and let me read it." Here his voice actually softened. "I want to hear it all, for your life has been most unusual. I am seconded in this by none other than the Angelic Doctor himself, Friar Aquinas, who was one of several of our Order to vouch for you. When he learned about your journals, he expressed keen interest."

"Father," I sobbed, "I will do all that you command. But may I go home now?"

"Yes, Lady Sofia. You are free."

Joscelin carried me outside, along the parapet, and down the stairs, though I tried to offer to walk on my own. "No, you are as thin as a rail, and I learned from the guard who brought me before the bishop that you were ill for awhile. Thank God you didn't die."

We said no more to each other until well after we had left the castle, I because I was too shaken and weary, and I suppose Joscelin because he seemed pained beyond words. I prayed that his pain was concern for my wellbeing, which in part it was. Sir Hugh and some other knights awaited us outside its gates, and he tried to hide his shock at my appearance.

They first took me to an inn where Joscelin called for a great washtub and plenty of soap. After gently undressing me and lowering me into the utterly welcome warm water, he sent my ruined clothing away. It reminded me of my escape into Derbent and the lovely bath I had been treated to then. But this bath I valued much, much more.

And when I was dressed in the clean clothes he had brought me, and daintily fed, and had given an outline of what had happened to me, my husband told me what I had missed. And now I understood his pain in full.

"When you were arrested, my mother, God rest her soul, did not faint. As near as we know, her heart failed her, and she died right there in the kitchen in Anna's arms. I came home at sunset, suspecting nothing, to a double shock, a double loss."

"Oh, Joscelin, oh no! How I wish it could be undone, all of it." Our tears began flowing as if from a broken dam on a river.

"Well, that is not possible," he sobbed. When he could bring himself under control, he continued. "I had no time even to grieve, for I had to set out to find you and bring you back. I only wish Sir Hugh and my other knights had not chosen that day for field exercises. We did at least find where you were being kept and learned where you were being taken, partly by means of shouts and threats; but what I could not do was get you released."

"So that was you I heard. I was certain you would come for me, but when nothing further happened, I thought it wasn't you after all, and then I fell ill and imagined you had abandoned me to my sorry fate. And I even thought it the best thing, for you and our family and Braissac were surely under threat as well. After what happened to your father...." I could say no more.

"Well, I could not get you released right away, but I did get your letter for once, thank God, and I sent Sir Hugh with your books. He paid your guards well for you to have plenty of firewood and better food—did you not receive them?"

"I did, some, but no one told me anything. I thought someone had taken pity on me." I could not tell him how he had been cheated, for there had certainly never been plenty of wood.

Joscelin snorted. "Money, not pity, changed your treatment. As for Braissac, your worst fears did not come to pass, though I was forced to act in haste. After burying my mother, I needed to protect Anna from possible harm. She was certain you would be freed, even packed garments for me to take to you, but that was all I could allow. So, having sent Hugh with my bribe to the castle where you were held, I personally took her back to Paris, to be betrothed to Gilles. At my request, she is under King Louis' protection now and therefore safe from any inquisitors."

I gasped. It was hard to take so many changes in all at once. No Anna to return home to, no Lady Alianore?

"And how did Anna feel about all this?"

My husband looked stern. "She accepted it at last. She turned twelve while you were gone, and that is the age of womanhood. She could have been arrested, too.

"But you and I do have many good friends, Sofia, including the king. It was he who wrote to the Pope, requesting that all these false charges against you be dropped and that you be freed forthwith. I wrote Friar Thomas Aquinas as well. And I served as emissary for the letter to the Pope myself. You are exonerated by no less than his authority!"

We both laughed a little, and for the first time, he smiled at me. "Sofia, I was not only beyond angry with you at first, I was horribly afraid for you. I was certain you had committed some terrible folly to get yourself arrested like that."

"Well, if being a Good Samaritan is folly, I confess to it."

"No, when I learned what had actually happened, I knew I'd have done the same, and probably with more authority and force. You were innocent of anything but trying to help someone in distress. If Mother Church objects to that, then we are all heretics!

"Anna explained everything after the funeral—before that, I was too wrapped in pain and haste to listen to her. How she blamed herself! She was certain it was on her account that we had even taken Grazide in. I had to order her to stop such nonsense. Still, in one way it was good that I could not get you released right away, for I might have broken my vow never to strike you again, I was that outraged.

"And once you are well enough, you must go on pilgrimage to Rocamadour, for a cloud will hang over our house until that is done. It will not be long before this Dominican priest is sent to us, and I worry that he will seek out faults in each of us in order to claim we are all heretics, thereby freeing the Church to seize Braissac and all my other lands. I would hate to think ill of him before he even comes to us, but this ordeal has made me into something of a skeptic."

The next morning we returned home. Once in Braissac, barely a day's journey away, I was put to bed, fed, and allowed to rest. But I was soon up. I felt a strange urgency to go on this pilgrimage as soon as possible, to be done with this horrible chapter in my life. And I wanted to find a genuine faith again; knowing that had Joscelin not interceded for me, I'd either have starved to death or confessed to heresy just to be freed from that cold hell. My exoneration had not borne any relation to my actual faith, nor had faith even mattered in the end; it was whom he knew, to whom he spoke, that got me released. Now I felt lost.

Nothing he could say would turn me from my course. "But you are not yet well enough," or, "But it is still winter," fell into deaf ears. Part of me briefly toyed with the idea of entering Lady Alianore's convent in her stead, but I set the idea aside. I would return to that question once I had gone on pilgrimage and performed my penance. Somehow Rocamadour would provide the answers I needed; that I felt in my bones.

Perhaps it was missing Anna so, and not hearing Lady Alianore calling impatiently to Olivier or Pierre le Brun to do this or that, but I needed to make a new life. I knew that the roads were safe again because while I was imprisoned, the bandits had been caught: a pair of rogue knights who had been roaming from county to county preying on anyone and everyone. Joscelin had had them hanged, and now no one dared molest his people, so there was no need to fear the journey. And there would no doubt be other pilgrims I could join.

The new priest arrived: Father Boniface, a pink-cheeked, youngish-looking cleric who always looked surprised. Even he thought I was rushing into this pilgrimage too hastily and being too harsh with myself. But after much argument, he and Joscelin relented, for I threatened to slip away in the night if necessary. And so in early February I went.

I set out alone, for such, I understood, is the lot of a pilgrim. I had confessed to the priest; had gone to Mass and taken communion with him; and he had blessed my pilgrim's accouterments—the coarse wool garments, the brimmed hat, the satchel for monies and food, and the staff. Both Father Boniface and Joscelin insisted that I take one of Joscelin's younger knights, a Sir Thierry, for protection, along with two of his squires, heavily armed; and I was commanded to ride on a mule, since my new priest insisted that my health and the cold days demanded this one concession.

The weather as I rode down from the castle that first morning was not friendly to my pilgrimage. While the days were growing longer and the first wild crocus stems were beginning to push out of the earth, snow was falling so thickly that by the time I had gone a hundred feet, I could not see my husband standing at the castle gates.

I rode through the village, and old Father Pierre came out from its alehouse to bid me farewell. For one who had lamented the sorry state of education in Braissac, he had seemed less happy than one might expect when Father Boniface had replaced him at the castle, and he must be comforting himself with a mug of ale on this cold morning.

Other villagers came out of their homes as well, solemnly bowing their heads as I rode by. "God bless you, Lady," someone called out.

Past the village the track turned, and both village and castle were swallowed up by the snow. How still and quiet the world seemed, how empty. The only sounds were the soft falls of hoof and foot.

We must have ridden for a good hour when I had to stop. It was so cold and I was already so weary that I wondered how I could ever have thought to try such a journey. My knight rode up beside me and said, "What is it, my lady?"

I slid off my mule and sank onto the ground. "I cannot go on. But I must go on."

He dismounted and came to my side. "What can I do to help?"

"Just let me rest here a moment, and then I will continue."

Sir Thierry and his squires retreated, and I sank into a kind of stupor, my head bowed. I was certain I had reached the hour of my death.

"Here, drink this," came a man's voice. A drinking skin appeared through a mist of snow and tears. Thinking it was water, I took a gulp and choked. It was eau de vie, and it burned just fiercely as my first gulp of arki had burned all those years ago in Argamon's ger. Had Dorje come back from the dead to offer it to me? In a way nothing had changed. I had in essence been a pilgrim then, too, seeking some kind of good in an utterly harsh world.

And then I looked up and discovered that it was neither Dorje nor Sir Thierry but my own beloved who had offered it to me. He too was dressed as a pilgrim, and as he wrapped his arms around me, he whispered, "I could not let you go alone. Your burden is mine, and it is only right that I expiate my sins, too. I am coming with you, Sofia."

And he did.

That first day I supposed ours to be a most unorthodox pilgrimage, because Joscelin had brought not only Pax but also his strongest mount with him so I could ride nestled in his arms for warmth when I needed. He had also brought more supplies, which he loaded onto the mule; and a warm fur-lined cloak for me, which he draped around me straightaway before lifting me up to ride before him.

"You don't suppose that when King Louis went on pilgrimage to Rocamadour, he traveled without servants and baggage and reasonable clothing! You are too extreme, my love. I tried to tell you, but you would not listen. Even Father Boniface could do little in the face of your stubbornness. There was nothing to do but to let you discover this truth for yourself. I always intended to follow, but I certainly caught up with you far sooner than I expected."

I had not thought of myself as stubborn since my childhood. What else did I not know about myself?

When we stopped at the first inn that night, crowded with other pilgrims on their way to Rocamadour, I soon realized that many people were traveling in even more comfort than we were. Drinking and eating happily, exchanging stories about their adventures on the road, what the best places were to stay, and so on, they seemed to regard their journeys as high adventure, as a way to meet people of high and low degree and be able to mingle freely with both. Clearly a pilgrimage was not simply a solemn journey but a chance to break from the bonds of ordinary life and to see the world. Some people were taking a sick or blind friend or relative, of course, and some had committed grave sins that they wanted forgiven, but for many the pilgrimage seemed more a celebration than a journey of remorse.

All this merry anticipation cheered me up and bore me forward with much more strength and resolve, not only for the next day but also for the days that followed, until we reached the valley below the city of Rocamadour.

We had gone in easy stages, waiting out a few storms, so the journey took over a week. But the weather had been clear if cold for the past day or so, and it had seemed that the last part of our journey, the ascent of the mountain path to Rocamadour, would be easy.

That was until we arrived.

I was prepared for a long climb, but I had not foreseen, looking up and up and up at the city, how menacing the last part of my journey would be, in a most personal way: the path leading up was so steep, it reminded me of the road to Alamut.

That last night we stayed in the best rooms in a little village inn, and in the chill morning dawn Joscelin and I rode to the base of the mountain and left our horses with Sir Thierry. From there we began the steep and, to me, terrifying ascent, for the road drops abruptly on the left as it winds up the mountainside. I managed to stay near the mountain wall, leaning on both my staff and my husband, and surrounded by perhaps a hundred other pilgrims. There was something rather wonderful about being swept along with this jostling crowd of believers, some of whom had already donned chains for the long walk up to the holiest part of the city. A few were already in tears, while others seemed merely excited. A few sick or lame pilgrims were borne in litters.

Caves along the way had been fitted out with statues to remind us of the Holy Birth, the Stations of the Cross, and more. All around me came the reverent murmurs of men and women recounting the story of Saint Amador, who was none other than the converted Jew Zacchaeus, servant of the Holy Virgin and perhaps husband of Saint Veronica, whose body had never rotted after these many centuries; or of the miraculous bell, dating back to the time of a great king called Charlemagne, which rings every time a ship is in danger and the sailors call upon the Madonna of Rocamadour and are saved; or of the many beautiful frescoes decorating the surfaces of certain chapels that would tell holy stories which even those without letters could read; or of the little Madonna herself, who would bless us in her sacred chapel.

It took perhaps an hour to walk up, and in my case almost climb up, gripping the mountain wall, to the entrance to the city. I had thought the brutal drop into the valley had paralyzed me with fear enough. Now, looking up, I felt just as overcome. How could anyone have built so many fine stone buildings—houses, inns, stores, churches, even a palace—on such a steep mountainside? And why had they? We went through the arched gates and walked the length of the town surrounded by the noise of hawkers, vendors, street urchins trying to pick pockets, and above all the noise of pilgrims praying aloud, some weeping for their sins, others for joy, while still others laughed and sang praises.

I was swept along by this sea of people and might have been separated from Joscelin had he not kept his arm firmly around my waist. The human sea carried us slowly but relentlessly to the base of a great stairway. "Two hundred and sixteen steps, they say," I heard people whisper to one another, before a reverent silence overtook each pilgrim as he or she was met by a priest who stripped them of clothing, gave each only a shirt or shift, and draped them with chains. Only then could they begin the final ascent. When it came our turn, Joscelin and I, with penitential chains wrapped around our shoulders and, paternoster beads in hand, began to climb the stairs on our knees and to count our prayers for forgiveness.

I had somehow imagined a swift and easy end to this pilgrimage, but I soon learned that it was not to be. A chill wind blew up and clouds swiftly moved to cover the sky. Great drops of rain began to strike us, and while some pilgrims looked up at the sky as if in gratitude for this further mortification of their bodies, I simply tried to wrap my pitiful cotton shift tighter around me.

We climbed higher and higher, and the uneven steps began to bruise my knees. All around me people were weeping or telling their paternoster beads or calling out for mercy. I put all my attention on climbing the steps and counting the special prayer Father Boniface had given me. Joscelin, who could have gone up and down those stairs twice by the time everyone else was finished, stayed close by my side, although at my insistence he did not help me climb them.

I glanced over at him every now and then, and he always seemed to be looking around him. I finally realized that while he too was praying, he was also keeping an eye out for evildoers. He had already mentioned that many criminals, feigning repentance, would join the genuine pilgrims in order to find the wealthy ones to murder and rob afterwards.

My shift was soon soaked with rain, and then, as we got higher, crusted with wet snow. My nose began to run, but there was no way to wipe it. One step had a jagged edge, and my shift tore. After that, when my knee came down on each step, it hit hard stone. Each stair step felt as if it might be the last one I could manage.

After awhile I fell into a kind of trance, much like the one that had kept me in thrall when Argamon first captured and enslaved me. So it came as a great surprise when suddenly there were no more steps. All around me people were struggling to stand, many of them in tears, crying aloud for mercy and forgiveness. Almost all of us had bloody knees and torn clothing. Joscelin helped me up, and I used his arm like a crutch as we slowly moved forward with the crowd, which now seemed like a great dumb beast crawling from one shrine to another, one chapel to another.

I saw nothing but the stones beneath my feet. I know we passed the tomb of Saint Amador and stopped to cross ourselves; that we descended into his underground chapel, which was built right out from the rock, to genuflect and pause, each pilgrim locked into his or her own world of prayer; that we did the same in the small chapels of Saints Ann and Blaise, that we prayed for some time in a large basilica called Saint Sauveur; went up a bell tower to visit a chapel dedicated to Saint Michel; and that, last of all, we came to the Notre-Dame chapel. People were murmuring to each other or praying to God; I overheard someone say that the sword of some hero named Roland was embedded in the rock above us and that its hilt was filled with holy relics. I did not look up, but I heard the ahs of the others.

At last we were inside. Along with everyone else, I sank to my knees, although I was so weary that it seemed more like sinking into a stupor than kneeling to pray.

This chapel was also built out from the face of the mountain, and it felt warm and stifling inside the cave-like room, what with all the overheated bodies and steaming clothes crammed inside it. Somehow Joscelin wormed us up almost to the altar, and when I finally looked up, it was right into the face of a crude, dark little wooden statue of the Virgin and her Child. Though they were robed in little velvet garments and capes and adorned with tiny crowns, the paint that had once enlivened them was flaking off.

I had seen so many statues of the Virgin and Child in our travels that I was expecting nothing new. But this mother struck me dumb. To my eyes she was already offering her beloved son to the world, knowing full well what awaited him, yet loving him and us all without bounds. She had such a gentle smile, and her neck was craned forward as if to see into the future or to look into each penitent's heart. I cannot say why this one statue would mean much to me, but suddenly tears were streaming down my cheeks, and all the woe I had felt since losing my home came flowing out almost as an offering.

And this offering she seemed to accept. I almost heard her say, "Yes, I understand. I am always with you as a fellow mother and a friend. You must never hesitate to help this world, no matter what the cost, for look at the cost I bore so gladly."

Other people came and went around me, while I stayed on, surely to the annoyance of other eager pilgrims; but I did not notice. I was visited by the past, by all the people whose lives had touched me: Papa, Baba Liubyna, Father Kliment, and my beloved Alexander appeared before me, and more people lined up as if waiting their turn: Kateryna, Oleg, Dorje, Lady Q'ing-ling, my fellow slaves, and especially Anna; Selim and his entire family; Rukn al-Din and Nasir al-Din, Adar al-Mas'udi; my orphans and servants; Helene and her two Gilles; Uncle Basil and all his kin; even Maffeo Polo and, to my surprise King Louis, who promised to remain Joscelin's steadfast friend; and Joscelin, Lady Alianore, and my dearest daughter Anna.

To each of them I said thank you and sometimes goodbye, and in King Louis' case, that I was sorry for feeling so jealous over his friendship with Joscelin. For the first time, I felt as if I understood my own life: it had never been mine but belonged to them all. And all the places I had passed through in life had been the same: through all of them, people and places, I had learned who I was. And through me even those who had died or been destroyed still lived on. What I believed, what salvation I might find, would never be based on vindictiveness and power and fear, on what any church might try to make me believe, for belief was not what could save me. Only caritas could do that, wherever it was found, regardless of religion. It was not any God who gripped us; it was we who gripped our ideas about God so tight that we could not understand that others might see in a different way and still be seeing truly.

This was something I knew I could never share with my husband, for he was and will always be a man of his times, no matter how gallant he is; much of who I was and who I truly am will forever be strange, perhaps even frightening to him. But I could never quarrel with that, for our love transcends our circumstances.

And at that moment I realized why I had been so desperate to go on this pilgrimage. As the Holy Mother smiled down on me, I knew I was carrying Joscelin's child and that it would be the son he needed for Braissac to stay in his family's possession. I also knew that I would have more children, until I was too old to bear any more, that I would grow old with him, that we would quarrel and make peace with each other, be ill or well together, laugh and weep together, that I had found what I was looking for: a simple life with a man I loved, and that I would die a happy woman.

I got up smiling and took my beloved's hand. We walked outside, where priests awaited us. There we whispered an amende honorable, were forgiven our sins, and were given a certificate of absolution and a lead image of the Virgin to wear on our pilgrim hats, almost unaware of the hawkers calling out to us to buy yet more trinkets of faith. We left our chains behind and walked down the stairs into our new life together.

And now I am almost done with my story. I have just sent Anna everything I have written so far, and she can make of it what she will. But other than this I will write no more, not for her, not for myself. Even what I write now I will burn: better it than me.

Six months have passed, and with them my old life. Shortly after we returned to Braissac, Paolo passed through with Fotis. The poor boy: he was so struck by grief over his sister that he screamed and tore out clumps of his hair. How I regretted my self-interest in keeping Irene away from Welf. She might have enjoyed some kind of happiness with him, and now it was too late for her, for Welf, and for Fotis.

We went to Paris after Paolo left with all the trade goods he had amassed. There I saw Anna and celebrated Lady Day with her. She seems happy enough in her new life and her betrothal to Gilles, and has settled into being a lady of the court. Lady Heloise has kindly undertaken to look after her. She is training her in Frankish etiquette and so forth, since Queen Marguerite is pleased to have her stay in Paris until Gilles is knighted and takes possession of his fief in another year. Then he and

Anna will marry, and I will be there with my newborn son in my arms, God willing.

But in essence she is gone for good. Though I miss her every day and rejoice that she is even interested in what I have written, a new life awaits Joscelin and me. I will soon go into labor, indeed felt the first pangs this morning as I looked out the window at the green world of early summer. Birds are singing, and the air is so sweet that I want to weep from gratitude. It is strange to know that I will survive what I had so dreaded—giving birth when I am so old—but I no longer feel afraid. I only pray for my son to be healthy, for he had to endure what I endured. But I have grown strong again.

I know that I am in many ways a heretic after all, for after my ordeal I can no longer accept that anyone possesses all the truth, much less has the right to impose his truth on others. And I have always lied a little, both to and about myself, and certainly to others; but in doing so, I have only been human. Above all, I know I am human. All the rest of it—what I must believe, what I must confess—is simply like the flaking paint on the little Virgin Mother. But her holy love in its many guises will always abide.

ABOUT THE AUTHOR

Rebecca Hazell is both author and artist. Her award-winning non-fiction books for older children have been purchased for distribution by MercyCorps and Scholastic Inc., and been published in Greek and Korean. She is passionate about history, both for its romance and for its value in understanding how we are always connected to and driven by the past. She has also written educational materials for high schools on such far-flung topics as Islam and Russian serfdom, produced award winning needlepoint designs, created science kits for children, and was a tailor and dressmaker/clothing designer in her youth. As well, she is a senior teacher in Shambhala International, a worldwide Buddhist organization. She has been married for 40 years and has two grown children. For more information on Rebecca and her other works, both literary and artistic, please go to www.rebeccahazell.com.

33180710R00206

Made in the USA
Charleston, SC
03 September 2014